A. H. Richards

kronos duet

Thanks to the Ontario Arts Council for their financial support during the writing of this novel.

Thank you also to Dan Ebbs, playwright and actor, for his valued editorial commentary; and for the initial and inspiring help of Marg Gilks, Editor.

Finally, deepest thanks to two special cats, Emma and Lucy – no longer in this world – who supported me with their unique and beautiful catness throughout writings, rewritings, and painstaking edits. Although each only read the varied manuscripts while I was sleeping – and liked them not a bit, except for the parts about them – during daylight hours, they were kind and positive.

1

ENGLAND, 18ᵀᴴ CENTURY

Gareth Pugh wished he couldn't trust his eyes and nose in the darkness. There was an infant girl lying in a rough bed next to his. And she stank. Her rags stank. The room itself reeked and what light passed through the oiled paper window barely differentiated bed from stone, body from dirt. He lay in a space that had surely never known a breeze, and he suffocated in a body that was not his own.

That wasn't supposed to happen. He couldn't recall it happening before, no matter how much Anis he took. And he couldn't recall anything going wrong in the morning's preparation. It had been just like old times. Though he no longer needed to eat, drink, or even inhale Anis to achieve his ends, he made sure to talk with it beforehand. It primed them both, bonded them, and gave them both pleasure. The nature of this intelligent fungus made you want to be intimate with it. So he had talked with it, silently, feeling its pulse deep in his mind. He had felt the same thrill of old – part dread, part awe – that was the precursor of mind flight.

But that was a distant morning, not this one. He studied the workman's hand that clutched the blanket to his chin. Blistered, with blood from scars coagulated in dirt, the hand spoke of hard labor. And he, Gareth Pugh, was trapped in this laborer, in an 18th century room. Trapped inside this great block of a human, who snored through a mouth tombstoned with diseased teeth. His head lolled backwards over the bed's edge, the mouth open, sawing prayers to heaven.

Gareth Pugh had simply taken the wrong artery in the Great Nobodaddy's mind, he told himself. Easy to fix, no?

No.

Time-space voyaging was fraught with nasty, bent surprises. Hopping time through the minds of others was fine if they were stable, decent people. The feat was a tough one, but relatively safe – with your real body left at home. Safe enough when he was in his prime, strong and patient. But his fifty-three years had sabotaged his control. He was afraid to venture out again. Who knew where the next leap would land him? And the madness out there now found its parallel in the cloying darkness which held him, undeniably, to this space and time. As if he belonged.

He definitely did not belong. He would even welcome Dr. Buckleigh, or the FBI, who had been doing surveillance at his home, with their nanotech bees and bluebottle flies He would welcome a return to his real-time body, to Toronto, to Buckleigh, and the never-ending renovation of the warehouse-home once known as the Wilson Candy Factory.

The cats would be dozing in the flower box, heads in their furled tails. And Adrianna, his daughter, would be in the kitchen perhaps, cracking a boiled egg while the tea-kettle sang quietly on the stove.

Thoughts of her clutched at his stomach. It was fatherly love, but it was also guilt. For all of her twenty years he had been abysmal as a father. And now, with this latest adventure, she would be right to abandon him altogether.

Stupid. Stupid. He never knew when he was well off. Just yesterday morning they had felt so right together, the two of them surveying the undergrowth sweeping up from the disused railway lines, down by the marsh behind the warehouse.

He imagined moving his lips to speak to her. "I love you Ade." But the laborer's lips responded to the dream urge, smacking in the dull, still air. The stubbornness of the fact hit him hard and plundered his courage. It was no longer the year 2035, and it did not look like he would celebrate Adrianna's upcoming 21st birthday. He was stuck – here, now, in a life defined by filth and pain.

kronos duet

TORONTO, CANADA: 2035 AD

For countless mornings, portly Dr. Buckleigh, Foundation agent, had watched Gareth Pugh standing at daybreak in the wasteland he called a garden. He had watched him disinterestedly, out of habit. Pugh was harmless and always ready to hibernate, rendered comatose by the drugs Dr. Buckleigh had supplied every day for over five years.

But this morning, he saw a different Pugh. Something was afoot. Pugh's body-language spoke of a purpose and determination that Buckleigh didn't like. Worse, he had *done* something. Pugh was not supposed to *do* something. Pugh had smashed his blue bottle of meds, thrown it into the mud and ground it in with his heel. And then, he had swiped at the bee, sent it spinning over the long grass. He must know about their nanotech spies, this one the last model Entomopter – an old war horse, but always reliable.

What if he did know? So what? It only meant that Buckleigh had to respond, gently. It wasn't as if he hadn't planned for this eventuality, as unlikely as he had thought it. He balanced his vidspecs on his nose and watched the Foundation Reconnaissance Vehicle – a stubby, electric one-seater that purred on the road.

"Buckleigh here." He spoke to the officer through the slender phone wand at his chin. "Any news on Pugh you can pull from Serv?" He used the agents' lingo for the Multi-Surveillance Server. "Did the old fossil talk to himself? He seemed agitated to me."

"Not much to tell ya." The driver replayed the current download on his car-screen, watched it closely for seconds. Buckleigh detected Pugh's voice.

"Not much to go on. Says something about getting a baseball bat and offing some bees n'stuff." The officer looked up at Buckleigh, grinned and circled his index at his temple.

"Senile dementia," he offered.

Buckleigh knew otherwise. He would have to watch him closely. And he would have to hide anything resembling a baseball bat.

3

Gareth Pugh lay silent, willing himself to think thin thoughts, the kind the laborer might not register. He hung within the white noise of the laborer's mind and tiptoed through the day's preparations. He had heaved his drugs down the freight elevator shaft. Without the dulling effect of the pills, the psyche would blossom again. He would become himself.

Even more, he would once more become his obsession, as he had five years ago. He would once more follow the path to the one great love of his life – loved, and dead this long while. The plan had been to go to her, if he could. And then, to alter the path they had been on, to straighten what had bent, to right their capsized life.

He had written a letter for Adrianna. How could you say enough? He had forced himself to stop after a few pages, signed 'I love you. Dad,' and left it at that.

After a drive to his lawyer and a consultation about his will; after digging up his strong box and hiding away the neatly packed currency; after a complete shave of his old head, he had slipped, silent as a razor cut, into the study with his silver box of Anis. He had opened the box at his desk and the odor of Anis came, better than fresh-baked bread. Its scent calmed nerves, sinews, blood cells.

Then he pulled out from the desk his leather head strapping with its network of brass studs worn dull by years of fingertips and skull sweat. He slipped the helmet over his head, feeling the studs match the pressure points in his skull. He pressed a thumb on the cerebral cortex, until he could feel the collapse, the signals passing through the corpus callosum, subtly marrying the two hemispheres.

He felt himself slipping from his moorings, that familiar sensation, like lily roots snapping delicately free, and then he rose over the cosmopolitan world. Dormant senses awoke and, like the soft hairs on the body of a moth, he touched at the gate to Nothingness. Then he disintegrated in a fusion of atomic flame. He became nothing, in a spot called Nowhere.

He had known this would not be a mere spree. More likely the final episode. Now he wondered, carefully, if he were dead.

Pugh had disobeyed. He had bloody well woken up, and gone off again: After five years of medicated coma, he had managed to wake up. And now he was gone. Sure, his body was still here, in that same room he had always used for traveling; but his psyche had gone, and he might not come back for weeks, months. Pugh had a plan, and his plans were always a threat. The Foundation would have to know, and soon. And a report of even a minor failure would damage his reputation. Buckleigh was too vain to let that happen. He would not report: he would solve the problem.

The Foundation had demanded perfection in his service to the political and economic status quo. He had given them decades of faultless service, protecting the power and wealth of the few who managed the world. Keeping the disadvantaged helpless, by any means necessary; making the self-realization efforts of the educated and 'empowered' classes' futile; spreading disease, turning brother against brother, making addicted whores out of abused women; Buckleigh had done his bit. The ship of state barely rocked, despite violent civil unrest and terrorism, because he and thousands of other operatives implemented the plans that made everyone but the power-mongers expendable and impotent.

Buckleigh spoke date and time into his phone wand, then voice-faxed a tel-call. There was still time to manage this. He thumped the button for the freight elevator. Pugh's two cats, damn them, appeared under his feet again, as if they had been skulking in wait all this time. Little bastards had it in for him. He kicked out at the black-and-white one, who leapt out of range and sat watching through amber eyes.

"Piss off, you horrible parasite."

He thundered onto the freight platform and heaved the gate closed. The cats blinked at him in unison, and seemed to smile in the wavering sunlight.

There was one immediate option. Buckleigh exited and walked to the Jaguar, clicked the key once. The car unlocked luxuriously and lifted the driver's door like silk. Buckleigh slid his portly bulk into the driver's seat, adjusting the phone wand. Voice operated, the phone responded to his arm implant, connecting with his private assassin.

"Hey, Sangster!" he cried when the man's voice came through. "Got a quickie for you, if you could use a few thousand."

"Who couldn't? Sure, as long as it ain't this Thursday an' Friday. I'm in L.A. then."

"Not Thursday: Tonight." Buckleigh looked at the time on the dashboard and stroked the starter button. The vehicle hummed into an oiled crawl. They flanked the building, turned onto an empty Sorauren Avenue where the Jaguar broke into life, pushing Buckleigh into the bucket seat.

"You okay for tonight, say within the next hour?"

"Shit. I was just ordering dinner." Buckleigh could hear Sangster pulling the cigar from his lips. "Seven or so? Where exactly? I'm down at the Harbourfront. Why don't you join me first? Amazing sea-food. We can talk then and I can do the business after."

"No good, Sangster. I want it done now, while you're sober. A steady hand with the hypo, one puncture, and you're done. The guy dies of a heart-attack. No guns, no blood. C'mon. Ten thousand ..."

Buckleigh detailed the warehouse layout, exits and entrances, the third floor where Sangster would find Gareth. Sangster didn't need to know anything else.

"I don't know, Bucky," came Sangster after hearing the price. "Spoiling my night will cost you double that."

"Okay, you shit. Twenty thousand." Buckleigh grinned as Sangster agreed. "Tell you what. You get it done, then meet me where you are now. Dinner on me."

Minutes later, Buckleigh's Jaguar slipped into underground parking. He smiled all the way to the restaurant, where he stroked the butt of the gorgeous hostess. Seated in a plush velvet booth, he smiled more, lit a cigarette and hummed happily into a snifter of brandy.

An hour later, he stopped feeling happy. Sangster had not arrived and a cloud of doubt irritated Buckleigh. He refused a third brandy. Waited another twenty.

A half hour later, he was on his knees on the warehouse third floor, puking next to Sangster's body. Behind Buckleigh's back, Pugh lay as stiffly formal as ever, untouched. In front of Buckleigh's face, Sangster's hand clutched the hypodermic, unused. The assassin's face was blue, white-blotched and decorated with laces of blood. His eyes bugged out, frozen in fear, and blood caked his eyelids, ears, nose and mouth.

Buckleigh scrabbled at the zipper of Sangster's blood-stiffened jacket and pulled it open. There was no chest, no abdomen, no pelvis – just crushed flesh and bone. Buckleigh retched again.

He groped his way out of the room and bent in the hallway, puked, then sucked in air. He needed cleaners, now. He spoke the alert for the local cleaners into his wand. Never had he needed cleaners before. Never. Not once. He had been proud of that. Proud of his aesthetic, elegant work.

That crushed splatter in there, not aesthetic at all. It was shit. Stinking shit.

He explained nothing when the cleaners arrived. He couldn't. He didn't know anything.

Hours later, Buckleigh surprised himself, as always; this time in the shower in his office. Brilliant man, he was. He washed the last of the blood off his arms. His mind had not totally caved in under pressure. He had a nice solution. Hot water massaged his neck muscles. No-one had killed Sangster. But something had. And he was pretty sure it was this drug, this plant, whatever it was: Anis. The early tests, using Anis stolen from Pugh, were rife with weird accidents, violence done to innocent, well-meaning people. Well, maybe not well-meaning exactly, if you were going to split hairs. But secretive about their more violent aims. They had remained objective, scientifically thorough. Clinically removed.

It had to be the Anis that had done those things: death to some, strokes, comas to others, imbecility to a few. They had found no evidence pointing to human perpetrators in these acts. And this one, Sangster's death – no human could have managed this murder. A truck, perhaps, but not a human.

Well now. Foundation agents were not expendable. Anis brought harm. So it was simple; do not expose Foundation employees to the danger. He needed someone else, and it struck him that he had someone, right in their midst. This new fellow Adrianna had befriended, just months ago. A university professor. There was something about him that had stayed with Buckleigh after only one encounter; a simmering violence, a hang-dog arrogance in him that Buckleigh was sure could be harnessed. Buckleigh could read peoples' insides better than a CAT scan, and he was right about this one. A smile slithered onto Buckleigh's face, parting an underbrush of thoughts. He had it. His mind canceled other options. He had this man's number, and he would dial it – connect right to the center of the man's vanity. This time, vanity's name was Professor Cabot Greenway.

2

Adrianna gasped through her phone wand. "Is that you Cabot?"

"None other."

"Sorry to bother you, umm, I need a second opinion. Can you come right away? Please? I'm afraid my father's dead."

He had the urge to laugh. It had to be his infatuation. Any excuse to meet with her was a triumph. He was expected at the Rasputin exhibit at the Art Gallery of Ontario, meeting whatsername, B-student, wanting A's, great legs, no boobs. Definitely seduction material, but she would have to wait. Adrianna trumped anyone, any time. Pushing his speech wand over his forehead, he swung the car into a u-turn.

He wondered at himself as he ran the red light. He hardly knew Adrianna – barely three months – and knew her family only vicariously, from opinions of colleagues at the university. By all accounts, he should have avoided her. He should have stayed engaged to Megan, letting the rest follow its natural course. But he had found Megan terminally dull; and more so with Adrianna on the scene.

And here he was, playing Sir Galahad, because of his hormones.

His father had been a right bastard, but he had been right: the world was decaying from effeminacy – queers and neurotic women running the show, and kids wielding the power of the state, suing you for existing. They never should have spared the rod; now spoiled children had become monstrous. The result was hell.

His mind shifted over to Adrianna's father, his possible death. He couldn't have cared less. He wanted her. And he was irritable with hunger. Teaching logic on an empty stomach had been exhausting enough. Facing a corpse and a grieving... what should he call her? Friend? Lover? Not quite yet... would drain the last dregs of his blood sugar.

He descended on the roofs toppling at the outskirts of Roncesvalles, the residences inching toward ruin. It was a place that had always given him the creeps. As bad, today, as were Jane and Finch in his undergrad days, centuries ago. Middle-class brick houses, fallen to ruin, with no middle, and no class – just gutted shells waiting for the wrecking ball to pulverize them to dust. And in them, squatters, drug addicts, pretentious artists, bad musicians, and here and there a bag lady or stinking old cow from the 'old country' who hung on to the house, refused to be uprooted from the substitute history they had taken half a lifetime to construct.

There really was no history anymore. Nothing beyond last week.

Life was tough. So what? He knew it, and he accepted it. There were winners and losers. He just happened to be one of the winners, instead of a decrepit leftover with body odor and mental problems.

Something hit the rim of the open sun roof. He pressed the button to close it, cursing himself for forgetting his normal precautions. Always, the locals chucked things, off overpasses, off balconies, or like this kid coming, his arm whiplashing. It was sport, trashing expensive cars.

He had not shut the sun roof fast enough. Cabot felt his head and cursed. Stinking raw egg. He'd have to wash that off before he met Adrianna. Where were the fountains in her building? There were some still functioning, he knew. She had shown him around the warehouse on his first visit. His mind's eye saw the layout, the bulging walls of whitewashed brick, the freight elevators, the long hallways of creaking floorboards.

He would be with her in a couple of minutes. Once he had remembered the location of a fountain, three thoughts elbowed each other in his mind: Was her father dead? What would he get to eat? And could he screw Adrianna that night?

Adrianna stood at the window with her back to Cabot, her body profiled by sunlight. Her fingers toyed with strands of her mahogany hair – a nervous habit. The room seemed just the place for ghosts, as though it had been shut up for decades. Dust floated in the sunbeams. The air hung with a kind of ennui. He saw books, shelved from floor to ceiling; a severe rotary dial telephone, soot black; a small acreage of carpet worn bare down the middle by someone who walked obsessively; and finally, ancient wingback armchairs, probably stuffed with horsehair and as comfortable as... horsehair armchairs. No holograph console; in fact, no technology at all beyond the light switch and antique telephone; no wall-size screencomp, no satellite con., only an ancient keyboard laptop, with dust-thick enough to finger paint through.

Cabot cleared his throat and Adrianna turned to face him.

"Oh, you made it." She crossed the room, her eyes flickering aside from his scrutiny. She hugged him and they teetered forward. He felt her breath on his ear: unmistakable scotch.

"You all right?" he tried. Pathetic.

She composed herself and stepped back, finally braving eye contact. A smile appeared and vanished.

"I'm together now. With someone to talk to, I don't feel so completely helpless..." Adrianna's voice trailed off. "Sit down." She offered an armchair, and sat in her own.

She stared at her lap, then raised her eyes. "How are you?" Her gaze returned to the window and remained, watching the clouds.

"I'm okay." Cabot felt anything but. Acute hunger and the leaden atmosphere conspired against him. At a loss, he watched her. Her detachment seemed completely out of character. But then, he had never known her in such circumstances.

"Ummm," he began. "Your father... is he...?"

The slightest tremor at her temple indicated her attention to his voice. He waited.

She turned to him. "He's in a little room down the hall. That's where I

11

found him, when I came up to see if he wanted any food. Just lying there, as peaceful as can be.

Dr. Buckleigh insists that we don't call an ambulance: my father didn't want to involve the authorities in such a situation." Her eyes were a sheen of tears.

"I can't force anything. Can't even send him to the hospital and put him on life support – if that's what he needs. After all the trouble we've... father has had... if I called the hospital we might have another scandal to deal with. I couldn't handle that, and neither could he, if he lives." She stared at her lap.

Descending silence threatened to fossilize them. Cabot felt like a beached fish. Out of the corner of his eye, he strained to catch a glimpse of her cleavage. He waited for her to come alive again.

He had always sensed some encroaching flakiness in her family. Adrianna's mother, unhinged, with the poison of what she considered pedigree gnawing at her sanity; Adrianna's dad, eccentric, reclusive and, apparently, some kind of fallen genius; and Adrianna herself, willful, embarrassingly outspoken, something that had got her tossed out of university and more than one job since her high-school graduation at a precocious fourteen. Cabot was a little afraid of her.

Caution dogged him, asking him what he knew of her, and urging him to remove himself. As soon as you got tangled with a woman, the shit arrived. And could she be any different? He didn't know her, and he hardly knew himself.

"Mind if I smoke?" he tried. Her hand signaled indifference. Cabot lit up and inhaled a lungful.

With her plain, ingenuous ways, Adrianna was almost as much a mystery as her father. Possessed of her parents' money and with unblemished good looks, she could have been a snob. Her poise alone indicated that she had been 'to the manor born.' The way she always ate 'European-style,' fork in left hand, knife balanced in the right; her smattering of foreign languages, picked up here and there during her family's travels; her unfaltering taste in expensive clothing. That was a woman who he would have, in any other circumstances, called spoiled, even decadent.

But spoiled was not the word for her. The gamin in Adrianna showed flesh, flailed limbs, made her as clumsy as an adolescent. That clumsiness fit with her earnest nature.

At their very first meeting, a university fundraising function, she had appeared to him out of the noise like a sudden, unexpected cease-fire in his war with women. Within seconds he hungered so badly for her that his light-headedness threw itself into overdrive and he got blindly drunk. The first few glasses of wine had generated a state of womb-warmth, then he bucked directly into greedily feeding the beast – Aquavit at the table; then scotch, brandy, beer, and gin and tonic. Unable to bring himself to talk with her directly, he had chain-smoked filthily, and finally threw himself into a cab just as he reached the frontier of self-destruction.

Cabot had made strides since then. Acquaintance had edged into something closing on friendship, and that had been enough to bring him here. Surely more choice delights were to come.

His stomach thrilling uneasily, Cabot made himself walk to a spot behind Adrianna. Was that a flinch he felt as his hand touched her shoulder? He had been too abrupt. Softer, softer. He counted himself back into it, like a musician rejoining at the right measure. His hand relaxed and he hung, between apology and lust, dumbfounded deeper into silence. Hopefully, she wouldn't mind it, wouldn't push his hand away. He was innocent. He was just being kind. He was inconsequential. Anything. Just let the hand soak her in. He made himself think of other things as his fingers hovered lightly on her shoulder.

Pugh Senior had reached a frontier. He had stepped right over it, far from academia and the media and his ex-wife's high-society. Dr. Pugh had, years ago, embarked on a quest to South America, searching out a species of fungus that folklore said was a supernatural being, which, at the world's beginning, had taken the form of a plant; a few steps up from a stone. Pugh's reputation as an academic had been just enough to garner him a research grant sufficient to sustain him through his odyssey. With a motley group of shamans and peasant pilgrims, Gareth had entered the rain forest gloom and disappeared.

Cabot remembered the library's iKiss database article, "Free School Makes

13

Slaves," with a photograph of a young man named Alex, a jazz guitarist of local fame. He had attended classes at Gareth Pugh's 'Free School,' spontaneous affairs that guided students through mind/body research. The jazz player had had the bad manners to get himself deathly ill on the Pugh premises. Alex, claimed the news blurb, had been discovered on a carpet littered with plant debris, next to a pool of his drying vomit. Comatose from poisoning.

Arrested and tried for criminal negligence, Gareth, naively, had represented himself. He argued, first, that the victim, despite being warned of the dangers of the 'drug' Anis, had overdosed of his own accord, while Gareth and his other students had long since retired to bed.

His second line of defense had been that he was a scapegoat for the community's neuroses. If he had, like Skinner, merely electrocuted rats, or harvested obscene amounts of money to conduct studies stating the obvious, he would have become a pillar of society. As it was, he was a victim of the emotional feeding-frenzy that passed for justice in contemporary society.

The accusations, innuendo and gossip, Cabot recalled, formed an impressive slag-heap. Pugh was a sado-masochistic homosexual; Pugh performed artificial insemination on cats so as to breed kittens, which he regularly sacrificed in satanic rituals; the Free School was anything but, its orgies of sex and lethal, mind-warping drug-taking costing its students dearly. Pugh was also an ultra-covert hireling to a military machine so secret and nefarious that no trace of its existence had yet been detected.

In the snake pit of accusations, slander and innuendo, Gareth's voice drowned. Even the public appearance of the now un-comatose Alex did nothing to calm the public's ire. The city quietly shut its doors to him, thankful for the excuse given to them by his supporter, Dr. Buckleigh, that he was mentally fatigued and needed prolonged rest. The university's board of directors breathed a sigh of relief when he tendered his resignation, and accepted his departure with all the grace they could afford. Pugh entered another uncharted gloom, and disappeared from sight.

"Have you got any scotch?" Cabot was almost to the well-stocked bar by the time he had spoken.

Adrianna poured them both a generous glass. They stood side by side, facing into the room. He wanted to kiss her, to hold her to him and, consoling her, cup his hand around her ample breast.

He cleared his throat, moved away from her.

"Ummmm. Shall we uhhh, look in on him?"

Her fingers touched his arm as he moved to the door. "Let's not go to see him yet. I'm just... I'm exhausted. I can't think. Or feel, right now." She faced the window, shut her eyes leadenly and breathed like someone already asleep.

Minutes crawled, then her voice jumped out of the silence.

"Let's get you something to eat. My guess is you haven't eaten much more than that chocolate on your breath."

She led him to the door, taking his hand so that his heart bumped at his throat and he felt the familiar stirring down below. His desire clenched in his stomach, and an entirely disrespectful notion stole across his imagination. In her grief, she might be all the more vulnerable to his tenderness, his kiss...

Along the hallway, sunlight slanted obliquely through a wall of windows. It was as if the corridor were suspended, unhitched and floating free. As if time had stopped itself. Cabot felt that they were watched; like on Sundays at church when, as a boy, he had struggled to comprehend God – knowing His eyes were on him that day – and had failed every time.

3

Afraid to disturb anything in the room, they hung in the doorway, looking into dusk light. A cot sat against the left wall. The muted light showed Pugh lying out, snug to his head a contraption of leather straps studded here and there with dull metal rivets. His head was shaved, with nicks of dried blood showing, scraped inexpertly down to patchy, stubbled baldness.

Cabot crossed to the body and clasped the slim wrist.

"No heartbeat I can feel."

Adrianna's own wristwatch had more of a pulse – or the building itself, reverberating from distant traffic. In the half light a pallid spider crawled tremulously upward on the wall alongside the cot. Adrianna watched Cabot brush it aside, then unbutton her father's cardigan and put his ear to his chest.

Cabot pinched the cheek and released it, watching for evidence of circulation. There were no signs of rigor; the arm as supple and deadweight as a slumbering baby's; the skin on his cheek elastic to the fingertips. At the points where the rivets had contacted the skin, minute reddish abrasions, like pox sores, circled the skull.

Adrianna waited. An eternity.

The spider reappeared at Cabot's left foot. The scene before her pulsed; a television screen tuned to nothing. She waited, chewing her lip. The blood drained from her neck and arms.

She heard his distant voice.

"I think..." he hesitated. " Don't get excited, but I think there might be a heartbeat. It's almost non-existent. But I think he's still with us."

"Doctor Buckleigh already told me that." Adrianna snapped, then pursed her lips, ashamed of her spite.

Cabot took her hand and urged her to his side.

"You want to listen? See if you can hear anything."

"Oh God no! If it stopped while I was..." Adrianna pulled away.

She knelt beside the cot and picked lumps of wool from her father's sweater.

"Short of slapping him or dousing him with iced water, I can't imagine what we could do to bring him out of this."

Cabot's words rang dull. Adrianna stared while he lifted one of Gareth's eyelids, inspected an unresponsive pupil.

She looked at Cabot, her eyes hugely dark.

"I don't know what's wrong with him," she said. "I don't know enough about this... It seems that he used to do this, years ago, when I lived with my mother. Dr. Buckleigh knows..."

"But we're going to have to telephone the hospital anyway. You can't wait days. If he has snuff... if he's dead you can't just..."

"No." Her voice was firm. "Only Doctor Buckleigh. That's the way it is. And the men here," her nod indicated the hall, "they're always monitoring him."

"They're thugs, not nurses Adrianna. All this makes no sense. Where's the heart monitor? The brain scan? I don't see any. If he's comatose, he needs hospital care..."

"He's not in a coma. I know. If he's not dead outright, then he's not comatose. Dr. Buckleigh talked to me... I don't exactly trust the man, but dad has always insisted I follow his counsel."

She swung away from him, her long hair a curtain closing on her thoughts.

"So what, then?" Cabot snapped, pulling her to face him. "We just wait for him to die, or pop up like a Jack in the Box?"

"I suppose so, Cabot. I'm sorry. I just needed you to confirm that he isn't dead. I needed a second opinion." She smiled wryly. "Dr. Buckleigh is a bit of a drinker and, well, a little too secretive about my dad."

Once again, Adrianna closed up as she stepped into the hall. She could feel his eyes on her. Her flesh suddenly seemed too soft, her hair too lush, her jeans too snug. Cabot's sigh trailed behind them, dissipating into the stairwell in the wake of their footsteps.

It had been a mistake, as usual, to telephone her mother. But the climate had become just too cold and lonely and her fortitude had crumbled. Who else to turn to but mother?

"Might as well have talked to the garbage man," Adrianna observed to the still life that was her father's study. Mother had sniped and ranted, her voice honeyed and bitter.

"I just couldn't believe it, when you exiled yourself there. I don't know why you didn't take the holiday in Europe I offered you. And now you telephone, with more trouble..."

"He needs me, mum. He needs protection – and no one else will help him."

Her mother exhaled cigarette smoke into the receiver. "Mother, dear, not 'mum.' That is so proletarian. Do us all a favor Adrianna. Don't waste any more time repairing that relationship!" Adrianna heard her bracelets clattering. "It's high time you exiled that man forever. I told you, there's something genetically askew with him. A bohemian, in the worst sense. I should know."

Adrianna held the receiver away from her ear.

"He doesn't even have the decency to paint, or play an instrument. If he were really an artist, I could see it. You were always good at drawing yourself, you know. Had a gift for it – and music... so I could see an attraction to a father with similar gifts, even if he was a horse's ass... which your father is."

"But what have you done? Allowed yourself to become completely mesmerized by a totally unimportant semi-lunatic, with no thought in his head that isn't anarchic, or, quite patently idiotic. Those awful books he writes. What was the idea in that last piece of drivel, some blather about the mind and light waves? He should try being a little more conscious of the real world..."

The real world was certainly dominant in her mother's mind. The conversation ended with her probing after just how close to death Gareth might be.

"We'll be there shortly dear. I assume you had the presence of mind to phone your Uncle Kurt. Remember, he is the trustee. Daddy and I will be there to make sure you don't get cheated..."

Why did she insist on calling that geek 'daddy? Adrianna hated the arrogant creep. Her mum's beau of how many years... probably some years before her separation from Gareth, knowing mother. Clifton fancied himself. Period. That's all he did, other than manage money at arm's length and pretend to write literature.

"Ode to Clifton, by Clifton," she smirked, dropped the phone into its cradle and settled into the solid wood back of the swivel chair. Where to start? Not by crying, surely, which was all she really wanted to do.

Her fingers wiped absently across the desk surface, cleaning a track through beige dust. The dust felt as slippery as talcum. And it gave off an exquisite scent. She put her fingers to her nose and savored it. Almost floral, but not cloying. Almost spicy, cinnamon and baking bread. Adrianna laughed to herself, feeling a rush of warmth envelop her. She turned her head, surveyed the room. It had felt, almost, as if her dad was there with her.

She smelled England in kitchen odor – boiled cabbage, grease and coal – and saw a series of images in a brief, intense dream. An aging housewife leaned, weeping by a half open door that faced stone row-houses across a narrow street. Through stained-glass above the door, a shaft of sunlight fell through ruby-red glass. The woman's right hand shook in sharp pain, then flashed to her mouth as a sob broke forth. The sunlight revealed a fraying hole in the shoulder of her blue wool cardigan; revealed her kneeling, resting her forehead against the door; revealed her stockiness, her buxom warmth under sea-blue wool, and revealed the telegram as it slipped from her fingers to the tiled floor.

For a moment Adrianna felt suspended in silence. Then, nauseating fear lurched in her. A malevolent chill gripped the air around her, leeching to her with the fevered violence of a sick man. Panic swallowed her breath as she strove to suck in air, to feed her blood.

A roiling blackness, and herself within it. A dreadful pressure. Terror. She could see only where her hands, where the desk should have been. In its place, nothing, while from behind, a grip forced her head downward and a claustrophobic, deadweight darkness enveloped her. She could hear the blood coursing in her ears. A strangled growl struggled in her chest and beat at her diaphragm, an animal's panic and rage. She barely held to consciousness.

Then the thing released its hold and Adrianna found herself, sweating cold and palpitating. Her eyes saw but her mind registered nothing. She gulped breath hungrily as her heart relaxed to a regular, paced rhythm. Then her mind switched on again. Ceiling above, smoke stained – the chair-back a dull knife-edge at her nape. Her hands trembled. Her body absorbed a fiery ache that beat from her sinews; that reached from her toenails to the back of her eyes, and finally released itself through the roots of her hair.

Her eyes took in the room, the stuffed chairs, the wood grain flowing through the desk top, the sunlight glittering off the gold lettering of leather-bound books. Everything captured in an opalescent clarity, so beautiful and certain that it was almost awful. Warmth reanimated within her. She laughed to herself and looked affectionately at her hands. Her mind glittered. What a miraculous reality!

She had learned something just then. She knew she had. But she could no longer recall what it was. Something had scared her – long ago, it seemed. She remembered, faintly, the image of a terribly sad old woman. Images came and fled, but only insubstantial mockeries, a poignant stab. She had returned to the determined hardness of the absolute present.

The beige powder on the desk. Was that the culprit? She dared not touch it again. What had her father found, or concocted? This led the way to her father; she knew it.

Adrianna stretched out hopelessly on her bed, holding the letter from her father she had found peeking out from under the reading lamp. She read in snatches, pained by every sentence. On the back of the envelope, an inscription: "To my daughter, Adrianna." She scanned the lines furtively. "...who, if she is to comprehend me as completely as words can make possible, must read this." To read, she needed privacy and time to gather strength. Her eyes flickered through the accompanying pages; fell on a segment without thinking.

"...I have decided finally, to return to this work. I am resigned. It may take me wherever it will. Light years hence, perhaps, and no return. But truly, I have no choice. This is the summation of my rather puny, ridiculous life. A profound end, at last, even if the means are less than ideal."

That was all? A letter? Adrianna felt cheated. Tears swam at the rims of her eyes and a sharp sting choked her throat. She wanted to disappear, to finally yield to her exhaustion, to fall into her bed's embrace and disappear. No family. No Cabot. No Buckleigh. Maybe Emma or Lucy purring at her side.

Adrianna tuned out as much as she could. All of her concentration focused on resisting the sobs grasping her stomach. She could feel the last of her spirit diminish, extinguished by cold despair that wrapped itself around her and settled like a familiar spirit. She gave it full room. Her rueful smile was tinged less with sadness than with a hard realism, a vacant and infertile realism. It had, over years, become so much a part of her that she had not noticed or questioned it. It was her father. Gone.

Her stomach held a chill. She could feel it growing. The chill emanated from her centre.

'I want a hot water bottle,' she murmured, and pulled her leaden weight up from the mattress. She made it to the kitchen. Impossible to wait for a kettle to boil. She filled the rubber lung with steaming water from the tap, and stoppered it with a slow wrench of her wrist. Hot water bottle. And sleep.

It was not until she awoke in the dead of night and unlocked her arms from the hot water bottle at her stomach that she noticed she had crushed the letter under her naked belly. Its pages, one by one, separated, and the last page detached from her belly as she breathed. Adrianna turned on her back and stared emptily into the ceiling.

4

Afternoon sunlight dappled her forearms and the scent of apple blossom lingered. She had settled herself, for what remained of the daylight, in a chair shaded by the lone apple tree Gareth had planted.

She looked up at the warehouse windows. Dr. Buckleigh had been quick off the mark, telephoning various members of the family, summoning them to Gareth's 'death bed.' He had more information than she did, and that bothered her. He was in charge – while she should be.

First a 'comatose' father, then the adventure with the beige dust, then her father's letter. Adrianna felt insubstantial. Exhausted of feeling. Even though she had found a pile of her father's notes, she read almost without focus, soaking meaning from the letter by osmosis.

"Dearest Adrianna. You know that I have always been some species of eccentric; and that would be a generous description, a romanticized version of the man who has certainly not been the best father to you. In short, I have constantly let you down. I do not look for excuses for my behavior. I know that no amount of babble will counterbalance the weight of sadness you have inherited from the foolish pairing of your mother and myself. Money, the best schools, riding lessons, tennis lessons, singing lessons... you know better than I how little they really mean in the grand scheme of things. And the grand scheme of things, obviously, is LOVE. I must admit that I have failed you in that, though I love you dearly."

Adrianna's eyes misted over and her mind's eye saw warm memories of her infancy... of her father crouching with her over rock pools, describing the crabs and fishes, and playing 'mermaid and treasure' with her. Her father carrying her upstairs to bed, humming an old vaudeville song... what was it? 'I'm hmmhmmhmm Bertie – I hmm hmm at thirty...' The song dissolved in a current of brief memories, then sank altogether beneath a bittersweet wave that brought tears. She forced herself to read on.

"I feel my utter failings as your father, but words fail. For me, looking at everything from beyond Earth, words lose their meaning. I have been to weird dimensions in my explorations, and to the warped spaces in between. Seeing them, seeing miracles, I find words inadequate, a kind of torture...

My mind opens out into a vast hostile and loving infinity – It has made me abnormal, so I have trundled along through my life as a father, with half the caboose off the rails.

No doubt, in the next little while, you will hear the name Anis – either via Buckleigh or your own researches. (I know you will look.) So let me give you a preamble.

Once there was a variety of strains of Anis. I've seen other species of Anis, in other centuries. One existed on the Yorkshire moors in the 17th Century. I found no more of it – which leads me to believe that various strains have died out.

Anis helps consciousness travel through time. Not the body, not a ludicrous machine. Anis is the limpet attachment to the moment. It never forgets, never distorts over time. This Anis memory can be transmitted to the person who ingests Anis – and a kind of dialogue exists between Anis and the user, so that the user could – if he or she were brave or foolhardy enough – connect with Anis' intensity to time and space.

Anis has its own version of passion, and, once given the go-ahead, it will careen through space/time with no concern for anyone piggy-backing. You might die, you might never come back, or come back insane. For that reason Anis must be controlled by your will and desire.

I have long since stopped using Anis as my time-taxicab, because I was born with a freak mind that gives me faculties of experience as intense as that of Anis. So now, I do time-travel by myself. But I have not yet found the linear path, one that would push me safely through infinities of existence.

You may find this with me, some time.

May this all get better in the near future.

Yours, out in the universe somewhere, with love, Gareth."

Adrianna lifted her head, only to focus on the undeniable image of the cat's anus, as the peaches-and-cream darling yawned and stretched at her feet. She laughed, then felt a brief Cabot-tug. Such a shame that the man had no sense of humor, if he wasn't drinking. Toooo serious. And sneaky, as if there was something dirty in him he was trying to suffocate.

Noise reached her from the dining room's opened French doors. Most of the relatives were here by now and needing food and entertainment. The will was not going to be read for some days, when Uncle Kurt arrived. She had to make haste if she were to grab some snacks and disappear before everyone assembled to be fed.

5

Motionless in the armchair Adrianna started out of her trance and stared at the cot, her pulse thumping.

"Dad?"

Not a flicker of motion. Not a blink or a twitch.

"Dad, was that you? Please... please, let it be you." Her voice rasped in her dry throat.

Of course it's me. It wasn't you, was it?

His teasing voice. But it was in her head. In her desperate head.

Wrong there. In your head like water in a vessel. But the water is its own.

Adrianna's eyes welled tears. The sadness had fatigued her into hallucination. She stared at the wall, reached forward and stroked her fingers across it. This is real. The pain in my knees and calves is real. Now. Is my head real?

Was this telepathy? How did he do this?

I'm so relieved that you can at least do this much. I've been waiting on tenterhooks for the moment when I could speak with you. You've been so preoccupied. But that was expected. And ironically it had a positive effect finally. You finally got tired enough for me to get through...

Adrianna's ears pulsed hot with anger.

"Ok. Now I'm pissed off. You waited? You held off contacting me. What am I talking about, 'contacting me'? Either you're dead, or I'm mad! This isn't you. There are only cold facts here. The family is here, waiting for proof of your death. Philomena is here, and Clifton and Beer Gut and..." But she could not will herself to break the hallucination.

She gripped his body and shook it once, abruptly. She was going to cry...

That does no good Ade. I can't be woken if I don't want to... sudden shock works. But I'm not ready for that yet. Soon, but not yet.

Adrianna slumped, sleep-invaded. She was always a possum under stress, she thought. She could feel her mind closing up shop. She managed words.

"You can tell me something I need to know right now."

Ask away sweetie.

"Were you there, a while ago, when I was in your study?"

You were all by yourself there. You may have felt me there, but it was not enough of me to help you. So just be careful.

She listened to a moment of silence, as if history had closed itself. Then she felt him gather his voice, felt the effort in his breathing.

Exhaustion is pulling me back... But know this. You are not dreaming. I am not dead. I have inhabited your mind, quite benignly. You must come to me. But... look, I'm fading here... I will make contact soon – when I've caught my breath. I'll need your help... He should be dead asleep if we are blessed.

"Who will...?"

Take a tiny scrap of Anis. Not too much or you'll manifest too physically, which we do not want. Ok? Will you do that? I'll guide you here. But now I'm tired.

She shouted through rising panic "Tell me something, before you go! Where are you?"

Right now, on my way to sleep on a straw-filled pallet.

"That's not what I...."

Sorry love. I'm too tired. I have to go... I'll call you here. Just be ready.

Adrianna opened her eyes.

"Selfish jerk. Why is it all about you?"

6

Adrianna hurried across the empty kitchen to the ironing cupboard that had been renovated into a staircase that climbed to the third floor. She went up, stopped in the dark, breathing in the cedar, hearing the sounds of the old building.

The fragrant stairs brought her directly to the museum room, a long space with high ceilings and floors of wide boards like the planks of a Viking ship. It had been a never-ending office room. Its windows backed showcases and cabinets and in those cabinets, costumes of Canada and England and India, through the nineteenth- and eighteenth-centuries and beyond. Old glass and oak counters from Eaton's or such ran the length of the room, crammed with household items and knick knacks and jewelry. Newspapers and magazines toppled on solid wood tables – the kind you never saw any more.

She found her favorite dress, Edwardian, in silken gray, with two rows of buttons (like blueberries amid the fine, dark-blue embroidered border) forming an acute v the length of the bodice. She unclasped the hooks behind, releasing the dress from its mannequin, and then stepped into it, carefully extending her slender arms through the tight forearms. Unbuttoning her jeans and pulling them off, she reveled in the touch of the heavy skirts on her bare skin. The fit was just a little tight at the tummy. She needed a corset, or fewer late-night snacks.

But it felt sexy as hell as she walked across the boards, fingering scarves and hats, pith helmets, boots, and jackets, on her way out the door. The thought of impending danger sent heat through her body.

—•—

Her father's bedroom was a cave. Dark, polished wood furniture and an immovable four-poster bed gave it a fortress safety. Adrianna felt the sensuous drag of her dress on the deep carpet as she crossed to the dresser at the foot of the bed.

Her father's 'snack supply' of Anis was secreted in a Mah Jong piece in the dresser drawer. With its minute golden clasp centered on one side, and on the other, two tiny hinges – the bamboo and ivory tablet was gorgeous. Adrianna prized it open with a fingernail. To breathe in too much, she thought, or worse, to blow it away with a careless sigh, would ruin everything.

Her watch told her it was time, heart palpitations be damned. She looked at herself firmly in the mirror, then held the box close to her nose and sniffed gently.

She stood on a street in a pitch dark night, amid the stench of horse dung, pig poop, maybe even human excrement. Her eyes adjusted to the dark and she saw its source: A slimy, narrow canal flowing down the centre of the street. It looked wide enough to float carcasses in. She shuddered, and stepped quickly away, then held herself, taut and small, in the shadow that clung to overhanging roofs. The smell of wet iron invaded her, and a floating stink of something like sulphur. But worse was the tensely ominous night. The shadows palpitated with threat.

Should she creep where it was less dim, near the centre of the street, and risk being spied by anyone who cared to look? Or should she hug the walls, where anyone might be lurking, where it would be too late to cry out, impossible to run once snared?

She took stock. This was maybe the eighteenth-century, judging by the darkness. Not a gas lamp in sight. Eventually her eyes detected the faintest glow from one window and another; pale, cold candle flames barely probing the night.

She wanted more light. Light was power. Her hands went for her pockets to find matches or a lighter, but found smoke-like billows of cloth instead. Of course, she was wearing the dress. It glowed from within, like ectoplasm, she thought. She could barely feel the material, or herself for that matter.

She started, her heart lurching. She could barely feel herself!

Panic fluttered her hands about her body. She felt herself choking. She wanted her body back, the old clumsy body. Her hip vaguely felt the snag of a spike that protruded from the wall beside her. She looked down to see the spike pass through her as her body turned.

She held herself still. "Dad! Help me! Am I a ghost? Please..." Her wail barely broke the air. She heard the wind rush through trees. She felt the huge night sky above, felt the glittering cold rivers and lakes that reflected moonlight throughout the countryside. She felt like a thing of smoke, on the verge of drifting apart. Even the sky, the stars, the sleeping world were hostile.

Come here.

The voice was warm, close. Her eyes searched about. Nobody on the street or in the shadow.

"Where?" Her voice whispered relief.

Just follow. I'm in your head, guiding your feet. Everything's okay. Just watch for poop.

She let her feet go. Four doorways, a narrow alleyway that stank and sent shudders through her. And then the house. She grasped the wooden handle and stepped gingerly into the smell and dark. Her foot stubbed on something alive that grunted. A human, or pig, or a dog asleep. She was at the foot of narrow stairs where denser patches of blackness betrayed sleeping bodies. Sodden, abandoned bundles groaned amidst a stink of gin. She stepped through the stench and ooze underfoot.

She felt her way, following his voice through the screechings of rats, bumping against walls. She emerged into grayer light, a small room with a window covered by a translucent scraped skin; the poor man's window glass. Adrianna's nostrils shrank from the fetid odor of bodies and urine, of near putrid food and the sweet stink of a newborn. Where was her father? What did this have to do with him?

She forced herself to look down at the lump of blackness near her leg. A body hugged a threadbare blanket around the shoulders.

Her father's voice whispered. "He's asleep now. We can talk Ade."

"Dad! My God, this is awful! These poor people! How on earth did you end up here?"

"Took a wrong neuron in my own mind, I suppose. Ended up inside this poor wretch at your feet."

He sounded so glib.

"Can you get out? Can I... Can I leave here too...? I don't know how to do anything."

"Never fear. But we have work to do. This man you see is poor and chronically hungry, and is going insane by degrees, partly because of syphilis. He is so beset by anger and fears and stresses that he cannot mend. And there's the rub. I'm in his brain, and the only way I can release myself is a shock, his, not mine. At deeper levels of sleep, I would be released into horrors and difficulties I can't explain right now. So I must 'bounce out' as it were, right now. I need a momentary shock, to him, not me. Though it helps if it's me too."

"Okay then." Adrianna grabbed a mucky, snarly cat that rubbed against her legs, and flipped it at him, end over end. Its hissing snarl changed to a howling screech as its heavy body pressed its sprung legs onto the laborer's stomach. Adrianna all but felt the tomcat claws dig deep. The laborer bellowed and swiped the air blindly. His club hand smacked the clinging cat, who growled, bristling.

Then, a shout. "Run!"

Woken up, the laborer's old mother screamed out from under her cowl.

"My Gawd! A witch! A witch and her demon!"

———•———

Adrianna ran. She ran through the misty dark beyond the edges of the town, she fell through a cropped field, climbed a stile, then crouched under tree shadow. The cat had bounded along beside her and now pushed its head against her hand and curled about, settling its rump against her hip.

"So, what d'you think," said the cat. "Clever trick, huh?"

"Fine for you Gareth. It's a silver witch they're hunting for." She stared far from the shadow. At the edge of the town, dark figures moved and called to one another.

"They'll string me up too," he said; "as a familiar; maybe disembowel me and burn me. If they catch us that is. Something I very much doubt."

"Why so cocky, pussy cat?"

"When I – this kitty, I mean – falls asleep, which as you know they do most of their days and nights, I can leave its little brain and we can go home."

"So we sit here and wait for a cat to fall asleep? That's your plan? And hope that when the horde finally descends on us, you can charm them with your cute kitten ways? You might be rolling on your back for them but I'm not..."

Adrianna's bottom was already damp and numbly cold. She wanted home, and oh Christ, there was now Cabot to deal with! What a turn her life had taken.

"So, the plan worked, Ade. Tom the cat, that was all we needed. Something for me to enter, and run like hell. The biggest treat of our laborer's working life, I bet. He's probably still fast asleep. He slept through all that shrieking. Gareth mimicked her voice, "A witch, a witch!" but the cat's throat didn't do it justice.

"Once we're home," he continued after a cat cough, "I will not set foot outside the third floor, physically speaking. You will have to feed me, you know; sneak food up while I'm 3D."

"Well, do me a favor then. Remain a cat. You'll be cheaper and easier to feed. And more fun to play with." She calmed herself. No-one had entered the field; as though none dared breach the wilder lands beyond the town's boundaries.

"This century-hopping game is kind of taxing, don't you find?"

The question was rhetorical. Adrianna picked a grass stem and chewed. The dark copse was less frightening now, with her father's company and the moon shining down like a blue painted egg.

"I must sleep," murmured Gareth and made himself more comfortable against her leg. "A little cat nap, and off we go."

His tiny nostrils expelled pencil points of breath against her hand.

"This will be my first good sleep in three or four days."

"You were in his head for that long?"

"Yes. Bad mistake. I'll have to be choosier next time, I suppose. Do a little psychic reconnaissance before setting up camp, so to speak..."

Adrianna had to chuckle. Such a tiny, sweet voice coming from the cat's throat.

"So why did you choose the cat to escape in? Why not just be yourself? Or can you not take your own form?"

Gareth purred, then sleepily replied. "I can be myself. But with them lusting for witch blood, I was not about to show up as Mr. 21st Century. I look insane at the best of times. Besides, I love cats."

"You love Olivia Hussey too, but you didn't turn into her."

"How do you know about...? Never mind."

Gareth nipped her finger, once, lightly. "Can you let me kip now? Just ten minutes or so, then we can be off."

"And how do you plan to get me out of here with you? Isn't it your mind traveling? We're not real are we?"

"You're half-right there. We're like holographs, but not quite. But just trust me. My mind will let yours know, when the time comes."

Adrianna hunkered down and kept watch. A weasely thing loped to cover and a small owl watched from a bough a few yards away, two huge topaz eyes set in an Elizabethan ruff. Then the owl soundlessly spread its wings and floated to ground, where it lifted a live morsel in a talon.

Then she realized what was so different. There was no traffic. Not a rumble, near or far. The moon licked everything with its silver tongue. Liquid darkness prevailed. Nowhere the vibrant, atomic glow on the horizon of the city. This was a proper darkness that belonged to the night creatures, to the silent, craggy mountain sides and the brooding interplay of shadow and silvered paths. She loved it, even though it scared her. Such a beautiful, honest darkness, made for roots to grow in, made for the minute sounds of mole claws and for the fattened, sleeping bellies of foxes.

"Time to go," said Gareth at last.

The real cat was slinking toward the woods. Reincarnate, Gareth looked a spectral figure, wearing his favorite green trousers, brown turtleneck and tweed jacket, all of them translucent. She could see the barely flattened grass underfoot.

Gareth sat beside Adrianna, resting his arms on his knees. He sighed happily, then took her hand in his. He spoke low.

"Rest your head on my shoulder. Envision home, the very space you are now actually sitting in back in Toronto."

Adrianna's eyelids were curtains weighted with lead.

7

Food, then a bath were her restorative. Adrianna crept down the cedar stairs and wished she hadn't unlatched the door. Cabot was crouched in front of the open refrigerator. She pulled the door tight. Her heart thumped in her throat. Her blood hissed in her ears. Then the knock came.

She caught her breath. He might have found the door but he needn't find her. She started up into the shadow. Too late. The door swung open, the light fell full on her and a half drunk, smirking Cabot feasted his eyes on her body.

"From what hidden tower do you descend?" He extended his hand with a mock chivalrous flourish. "Come, abide a while and sup with me."

"You're drunk." She stepped down and turned to lock the door but Cabot crammed himself into the doorway. His face searched upward.

"Very clever. Can't tell from the facade at all. Mind if I go up?" He got as far as the first step. Adrianna yanked him out.

"Yes, I bloody well do mind! That's private! Now let me lock up."

"Oh dear me. Now you're getting angry at me." He picked some leaves from her hair.

"You went out? I've been watching for you. How and when did you get out?"

Goosebumps rippled her flesh. Watching her?

He could not know, must not know anything. Her honest nature nearly won out, nearly brought her to speech. But she breathed deep and looked away, waited for the air to change.

Cabot returned to the refrigerator and began helping himself. He waved a bottle of wine at her.

"Your fridge is hospitable. Even if you're not."

Adrianna folded her arms and stared.

"I don't know why you're rude to me Adrianna."

Cabot stood before her and slurped a mouthful of wine. "You're rude, like now..." he offered her the bottle. She pushed it aside.

"I wonder, sometimes, what makes you think it's okay to be rude to me? I help you, don't I? I came here when you called and ..."

"I'm not rude to you Cabot." She spoke calmly and quietly, as she would to any drunk. Respect him, he might respect her. That was all she wanted. "I do like you, when you're not drunk... You seem like a nice man when you're sober."

"SEEM?" His face darkened with anger. "NICE? My God, girl, haven't you known me long enough to say... to feel... more than that?"

"You've been around for a few months Cabot. Hardly enough time to know someone."

She crouched at the fridge and her eyes lingered over a half quiche.

"Well, I know you well enough..."

"Do you?"

She was sure she could eat all of that quiche. In the bath, with a glass of red wine. She was so happy. Her dad was not dead, or dying. And she would see him tonight, if all went ok. She grinned at the quiche as if it were an old friend.

"You think this is funny, don't you?" Cabot's voice roughened. "Because I feel something for you, something more than you're interested in, as you make so evident..."

She tried to maneuver past him and he twisted her wrist so the skin burned.

"Look at me Adrianna! You never look at me."

He shook her, sending the quiche to the floor. The plate smashed, chunks of quiche skidding.

"You...!" She crouched to see what she could salvage. Tears pricked her eyes as she gathered the pieces.

Cabot was striding now, back and forth.

"You cry over a piece of quiche. But you feel nothing when it comes to me."

His drunken intensity, the perverse logic it engendered, was something alien to her. She could not argue, she knew that. It was dangerous, and a waste of time. She would not win.

He was pleading now, brainlessly pushing pieces of quiche into a pile with his shoe.

"I'm sorry Adrianna. But you KNOW how much you mean to me. All these months I've ... God! Why d'you think I broke up with Marion? Why d'you think I came rushing over here the moment I thought you wanted me... I mean, needed something?"

"Who's Marion?" Adrianna stretched her mind back – Cabot and some woman.

"Marion. Oh right. The woman you were going to marry."

"Yes, until I met you, and then..."

"Then what, Cabot? Did I lead you on in any way?"

"Well... maybe not...but you sure knew how to... Christ, Adrianna! You kept visiting me at my office... we kept bumping into each other at the library... what was that all about?"

"I liked you Cabot. I thought you were interesting." She walked to the door. "A friend. I wanted a friend, and since you were engaged, I thought you would be safe."

"SAFE! She liked me because I was SAFE!" He strode after her.

"I suppose that's why you always came around looking so damn good. That's why you kept accidentally showing up at the same dinners and parties I was at, and making eyes at me and seducing..."

"I NEVER seduced you Cabot! You seduced yourself!" She opened the door. "So you can either be my friend... or you can decide that's impossible and deal with it. It's your life." Quickly, before his drunken brain could respond, she pulled the door shut.

His voice came muffled. "Deal with it? You heartless bitch." Then came a thudding, as if he was beating his head against the wood.

"I'm sorry, Ade. I'm SORRY! I didn't mean that. Don't go."

She was gone. She locked the upper door, ran to her father's suite and scrambled the big key into the lock. Inside, she pushed the door tight and turned the deadbolt to.

Cabot laughed and leaned against the hat stand for a microsecond. He tottered a few feet to the kitchen door and shook his head, as if that would help. 'Well beyond it now,' he observed muddily. He was drunk and the whole world was treacle, laced with scotch. That was funny. He was a friggin' genius. He could paint that image... a submarine world of drunken brilliance, not brilliant as in light but brilliant as in... bloody brilliant. Now, where the hell had she got to? Disappearing all the time – too busy reading to spend time with him. It was time she stopped avoiding him, or keeping it casual, or whatever she was doing. Didn't she know that she shouldn't toy with a man?

He stepped off the freight elevator at the second floor, slid back the door gently. His heart thumped and his knees trembled in unison with his hands when he smelled the scented vapor coming from the bathroom. He dared not touch the bathroom door handle. He quickly scanned the hallway to the left and right, steadied himself with a hand pressed to the door frame, then bent to the keyhole, his hearing tuned to noises behind and about that might signal people coming.

He smelled bath oils and soap. Heard her humming through the rush of hot water, then the squeak of faucets. If she moved just a few inches leftward... oh... he prayed. He was rewarded by Adrianna's naked legs stepping into the claw foot tub, then a view of her bottom, already turning heat-pink, then her smooth, glistening back. She sank down and stared at the ceiling. He stood for a moment, checked about him, then returned to his spy-hole. He might have felt sympathy for her before the argument. But now his dick had control. He prayed to his cunning muses, "Let her show me more flesh. Her pubes, her boobs..." His eye stayed glued to the keyhole.

Adrianna soaped her legs. Cabot's ears listened behind him while one eye remained glued to her flesh.

"Anis, Anis, Anis..." she whispered it as if it were a lover.

Anis. Cabot knew that name... from where? Yes, he had it... from the internet. Anis had come up in the court case... they claimed that it was some kind of drug, some hallucinatory substance.

Then it came – the dreaded footstep. Someone poking around. Uncle Kurt, or that patronizing bullet-headed Dr. Buckleigh. Time to flee. Cabot did his best to saunter away from the bathroom, restraining the urge to run. He arrived at a landing, where a wide stairway descended. He lit up a cigarette as he disappeared down the stairs.

So what was the connection, he wondered? Adrianna had mentioned time-travel with all seriousness, and Anis in the same breath.

God! What an ass she had.

Gareth's room, dominated by dark wood, antique highboys, the Stonehenge-poster-bed, the dark dresser, the bookcases dense with glittering books; all formed a fortress. She sat in its protection and ate with the lamp turned to its lowest power. She lay back, sunk herself into the mattress, and curled the silk comforter around her. After such a hectic few days, this was supreme luxury. But she was so hungry! Shaking from it. Sometime, Cabot must be out of the way. Then, something to nibble on, at least. Then she would locate a bottle of wine for company. And if she met Cabot on the way back, she would slug him over the head with it.

Tapping came at the door. She froze. The knocking on the door insisted. "If this is Cabot," she snarled, "If he has found his way up here, I will break his friggin' legs."

She unlocked the door and threw it open. Gareth entered, tossing his leather helmet onto the bed where its brass buttons shone dully in the low light.

"Cheer up. Sorry I'm not that fella."

Adrianna didn't laugh. "You took your time!"

"Damn hulking guards outside my room. The 'nurses.' Had to get inside a mouse and come out a hole in the wall, down the hall from them. Then I got so weary. Lord knows whether it was me or the mouse that was worn out. Poor bugger running from the cats all day maybe."

They sat together at the foot of the bed, their feet inches from the ground. Gareth bounced. He fluffed Adrianna's hair.

"How about some dinner? I'm starving. And so are you. Do you dare bring some from Cabot Land?"

"I'll slip down there. I have to make an appearance for mum and the relatives too. Haven't seen them in a couple of days. Oh, and your mum.

She's here with Uncle Huw."

"I know. I took a quick tour before I knocked on your door. Mum and Huw didn't see me, but they felt me. I hope it helps them."

Adrianna crept down the cedar stairs once more. Her hand reached for the skeleton key at the door. Her fingers found nothing. The door swung open onto an empty room. She swept her hand across step and floor in search of the key, then swung the door shut. Perhaps she had left it stuck on the wrong side. But hadn't she locked it the last time?

There was no key. And there was no lock. Chipped paint and gouged wood showed that they had been violently removed.

8

Cabot didn't know if he was coming or going these days, and he didn't like it. He had always been as decisive as the next man, until this Adrianna business. Why he stayed he no longer knew. All signs pointed to him not getting another chance with Adrianna. He had thoroughly botched their last meeting, and women, in his experience, did not shrug off being called bitch.

Had he actually called her that? An ugly thickening inside him told him he must have. He really would try to be super nice to her from now on. After he had disposed of the evidence.

The nighttime pond smelled, its weed and rot perfume belying its shining jet surface. He scanned the neighborhood. Just himself and the frogs. In one quick movement he tossed the cabinet lock and its key up into the darkness. He listened for them to hit the water. Two seconds of frogs chirping. Then the lock and key bounced off his skull.

He swore under his breath, snatched them from the mud and flung them as hard as he could into the pond. Now his damn shoulder hurt. If he didn't stop getting mad over this woman he'd dislocate every piece of himself.

And he'd have to think up a believable plea of ignorance about the damage to the bloody door. Adrianna was sure to know it was him. Well, she deserved it. He didn't know how. Hadn't figured that out clearly, and probably wouldn't bother to. But she did deserve it. She deserved a hard spanking... first of all. Cabot passed into the dark at the back loading dock, then disappeared into the freight elevator.

For a fifty-something portly man who smoked over a pack a day, Buckleigh was surprisingly wheezeless and quite capable of standing silent and unnoticed in the dark. He was certain that Cabot was the man to use. No risk to Buckleigh at all. The red tip of his cigarette flared in the night. He watched the curling flecks of tobacco turn grayblack as the brilliant crimson died to orange.

He would not have to 'go in' after Gareth now. Cabot was a bit stupid, but he could be trained, and managed into doing the necessary things. His brainless testosterone-love for Adrianna would motivate him far beyond the scope of your average Joe.

Buckleigh followed Cabot's path inside the building. Tonight, he would telephone his 'betters,' and brief them on Cabot. Tomorrow, he would drive Cabot out to the testing site. Training would follow, and in a week or so, Buckleigh could finally drop this doctor act once and for all. Retirement, and far more than the proverbial gold watch, were coming at the end of this little episode with Pugh. And he couldn't wait. He itched for it, like a snake shedding its molting skin.

9

With just a tiny speck of Anis, catching Gareth's thoughts had been the first feat that thrilled her – then sending her own thoughts back, shucking off all extraneous impulses. She calmed herself, then was off again, with even more self-control. By the end of four hours, she could travel into other rooms in the house, then to previous days, reliving Cabot's arrival, and days before that, finding a rabbit down by the railroad tracks. Then in real time, she climbed into a tiny electric delivery car down the street and drove it around the block just for a laugh.

Then it was time to travel in unison. She prepared to breathe in a larger dose of Anis.

"What about Cabot. Will he do any more damage while we're gone? Maybe find our bodies here and..."

"The sabotaged lock was just Cabot's hormonal funk. He can't get to us, even if he can reach this floor. This door, and mine, is as thick as my fist and dead bolted."

An hour or so remained for them to prepare for their exit. She remained anxious, perplexed about Gareth's insistence on flying off again. Why did he want her to come along? Secretly, she wondered about the health of his mind. Was he grasping at straws, losing his way in his old age? What the heck was he doing this for anyway? And what, exactly, was he doing?

"You know, they'll add me to the list of loonies if I go with you."

"Doubt it. You look sane."

"Really, dad. This could be insanity."

Gareth, quite calmly, agreed. "It gradually sorts itself out Ade, as things tend to. And there is a payoff. The miraculous."

The miraculous? The universe way out there, wherever, whenever? She saw images of massed darkness, their two bodies cast off into the abyss.

"It will make sense, I promise. You will surely find answers. And killing beauty."

Adrianna's heart stopped. The idea of that species of beauty caught in her throat, blanked her out. Killing... she would rather hide within non-lethal mediocrity.

Gareth lay on his back. His hand reached for Adrianna's and his fingers curled around hers. "For me, being with Elspeth will be everything to me."

"Who is Elspeth?"

"I can't talk about her, even now. But I can show you. Tell you the story with my mind."

His hand searched at the back of her skull and she found her mind slipping into a comfortable numbness. He slipped the leather helmet onto her head and fussed with her thick curls for a while, making sure it sat right and did not hurt. Then his thumb pressed at a spot in the back of the helmet a few inches above her nape while his fingers formed a skeleton crown, gently but firmly pressing at points in the leather.

If her earlier Anis experience had not prepared her, adrenalin and shock would have mastered her. She saw what he saw, as immediate as real life – and felt no more knowledge of the room around them, the bed...

Adrianna stands on the steps of a church, a spirit among a stoic wedding party in the blustery cold. People are half-heartedly throwing meager scraps of confetti at Gareth and his wife as they step through drizzle down the chapel stairs. Gareth's father scowls at the photographer from the top of the stairs. Mother flaps her hankie and tosses the remainder of her confetti in the direction of her son and daughter-in-law.

Then, their silent house. Gareth sits on a hardback chair in the living room, hands on knees. He stares at the floor. His father paces. His mother sits on the edge of the couch, hanging carefully between one gesture and another. Her eyes are tearful, her face troubled, but there is in her an aura of hopefulness she hasn't shown before.

Father stops at the mantel with his back to them, toys with a china dog, then begins tapping its base against the mantel, finding outlet for the anger he can barely suppress.

"First [tap tap] there's your mental fits, getting in the way of you doing anything [tap tap] with your life. Then, you let this Elspeth girl throw herself at you and you just have to get married." He turns a scowling face at Gareth.

"And now you want to fly off to Canada, of all places. It's not enough your brother Huw has gone there, now you want to go gallivanting off too, instead of staying here, where your mam needs you, and ..."

"Oh, be honest, Dad! It doesn't really matter if I go or stay. You don't want me around. I'm just a bloody accident waiting to happen, like you always say."

Father is pure exasperation. His eyes travel back and forth between Gareth and mother. "I was joking, you stupid bugger! Wasn't I mam? I was just bloody jokin' all the time. Good God! A man who can't take a joke these days..."

"Really funny joke, Dad. You never criticized Barry and Huw. As long as they played rugby and got into fights, they were alright. But because I'm different, you've never had any use for me."

"Different? What makes you so bloody different? "Father spits the words in sudden fury, staring about him as if not knowing what to hit. "You're no different at all from the rest of us. It's just your bloody arrogance that tells you you are. A little bash on the head from a fall, you start having fantasies and spouting nonsense, and that makes you better than everyone else?"

Gareth clenches his fists helplessly. His eyes plead with his mother.

"I'm sorry, Mum. I don't mean to be mean to you, honest. Elspeth and I have been planning this for months. It's my only chance to start again, where people don't know me... you know?"

"It's alright son. It's alright. You do what's best for you and Elspeth. Your father will be fine."

Father swings about, witless, stares at mother, then at the floor. He shakes a fist in his son's face, his teeth clenched.

"Bloody GO then," he chokes. "Go to Canada. Go to bleedin' Mars for all I care, if you hate us all so much! But you go without my blessing!"

"He wasn't saying that, Cecil." Mother reaches for him as he stalks from the room.

"He doesn't hate us ..."

"Oh, bugger him. He's useless. Canada can 'ave 'im."

The St. Lawrence River. The very air smells different, of the sweetness of pine and silver birch that mass the slopes, that climb along the Laurentian mountain ridges like a welcoming committee, waving, waving in the sunlight so bright you have to squint. A river this wide! So wide that an ocean liner can purr along, a loaded, festive iceberg, all the way to the Montreal docks: and along the journey, farmers in check jackets and children barefoot and in boots standing in the fields that slope to the water, waving at the big boat, waving at the big boat...

The train pulls out of Montreal, a train as long as the ship but dwarfed by the land, the rocky, bulbous, tree-bearded land that hugs close to the tracks, then falls away like a clumsy bear barreling downhill; ragged land, all pine spikes and glittering leaves and bush coming to a halt at huge ponds that had no right to be there, all by themselves with not a house in sight. Ponds and bush and mutant telephone poles stretching forever, then the sudden shout of a railway station's walls as they fly by, into more trees and bluff and bush, then a town, where everything stands still for ten minutes while the train rumbles to itself and Gareth and Elspeth stare out at wooden houses that look as though they have just been nailed to the dry ground, and follow the tail ends of huge cars bouncing over hill crests into more town that can barely be seen for trees and brilliant blue sky.

They sleep and wake fitfully through what seems weeks, waking to eat sandwiches they made on the ship, and alien biscuits called cookies, far too sweet; and once in a while, make staggering trips to the cramped toilets, then more slack-jawed, rocking sleep, until the Canadian National angels announce the arrival of Toronto and they awake, thick-headed and diesel-fumed. And Huw is there, grinning on the platform, waving up at them as they crane through the windows.

Elspeth smiling through her exhaustion, flops into an ugly blue armchair that Huw describes as 'Swedish minimalist shite.' Furniture donated by neighbors and the furniture shop, (sorry 'store') just down the road (sorry 'block'). Nice people these Canadians. Give you more than the furniture off their backs – which is not surprising, considering they've got everything and more to spare.

Huw says, "You should see the steaks! Thick as your thumb. An' if you order steak an' chips (they call them French fries here), you get a plate as big as a car, loaded with food."

Suitcases unopened, planted haphazardly around Huw's beautiful pine floors, and the sun blazing through the huge plate-glass living room window, and the buzz of traffic pawing at them from twelve floors below. Elspeth and Gareth smile and look bewildered, hold hands, then share a Canadian beer while Huw talks and shows them Canadian bread, Canadian cigarettes, Canadian tomatoes and potatoes, Canadian crisps that they call chips.

And with these wonders floating in their minds, they wander into the spare bedroom and collapse, fully clothed, into a mutual hugging sleep.

Days rise up and fall away in the hazy, humid heat of a Toronto back yard. Mosquitoes attack, raising obscene welts on pale Welsh skin, and Elspeth runs, screaming, from the monsters they call June bugs. Everything a bug, from the ant to the praying mantis. Everything huge: they lounge in Huw's second-hand Impala and gawk at Sam the Record Man, Eaton's department store, the crowds lined up at the Canadian National Exhibition, (exhibiting what, they wonder... mummies? elephants? suits of armor?); the brick and stone mansions of Rosedale, Honest Ed's Emporium screaming like Ethel Merman on Bloor Street, and Casa Loma screaming back, Ethel Merman's modest mother. Gareth and Elspeth relish buying apartment junk from Ed's, lie together on Huw's living room floor reading the apartment rentals, building fantasies, shivering with anticipation of owning furniture, a one-bedroom with a balcony, a television and internet. Sometimes, out of nowhere, they are hit with the loneliness of it all, with the strange alienation, with a poignant dose of hiraeth, that unique Welsh longing that can't be explained to the non-Welsh. Then Gareth turns into a shipper-receiver for D.M. Best, piano suppliers and they buy Huw a replacement 'two-four' of Carlsberg and Elspeth cries on the telephone to her mam. Then they go, all three, to Fran's restaurant and order huge banquet burgers and blueberry pie a la mode.

Gareth reports to work on the Monday, learns to package piano strings and sets of piano keys. Within two weeks, a promotion, to assistant piano-key repair man. The summer streets shine brilliantly through warehouse windows. His workmates tease him about his accent, but tolerate his fits. "I'm narcoleptic," he says. The summer flirts and cavorts, a bare-legged adolescent girl, and Gareth grins sometimes, as the legs catwalk into autumn. Then the gritty weather, and the city's sex hides under woolens and boots. Gareth buys Elspeth a brand new winter coat and they roll up all the early back yard snow into their first Canadian snowman.

Late November, and Huw has pneumonia on his birthday. Gareth slumps in the kitchen and stares at November 21 on the calendar. Elspeth wishes they had never come; Huw would not be working construction overtime to help them along. He would be in his living room now, watching television in the warm, instead of in a hospital bed.

They bundle up against the sleet and walk to the bus, ride to the hospital, sit beside crisp bed sheets under fluorescent ceilings and hold Huw's sallow hands. His brow is hot beneath sweat; the pillow is soaked beneath his head. Gareth lifts Huw's head while Elspeth turns the pillow over where the perspiration has dried up. Huw's eyes fall back into fever. They sit a while more, each holding a hand, willing enthusiasm into the feeble heartbeat. When Huw is asleep, they creep out into the winter night where the hissing traffic drowns out speech. The bus careens past before they have gathered their wits, so they decide to walk. They cross a small park where a snow-covered bench shines, a glittering sarcophagus under freezing rain. Then they turn onto the roadway between the office buildings. After seven in the evening. Only the janitors alive inside. A short cut through deserted territory. An ice-wrapped twig clatters across hard-skinned snow. The vicious wind kicks and passes.

Gareth stands beside a gurney in a naked room. His mind has collapsed; his veins are closing down. He is willing himself to die, to shut down like an unplugged machine. But he has not died and he hears someone stamping snow from their boots in the corridor, hears the sound of overboot clips undone. This is Canada, then. No overboots in Wales. This is the morgue. That is the body under the sheet. He cannot cry, cannot even scream, even as they pull back the sheet and he has no more room for denial. He has to nod. That is Elspeth with the nine-inch slash through her throat.

Adrianna jumped, clamping her hand to her face.

"My God! What...? Oh, I'm sorry dad. If I'd known. My God! How?"

She wrapped her arms around him, instinct making her rock him. He pulled away gently.

"It rips me apart all over again." He smiled wanly. "But I had to show you, so you know, if nothing else, what's driving me."

But how, she thought, could he resolve her death by traveling back there? And where was there? Even if he got there, to a somewhere or other, what difference would that make? Elspeth was dead. He couldn't make her un-dead. It was not possible.

Gareth's voice broke through her thoughts. "A janitor found us when he came out to get his car. The cops said I had been hit first, from behind... 'blunt force object' as they say. I was out cold. They told me that Elspeth must have fought like a demon, judging from the bloodied tracks in the snow, bits of clothing... hair. She had skin under her finger nails. Bruised all over, arms, legs. Three men, apparently. They stabbed me once where I lay, just in the leg. But they really took it out on Elspeth. She resisted too much, scared the hell out of them, so they slashed her throat. She must have died within minutes." He rolled on his back. "They took our coats, our money, her purse. They didn't rape her, thank God. Just a gang of alcoholic losers, a little younger than we were..."

Adrianna felt the depth of his depression, and she suffered as it transferred to her. Overcome by unutterable loneliness, she felt alarm and tears well up. He had not cried himself through that trauma, raged the sick moments out of himself. Escape, complete escape from this time and space, with mad hope beyond reason; that was what comforted and possessed him.

Out of some other facet of his mind, her father spoke into her pain.

"There's my hope. To see just her face among those billions of dead. I can hope for that, I think. Just maybe God can fix things if I can't. Who knows? I'm guided only by my 'gifted' brain and gut instinct."

Would finding some god be an answer for her too? She knew it would not. She didn't care a whit about any god. She wanted her father's love. She gritted her teeth. If this insane journey was the only way to keep them together, then so be it.

"So where do we go first? Do we actually go anywhere specific, after 'God' I mean. Show me. Take me there."

Gareth stroked her hair behind her ear and spoke quite normally, as if this were nothing at all.

"Well, I don't really know how to meet up with God, of course. But I have a clue; the word Aberconway. I know of a monastery by that name, and it holds something too important to bypass... The Croes Naid..."

"Huh? Crows what?"

"The Croes Naid, in Welsh. They say that it's a piece of the cross on which Christ was crucified. And he may be the door to God... Don't you think?"

"I gave up thinking hours ago," she said.

10

Adrianna collapsed on the bed, into herself.

"Am I ready?" she said.

Her father's voice sounded in her head, sent from his cot downstairs.

"Perfect," he said. "I am with you all the way. Take your Anis. Number five should do it."

Adrianna held the minute silver container up in front of her face, turned its lid until the hole lined up with the five. 'Just like selecting a sewing needle' she said. Carefully she tipped it to her nose and inhaled. Nothing sharp. No pain. Just an awareness of baking bread.

"Oh, no doubt," Buckleigh intoned, his hairy-knuckled hands stroking the steering wheel as it turned automatically, "I could have been a very fine doctor, had I the inclination. But, as it was, you see," his right hand played over a keyboard, punching in numbers, "the handsome remuneration offered by the Foundation naturally resulted in my signing on, so to speak, and enjoying this lifestyle for, what, twenty years now, give or take. There, that's got it. This baby will drive herself now." He slackened the seat belt so he could angle his bulk toward Cabot who scrunched uneasily in the passenger seat.

Handsome remuneration, for what? Cabot thought. Buckleigh might not be a doctor, but he was paid like a surgeon, judging by the car: A new Jag, computer-and human-drive, with hybrid auto/manual shift and God knew what else. Buckleigh offered him a fat glass, scotch and ice tinkling. Cabot took it and offered a smile like a closed zipper. *What else* included a nicely stocked bar – Glenmorangie scotch, Courvoisier, tequila, little white pills…

the door sucked closed into a flawless walnut dashboard. And what else included an eerie sense of cocooning. Around his ears a subliminal hum erased the sound of outside traffic. If he didn't concentrate on something, the drone would put him to sleep.

His eyes caught the street sign, Page Street, as they turned. They were on Bloor now, heading east. Cabot imagined the Foundation offices, glittering brass doorways and marble floors. Faux-Deco, maybe – arrogantly conspicuous elegance, probably. He turned his mind back to Buckleigh's relationship with Gareth Pugh and voiced his thoughts.

"What is this Foundation you keep talking about?"

"Can't tell you too much there, Cabot. Let's nutshell it, shall we?"

'No', thought Cabot.

The Foundation was a United Nations cell. An intelligence-gathering unit like the CIA, Interpol on a far higher level. Global, yet entirely integrated, with a mandate with very complex ramifications; to discover and eliminate any threats to the world's economic and social equilibrium.

The network was impressive in scale, backed by the obscene riches of global corporations, in China, India and the E.U. and to a lesser extent a bankrupt but obscenely well-armed United States. In short, The Foundation believed it stopped the world, by all means possible, from going to hell. They were also fanatical about Democratic principles.

'Bullshit,' thought Cabot. Democracy had been destroyed long ago, first by stealth, then by the police state. Democracy and Fascism should, logically, not have been bedfellows. But they both pretended to be what they were not – and all was well with the world.

"So, I could gather, from your talk of civil war and such, that you maintain a kind of right-wing, capitalist, status quo?"

"Right wing, left wing, it doesn't figure here. We do what's necessary. And we have some pretty powerful people on the team."

"You mean presidents and such?"

"Those who control presidents."

"Nefarious bastards then."

"If you like."

"So, if you're not a doctor, then what are you to Pugh? A keeper? Keeping him healthy and sane enough to do his work...? This is all quite new to me, you understand... I've only dated Adrianna for a matter of months."

Buckleigh's dry grunt and sidelong glance seemed to say, "I know all about your two seconds of so-called dating with Adrianna." He stared at Cabot, menace in his rhino brow and his dead challenging eyes. "A keeper, after a fashion," he said "in that I ostensibly tend to his medical needs. That's past-tense. I tended to him and ensured that he didn't break out, so to speak. I kept him confined, sedated, safe and harmless. Made sure that he did little or no work."

Buckleigh pulled a thick wad of banknotes from the glove box, which he smacked onto Cabot's lap.

"Count that lot. And listen carefully to what I have to say. I'm going to be as open with you as I can. So, to begin with, money. The Foundation is generous even to its foot soldiers; and that sum you have in your hands could be yours, if you agree to work with me. There's two-hundred fifty-thousand there. So let me explain. I've been quote unquote treating Pugh for ... since he began exhibiting strange, at the university, before his arrest."

"Ahah. Yes. I've read bits about that." Buckleigh shot him a sour look and Cabot's mouth snapped shut. He would listen then. Not a peep. Two-hundred fifty-thousand dollars... that was something to muse on.

"Doctor Buckleigh keeps Gareth Pugh from researching, from exploring his natural psychic proclivities, if you will. Doctor Buckleigh saved him from a lynching after his court case, thanks to Dr. Buckleigh's connections. And Dr. Buckleigh prescribed a bucketful of drugs for dear old Pugh. That was back in the day, before his second wife divorced him and he sold the house." He indicated the city outside.

"He lived right here, comfortably nestled in with the other lefty, overpaid academics and such. Been through quite a lot of changes, this end of town, since I was a kid."

Cabot looked out as the Jaguar purred through the outskirts of Toronto's Annex. Once a haven for hippies, students from the University of Toronto, and every sort of artist and fringe-dwelling lunatic, at the end of the 20th century, the Annex took a swan dive into a pool of filthy lucre, and never again came up for air. It was, by nature, and almost without design, as impregnable as its polished marble foyers, behind which the lawyers and businessmen played their sociopathic masques. Money and the inherent fascism of your average rich prick, thought Cabot, made it a brass-hard environment, out-of-bounds and lethal for those not in the club. Cabot could smell the money exuded through every crack and Victorian chimney, every manhole, every chic patio and narcissistic house of fashion that they passed silently. The car swung left and headed north, at a lubricated, silent crawl, up Brunswick Avenue.

"So where are we going?" said Cabot.

"Not far now. This is one location we don't want anyone talking about. It's where we've done much of our research on Pugh and Anis." Buckleigh snorted. "By rights, I should have blindfolded you. But if you say any-thing, I can just have you killed. Our agents are wonderfully cold-blooded, I assure you." He saluted Cabot with his scotch glass and a sterile grin.

"And talking of killing, how would you feel about Pugh dying?" Buckleigh said blithely.

The death or life of Gareth Pugh mattered only inasmuch as it might affect Adrianna's mood. And that was too subtle a dynamic for Cabot to consider right now: Would she be easier to manipulate when miserable over daddy's death? (The female corollary to the 'pity fuck.') Or did happiness turn her into a slut? If daddy were alive, and Cabot could be the one to tell her, to prove it to her ... The potential fruits of gratitude boggled the mind.

The car came to a hushed stop in a driveway and unlocked its doors.

"You have some inkling of what Pugh was up to, do you not? Telepathy, psychokinesis, all the rest of that spiritualist bunk." Buckleigh maneuvered his bulk out of the car.

"Now, another Maldor the Magnificent we could tolerate, no trouble at all. Difference is, Pugh has formidable psychic gifts; always has had. Pugh is dangerous, precisely because he has chosen not to be a showman, chosen not to be a rich celebrity – because, you see, he takes himself very seriously. And there is always the possibility that others will too."

Their destination, 411 Brunswick Avenue, had seen better days. It leaned arthritically, and looked over the road through black-blind windows. Squat-ters could live here, or a faceless nuclear family, or a solitary Latvian grand-father. The last thing it spoke of was clandestine research and killer agents in dark suits.

Buckleigh touched numbers on the entrance key-pad, and the door slipped open with a lover's whisper. Cabot followed him into a hallway. Straight through on the right, the hall passing potted ferns, a vaguely humanlike sculpture, and huge framed paintings of nude women, stopped at a brushed steel door. On their left, stairs ascended. Cabot's nape prickled. The dense silence breathed malice.

Buckleigh mounted the stairs and he followed close behind, hoping that something got friendlier, somewhere. Pseudo-Doctor seemed comfortable enough, and continued his monologue unabated.

"We would have preferred a Gareth Pugh comforted, even debauched, by money and fame. Men like that are a dime a dozen, and completely impotent. But he went his merry way, believing that his gifts were from God, of all things, and setting out to prove it. Had this notion that most men could develop similar faculties to his, you see..."

"So do a lot of spiritualists," he countered. "That has never made them dangerous. Quite the opposite..."

"True, sir, true. But Pugh has always gone further than 'a lot of spiritualists.' He has gone deeper. Without beating around the bush Cabot, he has managed to pull off some incredible feats, and that's what got our ears cocked."

"Like what?" They had reached a landing, where Cabot could finally breathe calmly and orient himself a bit. The landing gave them one option, a right turn that ended in a blank wall.

"Have you tried Anis, Cabot?"

"What? Anisette? Of course..."

"Not anisette. Anis. It's the fungus that Pugh dug up from the jungles. It's what he dragged back out of the Heart of Darkness, my man." Buckleigh lit a cigarette and leaned over the balustrade, watching the spiral of the burnt match that dropped to the floor below.

"Anis is one of the problems. It boosts a man's psychokinetic faculty a thousand percent. And it does all sorts besides. For instance, it allows you to travel through time."

Cabot howled incredulously. He clamped his mouth shut, double-checked Buckleigh's expression, then stared stupidly after the fallen match. The man wasn't kidding.

"No joke, Cabot, even if I do exaggerate a little. You see, we're not exactly sure how it works, what it does. I snagged a chunk of Pugh's supply for The Foundation – we'd get it ourselves, from the source, but we don't yet know how to prepare it as Pugh does. Anyway, thing is... it seems to allow a person to travel through time. We have performed scores of tests on as many subjects, and our men say there's a damn good chance time travel is happening. It certainly looks like it to the imbiber, if you follow me."

"Which you need to do right now." Buckleigh walked on and beckoned Cabot over to a glassed-in counter that had appeared in the wall. A writing tablet slid through a slot in the darkened window. Cabot lifted the electric pen and signed his name on the screen. A talking wire-network embedded in the glass said, "Press your fingers, four at once, into the gel pad, then your thumb." The signature pad slipped away, replaced by a rectangular box the size of a chocolate tray. His fingers sank into a gel surface that gradually enveloped them and gripped tight. At first warmer than his body heat, the gel cooled, parting from his skin, allowing him to retrieve his hand.

"Now the same with your thumb." Buckleigh spoke as a second tray slipped out. "This all gets your fingerprints, super-detailed, along with your DNA and blood type." He turned to a keyboard on the wall and coded entry numbers beside what Cabot now recognized as a door, the subtlest of pin-stripe shadow delineating its outline.

"Blood type? How do they get my blood type from gel?"

"Look at your fingers," said Buckleigh and stepped through the opened door.

Just below Cabot's fingerprints on the index and large fingers of his right hand, two tiny gouts of blood sat like jewels.

"I didn't feel anything," he began.

"Much of the time, you won't." Buckleigh said. "We could suck your brains out here and you wouldn't know it."

Cabot sucked his finger.

"Pugh is putting some version of himself through time," continued Buckleigh, "a mind-projection of some kind, or an astral body close to physical. That's how he has cracked the code, so to speak. His mental-pro-jection-self can fly faster than the speed of light, past the Event Horizon that would crush a spacecraft or some physical object, if it could do so much as reach that speed, which it can't, thanks to the laws of physics. AND, there was another young man who claims he is close to doing the same – kid that went into a coma chez Pugh, and started the whole scandal that brought the old man down. We brought him here, tempted the little rodent with the same cheese I gave you in the car. And he showed us what he could do. Astral projection, distant viewing given nothing more than geographic coordinates – and even seeing, if not exactly going, into the past and bringing us back historical details which he certainly would not have known prior. After a month or so, he died." Buckleigh coughed through suddenly watering eyes.

Cabot's heart fell, and his throat constricted. "Died?"

"Yeah, but not to worry. We have perfected things, and sent other agents in and out for long periods of time – and not even sickness. But with Pugh, now, it gets worse. We know that Gareth has perfected Anis for this purpose. But now he does it all on his own, no Anis at all."

Cabot kept a straight face. Whoever Buckleigh worked for, whether he had something on Pugh, or was completely out to lunch, he had money to throw around. Cabot watched as the door opened on two nurses pushing a trolley toward them. The smaller, pretty one smiled at him in that 'drop-your-pants, this-won't-hurt-a-bit' fashion and stepped behind his chair. The other manhandled his arm, pushing up his sleeve.

"Not to worry, sir," chirped the pretty one. Her fingers were in his hair, fiddling about like a squirrel burying a nut. "Just a little bit of prep."

Cabot glanced alarm at Buckleigh, who beamed, woodenly, as always. "Meet you in there," he said, and rushed back to the stairs. He waved his pack of cigarettes. "Gotta get one more in. They don't let you smoke in there."

The nurses scoured bald spots on his arms with abrasive pads, and pressed small rubber cups to the bared skin. The pretty one breathed in his ear and scrubbed at his temples. That done, they rolled up his pants and repeated the process on his legs. The sanding complete, they took from the trolley a tangled skein of many-colored wires and connected wires to the cups so that, by the end, Cabot stood wired from head to foot. Another nurse had arrived with a wheelchair, which she slid under his backside, and wheeled him through the swinging door.

A bare wooden table. A camera eyed him from a spot high in a corner. The nurses plugged him into various jacks under and along the edge of the table.

"Don't move much if you can help it," said the pretty one. "You don't want to break the connections."

"Don't I?" Cabot thought otherwise. This was invasive, $250,000 or not.

"What kind of tests are you doing? You could explain a bit, you know," he tried. But they were gone. Buckleigh's phlegmatic cough sounded from around him.

"Not to worry, Cabot, old boy. We're just scanning the old brain. First, we'll relax you, then start playing a bit with different stimuli, focal points, that sort of thing. No paradigm-shifting much beyond the Alpha Level, really. That's not what the docs call it, but it's the common parlance, y'know. Nothing to be anxious about. A retarded hen could pass with flying colors."

Cabot did not feel comforted. His neck and shoulders were painfully tight, and the light was beginning to burn his eyes. As if on cue, the light dimmed and a hum probed his mind like loving fingers, kissing lips. A smell of fresh baked bread percolated the air and his body and mind seemed to lean against one another, then infiltrate into oneness. Cabot could not tell them apart. Now, mind felt and body knew.

The slightest movement toward thought spread out like ink soaking into paper, as his cells received and gave signals. His body knew as much as his mind. The body thought, saw around corners of thinking that the mind alone could never even conceive.

He was in a universe of knowing so huge it could crush him like a house-fly between a thumb and finger. It would have terrified him, except that it was him, and at the same time indifferent to him.

"Hey, Bucky." He addressed the wall speaker. "This is better than heroin." His words fell away, pulled adrift from gravity. He watched them, fluorescent words floating like amoeba that traced closed eyelids.

"I could fart universes," he tried, and spluttered a laugh.

"That won't be necessary." Buckleigh's voice was facetious.

"Cheer up Bucky, old man. It might never happen." Cabot felt cocky. "Deal the cards, my friend."

"It's time to think of nothing for a while. D'you think you can do that?" The voice reeked of boredom.

Cabot tried shepherding his random thoughts into a fold of silence. It was hard at first, like forcing a tangle of barbed wire through a hole in a bush. Images sprang out, pricked at him, coiled past his ears. But then, suddenly, everything stopped. He was less than a piece of plankton afloat on a still ocean. Less than a dot. Left of him, to the right, all was breathless gray. Up and down, the same. And through this came Buckleigh's voice, flat and horizon-wide. "What can you see?"

"Nothing, and anything. It depends..." He considered for a second, and remembered himself. He was at the centre of this – the linch-pin ... "on what I want."

"Does it really?"

Fat Buckleigh, envious, obviously. Cabot was sure the old fart had never done this himself.

"So, this is Anis, I assume?"

"Got it in one," Buckleigh affirmed.

Cabot was water dripping from a petal... He was bigger than the Milky Way. There was a wind. He remembered a surrounding hum, somewhere distant, in a room. Antiseptic walls, but filthy nevertheless: his inner sight saw like a microscope – bacteria, hand prints, smears. If filth could shout, we would all go deaf, he thought.

His mind swung about, a razor-sharp keel tacking with the wind.

'I'm ready,' said his mind as he tacked through into wider horizons.

Buckleigh read him some coordinates. He watched the numbers and letters drift back and back in his head; they were floating ships approaching a great white wall – no water, they were airships, swallowed by white. It was new geography to his mind.

It was infinite history soaring on wind, blowing back through centuries. And he knew himself but faintly, as a remembered Cabot. All time coalesced in one moment and place. And now, perhaps five seconds in, he was beginning to feel pain inside his veins, as if his blood were turning to sand, cell by aching cell.

"Is it hurting yet?" It was Buckleigh again.

"Yes. More like a migraine every second." If only he could throw up, but without himself there, even that release was impossible.

"You're not trying hard enough. You have to get yourself over the first hurdle. Tell us where you are, what you see."

"There's just white, and this pain…"

"Not true. See further. Look out, and the pain will pass. The psyche usually balks right here, faced with the alien. You have to have something to see. That's why the coordinates. They're your anchor. Remember them?"

Gratefully, Cabot's mind remembered and latched onto them. Numbers, lines of latitude and longitude, stretched like a ladder over the void. He clung, repeating the numbers like a mantra. The migraine slackened, and he saw geography, a definite place. It was earth again and his mind laughed as the pain dissolved: his eyes and ears awoke, hungry, and led him one step further, into near physical manifestation.

He stood on a path at the crest of a steep hill that overlooked an ocean to the left. The damp cold wind, the smells, hinted that it was England; and the tilt of his wide mind confirmed it and gave him a date - 1896. A long beach of hard sand. Hugging its curve, a railed promenade peopled with silent strollers bundled against the cold. To his right, fronted by sections of lawn that connected to the promenade, clumps of row houses stepped down the slope, some whitewashed, some tan sandstone, a conglomeration of chimney pots standing up from russet and slate roofs. And right before him, two sea-worn benches. He sat and watched the bay, heard a dog bark and a woman's thin voice from the beach, calling a child, "Rachel, come along, there's…" and her voice was tugged away by the wind.

Cabot rearranged his backside on the hard bench. His heel tapped something beneath him. A hat box. He reached down and pushed the lid aside, revealing an elegant wristwatch. He clawed it up. A Rolex. That made no sense at all – a watch from the 21st century… unless someone else…

"Someone planted it here!" His voice leapt, loudly out of place in the English Sunday quiet. It was gloomy – he wanted to get back home. He spoke to an image of the room in his head, grounding himself in it.

He awoke with his face squashed into the table and drool pooling from slack lips. He detected cigarette smell and opened his eyes on Buckleigh swatting him with a handkerchief. The man lowered his face to inches away from Cabot's and rumbled a laugh, scowling into him with huge eyeballs.

"You dun good, Perfesser," he said, and slid a mug of coffee up to his nose. Cabot slumped back in his chair, yawned himself awake, and, for fear of snapping any of his network of wires, gingerly reached for the coffee.

"Happy to be back? Good. So tell us where you were, when – all that."

Feeling smug, Cabot described the scene and reached in his pocket for the Rolex. "I guess somebody else from here planted this there," he said and held it up to Buckleigh's face.

"Yes." Buckleigh took it, studied it for a moment, then placed it on the table. "One of our agents spent a little longer there than you, manifested more solid, thanks to the Anis. She was dressed in period clothes, so she made her way to a haberdasher's where she got the hat box, then put it where you found it, with the watch inside. You may even have passed her on the path. D'you recall a woman walking there? No? Well, maybe the timing was a bit off – even our best subjects can't control that acutely. She just got back here a few minutes before you did. So... what time was it? By your Rolex?"

"I don't know. I wasn't thinking about that..."

"You must be observant, always. An astute mind would have registered the time there." Buckleigh's hefty index finger poked at Cabot's shoulder. "The more details you record – tiny details of things we know are there, for example – the more certain we are of our results..." He lifted Cabot's coffee and took a swig.

"Reminds me, I need a smoke. So, onward and upward as some superhero said. Onto the second stage for you. You up for it?" He spoke as if it was all as commonplace as a game of Crib. "Oh, by the way, check the watch again. This kind of thing happens once in a while: we don't know why."

Cabot's Rolex looked like Salvador Dali's melting clock.

"Spoiled your spoils, my man." Buckleigh sounded happy, in a sterile kind of way. "Time travel can warp lots of things."

Cabot eased his aching back into the Jaguar's bucket seat. The day had been more than grueling. The testing had continued for the rest of the day, this time using photographs to direct him. Buckleigh termed it Photo-Realism. A photographed location, with which the Anis-fed mind fused. Cabot could feel it feeding on the image, devouring its atoms, reaching deeper, until deeper became manifest reality. They had manifested in a little town in Vermont, U.S.A., then in a desolate place called Chernobyl, and in a place that had once been Afghanistan, where Cabot was asked to find a small metal cylinder. He had discovered it sticking up from rippled desert. A crying windstorm, caustic with sand, cut him off from humanity. Sand that would shred you and bury you in minutes. He accepted near total burial.

He had attempted to transport the cylinder, but had failed. Not his own fault: he had carried it, but it had morphed into some residue of metal, and something powdery and yellow that clung to the skin of his hands. They had showered him down after that, scrubbed him under hot water with hard-bristled brushes on long poles. That had spooked him for a while. But a sense of triumph buoyed him up. He didn't care what the powder might have done to him. He had become something else, a stronger Cabot, a new creature and better. He had twinned himself with the Anis, testing the limit of his own fears until he reached the tipping point, when they arrived.

It seemed that he could collect portions of himself, draw them back into play in each new environment and time, so that Cabot once more found dimension in himself. Then he lived there, packed with hunger, energy, and a peculiar hint of a power he could not find the shape of. If it was Anis power, well, evidently Anis did not want to usurp him. It just wanted. It hungered for time and space, and, in the symbiotic relationship they created, found satisfaction, just as he did.

Now that he had shown some talent for time-space manipulation, they wanted him to apply himself full-time – to 'go in' after Pugh Senior and Adrianna.

Cabot turned away from the car window. They were cresting the overpass that hooked itself onto Sorauren Ave., where stood Wilson's candy factory. The pseudo-doctor put on his best chauffeur's voice.

"Would you prefer to return to the Pugh Mansion, Sir? Or is Home Sweet Home more to your liking?"

Cabot needed no contemplation on that one. Dig around in Gareth's belongings and secrets (well, more to the point, in Adrianna's stuff, underwear and all) or return to a lifeless condo to drink and play holo-porn games...

"Well, I think that, given the proposition you've made me, I should make the warehouse my base of operations, no?"

"Possibly, possibly. But there you'll have to avoid, and or manage the relatives. They absolutely must not get involved, or even curious. Got it?"

"Why not just kill them all before we start?" Cabot was only half joking. "Just shoot Pugh through the head?"

"Discretion, man. We are not the mafia. We don't whack entire families and have them concretized. The police must be left alone to do their day to day work – and we don't want them doing any of it to us at the Foundation. Strictly below radar, you know."

What the hell was radar? Cabot thought. Sounded like some inedible Chinese delicacy.

The Jaguar idled while they waited for a clear space through traffic.

"And besides that, we have found that Anis seems to be a little bit protective of his earthly body, back there in the warehouse. Tried to have him bumped off a little while ago and our assassin bought the farm in a nasty way. However, Anis never harms others who are using Anis. It would be like committing grievous harm on itself."

"Sure of that, are you?" Cabot wanted to believe him – if there was more money in it. And after all, he could just use the Anis, pretend to have killed Pugh... or, he could actually devise some death for Pugh that would not directly involve himself. For the right money. That was key.

Buckleigh chimed in again. "Well, here's the kicker, Cabot my friend. Can you guess what Pugh is after, with Adrianna in tow?"

"No idea. A cure for cancer? Hitler's parents?"

The Jaguar hummed at a standstill in the parking lot.

"Worse. He's looking for God. And he is convinced that he can prove to the world that God well and truly exists. Prove it, Cabot. With living experience of the fact. He and Adrianna are just the beginning... the Sputnik of time-travel history. He is determined to find proof, and then return to teach others to travel."

"The proof of God might be comforting to some..." Cabot began.

"Comforting?" Buckleigh blurted his disbelief. "Have you any IDEA what such knowledge would do to us, to our bloody world man? Good Lord, think of it!"

Cabot was not interested in thinking.

"What would happen if people knew without a doubt that God existed? Can you imagine the upsurge in religious yearning? Think, man, of how that would affect politics, governments, economies. A huge paradigm-shift in the human soul, in human desire. Good Lord! It would make the religious fundamentalists look like choirboys!"

Buckleigh's eyes locked onto Cabot's.

"It would be a plague on all our houses. It would mean any old Tom, Dick and Harry refusing to acknowledge the authority of earthly govern-ments. Insisting that God and God's laws come first. Demanding that we care for the poor, the millions dying of Cholera and Typhoid, and starving; demanding that we do not spend trillions per year on military defense..."

"Or military aggression..."

"It's those trillions of dollars, Cabot, on military power, aggression, that maintain entire cities and towns this world over. Were it not for military initiatives, major cities would collapse for want of contracts, industry and cash flow. Entire populations would suffer, unemployed, hopeless. Imagine the backlash from simply that change. Then add, ahh... planetary ecology, pollution, millions demanding that we actually stop polluting, now. We can barely manage to pretend to care about pollution, what with all the other priorities we have to juggle!

"Human society just could not stand the strain, Cabot. You think the status quo stinks? Just conceive of the alternative. All because of the naive earnestness of one little man."

"Let's look at it another way... purely personal, for you. There's Adri-anna involved."

"She does what she likes." Cabot couldn't keep the resentment out of his voice.

"She does, sir. She does..."

Cabot huffed, about to speak.

Buckleigh held his hand up to forestall any further objections. Cabot hated it when people did that.

"You're an intelligent man. And that's why I have divulged all this to you. The Foundation wants you to help us, and you want her. I think that's a good marriage, no pun intended."

"And you think you can help me get Adrianna?"

"In carrying through what we need, odds are you will have Adrianna in the palm of your hand. And if not, you still have the money."

"Why me? There must be plenty of others... And anyway, what the hell am I supposed to do when I'm there, wherever it is I'm going?"

Buckleigh gave one of his satisfied grins.

"For one thing, get close to Adrianna. There's no saying what will come of that. Be there for her, support her... whatever... we don't care if you tie her up and abuse her, as long as our first objective is met. Just imagine, Cabot. Adrianna living in another time and place, maybe somewhere where she is more likely to acquiesce to your needs, your demands..."

"Adrianna? Not likely."

"Pick any century you like. Some century where she has virtually no rights, no power."

Cabot saw. Any century. A time before the notion of equal rights for women had ever reared its ugly head. A time when women were chattel. An Adrianna cowed, helpless, and shaped by the whims of men. The notion sent a thrill through him. A time with no police. Where a man could do almost what he liked with his own woman, his wife or lover. If he could corner Adrianna in such a time, there would be no end to his power.

And, after all, he just wanted her to love him. And, given the right place and time, he could make it happen. He could prove himself to her. And she would be so much more likely to depend on him. His groin stirred at the thought.

As though he had seen inside Cabot's head, Buckleigh spoke. "Imagine, the 15th-century. Adrianna would have to behave, or else stick out like a nail just waiting to be bashed down. And think of it, Adrianna the bashee, and you the basher. No one would stop you. You would be in control there."

Cabot considered. That scenario was the closest to magic he would ever be. It could be like a dream; a dream he controlled.

"Before I say yes, tell me the other half of the scenario, your 'first objective,' as you say."

"Simple really, for a man of your intelligence. We want you to watch Pugh, and find a way to dispose of him." Buckleigh waved a hand. "I don't know. Make it look like he has died, disappeared, conducting his foolish experiments. You keep him from returning, he dwindles to nothing, one way or another. The family gives up on him. He's legally declared dead – no crime, no culprits. We box and bury him. That way, he vanishes, as far as the public goes. And we deal with Adrianna when she returns. With him gone, she'll crumble. Unless, of course, you decide to trap her back there. It's entirely up to you Cabot. We trust your judgment."

Cabot pushed himself tight into the seat. This was huge. Maybe dangerous. Maybe not, if others had used Anis this way before. He was no dummy – he could handle it. And best of all, Adrianna at his mercy... But he would play hardball. He wasn't about to be a pushover for these anonymous Foundation specters.

"You know," he said. "The money is not really enough for what you ask of me. I'm taking a huge risk here, notwithstanding your assurances regarding Anis..."

"We thought you'd say that," returned Buckleigh

He tossed another envelope into Cabot's lap.

"That's another $100,000 for you. Play with it. Stick it in the bank, buy stocks. We don't care. Take a few days, spend some money. Then, do the job successfully, and we have another $200,000 on your return."

Cabot toyed with his bottom lip. More than five years' pay for a little game; for the experience of his life, with Anis and, more importantly, with Adrianna. He fantasized ... giving it to her over the kitchen table, her gorgeous ass...

"Okay," he said. "I'm your man."

Buckleigh leaned forward and extended his hand. They shook.

"We thought you were," he beamed.

11

The scent of Welsh cakes, their sugar and raisins, would have been heaven. Much better than the sad odor of dust they inhaled up here in the room's corner, hanging about like a couple of forlorn out-of-body candidates.

Gareth seemed content, judging by the age he was taking, 'inhaling the history,' as he put it. Adrianna's patience ran out.

"This is your choice, is it? Drifting about up here with our spines scraping the ceiling?"

"Mmm? What, Ade? Grumpy already?"

"You have to make this fun, dad, or I'm not coming along..."

"Okay."

Adrianna could feel him unshackling his mind, like a paratrooper preparing to leap. He took a deep breath and pushed off.

"Let's catch up with Elspeth then."

They moved, and the air rippled like a car windshield washed with rain. She could see a squat dresser standing next to an unmade bed, and sunlight reaching through the four-paned attic window. Its buttery glow suggested late afternoon.

The house was quiet, wherever they drifted, their only company the creaking of walls and roof and floorboards; an ancient house, bruised by a wind that moved eternally here on the hill crest. They passed the front bedroom window and Adrianna saw a blurred impression of the outside landscape; sun like an apricot, descending through a slate-blue evening over wind-sculpted trees and hills the color of dark Atlantic swells.

Where was Elspeth? The sounds of the BBC from a transistor radio lured them down dark, polished stairs to the kitchen. 'Elspeth's mum,' came Gareth's mind. Adrianna hung beside him as the old lady sat smoking. A teapot steamed under its tea-cozy, next to a chipped milk jug and two cups and saucers.

"Elspeth, my chick? You want a cuppa, love?" Mum craned her neck back to the small hallway that led to the steps outside. "Come in and shut the door girl. There's a nasty draft."

"Right mam. Lovely night though." The door creaked, the latch clanked to and Elspeth stepped into the room. She threw herself into a wooden chair, hooking her feet – in Wellington boots – on its rungs, and wrapped both hands around her cup, blowing steam away.

"Makes it so nice to come inside, too. Nice to be cozy, innit mam?"

Gareth's mind wrapped around Elspeth as if magnetized, and it took an effort of will for Adrianna to detach herself. She pushed herself to the opposite side of the room and studied Elspeth, her sight clarifying as she stared. 'Close to Rubenesque,' she mused. The kind who would either have to worry constantly about her weight, or just not give a damn. But now, in late teens, early twenties, she was blessed with a happy voluptuousness, all rosy, wind-buffed cheeks, bright eyes under tangled hair, large, impertinent breasts that strained the top buttons of her dress, and freckled arms, one medallioned with a smallpox inoculation just where her frocked cuffs ended.

Adrianna liked her. Elspeth would fall into the 'not give a damn' camp. She liked her voice – strong, and sweet with Welsh cadences. She basked in the sound of her chatter, in the way she stroked her mum's hand, in the scent of hot Welsh cakes on a plate.

Where Philomena was angles, Elspeth was all curves; where Philomena exuded the icy clarity of control, Elspeth emanated kindness. If Philomena was calculated drama and faux eroticism, Elspeth was naive power, a thing lovely to feel.

'She has no wiles,' thought Adrianna.

'You see?' Gareth had joined her mentally, his rhetorical question brimming with his admiration for Elspeth.

"You staying here then? I have to take a break from your happiness for a bit. Gotta go look around outside."

Joining her outside, Gareth was not happy. He wavered agitatedly.

"Something's wrong. Nothing's clear. You must have noticed that? Like looking through warped glass."

"I did notice it, yes. But only until I released myself from you. In the kitchen, I saw Elspeth perfectly clearly after a bit. Thought it was my eyes becoming acclimatized or something."

"If that's so, then I have a serious problem. Can't see a damn thing – and my head is throbbing."

He sat on the windowsill and folded his arms crossly. She wondered what Elspeth would see from the inside; perhaps a warped image, light playing on the glass.

"I just can't connect properly." He pushed a clenched a fist against his chest in frustration. "It's as if I'm being resisted. I feel a pressure every-where – mostly in my head, behind my eyes, but it's also physical – it repels me whichever direction I face. I feel unwelcome, like something being shoved back through a letterbox. And my head is just spinning – endless noise and chatter."

He growled and struck at his forehead.

"Maybe we should go then? Try another time?" asked Adrianna.

It suited her just fine, some relief from all this effort. It was histrionic, not historic. She did not like her father's strife, the attenuation of the mind that seemed to be taking him over.

"Come on," she urged. "I think it's time for cocoa and rum, and a night of doing nothing."

He shook her off.

"You go. I have to stay. There's a reason I came here, and I'm not... crawling off because..." he stared angrily skyward, "because SOMEBODY doesn't want me here!"

"Now you're being really silly, dad. As if anybody, least of all Him, cares that you're here." But Adrianna didn't feel too sure herself.

"I know what I'm doing!" He waved her away. "I can't argue with you. I have to stay. You'd better go."

"Well, give me something then, to guide me back to you when I'm ready."

He slipped off a ghostly ring, turned her palm over and dropped it into her palm. Its weight was a mere breath.

"Try focusing on it. If that doesn't work, I will call you back if or when I need you."

He made it all sound so simple, so comfortably banal, this flipping through time like a grasshopper.

And she hopped, with his ring folded tightly in her palm.

Gareth lay prone in wild grass that swayed and squeaked near his face. Stones pressed through the damp earth under his raincoat. The coolness was good for him. Turf and rock hills tumbled to the valley beyond his outstretched legs. He listened to the slow bubbling of the mountain spring into its deep pool. Always, when troubled, Gareth returned to this well and the whisper of the moving air across the slopes. He vanished into a few seconds of blissful rest, in an unblemished time. Then he awoke, completely renewed.

He searched for the hollowed stone, and found it tucked into a cleft in a trio of rocks. It was the same cup he had always used, the same used by travelers for centuries. He scooped from the depths and gratefully drank his fill.

He drank more and forgot to think. His inner plumbing gurgled, cold water seeping through a warm stomach. He remembered his problem. Elspeth. What was he doing wrong?

All he could do was try again. He didn't know what else to do. Years before, he had tried to reach her, meeting the same failure. At least this time he had broken through a little – he could see her once more, the very Elspeth he had known, the very same time and place. He could taste it, in his skin and in his soul.

This time then. He would get through. He could be stubborn too.

And wily. He decided to literally try a 'different angle.' The thought sped through him, he acknowledged it; and let it go in a flash. If the big Someone was watching him, then furtive speed was the answer. A different angle. So be it. No thinking on it. Gareth spread thin like flung mist, and warped sideways. He was not returning in a straight line back. He was a dolphin feeling a tidal change undersea.

Then Elspeth was ahead of him, walking to the bus stop. Her image was clear and strong. She strode downhill looking about her with her familiar half smile. Gareth floated beside her like a child following the tack of a tiger inside its cage. If only he could touch her.

She halted, her head tilted, her eyes hopping from plants underfoot to ragged rocks, to sky, then back to the path. Was she sensing him? He didn't know if that was possible. Her eyes, frank and soulful, looked right through the space he inhabited. They devastated his sense of being, as always. Eyes beautiful and serene, laced with slow eroticism.

He followed her into the close streets where the petrol fumes and house smells told him he was manifesting strongly. She wound from one row-housed street to another. At the main road, she crossed before a bus. It swayed past him, momentarily blocking her from view. Always the same stink from those buses, the stink of its seats and diesel fumes and the stale odor of cigarettes. He was really there with Elspeth, in an age before they had banned cigarette smoking from every public conveyance.

The bus gone, he searched for her, and saw himself first. Gareth Pugh, aged nineteen or so, whistling and strolling along the pavement beside the new Boots Chemist. Elspeth saw him and her face brightened.

"Hiya," she said, and strode past.

He pulled a hand from a pocket and waved at her, then skipped around the Walls ice-cream sign and rattled the tea-shop door, disappearing inside. Elspeth walked on to the corner where she met a ragged-haired young man in a brown coat. They kissed, then turned and walked arm in arm to the pub.

Stunned, Gareth peered through the tea-shop window at himself. There he was, skinny, with uncut bangs hanging in his eyes, worn tweedy jacket, his fraying elbows resting on the table. And Alison, all goldensoft and freckled across from him in a pale blue dress and leather jacket, and scarlet glasses, without lenses. She laughed at something he said, then took his hand. He lifted hers and kissed it.

"Sap," thought Gareth. What the hell? Why was he not with Elspeth? And who the hell was the fellow she was with? Everything was upside down. Anger and fear attacked him, waves of damp fever, chased by panic. In his jealous mind he saw Elspeth kissing the other man, at home under the blustery wind, leading him upstairs and wrapping her limbs around him in the dark.

The day disappeared and rain hissed. It plummeted through fathoms of darkness. He lay nailed to the street, naked and white as a maggot. Above his stripped body, the moon glinted, a toppling sickle. Rain bit into his skin, battered his eyelids. Elspeth walked over him, dark thighs and flashing heels. Then she was gone, trailed by the remnants of a melody.

And then Gareth was crying, rocking her in his lap, smoothing hair from her face as his lips kissed her again and again, like an animal drinking. Dead Elspeth, fragmented, breaking apart in his arms and each part becoming a muscular whole, another Elspeth, holding him and twirling him, sweeping him this way and that until he felt he would be sick. Sweeping him through years and dimensions. So many invading images, tangled with shreds of thought, all foreign.

Then Elspeth was a child running across the public school playground, running out of the gate and into the metal face of a passing lorry. Gareth cried out, his yell rasping against his throat.

The image was superseded by another, almost identical but seconds later. Elspeth running, the same lorry already passed the gate – and Elspeth skipping to her mother. Living into another weekend, into her ninth birthday, where she gloated over freshly baked jam tarts.

Then seventeen, passing her typing exam; eighteen and jumping off the bus near the Mecca Ballroom, her first day as their secretary, balancing on high-heeled Converse runners, wiping nonexistent creases from her leopard spotted skirt.

Another wedding – not to him, but to the man in brown. An antique honeymoon car packed with luggage, rumbling up the steep lane, coughing farewell fumes at bleary eyed sheep. Elspeth and husband en route to Cardiff.

Then Elspeth at home, sobbing quietly in the kitchen, her fingers absently turning her mother's ashtray on the table. The ambulance gone – Elspeth has the house to herself, forever. The wind moans. Gareth cannot touch her, cannot give her any warmth. These are some of her lives. Hers alone.

He strained against the weight of water, pushed until his sinews ached, so that his fingers might feel her, strained to break through a dense, implacable weight. It repelled him, and yet let him see. It let him feel agonies of loss, but would not let him control one iota.

He fell exhausted into a trench where he could feel no bottom – fell slowly into a slow tide, until he hit a final blackness, the blackness of loam.

Pungent earth, the scent of injured roots, underground networks of tangled lace torn up, seeming to bleed – dense earth holding two naked bodies, clammy cold. Two bodies, with skin translucent white, coupled together in the black like two Welsh love spoons, their hair matting, weaving together, cobwebs in duet. Gareth and Elspeth preparing to rot, and the sky outside wheeling, as always.

Gareth's breath jammed in his throat. If he had been physical he would have vomited. As the images subsided, the sound of bubbling water took over. He was sitting in the grass, breathing tremulously. A hand gripped his shoulder and squeezed. An aged hand, liver spotted, with fingers like polished wood.

He looked up at her, then smiled through tears of joy.

"Gran. I've so missed you." He was ten again, sobbing on her bed, for days on end, refusing food.

"I've missed you too, lovey. What have you been doing to yourself?"

"I should be asking you that. You're the dead one."

"You push yourself too hard, lamb. There's nothing you can do."

Her voice soothed him, took the blame from out of his gut like a huge splinter. If he was powerless, well, what of it? It was all gone. The straining, the desperation. Everything was as it should be, and breath seemed to enter him effortlessly.

Grandmother settled beside him. She talked in time with her hand, which dabbled dreamily in the brook.

"Dead, yes. And more comforted than I ever was in life. So good, it is, that even where we are now feels like a bit of paradise – which it definitely isn't.

"I'll tell you this, to start. You get what you believe in, when you die. You get what you believed in while you were alive, in a way. Although, not all of us are sure of what we believe while we live. So it's lucky that all the confusion strips away once you pass on – strips away like old bark, and there you are, all glistening with your own sap, your own down-to-earth self. That's your beliefs, coming alive. Once your real beliefs shine out, there's a world grows from them, Gareth. And that's the world I've been living in for the past while... a whole life, really, with some other people like myself. It's quite nice really."

She gazed outward, squinting through the sun's brightness.

"But I think there has to be something else coming. Can't be this nice forever. I get the feeling I'm being allowed to rest for a bit..."

"Well, it was a hard life for you... down there. Where are we now then? I'm not dead, am I? I know this place well..."

She looked around. "It's not like where I live – which is the closest to paradise I've ever been. But it is somewhere quite nice you've got for yourself here."

"For myself? I don't understand."

"Oh, it's simple really. You're not dead – but you've been playing around in the 'netherworld,' as you might say. And I suppose this is one of your little rewards, one of your safe places you've created for yourself in all those years of playing around."

Her hand tapped against his in good-humored remonstrance.

"Your deep down beliefs... how can I put it... they're like roots in your mind. Deep, deep down, so deep that you can scarcely feel them during life... they direct your actions. Your big actions, not the small ones. They tell you things like 'Go to Canada.' 'Become a priest.' 'Learn to sing.' Even the nasty things, like 'murder children...'"

She picked up his hand lightly, and traced the brook's spring freshness over its back.

"This place is the loving home you always had at the centre of your heart. Whenever things were terrible down there, whenever you were afraid, or lost, you would come to this place, in dreams, or by finding similar places on earth... like the rock pools you used to linger over all day. This is your place of peace."

Her eyes twinkled. "It's not a paradise, like my place. But it's the best you can do, in your mongrel state."

"Mongrel...?"

"Not alive, not dead. You've managed to infiltrate another place. You've used those mental powers of yours to get here... here and there and everywhere. And doing so has changed the way you are made. That's it, love. Your mind and beliefs have created this, and recreated you to some extent. And they will continue to do so. So you better be careful, my boy."

"I'm always careful."

"Oh, you think so... but you don't know. There's so much more to contend with than you can comprehend. I see it, from this side, and I certainly don't dare go near it – I don't meddle. I just wait..."

"But you're dead... that's what..."

"What I'm supposed to do, you think? Well, maybe. But maybe not. Anyway, it's what I chose, back then, and little else has happened since. And all I'm saying is, you'd better be careful what you choose. Like this chasing poor Elspeth, for example."

"You've seen me...?"

"Of course, you muggins. Why do you think I hang around where I do, half gone, half not? What do you think grans are for but keeping an eye on bad boys?"

"But how can that be bad? All I want to do is comfort her. I want to be with her for a while. Maybe even alter the life she had for the better, so she doesn't have to die as she did."

"You know that can't be done, you daft man! If you didn't clutter yourself up with silly wishful thinking, you'd have known that ages ago. The truth is as bald as a baby's bum, Gareth. And only you can choose not to see it."

"So I can't reach Elspeth? I'm not allowed?"

Gran puffed out exasperated air.

"I gotta go soon love. So I'll make this short and sweet. So LISSEN, will you?"

"I'm listening."

"Okay then. Now here's some rules, for bad boys like you who won't behave. You CAN'T visit the Elspeth you knew. You can't go back into your own past. It's impossible, both physically and... metaphysically. Remember all your, what'd' you call it? Your quantum physics. You can't re-enter your own life. Just like you can't be a particle and a wave at the same time.

"But you can. I've seen it."

"Never mind. What I speak of is real to you... The best you can do – and this is infinitely more than an ungifted human can do – is to observe other potential lives."

"You are the same Gareth that lived one particular life, so how can you re-enter that life? It is done. It exists, perfect in and of itself. Its very manifestation is evidence of that: otherwise it wouldn't manifest at all. It would be something else. Your own logic should have told you that. Your own experience, boy."

She was right. He moved through time, he 'existed' on the sub atomic level, and the same rules applied to him as did to quanta. It wasn't the real, corporeal him that traveled, that encountered Elspeth's world, his old world.

"That's why your vision was cloudy. You can't retrace those steps, because they've been lived, and to tread all over them and try (even with psychic gifts) to alter them, botches everything up. That window through which you saw Elspeth in your particular time, that window wouldn't let you in, true. But it also saved you from harm. Going through that window would kill you or make you irretrievably mad."

Yes. Only alternate worlds would allow more manifestation. Not only the world changed, then, but the Gareths changed. The new dimension would accept him as a visitor, 'knowing' that he could never manifest completely and alter anything. On the sub atomic level, worlds were discrete.

To think there were other Gareths, not controlled by this Gareth. If so, then those other Gareths were not affecting him either. Separated from them, he felt suddenly isolated in the universe. Irretrievable in vacancy.

Her familiar voice grounded him in her love.

"You were shocked at seeing Elspeth with another man. Well, it should have dawned on you that you were watching another life. Her life, to be sure, but another one where you were on the border, not the centre of her. There's an infinite number of possibilities and choices. And in the one you saw, she had chosen another man, and you had chosen Alison."

"Forever?"

Gareth felt cheated. Without Elspeth, without his desire for her, what could he do? It had shaped his life, it had sculpted him. How could he be with Alison, when his love for Elspeth was so great? Had love cheated him then? Was it all a lie that he had been dragging around all these years?

"What d'you mean 'forever'? Don't be so tup, mun." Gran bashed his shoulder. He had to laugh. He hadn't heard the Welsh 'tup' used for ages: 'tup', stupid, half-witted, daft.

"You aren't with Elspeth forever, or Alison. Or anyone else you choose. You might prefer to think that Elspeth is everything. And that's very nice for you. It adds the kind of dark, Celtic tragedy you like in your life. So much so that it colors even your ideas of the afterlife, and of this in-between world. It has all been a nice obsession for you, in the way that mastering the cello would be for somebody else."

Gareth sat, chastised, not knowing how to respond.

"And you can continue doing this if you want. Flapping around willy nilly and banging your head against the window like a fly. But you can't get in – you can only watch, at the best of times, and you can't change anything. SO... the thing you really want, to be with your Elspeth again, that just can't happen my boy. You really... honestly now... you don't have a hope of that until you die. And maybe not even then. Who knows what will happen when the bark peels off..."

"So was I wrong all along? I don't understand. This was so urgent. I couldn't say no. It was...truth. It's ... my art. Without it, I'd be useless."

"Is a tree useless? Is a buttercup?"

"You don't understand. I'm human. I need..."

"We all need, Gareth. You're right. That's being human. But have you thought... maybe what you have done so far is just the start of things? Maybe Elspeth isn't the point after all."

He was not free of the pain that shadowed every mention of her name. He didn't want to be free of it. The greater the pain, the more profound the bond. Yet he glimpsed, for the first time, the sense of a wide open sky, free thoughts, clear thoughts... as clear as the water that bubbled...

He slept. And when he awoke, gran had gone. And the stream was not a stream but the sound of the tap running. And Adrianna was gently pressing a cold, wet cloth into his hand.

He felt tears running down his face.

"My jaws ache from being me." He unclenched his grinding teeth.

"What is it? Did you meet Elspeth?"

"Not Elspeth. I met my gran. Out there in nowhere land, as sure as this mirror here." He stared into it in wonderment, as if Gran had been transmuted into it.

12

Minutes before, there had been a thick Welsh rain curtaining a bleak landscape. Now the sun had come out. Adrianna slogged along behind her father, uphill through wet gorse and bracken. She hadn't got this Anis thing down yet. She'd taken too much Anis to simply drift, but not enough to make a robust march through rough ground. The wind buffeted her left and right. Half-way was nowhere to be.

"Can we slow down, Mental Gareth?"

Gareth stopped on the crest and walked back to her, a scarecrow in a black raincoat. She caught her breath, stared at the turf through Gareth's boots and felt the faint touch of his wraith-hand on her shoulder.

"Okay Ade. We'll take this a little slower. But we must find some shelter before these nasty clouds break."

The mountain ridge they stood on overlooked the panorama of North Wales. It would lead to the monastery at Aberconwy, her father had said. But that was on the coast, of which she could see not a flicker. As far as her eyes could see lay fold upon fold of ancient mountains that checked the advance of small armies of trees. Gorse and brambles stubbled the undulating face of the land. A group of sheep cropped what rough grass they could find, under a hawk rocketing overhead on a draft. It was all much wilder than she anticipated, a land that had the run of itself.

"It doesn't look like the Wales I'm used to," she said.

"It's feudal Wales, Ade," said Gareth. "That is, if we're on track. It's a raw land, untamed in comparison to modern Wales. Much of this wouldn't even be farms and hedgerows until ... oh, I dunno, maybe seventeenth-, eighteenth-century, when they enclosed it."

"So you're sure we're in the right place and time?"

"I know North Wales when I see it." Gareth faced outward abruptly, cutting off conversation. His hand rummaged in his coat pocket and withdrew a piece of stone, which he held up to view.

"A piece of the monastery at Aberconwy. If this is authentic, then we are here. And if the monastery is here, then we are at the right time."

"Duh! Obviously...when you put it that way..."

"I'm serious. You see, in 1283, Edward the First of England controlled the land, and he ordered that the monastery be uprooted, moved elsewhere. If it's here, it must be pre-1283. Doesn't matter exactly when. I'm just after something that's in the monastery."

The wind beat against them roughly and behind them came the sound of slate slipping. They turned to face the shaggy figure of a mountain pony on a hillock, its muzzle turned toward them.

"What a beauty," whispered Adrianna. She watched it watching them, its long, rough-haired mane blowing thick across its face, straw colored against chestnut; and those huge, deep eyes, staring through them, then its forelegs shifting as it lifted its heavy head away.

"It knows where we must go," said Gareth.

The forced cheer in his voice indicated to Adrianna that the horse knew nothing of the sort. "I was kind of hoping you did too," she ventured, eyeing him as he set off down the slope.

"Of course," he shouted through the wind.

The threat of rain drove her. She toiled after her father's back, forcing fear from her mind. A small voice inside her told her she had no reason to be here. She was directionless, as with everything. Had she agreed to this misguided adventure as a way to avoid her aimlessness in normal life? Something told her it was bigger than that. It was love for her dad.

And need. That was bigger than herself.

She could not name the need. It shut itself off from her. She saw the opening valley floor, the riven stones through which they clambered. Her nostrils flared at the wind and its flavors, the soil, the burgeoning rain, the bracken and moss. And it struck her that nature was richer than she had ever known 'at home.' Nature permeated the atmosphere, commanded the stage. Even in her semi-spirit state, her feet were aware of the spring of the rough turf, the stones and soil.

She caught up and grasped Gareth's arm happily. Even he felt more substantial. She wondered if it was a delusion, a trick of her tired mind. Fatigue usually had the opposite effect, especially on Anis – everything became mist. She would find a mirror, or a pond surface somewhere, and take a good survey of herself.

They had come to the edge of a copse of young trees, where a handkerchief of land showed signs of primitive cultivation. Sad green leaves struggled upward under the shelter of a collapsing fence of interwoven boughs. Human hands had woven those boughs together. She stared about, listened into the waving trees, over the nearby hillocks, for signs of humanity.

Gareth looked pleased.

"Search around a bit, and I'm sure we'll find a good bit of shelter."

Well, she was not going to bed down out here in the wilds, with beetles crawling up her legs. They'd wake up sick with the damp and cold, and that would be the end of their journey. Adrianna squared her chin and said so.

"We'll find somewhere warm and dry," Gareth assured her, peering into the thick gloom of the copse.

"Damn right we will," she countered. "And it will look a lot like a house."

She strode beyond the scraping of tilled land to where she could see the valley opening outward. Let him crawl under a rock. She was going to find a stable, at least. A hut with a decent roof.

She was momentarily stunned by the sight. Too far to walk to, but unmistakable even in the raining gloom, the dark hulk of damp stone broke the horizon: A small castle, crammed onto a tor. Two towers, maybe three; one rounded, the other across from it a massive rectangle which she realized was a keep; with a circular band of stone wall coming off it, joining the towers, and shored up by earthworks.

Even better, dotted here and there across the hillocks that rolled to the tor, were little houses, the bluish smoke from their fires ribboning into the thick Welsh sky. Surely good old Welsh hospitality would apply even here – wherever and whenever they were? Adrianna pointed outward like an excited child as Gareth joined her.

"We're going there!"

One thick Welsh raindrop hit the straw roof of the hut and then the downpour was on them. She blinked through the rain. The sky flew like soot, unloading its stinging dark rain. Adrianna crammed her face to a crack in the plastered wicker, spying into the black interior.

The howl, raw and beastlike, pinned their backs to the hovel wall. They faced a black shadow that hovered, tensed, mere feet away. Adrianna saw brutally thick forearms on a squat, humpbacked body, rough clothed. The man's eyes moved from one to the other like dagger thrusts.

"Who be ye? Art not from Dolwyddelan... so ye must be foreign."

Gareth had gathered his wits. "Dolwyddelan?"

"My Master's castle, yonder." The man jerked his head.

"No sire. We are not connected to His Lordship. And yes, you are right. We are foreign to these parts. In fact, we are sufficiently foreign to be lost." Gareth dared a step toward the man, his arms slack, hands showing empty. "Do you own this house then?"

The man's eyes softened into a perplexed wariness.

"A serf owns nothing but his belly sire."

"You are a bondsman then? Well, you have the bearing of a gentleman."

That's pushing it, thought Adrianna.

The serf peered at them through the rain and spoke after some study.

"I sense no cunning in you sire, or mockery in your tone. Still, you must be from some strange parts, if I might say, to call such as me a gentleman." He pulled the wicker door up and aside, allowing entry into the earth-smelling darkness. "But enter in and take what comfort you can – the storm will not leave us soon."

The man unloaded the hump from his back and Adrianna recognized it as a coracle, a tiny boat of skins and frame shaped like a walnut shell. He leaned it against the hovel and tied it secure, all the while talking about the lack of travelers in these parts, and his fear that they were the bailiff and his gang, come to nab him for poaching.

He spoke the most execrable Welsh, a guttural, twisted kind of noise, with a peppering of ancient English, French and Latin, but Welsh nonetheless.

A. H. Richards

And that was the biggest surprise to Adrianna; she did not speak Welsh. She glanced quizzically at Gareth, indicating her mouth and ear. He gave a short nod and whispered in English.

"It's the Anis. You'll find yourself knowing things. Anis has been everywhere. You'll know things you never knew."

The hovel's interior was illuminated only by a meager rush lamp that their host lit with a burning stick from the fire at the room's centre. The slate gray sky and its driving rain had been sufficient cover for their otherworldliness outside; there was hope that the dismal light would hide them here.

"I were fishing, like, for me dear wife here, who has lain abed for many a day now." Their host looked almost jolly, safe within his home. He knelt down on a pile of mucky straw in which lay an equally filthy woman, her body wrapped in a torn rough cloth that tied about her waist with rope. Her head was covered in a similar cloth that might have once been blue but was now dominated by mud. She was awake, but merely stared from her husband to the visitors and back again, wordless with fatigue.

The bondsman pulled from his rags a large fish, still bright with life and beating like a muscle against his tight grip.

"I told ye, did I not, my love?"

He shook the fish proudly at them.

"She's been poorly for days now, and wanting only a trout, says she. Well, a few days of her wanting only trout was enough for me. So I went an' got her one, I did. Snatched it with me bare hands, I did, right out of m'Lord's river. Clap me in the stocks, cage me as a jailbird if they will, but the wife will 'ave 'er trout now."

Without so much as cleaning the fish, he slit its belly, pulled out its guts and then skewered it from mouth to anus and set it across two forked sticks over the sad fire. He motioned them to come closer.

"We 'ave an extra stool for the lady. And if you, sir, would make do with straw, I'm sure we will all find ourselves in dry comfort soon enough."

Taking care to remain in shadow, Adrianna looked about in feigned pleasure and repressed her wrinkling nose. The air was fetid with sickness. She felt cold air on her hand, and edged herself nearer until she could breathe the draft. Automatically accepting the rough bowl offered by their host, she drank something like ale, but thicker and more pungent than any she had ever tasted, rich enough to flush some warmth down to her stomach. Then the realization hit her as the ale seeped in. She was fully physical. How else could she hold a cup, and swallow, and taste?

Anis was supposed to wear off so that you gradually became more ethereal over time. It had been a day, at least, and yet she felt more substantial. She passed the bowl to her father, quizzing him with her eyes and weighing the bowl before him. 'Look,' she thought, 'feel,' making a clear image of her meaning in her mind.

Gareth passed her a quick, dismissive smile and a slight nod, then turned his attention to the bondsman.

A second turn of the bowl and Adrianna found herself slothful, staring into the banked flames of the fire. She ate morsels of trout with her fingers, wolfing the rich flesh at first, then deliberately slowing and grinding every mouthful until it dissolved into her. Fatigue and the fire, the murmur of voices, the ale and the continuing rain submerged her into a pleasurable drowsiness. Eventually, she lay her food board under the stool, scraped together some straw, and curled up on it, thankful for warmth and golden flame and for the thick billows of the long dress she had chosen for the journey. She fell asleep to the rumble of her father's voice, speaking a Welsh that felt as familiar as her fingers. A steady drip drip leaked through a hole in the wall beside her head.

She groaned awake, squeezing her throbbing neck. She had fallen asleep twisted up in the draft and her entire spinal column felt assaulted. But at least her clothes had dried, although they reeked of fire smoke. Daylight nudged at the hole in the wall. She sat up. The wife lay just as she had the night before, weakly poking a stick into the low flames.

"I slept well miss," she said. "I'm grateful for your hospitality."

The woman nodded shyly and, showing a toothless smile, pointed through the opened door to Gareth's back. Adrianna stepped outside to a water-softened morning, mist in hillocks and dew dripping and glittering. She squeezed beside Gareth on his rock.

"She seems better. Looks like a tough beast, that woman," said Gareth.

"If I didn't know better, I'd swear they were the missing link. Tough as Neanderthals, to live in these conditions."

She was reminded of Cabot and wondered where he was now.

Gareth poked at the earth with his foot.

"It's strange," she began, putting words to her worries of the previous day. "You'd think Anis would be fizzling out gradually, but it seems that you and I have become more physical with every passing hour..."

"Yes. I've been pondering that." Gareth glanced at her, then at the ground. He picked a stone loose with his toe.

Her eyes caught his and held them. "Please tell me nothing has gone wrong. That we can go home as usual."

Gareth watched a couple of goats clambering a bluff to their left. His fist rubbed the stubble on his chin.

"Dad! ..."

He turned to her and spoke with measured calmness.

"Here's my tentative hypothesis. Since being anywhere in this state – with or without Anis – depends greatly on desire..."

"You're kidding me..."

"No I'm not. So let me finish. Desire is far more crucial, more fundamental to our existence in any plane than you would imagine. Desire, Adrianna, is something constantly unattainable – or the object of our desire is. (Which is a funny turn of phrase, since so often what we desire is not an object at all...). It is the sum total of all that is memorable and beautiful about an existence, and its unattainability just intensifies its power. Anyway, my point is, I know from my varied and odd experience the significance of desire, whether it is conscious or not. Artists know it. Visionaries, like, say, Joan of Arc, they knew it. And, to put it simply, I think it is my desire that is ensuring that I manifest here as strongly as I do."

"And me?"

"Your desires, probably neither of us completely apprehend. Your deep need to bond with a father who has given you far less than you deserve, for example. A hunger after something bigger than the self you perceive as being Adrianna – the Adrianna you don't particularly like."

Adrianna pondered his words. True, she didn't like herself much. But wasn't that true of most women? It wasn't enough to account for this. Was it? What he said about desire opened something in her, seemed to find its positive response somewhere within, far distant. It itched in her mind like a sliver irritating the skin. Something in what he said was right. Maybe Joan of Arc knew what it was but Adrianna was stumped.

"Have you heard of the Welsh term 'hiraeth'?" Gareth stood and walked a few steps.

"I've heard of it – in some Welsh songs or something."

"Yes. Well, hiraeth is a uniquely Welsh term that expresses an indefinable, poignant longing. Poignant, and yet at the same time, for some, a close-to-visceral experience, like growing pains in the arms and legs."

Adrianna was reminded of the very real itch crawling about her waist. She rubbed her chafing dress with quick fury.

"I have always felt an intense hiraeth. In my spiritual feeling, my love for Elspeth, and for you, and ... How to put it? ... I have always been insanely in love with existence itself, with the poignancy of our lives. That is the desire, the power that has led me here. And that, I think, translates into me being earthed here, as it were. It delights me anew, with life, with the friction of the mind against new air..."

Was it something like hiraeth that worked on her too? Surely not; unless hiraeth also meant trepidation and nervous excitement.

She poked his stomach. "So. I think we should buy some food from these people, then go find a monastery."

She started back to the hut, then turned and waited for him to move. He was gazing dreamily out at the lead-toned horizon, where rain clouds had parked themselves close to the ground. Slowly rising behind them, the sun painted gold on the gathered clouds.

Gareth spoke, almost in a whisper. "No matter what, I will see to it that you get home."

13

Arriving, Cabot barely displaced the air –the peasants had walked right by him on the path.

A bloodhound sense had brought him here. A success; but he felt glum, in a nasty sort of way. Maybe it was the rain and gloom. Maybe it was the predictability of everything, the absence of anything close to adventure. Time-travel and medieval Wales had become pedestrian certainties.

He peered out the window. Earth and sticks, this world, with bits of rock thrown in here and there. He had expected a lot of stone – cottages and castles and churches – but apart from the small castle on the tor over there, stone architecture was rare indeed. For the masses, it was still earthworks and wattle. The world stank of it.

A slug as long as his finger lost its grip on the wall and dropped into the dirt. This hovel was certainly uninspiring. He felt no thrill in breaking into a mud-floored cave and staring at a fireplace and stool. No secret life to uncover, nothing hidden away in a cupboard, nothing nasty or secret. The atmosphere of dull exhausting work sat like boredom in the air.

He stared stonily at the sheep dung on the packed floor, at the primitive threshing and cutting tools leaning against the walls. They lived with their animals here: half the house for the humans; half for the goats and sheep and pigs. Luckily for him, they were up early to work and the animals were out to graze.

Cabot's predatory urge was rising: the verboten side of himself he had come to love. It made him feel like the Marquis de Sade at a Boy Scout Jamboree. It shot adrenalin through him; the urge to fight, to trap and terrify – the urge to penetrate the sanctity of others, to appropriate what was theirs.

He touched the pouch of Anis he had set on the earthen sill. Maybe he should snort some more, perhaps make himself more substantial. He craved action. There must surely be some advantages to being who he was, where he was? A predatory man in a pig-ignorant world, living in a spirit-like body... Surely he could entertain himself in all sorts of ways while waiting for his opportunity with Gareth and Adrianna?

The door's squeaking complaint almost caught him off guard. He slipped into darkness and watched as the figure entered; a child with a wan little face peering out from a ragged hood. She would be as rough as the rest of them in no time – her child-skin calloused and eaten at by weather and disease. Cabot followed the motion of her limbs as she crossed the hut, stood on tiptoe and reached up for the pole that hung by a strap on the wall. Tending pigs, or planting, or something. Then he saw her little naked hip jutting out from a rip in her filthy shift.

He was on her before she could turn, before she could so much as breathe an alarm. His hand clamped around her face, big enough to cover her mouth and chin and hold her firm. It surprised him how much strength he had. He crushed her to him with his right arm and forced her legs apart with his knee. She struggled, but it was nothing. It was a dream, where she was plastic – a floating, malleable thing. He absently wondered if this was another effect of Anis, while his fingers, seemingly three times their length, pulled at her limbs, probed for the centre he wanted. He slammed her hard against the mud-plastered wall and, relishing her cries of pain, pushed himself into her.

It was a dream. He could do with her as he wished, but he could hardly feel. Her squirming body was here one second, hot flesh and blood striving against his, then free of him, floating, so that he was forced to manipulate her again, hold her with his body and mind. He twisted her this way and that, manhandled her like plasticine, dragged her across the floor and flattened her under him. And it was all thrilling, an acidic, dreamlike, adrenalin rush that engulfed him. Beast-laughter echoed through him – struck the dull twilight of the hovel.

And yet, when he was done... he was not done. He watched her struggle away from him over the straw, grasping for a scythe. He watched her dirty face, her wide, dark eyes under rough hair and heard her croak something that must have been Welsh, then make the sign of the cross in his direction. She sank, convulsing, sobbing, to the floor. He couldn't have cared less. It had been good, shades of what he might have with Adrianna. But it was incomplete. His brain was a fog as he snarled at her and strode out into the day.

He looked about quickly, relieved to find no other humans. All were out in the woods and fields. And she took him for a spirit, a devil, in his half-state; her terror would ensure that she cringed in that dump for a while.

He zipped his fly and took to the narrow footpath. Luck was with him this time. And there would be a next time, he assured himself.

He wiped his mouth with the back of his hand, expecting to find saliva. But nothing. His heart bumped. Getting thinner like this signaled that time was running out. His hands clawed open the Anis pouch and he held a pinch to his nostrils, inhaling greedily. Shortly, he would be solid enough.

That was probably what he had been missing in that little episode. Anis. Next time, he vowed, he would make sure he was fully physical. Spirits didn't have orgasms.

You live and learn.

14

They bade farewell to their host, and walked in the direction of Aberconwy, northward through the magical beauty of waterfalls and brooks. Cooling mist enveloped them. Pheasants rustled in the furze, and far off, where the curtain of rain petered out, the plaintive cries of gulls floated from the bay.

The man on horseback appeared, seemingly out of the rocks themselves. Adrianna recoiled, made ready to run, but her father showed his usual glib calm and fell into conversation without missing a step.

Their dress and stature did not elicit the hostility Adrianna expected from this stocky man. Their foreign demeanor, in fact, seemed to count in their favor, for the man expressed a humble kind of awe at their stature, and at "my lady's radiance" and then insisted that he dismount and they both ride. Adrianna swayed gently in the saddle behind her father and relished their luck.

"I be yeoman of the Court, "he said. "I be Gentleman Usher, seating His Lordship and his guests at table. 'Tis an important position. You have to be the right man for it. Which I be."

The yeoman was obviously proud of his role, betraying a smidgen of superior feeling as regarded his fellow yeomen.

"My work is clean, and I have not the odious tasks of some, like our Yeoman of the Ewer who must needs always be washing this hand and that."

"Have we far to go, then, to the castle?" asked Gareth.

Adrianna watched the misted hills far off. She was famished and felt a creeping ache in her tired legs.

"We now pass close to the Druid's Circle, which will not harm us if we are respectful – and from there it is but a sparrow's hop to our castle at Conwy."

Her father stiffened.

"Conwy Castle, did you say?"

"You have heard of it then? It is a great place of great power, and you will be fed well and bedded comfortably, if I know His Lordship."

Adrianna whispered to her father's shoulder. "What is it?"

He shook his head and shifted his weight in the saddle. Talk ceased for full minutes. Adrianna listened to the soft thud of the pony's feet on beaten turf, the squeak of leather saddle and bags, and stared across to where Snowdon's mountain range began to dwindle toward the coast. There was no forcing her father to talk if he did not want to.

"The Druid's Circle been here far beyond the memory of even the oldest person alive. There be dark figures there, dark people who run stooped and cry out, now like wolves, then like frighted cattle." The Yeoman was enjoying his storytelling. "I never seen them myself, never dared go near the magic ground, but I heard the tales. There be the Stone of Sacrifice and the Deity Stone stood there, where people die who dare to blaspheme.

"It is said that the place be a door to the underworld, and to other times. It is just the place for the faeries and demons to make entry into our world, and to twist time as they do... so that these beast-men follow them out, from their time so distant.

To be honest with ye, I feared when we first met that you yourselves had been brought up from the underworld with the faeries, as you might say. For there is to be a great feast at the castle this very night, and as you will most likely know too, the Tylwyth Teg most often show themselves at feasts and festivals and rituals."

He looked up at Gareth, and his dark eyes flickered gently at Adrianna, then resumed his forward gaze.

Adrianna noted how her father shifted about, impatient or uneasy. His mind was working overtime.

Finally they halted and looked down from the hills, surveying the enormous castle that dominated the bay. She counted the castle's towers that defended the walled-in town.

Twenty-seven towers, grimly intimidating. But, unlike Snowdon's jagged heights, here humpbacked mountains folded this way and that, softly descending to the bay. A gray-green ocean, as if pressed under the waterlogged sky, lay calm, its waves rising and falling like shallow breaths.

Then they were on the narrow path, and through the castle's main gate. Gates followed gates, and bridges led to towers, then to grassed enclosures which presented more gates. Conwy was a formidable stronghold, with, as their yeoman had told them, walls fifteen feet thick, proof against any enemy. Now, those walls blocked out sound from the wild world behind their backs and magnified the noises of human commerce. The inner court-yards of Conwy castle were thick with bodies and machines and cry and song: From wild looking warriors carrying spears, to archers with Welsh longbows strung over their shoulders, to hustling women loaded down with baskets of vegetables and fowl, or indistinguishable, raggedly-clothed forms heaving two-wheeled carts nearly splitting apart with great sides of beef and mutton, freshly killed chickens and glistening fish.

Few noticed the trio passing through, and those that did merely gawked in gap-toothed awe, primitives whose eyes and minds had never moved beyond their valley's border.

The smell of leather and horse dung, spiced with the faint tang of urine, encircled them as they made their way toward the heart of the castle-town. Once in a while, a reprieve came in the scent of mountain flowers on a flat cart, or a cool breeze whistling gently through an archer's slit in the walls.

Adrianna felt a new, tense caution in herself, a kind of animal alertness. At home, there was always a neurotic, subconscious tension, generated by the constant thrum of cars and trucks and sirens, the general high-strung tension of the city – but here, she felt a bright, hungry alertness to whatever lived, to shadows on the periphery, to the scent of weather and wildness flying amongst the warmth of beasts. Adrianna liked it, despite her anxiety over their inevitable meeting with the lord and his court.

Her sight moved to the smoke-gray sky flying beyond reach, then passed along the battlements and down the massive stone walls that crowded at her side. Their strength meant protection and comfort to these people. But she felt their power to imprison her.

15

Everyone, it seemed to Cabot, disliked and distrusted the miller. Shunned by grim or suspicious faces, fawned over by the obsequious, the miller remained a stiff-necked brute, proud of his position, and ever willing to batter the first man who dared cross him. Well-fed, domineering, with a square body as impregnable as a keep, the miller was proving the best choice of all for Cabot's first foray into town life and Cabot was immensely enjoying his sojourn inside the man.

The miller lived to eat. Although food, for the serfs and most townspeople, generally started scarce and tasteless and got worse from then on, the miller always dined on the best of everything. It was as if his density created a gravitational field that attracted trout, and mutton, and sweetmeats, the occasional hare and even pig. Were he to lift his fat hands in the morning and brush fingers through his copious beard, they would retrieve pieces of yesterday's sustenance – flecks of chicken, goose liver, bread crumbs. The target of the town's envy and malice, he was also indispensable, and thus the household god to whom all paid their due in victuals.

It was his lot and good fortune in life to grind the townsfolks' corn as well as His Lordship's, a position that allowed him to cheat those whom he disliked without compunction, dealing out ill-ground meal enriched with a generous supplement of sawdust and dirt, while hoarding the best of the flour for his lord and, most importantly, for himself. He took his own, and left the townsfolk just enough to stave off sickness and death a day at a time. What did it matter that they sickened and died anyway? There were a thousand ways to die, and sickness came and went, as abundant as his farts. What did he care – and why should he? He lived, and thrived, in his own fashion. And though there were many of his betters with their boot on him, to whom he had to grovel and play the toady, there were enough squirming under his own fat boot to feed his pride.

Better yet, as the lord's tenant and servant in matters of grain and bread, he could batter others almost with impunity. Which was what he was doing this afternoon, his boots solidly planted in the muck and his beefy forearm smashing into his opponent's neck. His opponent, not of the diminutive persuasion by any means, had finally come to the understanding that he was beaten and crumpled to the ground, retching up a mixture of ale, coarse bread and cheese. The ale had made him sufficiently foolhardy to challenge the miller's character in front of a fair-to-middling crowd. Now, he kneeled in the dirt, covered by the miller's shadow, and the miller grunted out a satisfied laugh.

Cabot could feel the sting of a gash on the miller's right leg, brought about by a meeting with the edge of a scythe during the tussle. He reveled in the throb of a bruise on the miller's forearm and a bump on the forehead that must be turning color. He had always wanted to be a boxer, had secretly wished for the skills and physique to kick the crap out of somebody, just for the feel of it. Thanks to Gareth Pugh and Anis, his wish had been granted in brilliant fashion.

Excited though he was, his own thoughts had to remain dormant, lest the miller imagine he was going mad. Cabot reclined happily, anticipating an interestingly sensuous day, one that knocked all his time in the sterile halls of academe into a cocked hat.

The miller wiped the crust of blood and earth off his upper lip, snorted rich mucus onto the ground and presented his proud, full belly to the crowd.

"I don't like to fight, as ye well know. I keeps meself to meself, and me nose to the grindstone. But I was severely vexed then, I was. An' now I need a good draught, an' 'ope to be left in peace to drink 'er."

A belligerent stare from under his furry brows ensured that he was well understood by all and he sat his monstrous bulk once again at the eating trestle, his wall-wide back turned on his victim. Then, his mighty flagon of ale sucked dry, the miller heaved himself up and strode to his tethered pony. Mounted and kicked hard by the miller's heels, the sorry beast set off at an amble that evolved into a game trot under the miller's cursing threats.

Before long, they had left the scene of the town's feasting and advanced through light forest where the sun glittered through foliage. The miller watched about him but took nothing in, so intense was his thinking.

The miller was uncomfortable, for the first time in his life, with his natural aggressiveness. It would not do, given the circumstance he found himself in, and the way in which he wished to shape things. Today he had promised himself to venture to her home, and there to propose marriage to a woman half his age. A woman to whom, he sensed, brute strength and certain power held little charm. Some hard women relished a violent man, found his ability to cow other men a heady thing. And some pretty women swooned at the sight of blood and had to be pampered, even loved and cared for.

He wanted neither kind of woman.

He wanted a woman who could be taught to behave, if she did not already know; a woman who could work hard, and give him pleasure at his whim, and yet who thought little of herself and asked nothing in return but a roof over her head and a baby in her belly.

That was what he wanted, but he was not sure that this was the woman to give it. She was neither a hard woman nor a beautiful one. And yet somehow she was a woman who intimidated him, even while she beguiled him. She intimidated him through his very skin, because, in some way he felt that she knew what she wanted. That she wanted nothing at all, that she had a sense of purpose, unnerved him.

And she beguiled him for one reason only, and that not her looks. What seduced him was the plot of land she owned. Ownership of such land, once the fee for clearing it had been made to any Lord or King, was rare but certain. And this piece of forested scrub was now cleared, ploughed and yielding crops. Desire for the land had set the miller's mind aglow. To marry this woman would not only mean warmth in his bed – long cold since the early death of his second wife – but would reward him with the largest plot of arable land in the town.

Himself with all that land, and his mill, and a wife to bear sons! He enjoyed just the dream. He was determined to make this marriage a reality, and had approached His Lordship on the matter. Knowing that a widowed woman owning the land of her ex-husband was much less profit to His Lordship than a married one who could produce sons to till and sow and, when necessary, fight in his army, the miller had counted on his Master's blessing. And he had not been wrong.

Now that blessing, and a rush of blood to his groin, made him feel momentarily certain of a good outcome. He could all but taste the pleasure of owning this woman. For that was what he aimed at – to impress her, to seduce her back into wedlock, and thence to master her and her land. A woman to milk the cow and feed the pigs, to cook and to mend his clothes! To dress herself fine, and him too, with good clothing that only a woman would have the patience to make, and to be the prize that he showed off to the rest of the townsfolk!

He felt sure that she was somewhat impressed by his position – and what woman in her right mind would not be? A widowed dame, more than any, must make designs for her security, must calculate her chances on a slate of hard realism, not on a bed of whimsy, if she was to gain any kind of comfort in her life. She could not last alone, this woman – he knew that, and she knew. And thus he must be attractive to her. And, if he could, he would have her this morning.

But there remained one stubborn obstacle, and at the thought of it the miller's hand went to the hilt of the long knife at his belt. The obstacle, a rival for her affections. He was a neighboring bondsman who owned cattle and pigs, a plow and an ox, as well as a well-maintained house with good land that yielded well. This interloper stubbornly remained high on the widow's list of suitors.

Well, in fact, the bondsman came first, and himself second, and there were no others. All other men in town had had the good sense to retreat and demur once they understood the miller's goal.

Now, as if on cue, the miller could spy, through the thinning trees, the cottage of his intended, and could just make out the open front door, and a hen bobbing out of shadow into the weak sunlight. Surely she would be hospitable to him, as was befitting. And surely he could win her.

Cabot looked forward to a brawl between the two men. It seemed to him that the miller was a little too cautious, even obsequious, about this woman. He might be too well behaved, and that would lead to very unsatisfactory sex, if it led there at all. A contradictory brute, this miller; hard as nails, and belligerent, yet made confused and insecure by a woman. That situation did not promise enough power for Cabot.

There she was, standing in the doorway with a rough broom that looked sturdy enough to go to battle with. Relatively tall for a woman, with a solid, squarish face framed by long plain hair pulled back in a knot, she nodded silent acknowledgment as the miller dismounted. Her face, looking as if she paid it no attention from one week to the next, was wholly unremarkable, even to the eyes, which seemed to have made no final decision as to their shade, changing from deep set black to a dull brown as she stepped into the meager sunlight, then to the shade of sun-dried mud. The welcome she gave the miller was one of practiced courtesy, but Cabot sensed not an ounce of warmth beyond that. She clearly knew she was being courted, or hunted, and had no illusions as to why.

With the miller seated on a stool beside the lintel, the woman disappeared into the cottage – while he picked at the plaster-covered wall – then returned with a cup of ale, which she watched him drink as if watching a wasp sun its wings on a rock. She seemed bemused, but itching to be left alone, as if her floor sweeping were of more consequence than this ox before her.

A small pig trotted nonchalantly across the yard and rubbed its bristly back against a leg of the stool. By the time the miller had contorted his bulk to kick it, the woman had shooed it safely away, revealing her ample bosom as she bent. The vision galvanized the miller and without forethought, he blurted out words he had never practiced.

"You have been widowed now almost a full year. And I would have a wife... I would have you for a wife, if you would say yes."

The woman stood looking after the pig whose rump disappeared into the copse at the edge of the yard. She spoke without taking her eyes off the spot where it vanished, and with hardly a movement of her lips.

"And why should I feel so inclined, Master Miller, to marry you or anyone?"

"Well, I... I was thinkin'..."

"'Tis harmful to think overmuch, Master Miller." She took up her broom and amused herself by sweeping leaves and twigs at her feet.

The miller's eyes flashed hotly at her teasing. He did not like this tendency of hers to tease him as though he were a dumb brute just learning to speak. He planted his feet and stood up, as if to enforce his superiority with a reminder of his size.

"Yes, I was thinking. I was thinkin' that as you are out of the way an' all..."

"Out of the way?"

"Alone like. An' that not by design, I was thinkin,' but due to your former husband's solitary manner... I mean no offense by that..."

"And I take none." Sweep sweep, a clout of lank hair falling across her face.

"I well knows that you be able to fare for yourself an' all. But a woman do need a man, Blodwyn, just as she do need babies, an', an' the comfort of a good home."

She darted a look his way, surprised at his use of her Christian name.

"A home, I have, Master Miller. A safe and a clean one, with neighbors willing enough to come to my aid when needed."

The miller flushed red and his ears began to burn.

"Oh, I'll wager they be willing miss. Some more than they should!" he spluttered.

"What mean you by that remark?" She stood square to him, her broom at attention.

"'E means there are others who would be courting you, Blodwyn-all-Alone."

The man who had spoken was middling of height, and trim, with powerful arms showing from his jerkin and strong legs beneath dark, mud streaked breeches. He stepped forward from the copse carelessly, as if there were just her and himself, and no threat from the miller at all.

The two seemed to block the miller out of their circle. He was the foreigner, about whom they two shared a common, secret distaste.

The newcomer set the little pig he was carrying free on the earth.

"Your piglet got 'erself almost drowned in the brook. I did fish 'er out and saw she were yours. So yere she is."

"An' here you are." The miller stared, snorting through flared nostrils. The pig, he noted, was bone dry. His head buzzed, all the way down to his shoulders. That always signaled the urge for release, in a powerful punch, or a bear hug. Unused to being denied, and ignorant of social etiquette, he stood gawping impotently, confusion demanding all his energy.

Cabot anticipated a fine bout of fisticuffs. How charming that would be, to grapple in the dirt with this interloper. It was so easy, and so enjoyable, to take the side of this lout he inhabited. He awaited any snub, the excuse that would set them fighting.

The neighbor had other plans.

"'Ow do you fare, Master Miller?" he said. And, "'twill be a pretty day, if the rain 'olds off."

How could you punch a man who was so sanguine, whose smile embraced the world with such sincerity?

"Aye, 'tis fair enough if ye're flapping about in the sky," grunted the miller. "Not always pleasant for those who toil down 'ere."

Silence hung around the three, and Cabot wondered if they would ever break out of the frieze. A cuckoo sounded from beyond the copse. A piglet – perhaps the same one – snuffled about with two young relatives. A hen murmured to herself and stared brainlessly into the dirt.

Finally, Blodwyn pushed her broom into action. The neighbor relinquished his focus on a distant armada of cloud and spoke, just as the miller felt compelled to break the oppressive quiet with some violent act, like booting a piglet across the yard.

"Well, Blod, I think it's time I repaired the fence, as I've been promising this long while," said the bondsman.

Her response, a soft, easy smile that had secrets written all over it, stopped the miller's insides cold. So that was it. She and the interloper were intimate – and with a warmth and naturalness he knew he could never share with her. Foolish bitch!

He threw himself onto his tethered pony without a bye-your leave, yanked the reins roughly around and dug his heels into her flanks. A snap of leather, a whining creak from the tether post, and the miller broke free, leaving the post leaning at an angle. "Good riddance to the two of them. Blast their stupid lives," he cursed to himself. The stupid old wench did not understand what she was giving up in shunning him.

Passing through the forest, the miller worked himself into loud indignation. "Damn her! Damn everything! Damn you bloody trees an' all!" He gave the hostile eye to a squirrel. His hand gripped his gold neck chain and he pulled it from under his shirt, shook it at some poor sod ahead on the roadside scavenging for firewood. The path had narrowed to the breadth of two men, and the horse's flank narrowly missed the scavenger's head as the miller leaned over him, rattling his riches in the decrepit fool's face.

"That's riches for ye – that's power!" he barked. "Ye don't see the likes of me scraping for firewood."

He yelled at the branches overhanging. "A man respected by His Lordship 'imself! And playing second blasted fiddle to a yokel! Damn me, I need a drink!"

Then the horse balked, its reins grasped by a hand on skeletal arm. A rough looking yokel, someone the miller did not recognize, looked at him pleadingly.

"My companion, kind sir, 'e is that beat from walking a full two days sire, that 'e seems fair nigh to collapsing o' hunger and thirst. Will ye have mercy on us sir and carry 'im on yer mount as far as the next inn?"

The miller urged his mount onward, finding it held fast and still by the scrawny arm.

"Your hand off my reins, villain, or I will break it for ye."

There came the whistle of a stone in flight, and his head exploded with pain and his eyes saw a cloud of blackness. His body went limp, and followed his skull sideways and down, smacking the ground heavily. Before he could properly clear his mind, they were on him. He could not count them, nor pick out one clearly enough. It took all his concentration to hug a nearby tree and drag himself upright. Then he flailed at them out of the dark cloud that obscured his sight. Blurred men, dancing at the edges of the cloud – and the sound, somewhere, of his horse snorting, its feet stamping in the mud and stones. A club smashed into his shoulder before he could raise his arm to fend it off. Then another hit, sending sharp pain flying from ankle to thigh. He knew he had drawn his knife. He swept the air before and around him, hearing cries that might mean he had struck home. But the cloud would not lift, and there was the smell of blood in his nostrils.

Cabot scented it too, and felt more – he sensed the miller's diminishing strength, knew that he was not in control. His fate was in the hands of those who beat him, who were sticking him with their knives. He felt the miller sink to his knees from a powerful kick to the stomach, his breath forced out of a slack mouth. Cabot knew he was near death, could feel a kind of resigned, dumb stillness inside the man as the knives dug in and the pain became familiar, then a mere numbness, and the knives kept up their work.

Cabot panicked. To get free, that was all that mattered. But to where? To whom? To escape, must he fly from the miller into someone else? Or become a plant, or a stone?

The stabbing had ended and they kicked the body into a ditch. He could feel the last of the miller's consciousness ebbing into the close-up funk of rot and mud. He felt the blood pumping from the deep slash in the throat, felt its heat as it soaked down the neck, heard its fountained spume pattering onto the ground. Then he leapt.

Into nothingness. He seemed to be free, which mattered. But he was lost, which mattered more. Dimly, there was the sound of hooves meeting packed mud. And the sound of wind through branches and leaves. And the diminishing cries of the robbers as they vanished down the road.

Cabot realized that he was nothing. He floated, and there was no pain from the murder. A brief memory of the nightmare, but mostly silence. He might as well be a leaf, or a gnat.

"So much for that fat bastard," he thought, happy with the knowledge that it was himself, thinking. A pity about the situation though. He had begun to like the miller. Now, he was homeless, and not a little tense, unnerved by his predicament. Was he dying himself? Was that what his weightlessness signified? Had they actually killed him? Had he leapt too late? Or had it been his soul leaving the body?

Naw! Couldn't be, dammit! Souls didn't exist. And yet, he was as still as a breathless morning. And the forest, if it was still present, was equally muted.

Then he had it, and a squeak of joy ran through him, as if blood were flowing. This must be how Anis behaved without a focal point. If he simply allowed it to play itself out... ah, he was remembering now! Let it play itself out and he would find himself at the warehouse, with the relatives and Dr. Buckleigh.

A nervous tremor passed through him at the thought of Buckleigh – guilt over a job badly done. In his fervor to master Anis – or so he reasoned now – he had strayed from his task. He had failed. And employers didn't take kindly to failure. Cabot saw the promised riches snatched from his hand. Something had to come to him. Some way of convincing Buckleigh that he was in control of the situation. He thought of Adrianna and Gareth. If only he had stayed on their trail, not strayed so far. Then things would be drastically different. He would not be dissolving like this, en route to...

Then he had it. Eureka! The Euclidian bathtub moment hit him. He knew how to salvage this. He knew what he would say to Buckleigh, and what should be their next move.

16

She lost herself in the many courses the court enjoyed – duck, chicken, roast veal, a heron, and some tiny little birds covered in a milky sauce, then a boar's head, swan, some rabbit and even hedgehog. Adrianna grew sleepy from an excess of food and gave up attempting even petty conversation. She was overwhelmed and felt as insignificant as the poor little hedgehog lying on her plate.

Their hosts had forgiven them their lack of feasting, apparently concluding that the pair were quite mad. Gareth had told the truth about their homeland since the truth was easier to recall than fabrication. Their fellow diners' faces told the story. A place called Canada. At three thousand miles distant across the Atlantic Ocean, indeed! – which, the Good Lord knew, ended at the very edge of the world! Gareth had not minded. Being mad, he could tell them anything, and none would be any the wiser or more suspicious of them.

Finally, dazed and with ears ringing, their aching bodies followed their assigned and foul servant to their chambers. Their gaunt overseer indicated their beds, opened the scenic canopy that served to separate them, arranged the footstools and chairs in a geometry that suited him, then tugged the chamber pots from under the beds, and with indecent pantomime showed their purpose to the two obviously uncivilized demented persons. With a superior air, he swept out.

Adrianna unbuttoned and threw her dress aside and dived under the covers. She watched her father through half open eyes. He seemed particularly interested in the scene depicted on a wall tapestry – as far as she could tell, a pastoral landscape surrounding the castle itself, from which burst soldiers and flags, rabbits, stags and peasants. He stared and searched its breadth, his fingertips tracing each piece of architecture, while his body sagged by degrees and his anxiety increased.

"Blast it all!" he cried and threw himself onto a footstool.

"What?" she managed, hoping he would not want to talk.

"Ah, it's all wrong."

"The' tapestry, wrong?" she murmured.

"No. Not the tapestry."

Adrianna forced herself up in bed.

"Tell me, dad."

He was pacing along the wall.

"Everything I've tried has been going wrong! I don't understand why, and I'm torn." He stared at the tapestry, as if willing it to alter.

"It's all so messed up. For the first time, I'm concerned that there is something wrong with my whole plan. First, I couldn't get near Elspeth – and now, we can't get to Aberconwy..."

"Okay, so what's so important about Aberconwy? And why can't we get there?"

"It's the history of Aberconwy, you see. It was my grandmother that put me on to it. She reminded me that the purpose of it all was not simply to meet Elspeth again... Anyway, Aberconwy... A very sacred place, which the Celtic monks who founded the monastery protected and loved fervently. They and the townsfolk fought tooth and nail to keep this place sacred – against various English armies. Armed with pitchforks and home-made swords, they fought alongside Welsh soldiers to tear apart the English soldiers who once pillaged the town and monastery. Tore them limb from limb, literally.

"But then the end came. In 1283, Edward the First of England controlled the land. He ordered that the monastery be uprooted, moved elsewhere. And in its place, Conwy Castle was to be built. The very castle we are in now. That's why I balked when the yeoman first mentioned the castle. Aberconwy is gone, to all intents and purposes. Its relics and riches were stolen by the English and removed, maybe to Westminster, or...I don't know.

"So what does an ancient monastery have to do with us?"

"It was Aberconwy that was to be my path to God. Vain thought, perhaps... but one that was as possible as anything else, I supposed. And the secret of Aberconwy is the Croes Naid... The True Cross, in Welsh. See, legend has it that the monastery of Aberconwy secreted an authentic piece of the cross on which Christ was crucified. It was said that Joseph of Arimathea, who was supposed to have visited here more than once, brought it here.

"The stone I was carrying when we arrived... I thought it was a piece of the monastery. I thought it was leading me to the proper time and place... where I could somehow touch the Croes Naid. And if I could just touch it..." his hand crept upward in the dim light, "I believe I could have gone back there... to the very place and time when Christ was crucified. I could have met Christ... and through him, dared glimpse a shadow of what God is.

"It's truth, Adrianna... the truth has been my central motivation for as long as I've had thought. It has hurt me, damaged me in some ways – driven me apart from other people all my life. But it has been there like the air itself. Like a huge, dark ghost hugging the air behind me. It has never been absent. Even when I fell in love with Elspeth. Even when we made love."

"Dad! Please. That's a little more than I need to know."

He carried on heedless. "The Aberconwy thing. It's the truth of our family's existence, our meaning. That's all bound up, wrapped up in the most beautiful, indecipherable way."

She sat on the edge of the bed and took his hand. There was nothing to say. Her mind and throat had become blocked, as if the sheer scale of what her father intended obliterated the little words of comfort she might dream up. She waited, then found herself weakening, her bones and muscles turning to water, and she curled up sideways and fell into exhausted sleep.

Gareth had not been able to think his way through it. In the dark night, a great weight of emptiness conquered his body and mind and he had sat, unconscious of anything. He needed sleep, but was denied it, coming out of his stupor with the sound of birds heralding another day, and a damp wind pushing through the window.

His thoughts, if they ever again took on a semblance of order, would have to wait, at least until this day had passed. The lord himself had commanded their presence on the day's hunt. And so the day had been stolen from him.

They set of at a relaxed trot through the misted air, to the sound of horns bleating near and afar. The shaggy, streamlined hounds bayed their short cries and pulled the hunting troupe eagerly onward, across the hills, through sections of rough farmland with cottages clinging to the edge of the town sprawl, and on into the wilds.

Beasts and birds leapt from the bushes and undergrowth, scrambled up the wooded scree, rumps and tails flashing as they vanished over the brow or into hidden tunnels. Gareth found himself stupefied at the abundance of wildlife scared into life at their raucous passing. He expected the trout themselves to panic out of the brooks.

Then, at a tight chorus of bays from the hounds, they were on their prey. Wild boar was the lord's kill of choice this day. Drawing up the rear, Gareth searched through an army of horse's legs to catch a glimpse of the boar on the run. Pity seized his stomach at the sight of the creature, nose downward, snorting its fear, its short legs working in a furious blur as it charged up from the bank. It dodged to the left, then spun hard right, its rump almost swiping the teeth of the lead hound, its trotters disappearing around a moss-carpeted oak.

For what seemed hours to his legs, and only seconds to his mind, Gareth raced after the troupe, straining to stay in the saddle. At his side, Adrianna cursed the brutes that tormented the wild pig, the crowd that had, on a whim, made this day fateful for the poor beast. And they rode, all blaring and color, with banners crackling above them, until finally they pulled up short and formed a ragged circle to watch their master leap amongst the needles and tumbling rocks and step forward of the hound pack with his knife drawn. The boar was now all but dead with fear and exhaustion and sat half broken – wounds from the dogs' teeth welling and seeping blood where one leg lay crushed under the weight of its body. It snorted, pawing into the dirt as its killer advanced, its eyes jumping from the straining dogs to the man and back again, not knowing from where the final danger came. Then, with one last desperate burst of courage, it stood and half charged, half fell between his legs, aiming for a gap in the circle, and freedom. But its fate had been designed all along by these men. The lord spun about, laughing with triumph, and grabbed the boar's hind leg as the hounds lunged their leashes taut. Trapped, spent, the boar fell on its side and the knife slashed before it could right itself. One deep cut across the bristled throat and the vermilion blood spurted and his murderer's hands came up soaked in its dye. The men and women cheered, and then the pages rushed in and trussed the boar for transport and the hunters swirled about and plunged on into the forest.

Pained by the killing, Gareth and Adrianna hung back. They had not spoken all morning, only communicating with quick, pained stares. Now they reeled mentally from images of the hunt, sank mindless while their steeds nodded onward.

Gareth found himself dumbfounded. It was not a mirage, not delusion. He heard their obscene, rough humor, heard words he had never before encountered, smelled the sweat of men and horses and the heat rising from the hounds. He was here – not in Toronto, not daydreaming – actually alive in the thirteenth century, with his daughter beside him. They were following a path to a castle inhabited and bustling with business and smells and bodies.

He knew he had further, deeper to go yet, if he could maintain his spirits. The night before had been draining and painful. Now he found a reincarnated sense of purpose and confidence. So what if Aberconwy had disappeared? It did not matter whether he found the Croes Naid or not. Didn't matter how he chose to get there or what he chose to see. It was all the same to the cosmos, to the God-thing.

He felt that he had moved so close to a self-destroying truth that he had almost no ego left. He had to admit that he knew nothing. In the midst of being, he remained stunned and stilled by ignorance. That told him everything by so forcefully telling him nothing. Except, 'You are here.'

Gareth laughed and clapped his hands. Adrianna stared into him darkly, searching him, and knowing he would not be forthcoming.

Well, Gareth thought, it was his destiny after all, not hers. Only he could find his own meaning in this. It was up to him to complete the task, to come full circle in this thing. Adrianna had her own journey.

He chuckled.

Adrianna stared.

It was not fair, was it? he thought. And where was she to find her completion, her happiness? And was it his business? His heart ached –

all the moments not known with her. All the moments he had murdered in embryo.

And yet, it could be no other way.

Alone, he could do this. With Adrianna there, he simply would not dare.

He looked into her eyes and his welled with tears. Any more and he would lose his resolve. He held her hand, ran his thumb across her slender fingers, then raised her hand to his lips and kissed it softly.

Then, before she could speak, he signaled her to stay, swung quickly about and spurred the horse to a gallop, praying that she would not follow.

17

"Not dead, you say?" Buckleigh pondered his cigarette's glow. "And not disposed of any other way. Must say, Cabot my boy, that I'm disappointed – verging on pissed off. Didn't expect you to return until the job was done."

He mashed the cigarette into a plate that recently held lunch. Cabot watched a cluster of crumbs smolder into nothing. He accepted Buckleigh's bald stare with silence. The old fart hadn't even offered him a drink. After he had spent a day in the guts of a sociopathic murder victim. With measured calmness he made it all the way to the liquor cabinet, where he pulled down the first bottle that came to hand and poured himself a generous glass.

"Certainly, have a drink me lad."

Buckleigh's voice and demeanor could be simultaneously sincere and supercilious. It unnerved him, as always. He gulped some noxious concoction of Drambuie and Grande Marnier. He hated both. He poured it back into the bottle and chose the scotch hidden in the back row.

"I have an idea how we can get rid of Pugh," he said.

"I would hope so. Assumed you didn't return just to drink his booze."

Cabot stared at him with what he hoped was a stony expression. Buckleigh stared back his usual challenge.

"Well, we know that Pugh is... ahh... psychokinetic, I think the word is."

Buckleigh added a decorative smile to his wooden stare.

"I was thinking we could use that..."

"Okay, then divulge your magnificent plan, my boy."

The 'my boy' stuff was getting on Cabot's nerves. He closed in on Buckleigh enough to share a dose of whisky halitosis.

"Here's what I do," he breathed. "I bring something back with me... you can transport things, y'know, if you ingest enough Anis – makes you almost completely physical," he said knowingly.

"So, you transport something. Like what, a gun? You could grab one on the way, just stop off in 1930s Chicago." Another sardonic grin.

"Not a gun. That's for amateurs." Cabot flourished his scotch, slopped a little over the rim. "We need something to help him do it himself. No killer. We need something that can transport him to his death."

Cabot detailed his experience as the murdered miller, and Buckleigh's attention deepened until, when Cabot described seeing death, feeling it encroach and him finally escaping its clutches and returning to the present, Buckleigh even seemed slightly impressed.

"So, given that Gareth can, apparently, get stuck there, the plan is simple, given Pugh's psychokinetic powers. We find something from the past, something easily transportable that I can somehow get him to touch, and something linked closely with death. Give him the Siamese twin to death – and, voila, he transports himself to his own end, something nasty that he can't extricate himself from."

Buckleigh dragged a cigarette slowly out of its pack, lit it and sucked in a lungful. "Y'know, Cabot dear, I'm thinking that just might work – if you've got the smarts to get him to take the bait."

"I can do it, no problem."

"That means I have to consult 'my betters,' said Buckleigh.

He puffed himself deep into the armchair, spoke the connection and huddled in conversation. Minutes crawled along as Buckleigh brainstormed with his Foundation contact. Cabot cuddled the bottle of scotch and snuggled comfortably into an armchair.

Cabot smoked and drank, smoked and drank until his eyes fell shut and his head slopped over to one side.

A hand shook him roughly, bringing him back from a sunny afternoon floating in a Cambridge punt. Buckleigh stood before him in a dripping coat. He held up a piece of black cloth, smaller than a quarter of a handkerchief. "Wakey wakey, Sir Drinkalot. While you were aslumber, I found us the Unholy Grail.

"Such great good fortune that one of our operatives is working at the Royal Ontario Museum, as an archivist. And there happens to be a very useful traveling exhibit there these days." He kissed the square of black cloth. "Cut from the inside of a very significant coat – what's left of it after the, umm, incident." He stuffed it into Cabot's slack hand, pressing his fingers closed around it.

"Who's coat?" Cabot grinned like a gleeful schoolboy.

Buckleigh told him.

"Good thing you're not psycho-whatsit too," said Buckleigh. "Or you'd be in big trouble about now."

18

"His Lordship is to understand, then, that this man, now disappeared, be your father, and that he be no warlock, no sorcerer?" The clergyman's soft speech held focused malice.

On her knees, dumbly confused, Adrianna stared at him, then down at the flagstones of the hall. She was cold to her marrow in this cavernous place.

"Why else, maiden, would a man ride to the Druid's Circle but to perform witchcraft?"

Adrianna croaked. "You say that he has gone there. How d'you know it was him your spies saw?"

"Not spies, lady, but honest, simple citizens, alarmed at a foreigner's dress and antics."

The clergyman leaned in conversation with one of those simple, very ragged, citizens, then turned his rheumy eyes on Adrianna.

"This man does swear on oath that your master did circle the Druid stones on a steed made of smoke, himself glittering all the while, like the very rain itself in sunlight. What say you to that little trick? It is enough to have him stoned."

'Someone must have been stoned,' she thought, but said, instead, "Visiting a stone circle does not make a man a sorcerer, surely. And as for a horse made of smoke, that's preposterous."

"Have a care! Your impudence is enough to have you drowned for a witch!"

The man who spoke, as tall as Adrianna and, despite his mail coat and cloak, as thin as a pole, had not spoken before. She felt his eyes hungrily roaming her body and drew her arms up to cover her chest.

"I am no witch."

They had already made up their minds. Pleading her father's innocence was achieving absolutely zero. Telling the truth would surely mean death, and she did not feel quick witted enough to concoct a believable story. At a loss, she merely shook her head.

His Lordship spoke softly from his throne, accustomed to an audience hanging on his every syllable.

"We will not stone, drown, nor burn this pretty woman," his eyes lingered on her, demanding her attention just long enough to send her a twitch of a smile. He spoke to the men flanking him. "At least, not until we have secured her master and his confession. And even then, perhaps she shall live." His eyes stroked her languidly, toying with her.

"Her fate depends on how she pleases her lord – witch, or no witch."

Adrianna sensed a superior intelligence in the man – the intelligence of one who might not lay any store by witches, warlocks, or demons of any stripe. But the intelligence, too, of someone inventively sadistic, who did not brook any opposition.

"She must be locked up, and will be denied the right to walk among or converse with anyone. She will be kept here, out of the way, for her own safety. The townsfolk, alarmed as they be, would cause her harm, and what is worse, would disturb the peace, a peace hard won in this wild outpost."

The clergyman puffed up like an angry owl.

"Ye cannot lay any stock in the word of a woman, m'Lord. Deceitful they be by their very nature. Spendthrift with fancy and illogic both. Why, 'tis their bottomless vanity that's at fault, same as spent in a trice whatever goodness was in Eve, first woman of all. An' that goodness being from Adam himself, on loan, as it were."

The clergyman winked at the men at his side, proud of his subtle wit.

"Aye, woman she be," answered His Lordship. "And for that reason alone, we must not expect overmuch in the way of wisdom or truth. We must find her father, or master, and thus clear the smoke of sorcery from this court in one short breath. So, less of your wind, good priest, until then – if it transpire at all."

The clergyman stared, bulbous eyed, at the air before his face.

His Lordship looked her over appreciatively once more.

On a signal from him, a servant stepped to her side and clamped a claw to her upper arm. The stink of violent boredom dripped from his voice as he pulled her away.

His eyes glinted the otherworldly black of birds of prey. Her skin crawled with revulsion as he steered her through dark hallways; just herself, him, and dull echoes behind and before. She closed her eyes, strove to imagine her father. Perhaps he would hear her, whatever he was doing.

She was thrust into an unlit, gloomy hole. The slammed door sent reverberations down the wall as the iron bolt locked. The chill evening closed in on her. She rubbed the grip of his claws out of her bare skin.

It had to be her. Who else? Bewitching, they had said, and taller than a man, with pale skin, like wax. Well, well. Cabot rearranged his cloak, removing its tail ends from beneath his backside. This cloak business took some getting used to; like an outsize car coat, always getting in the way. Although, it did make one feel debonair. There was something crafty about a cloak on a man – brought one to the nasty borders of drag, where one could play the dandy, or the villain, or the fop, with impunity. Cabot offered sardonic thanks to the demigod Anis.

The inn, if one could call it such, was merely four rough walls that held the roof from crashing on one's skull. Underfoot, a layer of straw barely covered a foundation of offal. In the warm air, a pungent mix of straw, bitter ale, body odor and shite commandeered the entire space – as it had almost every inn at which he had stayed. Bad air and prickling hostility under wraps. Cabot's hand had barely left his sword hilt from the moment he entered, though he knew he would run sooner than yank it from its scabbard.

Worse, his neighbor down and across the trestle had been talking low with his comrades and sneering his way as if Cabot were a dandy beneath contempt. And it didn't help that they had not yet invented the epithet. Etymology would certainly fail to deflect flailing fists or a cudgel aimed at his skull.

He offered what he hoped was a supercilious sneer, to no one in particular, but aggressive enough, he hoped, to keep ruffians at bay. He was master of the Parthian shot – here and gone before the foe could react. It had worked in academia's battles of words, but he dared not speak this time. He was wearing the clothes of some poor wayfarer he had hijacked on the road, clothes which could, perhaps, be recognized. Theft was not exactly tolerated here, and murder even less, he supposed. Always best to keep moving, remaining shadowy, peripheral.

He would not even have been abroad in daylight had he not heard rumors, the night previous, of this woman. It was her – had to be – and haste was necessary if he was to snare her, rather than this Big Man at Conwy. He was forced to move abroad in daylight now; for once she was well in His clutches, once he had 'sampled her wares,' so to speak, chances were he would not relinquish her.

Cabot sucked down the ale dregs, slammed the tankard down on the table – which was not as spectacular a gesture as he had hoped, the tankard being made of treated leather – and strode from the cloying air, picking at a thread of straw that had somehow lodged between his teeth.

19

Gareth tied his horse to the thickest gorse bush he could find and left it happily crunching on prickles while he approached the circle of stones from the north east. His feet instinctively followed the prehistoric trading path that wound up the slope amidst rocks that stabbed out of the buckled ridge like rough-hewn axe heads. Even in prehistory, it was said, there had been axe makers here, and later, a thriving axe factory that supplied finely crafted weapons and tools to people all over the isles.

The Welsh - diminutive, dark people who survived in a land of sacred wells, saw one's destiny in the gathering of crows; knew beyond question that the Tylwyth Teg controlled time; told tales of bottomless waters in the mountains and of the trout, called Gwyniad, that had never, ever been caught on rod and line – these people, who warned against laughing at a toad lest it count your teeth and make them all drop out, had forgotten to protect their sacred relic, the Croes Naid, from the profane invaders, and the spirit of the crucified son had departed from the land, leaving chill, gusting rain such as blew across Gareth's path now, a damp, sad welcome.

There were hauntings of pasts that had once been futures. He could smell them now, as he passed by each stone and touched it as one would touch a long-known friend or ally. The sacred was in them, and he would meet it, he would pry it out of its heavy, massive past, whether it transported him to centuries before, or millennia. Gareth breathed deep, and heaved himself onto a toppled stone as big as himself.

It was a compact circle, this ghostly ring that drew ragged, boisterous time into itself. A lonely circle on an anonymous, ancient ridge. So few knew how the stones closed the circle of human time. Gareth sat amidst its silent, blind sentinels, fearful of their power. He strove to silence his body's shouting muscles and bones, for only then could he submerge, undetected, into the circle's sacredness.

To awaken those guarding this gateway was all too easy. Your restless mind, the noise of wounds, psychic and physical, made a continual racket. The guards, darker than brooding night, could be stirred like the very roots of mountains. They could snap one's mind, one's entire destiny, as if it were a matchstick, and throw it away without a second thought. Here, the metaphysical became physical. To play carelessly was to court an alien death – not the comfort of a human death but a horror that would negate your every atom, after it finished tearing you apart like a child stripping a spider of its legs, after shredding what you thought was your soul. If such a death was handed to you, it could not ever be undone.

The guards, barely stirred from their depths, were aware of him. A guard's eyelid twitched in his dream of Gareth, and his subsonic voice rumbled, tectonic plates shifting. Gareth saw the figure of a delicate deer kid, a still-life, sculpted of alabaster. A creature so perfect that a brushing wing would desecrate and topple it. Then a wound appeared on its flank, at first like a butterfly, a brushstroke of blood, then ripping through its flesh, tearing fiber from fiber in the skin to reveal the sundered cells, the arrested blood, then its flooding from flesh to ground.

The guards blinked another image. An ice shard, as long as a whaler's harpoon and as tough as steel, tearing through blackness, its chill vapor cracking the air. And the blackness erupted like a wound, bleeding human sound, the wailing of women, babies rent with the terror of their own cries; an eruption of groaning flesh and war, the gut-poison of love betrayed, the deathly vacuity that was the universe speaking back nothingness. Agonies churned out in endless rolls like the seas parting in two huge tidal waves; agonies imprisoned in the marrow, devouring bone and flesh. The agony of child murder, of wasted life and no return.

Gareth was no longer Gareth, was becoming the stone on which he sat. Forewarned, his spirit, the minuscule egg of himself, prayed for the guards' momentary mercy. His spirit guided him into a silence so total that action, even the growth of a finger nail, was halted.

He was coming within echoing distance of the sacred, and he was the wall off which it echoed. He was a mite, a micron, and less, and less. Until he was not even a question.

A mouse does not challenge a mountain. It knows its place. And yet, as the Welsh knew, a mouse, transformed, could enter the very foundations of the world.

Gareth asked nothing. He was rendered infinitesimally small. He was Anis, and he was his faith in Being. Nothing else. More silent still. An insignificant atom passing through a hairline fracture in thought. And it was not even his thought. But it carried him and he was not hurt.

Whatever he had become part of, he was loved.

STOP.

Its voice was of woman, of angel. Of peace.

And he floated for a while, an embryo of stars in pattern, as if drifting, but following a calculated path, beyond his comprehension. Out, beyond anything he had yet seen.

20

She awoke after an endless night of trying to contact her father. She had tossed and turned, thrown off the rough blankets and despite the cold, paced the floors until at last she sank weakly into an hour or two of inadequate sleep that denied her comfort. Then the claws awakened her roughly.

A second trip through passages unknown, this time with what must have been half the castle's servants gawking at her and querying the servant whose talons threatened to cut off her blood supply. At last, the dizzying array of faces, shadows and noise stopped and she found herself struggling to rise from her knees – once more in the grand hall.

His Lordship sat enthroned as if he had not moved since their previous meeting, his purple cloak draped artfully over both arms, folding in ordered ripples across his lap and to his ankles. On his right hand, a leather glove into which dug the claws of a hooded falcon, its bell rattling tuneless across an acre of empty hall.

Adrianna gathered herself and walked towards the throne, wondering whether the protocol was to remain kneeling. A stiff-looking man hid in shadow at the lord's left hand. Evidently no close friend of the chieftan's, judging by his unease, he seemed eager to catch her attention. She felt him staring as if through her clothes. Why did they all do that, these men? Were they all losers and perverts?

Having made it to within a few feet of the men she decided to kneel again, a choice which evidently pleased His Eminence, who tilted his head to her and gave her another secret smile, half patronizing, half amused.

"It is not yet the time for punishment, it seems," he said. "The furies have passed you by, gone to torment older witches... the ugly crones who deserve torture."

Still smiling, pleased with himself.

Adrianna inclined her head, as was probably befitting, and said nothing. There was something about this visitor that spooked her, something too familiar in his stance and demeanor. Who did he remind her of? So far, he had not uttered a noise, not so much as moved a finger, as if doing either would land him in the stocks.

His eyes would not unlock from her; while His Lordship seemed content to torture her in his own way, waiting her out with his clever smile. Her knees were beginning to hurt again.

At length, he spoke.

"I am surprised, pretty one, that you have not exclaimed, not risen to greet your keeper."

"I am afraid," she began, thinking he meant himself. "Afraid that I would do something wrong and invite your anger."

"Ahh. Well, humility is a good thing."

"But madness is not, sire," blurted the visitor in a choking voice, then stopped himself, wary that he had been rash. He glanced uneasily at the lord, then at her, as if she would help. She certainly would not. She was in deep enough as it was.

She now knew what it meant to 'look daggers' at someone. His Lordship was a consummate professional – a quick, poisonous thrust from his eyes to the visitor, then, as cool as ever, continuing as though no-one had spoken.

"Yet, you know this man, I think?" He indicated his company. The hawk's head cocked as his arm moved.

"He is..." Her mind struggled on the verge of panic – then, yes, the visitor himself was mouthing words to her. She could not see his eyes beneath the shadow of his hood, but his lips she read clearly enough.

"He is my keeper," she said, speaking the words his lips spelled. If this was one of the lord's games, then it was best to humor him.

"Aha!" His Lordship laughed, slapped a knee in mock triumph. "There, then, that little mystery is solved, and both of you spared death and dismemberment." He grinned playfully at the visitor. "On then, keeper. Let us witness your magic."

"Conjuring tricks now," thought Adrianna. "Couldn't they have let me sleep?"

The man began to talk, his voice shaking at first, but gaining confidence with every word he was allowed.

"As I explained to Your Lordship, and your colleagues... umm, I mean, your ... umm... courtiers', retinue... my treatment is novel. It is as exotic, perhaps, to these shores as is my country." He stepped down the dais, managing not to stumble, and stood with his back to her.

"Bleeding and leeching, you know of, as effective treatment for weakness, the ague, and so on. Well, to that, we have – that is, my fellow surgeon/barbers and myself have – added the additional power of what we call 'psychic magnetism,' a physic that, in our country, functions most exceedingly well with those who are, like this woman, moonstruck."

She recognized him and the object he held in his hand. A yelp of surprise escaped her and her hand clamped to her mouth. Wild eyed, she stared at him.

"Yes. She loathes and fears this treatment. But she must live with it – and we must be firm."

Cabot bowed to her as he began slipping the leather helmet over her head, taking some care and time to ensure that the golden rivets did not snag her hair.

He whispered. "Yes, it's me. Just play along and we'll get out of here. I'll explain later."

He faced the lord, his large hand spread over Adrianna's skull, its pressure making indentations in her skull.

"You see, Your Lordship, this device enables us, through pressure on various parts of the skull, and by means of constant inhibiting pressure on precisely the nape, here," his fingers pinched her nape and she cried out once more, "to exorcise and eventually subdue her violent humors and the untoward behaviors she generally exhibits."

"Faint when I tap you," he whispered.

She followed his cue, a little too eagerly, her skull hitting the stone floor before he reacted, protecting her head with his arm and gathering her to him.

"I can't believe I'm actually glad to see you," she hissed.

"Keep it up. Do a bit of moaning and frothing or something."

Adrianna imitated something close to a fit, thrashing her legs, tilting her head back. Her hair had caught in some buckle or other on Cabot's costume and tore out, bringing tears to her eyes. She sobbed, quite professionally, and managed to dribble some convincing saliva.

Cabot whispered again and she followed his cue, ceasing all movement when he squeezed her skull with both hands. Not an easy feat, since he had managed to press a rivet deep into her forehead. The pain was well on the way to inducing a real fit.

"I must tie you, and be a little brutal. That way, he'll trust that I can control you."

Cabot yanked a cord from within his doublet, tied her wrists fast with it, then, winking, presented another cord in which he had fashioned a huge knot. He thrust the knot into her mouth and tied the loose ends tight behind her head. She tasted something like tar on the rope. Cabot sat her upright and she hung in position, swallowing her welling saliva as he talked.

"Both she and the man who poses as her father have the same sickness. Moonstruck more often than you or I are struck with hunger, the two often escape our little hospital and travel, ohh, leagues and leagues, acting their parts in some lunatic play only they understand. Their speech is as alien to us, though they are born and raised in our country, as my speech surely is to yourself, my Lordship. We are still striving to recognize the signals, of language and bodily gestures, that give away their plans to break out, those signals of what they will do next. But they are very clever, very wily – and so far, only the roughest treatment seems to have effect. Only this scares the demons out of them, temporarily."

Adrianna began panting, kicking out, twitching various parts of her body in what she hoped was a convincing imitation of lunacy. Not daring to meet the Lord's gaze, she stared wildly about their prison. Immovable stone, massed weight over minuscule windows, hanging cloth, low-burning tallow. If His Excellency remained unconvinced, Cabot was destined to be a fellow prisoner.

"It is strange," said the lord. "Before you came, she did not exhibit any kind of lunacy, no tremors, no spitting..."

"That is her wiliness, Your Lordship. She and her partner can be very convincing. I would imagine they were extremely calm on meeting you, very polite? It is all part of their charm, you see. They have convinced many a surgeon that they are not the slightest bit ill."

'Enough with the narrative,' she thought. 'Shut up while you're ahead.'

"And, in fact," Cabot resumed fiddling with her skull, "this little leather contraption helps summon her demons, even against her will. I call it my Be-elzebub Trap."

Did it augur well that His Lordship rose and walked to them, that he inspected the helmet, that he stared momentarily into her wide eyes?

He strode back to his throne. He rested his chin on his hand. Adrianna gave up flailing. She could hear Cabot breathing, hear his heart thumping against her skull.

It was done. She was released her into her surgeon's care. And they rode, Adrianna still bound and gagged, but held by Cabot's arms that gripped the reins, protected from any violence or mishap. A sudden rush of gratitude swept her at the realization that Cabot was a modern man, a man from her own home, with higher sensibilities than these brutes. She held back tears, her mind filled with a comfort she had not known, it seemed, for months. A comfort and yet a yearning at the same time – the yearning to get back home, to be where everything was familiar, where she could simply breathe effortlessly, be her own, leisurely self. They galloped onward and she offered no complaint, sure that, when they stopped, they could find a speedy means to get back to Toronto. After all, Cabot had managed to get here hadn't he? So he must have an escape plan, which would include her. She could leave, despite her stubborn physicality. Surely Cabot would know how...

And then her heart stopped and she knew that she could not leave.

Her father.

Sadness covered her mind as they rode on through forest and farmland. Cabot had eased back, recognizing that they were not to be ambushed by the

King's soldiers and killed. Good enough for them; but what of her father? Had he actually broken down, become unhinged? Or was he, right now, a victim of robbers, or warlock hunters?

Her father was no fighter. Not that way. He could be dead.

They finally stopped, and Adrianna began to speak of her need for Cabot to join her search for her father.

"Shut up." Cabot dragged Adrianna down to his shoulder and walked. She pushed against his back, hoping to see where they had arrived, but was roughly stilled. The voice of an approaching stranger told her that they must be cautious, and she lay quiet.

It was a stable boy. Cabot spoke curtly and she heard him pull coins from his doublet and pay the boy. Then they moved on, under a lintel, into an inn.

She tried, 'Let me down, Cabot,' but the gag turned it into gargled noise.

"Shut up," he ordered again.

She heard the smack of money hitting wood, saw the trestle table, and a rotund, perspiring fellow seated, shoveling the coins into his hand. He did not look up. The mistress of the public house led them up complaining stairs. It was all passing by so seamlessly that it seemed choreographed. Had Cabot planned this far ahead? Even establishing a place for them to stay? She would have been impressed, but for the irritation of his stony shoulder pressing into her abdomen. She squirmed and kicked, her fingertips pulling at the plaster as he carried her upwards.

"Begone, demon!" he snapped, banging her forcefully against the wall so that her head scraped. There was no need for that, surely? Or for the stinging smack he delivered to her thigh. She noticed, then, that her left leg was almost entirely exposed, naked to her buttocks, trussed as she was. Was this Cabot's voyeuristic revenge for their argument at home?

They stopped inside a room and she crashed, winded, onto a wooden chair that tipped and hit the wall. The mistress cried out instinctively and reached to right her.

"She deserves not your sympathy ma'am. A dangerous creature, she is," Cabot snapped. "All seeming innocence and sweet as a fig. But her demons are fierce, an' she will tear your eyes out soon as look at you. Do not meddle with her. It is best."

He tied Adrianna's cords, binding each wrist and her ankles to the bed, the rope loose enough to move her. Intimidating the mistress into the doorway, he pressed coins into her palm and pushed her away.

"Pay no heed to this woman, nor to the noises – awful though they may be – coming from these quarters. She will scream and fight, I warn you. The exorcism of her demons is frightening to her, and not a little dangerous to me. But interrupt us not, for that will break the spell of her treatment. You do not want to incur my wrath as well as that of her evil spirits."

The mistress bounced a curtsey and fled, gripping her coins tight.

Cabot turned his gaze to her and Adrianna was shocked silent by the thin-lipped coldness in his face. Her heart jumped against her chest and beat in her throat like a mouse flailing to escape.

"You're scaring me," she tried. But the gag baffled her words and seeped its tarry flavor down her drying throat. She struggled to swallow away the dryness but found herself choking. A voice from some recess of her mind shouted at her to move, to stand, but just as she broke from her stupor into life, he had her in his grip. He was on her, seated on her back, his thighs gripped tight to her sides.

"No more charades, Adrianna." His voice came hoarse, laced with venom. The bed creaked. He tugged her hips furiously and breathed tightly. All of it came to her with super clarity, magnified by her dumb, shocked fear. A stupid, useless thought came to her. 'Why?'

The why cried in her, turned to real sobs as her fear outraced her fatigue. The room, the bed, her suffocation – all spun together, tilting. Disbelief was a fist smashed into her face. The room was swallowed. She was in a space in time called fear. Utterly vulnerable and alone in a senseless place of impotence.

She heard his animal noises, brutal and horrible – noises she knew were in humans, but that stayed in reserve, reined within nightmare, not like this, invading her in the real, small day. She screamed, an eerie, wandering cry that beat away into a void. She had turned into a little, helpless beast. She was a deer, her hind legs cut down by the wolves' hot, crushing jaws. She was the little slaughtered pig.

She was nothing.

In her mind, somewhere, she heard Cabot's voice over the rending of her dress.

"Clever bastard, I am. Thought... I... was...nothing. Huh? Didn't you? Yes, you did. Simple-minded Cabot, there at your beck and call. Your trusted, masculine figure, Cabot. Help you through... your DADDY's death."

He clutched the slim belt at her waist and pulled it with all his force, biting on his words. Her stomach lifted from the mattress. He yanked harder, forcing the last of the air from her lungs. Then the belt snapped and his hard fingers were tearing through her dress. He ripped it apart, from her shoulders to her buttocks, exposing her flesh to the air. Sweat dripped from him, hit her back and ran down her skin to the mattress.

"No-one... not one single person will come to help you now." The words broke out of him in pieces, his breathing fast and taut. The stink of his body, adrenalin driven, clung to her even as she buried her face. The rabid, raunchy odor of his armpits, the odor of blood and unclean male sex permeated the air.

"Helpless, stupid woman, Adrianna Nobody." His knee dug violently into her right thigh, pressing agonizingly deep. Somewhere, distant, she felt her leg being forced to the side, forced to the limit of the cord's restraint. And his fingers, clutching, his knuckles burrowing into the softness between her legs, scraping against her as they fumbled to grip her underwear at the crotch. Vulnerable, opened flesh, tied and helpless, and the agony coming, worse than the slow plunge of a blade.

He was laughing now, a phlegmatic laugh that, with his forced breath, turned into a violent cough. He spat to the side, then, still chuckling, leaned close into her and pulled violently, tearing the crotch and heaving her torso upward in one motion.

Obscenities spat and a babble of animal, murderous noises, and she felt, helplessly, the tip of that horrible, hard muscle, swollen and polished like something no longer alive, no longer human, a weapon beginning to press into her, slowly cutting into her dry, tight flesh.

She howled. Her rage leapt up, her scream as bitterly sharp as acid, its noise filling the room, conquering her mind. A moment, an unforgiven moment in time, and he would be in her. Why? Why had she been chosen, out of all the helpless beasts in this world? Raped. Abandoned even by God. Or else this could never happen.

She felt her strength seeping away with sudden speed, felt the muscles against which he thrust, sapped of their will. Her head was bleeding, dripping blood in her eyes. He had smashed her forehead against the wall. And broken her lip open. Her mind collapsed with her muscles. Her will, her strength to hold him off seeped out of her like the blood dripping from her cheek. She would die. She hoped she would die.

A howl of rage. It filled the room like the roar of a waterfall, came down on them like the maw of a giant lion. She felt the weight torn from her back, heard it fly, then the splintering crack of the chair. The smell of violently churned dust filled her nostrils. Dust from the straw floor, from the walls, as Cabot's body pounded against them.

Her body had curled up tight, its restraints somehow broken by the whirlwind of action loosed in the room. She ventured a quick look through eyes that were terrified, cringing slits, and saw a cloud in motion. A collected thickness of shadow, agitated and howling, stood over Cabot's body and she could hear, more than see, the beating of its limbs, if they were limbs at all and not wings – beating against the limp body of her rapist. She heard noise, a rasping, crying choke of noise coming from the shadow, and she watched, her stomach heaving under her in fright. She watched as the shadow's form thickened, defined itself, becoming arms and two legs, a blob of torso. Color bled into it, or bled out to its surface, like myriad flower petals unfolding.

Then she knew the form, knew the cry of rage, knew who was binding the legs of her rapist, pulling his arms behind his back taut enough to break; knew who it was staring into her. And his pity, his sorrow meeting her pain, engulfed everything in her and her mind collapsed behind burning tears of relief.

"Daddy!" she sobbed.

21

Cabot came to. Gareth knelt in front of him, tightening the knots that fastened his arms to the bed frame. His legs were bound together by a strip of bed sheet. Some cringing was in order, he thought. Tears and abject shame might go a long way. Tears came on cue, and even a little lip trembling. The stabbing pains in his sides and abdomen pushed real sobs from his throat.

"I'm sorry," he managed. "Forgive me." Gareth was the kind of fool who might respond to such a plea. Despite the pain, his lip began to twitch with the ghost of a smile. He wanted to burst into laughter. Abject, he reminded himself. Abject. And don't look at Adrianna. She will only make you angry again.

"Forgive me," he whispered once more, through slack lips, his limbs lifeless – a fine portrayal of the exhausted, injured victim.

Gareth stared him down. Stony eyes, the malamute blue drained gray with rage.

Wasn't pity a natural human trait? So he had tried to shag the man's daughter – who wouldn't? No hard feelings... no pun intended. Cabot spluttered the beginning of a laugh and leaned forward to shadow his face. 'That won't do Cabot, me old swordsman.' His hand slipped into his pocket for a handkerchief, a rag to wipe the spittle and blood.

Then he had it.

He remembered, and thanked Buckleigh for what was in his pocket. Now was the time to put it to use. Cabot's fingers curled around the scrap of cloth. Gareth shuffled to his other side, his hands testing the strip of linen that bound him. Then, holding Gareth's eyes, he slipped the swatch of black cloth into Gareth's jacket pocket.

He closed his eyes, sucked welling blood from his lip. For the first time in what seemed like weeks, he felt truly exhausted. It was pleasant, creeping up through his pain. His brain registered noises around him – Adrianna still sobbing, her father's stupid, crooning voice, muffled laughter from drinkers downstairs – then his mind fell into an abyss.

He slept.

Dreams rushed him: of overhead beams rending, a collapsing ceiling opening a view on a pulsating sky through which screamed jets, or huge birds of prey. Then his ribs caving in from the blow of a boot, while the door of the room toppled, fell inward onto him. The clamor of figures entering, of bodies standing on the door, looking for him. And himself crying out, his voice hopeless, his will to move thwarted.

He awoke to the pain of straining bones. He had slipped sideways and his weight pulled his arms taut. He righted himself and faced an empty room.

They had gone, and he sat in the company of dust.

The blood had caked on his mouth. He was starving. He needed Anis soon.

Thump thump. He pushed himself upwards, using the bed's leverage, and let himself drop. Once, twice. Again. Banging on their ceiling.

'Come save the doctor,' he muttered.

22

They cantered on, the horse's hooves marking time for her father's voice. He sang to her, soft and low. Adrianna had not stopped sobbing for hours, her mind recycling the violation, echoed by the insistent fury of the horse's hooves. She cried with incomprehension, and a rage for revenge. She saw visions of herself fighting back and winning, clubbing him senseless. But reality insisted and his violence to her replayed. Her mouth and throat had burnt dry.

Finally her mind barely pulsed and her rigid body collapsed in her father's arms. He cradled her, letting the horse travel without rein, and she stared at nothing. She should be dead.

She had brought it on herself. She must have.

She should have died.

She awoke with a start, feeling arms around her, and gasped like someone drowning, kicked and pushed against the strength that held her. Until her father's breaking voice, his deep tones reassured her. It was him. She was safe.

Her mind wandered, occasionally doing back dives into a sleep like an ocean swell, then resurfacing to vaudeville songs. 'Burlington Bertie' crooned over her. 'How much is that doggie in the window?' The words missing in patches, her father's rumbling hum sounding in her ear that pressed against his chest. "Sleep lovey," he murmured. "Sleep, dad will protect you."

She wondered how he kept the rage out of his voice. He was like stone, like the Dolwyddelan keep. Isolated and unkempt, on the verge of ruin. But still formidable. Enough for any challenge. She listened to the hooves on turf and his voice, and let herself go.

She was deep in the ocean, the rumbling of the surf sounding rhythmically above her head. And somehow, she heard too the rattling of pebbles clattering as the surf pulled back. The earth breathing, a slow sucking, in and out, and the clicking of machinery. From where? Click, clock. Clip, clop.

The hiss of the sea dragging its fingers, as she had dragged her fingers along the wall.

No. No.

Just the sea. And sunlight, blessed sunlight and white cloud like churned cream, and the scent of her father's jacket filling her head.

She would not cry any more. Not for a while. She would try to be strong. Keep the crying for the stark loneliness of night that she knew would come.

She felt her fingers tighten on her father's arm. She watched him look down on her. She heard his voice. She managed a word or two.

"Where are we going?"

"Stonehenge," he said. "I managed to transport us both as far as Bristol. Mind's done in now though. I used some of that bastard's money to rent this horse, and the horse is now in charge."

Stonehenge. Why?

Gareth answered her unspoken query. "Time and space are radically changed there. That's what it's for. The Druid's Circle pointed me there – gave me my first foot in the door while you..."

His voice choked off. She saw the tears trickle down his silent, grim face. Her hand squeezed his. 'This is not your fault,' it said. Nevertheless, he would always think it was. As she always would blame herself. Unless there was some way to change...

Stonehenge. Time and space altered radically. Fair enough. But she had seen enough radical change to last two lifetimes.

Their route was guided only by the horse's instinct for sure footing, and rarely graced by anything resembling a highway. It took them past towns with peculiar names: Chew Magna, Clutton, Midsomer Norton; insular gatherings of wattle houses strung together by paths of regularly tramped earth, and, sometimes, overseen by a humble church.

When they reached Bath, Adrianna sat up and marveled. The city, with its elegant Roman bathhouse and architecture, its straight roads and urban planning, had withstood the ravages of war and change after the legions returned to Rome. Still offering luxury that was rare in the isle, it had become a cosmopolitan hot-spot, frequented by foreigners and the bravely eccentric souls who bathed more than once a season. The mercantile streets bustled with shoppers and gawkers and important personages, from France, and the Roman provinces, from Scotland and the colder climes.

Through this compendium of tongues, Adrianna and her father passed unheeded, drab amidst the vibrant color and noise of the marketplace. They bought a little food, then carried on. With every hour behind them, they became lighter in spirits. They dared to hope that, securely bound and gagged, Cabot would remain, powerless, until his Anis petered out.

The horse carried them onward until they finally found themselves in a grove on the city's outskirts. They dismounted and collapsed under the shade of a sycamore. The pony cropped fresh grass. And then, finally, they ate their first meal since escaping, passing back and forth a loaf of fresh-ly-baked, rough bread and strong Somerset cheese.

Adrianna chewed and watched an ant's progress up a grass stem. In her own, real time, there would be ants crawling up stems. Ants that looked no different to this one, shining black, fussing mathematically on its journey. Tackling the gritty bread reminded her of the unbelievable luxuries of her real life: the heavenly taste of bread that all but melted in your mouth and left behind no stray grains; the luxurious bite of red wine; and Emmenthal. Even the memory of cold-cuts was almost erotic.

But they were here, for now. Although Gareth made it clear that he would abandon his quest immediately if she wanted, she hushed him, made him sit down and eat more than the morsels he had gobbled. He needed to stop thinking, needed the brain-massage that a few moments of pure sensu-ousness would give.

And as much as his body, like hers, craved nourishment, he also craved a resolution to this ambiguous quest. She could not deny him that, and knew that she would not forgive herself if she surrendered now, slipped home like an afterthought, as though this were a matter of no consequence.

She decided to harden herself, to make this matter important to her and to see it through. She had determined, searching through her misery, that lessons had to be learned – from the seeming accident of her joining with her father and arriving here; from the horror of Cabot's attack; even from the lightheadedness – yes, lightheadedness it was in comparison – of her previous life. And lesson number one had cried out at her. "Make yourself real!" it said. Those were the only words she could find to clarify it. She had not been real enough, had taken life for granted. And now...

Something had happened to her, something had germinated in her from that sickening incident. She looked about her. She knew she would not remain here, but for now the rough bread was right, the crowding scent from the wild flowers and grasses was right; the gentle lapping of a nearby brook at its banks, and the very nowness of her bottom planted on the ground, her mind solid, sure of itself but thoughtless, all of this was just right. Maybe it was just the comfort of nourishment after such desperation; the beautiful, kind, mundane, coalescing into strength.

She decided she would not quit, or run. She would commit, to this quest, to her father, and to herself, from now on.

She bit into the cheddar in her hand, and tore off a hunk of bread with her teeth.

"Bloody hungry dad. We need wine, or beer, too."

She smiled at him, and could sense his heart uplifting. He shook his head and smiled back, as if in wonder at her.

Maybe, she thought, with calm clarity, she would simply kill Cabot. Nothing melodramatic, no emotional hyperbole. Just chuck him off a cliff or something. The end.

Gareth's mind also seemed to have righted itself, got its priorities right. He was tearing chunks from his fistful of bread like a wolf gutting a lamb and exclaiming rapturously over the tangy cheese.

"You're right. A beer would be heaven." He rolled his eyes and swallowed.

She chewed, and glanced at the primrose blue sky. She was damn well going to be happy, and strong – for as long as she could. And even if the horrors came back and she cried again and again, she would survive it. She would. She chewed and hummed into her bread.

Gareth's forefinger tapped the ground decisively.

"We won't be here much longer. I promise. Stonehenge by the end of the day, I think. Then another long rest for you, as decent a meal as we can scare up – I still have a few pennies left – and then, I think we can make our final plunge."

Stonehenge. She could see it in her mind's eye, in all its prehistoric glory, a steadfast ruin in gray, megaliths gathered on the naked plain like a herd of giants communing. She stared at her father and felt the glimmerings of fear. Not a familiar fear. Not the fear of the unexpected that she had become familiar with these few days.

A lump formed in her, somewhere between the throat and the heart.

It was the fear of the expected.

23

When they broke out of the trees into a clearing, the sight shocked her. Not fifty feet away, the massive standing stones of Stonehenge dwarfed them. She felt their menace, a claustrophobic, predatory closeness.

Gareth urged the pony forward. It obliged for a few steps, then drew up, its ears twitching. Another press of the heels and a few coaxing words and the pony repeated its action, coming to rest as if by force of ennui.

Adrianna felt an undeniable repulsive force; the more they determined to push forward, the more strongly it resisted.

"It's me," said Gareth. "They, or it, can feel my desire. I told you, didn't I? Those stones, even the ones not from Wales, comprehend hiraeth." He dismounted, grinning.

"Har har," she said. Her father's humor was seldom of the knee-slapping kind. And right now, she felt more than a little jealous of His Psychic-ness. How come he got to sense everything so much stronger than her? How come they talked to him, and only whispered to her?

"How come you have all the fun?" she asked, dismounting.

"Not fun."

His look, when he turned to her, reminded her of the cats when their night eyes glowed in lamplight. "It's just my calling. Some people collect garbage, some people drive cab. I go loony."

His last words dropped into the still air like a pebble into a pond. He walked on, through concentric circles, at each step becoming more obscure.

It had let him in, conceding the stage to him. And though it menaced her, it waited. Quite prepared to crush the soul, she thought, like a mountain falling on a rabbit; but content, for now, to watch.

She could feel that, at least. It was more aware of her insides than she was. She could feel its presence, and could sense the oddest things that she knew were not her imagination. Like her father's figure, flickering like sun upon water as he closed on the largest trilithons. Like the barely perceptible noise, as if of wind passing them, as if the planet itself were a ship that moved them through doldrums, with a cosmic breath drawing across its timbered sides.

Her father's body reappeared and she drew up, realizing that she had crossed fifty feet in what seemed a microsecond and yet, a year.

"Glad you stayed away from the drugs as a little girl?" Gareth was grinning again. He seemed overjoyed, half in, half out of a blissful trance. "You need all the brain cells you can muster for this place..."

His gaze slowly shifted upward, as if gradually pulled, or directed, and his mouth drew into a Cheshire cat smile. Adrianna searched upward. What was he seeing?

Despite the sunlight that drenched them, she felt the chill drift across them like waves of mist. She hugged herself, then jogged to the pony, and tugged the blanket out of the saddle. Well wrapped, she returned to her spot, not trusting enough to advance as boldly as her father. She watched him wend amongst the standing stones, appearing, shadow-like at the side of a trilithon, then gone, to reappear at some unpredictable spot.

Eventually, he became aware of a pattern, a fogged choreography of sorts. He began mouthing words to his footsteps and winding through a curved line of small upright stones like a cat through human legs. His shoulders hunched against the cold. He pulled his crossed arms tight around his chest, stopped, shivered forcefully, willing warmth into his thin body, then pushed himself forward again. He thrust his numb hands into his jacket pockets. And...

He had not expected this. The cold had gone. But so had Stonehenge. And he was in a menacing blackness where he hardly dared open his eyes. Somehow, he knew, he would be shocked. He felt weaker than ever before, not up to any challenge.

He reached into the air, blind as a mole. He was an embryo, not even aware of his nails growing.

His heart thumped violently and black fear conquered him.

———

Now she recognized the sound of wind… Maybe it was the sound of spirits in the stones. Her insides laughed at the thought, gave her the impulse to jump. Something so absurd, and yet concrete, visceral. And if time-travel, then why not that?

She began to walk now, urged on gently, pushed by a quiet beat. She searched for him, listened for his voice. Her stomach clutched and she pushed herself first left, then right, straining to move faster against the beat that controlled her.

'Think,' she said. 'You will have to outwit it, be quick and slide yourself there, where he is, before It even knows.' Where was he last? The Aubrey Stones, that's what they called them. Good, she could think properly if she tried. Her foot struck against hardness. She stood at the edge of the circle of Aubrey Stones. Her eyes strained ahead, followed its curve until it was intercepted by a standing stone. No dad.

She spun, stared the other way. Nothing. She fought down panic, swallowing dryly. BE CALM, she told herself through tense jaws. She managed to draw a deep breath. Minutes passed with not the slightest sign of him. He was gone, and she had not managed to follow.

Why did he not call her to him?

She waited, tense-nerved, fearing the place's menacing presence. Her eyes scanned the sky, the flint-gray of oncoming winter. She had lied to herself in her urge to be brave. To commit to him; she had denied her intuition of foreboding.

"Stupid cow!" she cried, as if the turn of events were her fault.

He awakened to feel his horse teeth bite into cake, sending sweet custard dribbling down his ragged beard. But he'd never had a beard – how was this… Then the face smiled up at Yusupov, his fingers crossing his thick lips, and Gareth was all but gone inside this incredible, lustful power. He listened through the ears, watched through gluttonous eyes.

The man licked his fingers, wiped his beard straight, licked his fingers clean. The cake's saccharine sweetness utterly annihilated the tea. Grigory Yefimovich Novykh, the infamous Rasputin, wanted wine, something to cut through the fatty richness. Then maybe some more cakes.

It was gluttony, one of the seven sins – but what could he do? They called him Rasputin, 'The Debauched one,' but there again, what of it? His taste for life, for women, for God, it was all a kind of gluttony; he was never sated: From the moment of birth, greedily sucking air. The hunger of the limbs for touch, the muscles for action, the tired body for sleep – each a momentary addiction. God could not condemn him for his huge self. God had made him. 'Enough of him for everyone,' as his wife Praskovaya would say.

If she could defend his lusts, then what man or woman could condemn him?

"Wine, then." He said it generously, as if doing Yusupov a favor. That was how you did it. It made them happy, made them feel superior, that it was their wine, their food, on which you were besotted. More victuals, more drunkenness, more pleasure than your lowly self could afford – it was your duty as a peasant (even a Starets like himself) to be awestruck and rendered stupid by their wealth. But it was wasted on the rich, all this money and food and sumptuousness. He was drowning in God's pleasures.

It was no sin. Just enjoyment. And God might punish at will after death, if He was so inclined.

But there would be no punishment. Rasputin knew this. God had made him superhuman, larger, more powerful than others, for a purpose. For Mother Russia for Mama and Papa; none of it for himself. He was just the vessel. And the vessel needed fuel, sex...

Grigory wanted Yusupov's wife. And he would have her – perhaps not tonight, but soon.

"Good. Wine is good." He held his glass out, spying his warped reflection in its ruby contents, watching the wine rise as Yusupov refilled the glass.

Why was this little prince so nervous? He was not a well man: Always disconnected from the earth, as if ready to flitter off at any moment, to flee at any threatening movement. Prince Yusupov couldn't help it. He was a sick man – a pervert who preferred boys' backsides over a nice, curved woman's rump. Little, bony Yusupov. There he went again, slopping wine on the tablecloth in his haste to leave the room. Grigory was sure the man would blow apart – some internal pressure, like in a steam boiler, straining against his insides.

'Garrettpyoo.' The voice in his head was back, asserting itself. Perhaps it was one of those brainless demons, talking to itself in the dark. That was harmless, but distracting.

"Grigory wants no company." He shook his head violently, sucked down the wine, drained the glass.

Yusupov faltered with the bottle part way to Rasputin's glass. "Grigory, my wife was so pleased that you accepted our invitation, she..."

Grigory glared at Yusupov, uncomprehending. The voice, this Garrettpyoo, had momentarily stolen his attention. "No," he commanded, and the voice inside dwindled, then submitted to death, as if crushed under an avalanche. "You go, all you brain visitors. Grigory is getting drunk."

Rasputin's mind returned to the important things. He raised a stiff arm, thrust the emptied glass toward Yusupov's face. The prince stood gawping – a most feeble man, clearly not making his wife happy. But a sinister fellow too.

"You say... about your wife, your lovely wife...?"

Yusupov was pale. Not a well man. Twittery. A buggerer of boys. Now there was a sin. Bugger his wife – a good thing. Why skinny boys, square boys? No breasts. No twat.

Yusupov had sprung to the foot of the spiral staircase. He smacked his palm on the banister, as if hitting let out some of the steam from the boiler.

"Hit me." Grigory rose, laughing, banging his chest. "You want to punch? Punch me. Come, my friend. Hit me. I make you well again."

Yusupov stared, a frightened rabbit – no brains.

"I make everyone well. I touch. They heal. Mama and Papa know. Alexei, Tsar's son, knows. Even you hit me, it makes you well."

His eyes followed Yusupov up the stairwell.

"Come back! We drink, then sing gypsy songs, yes? Then your wife join us and sing..."

Humming, he returned to the table, stuck his index finger into a cake and licked off the custard.

"Go away!" he barked. Garrettpyoo again.

"No demons. Almighty God, be my friend. I drink tonight. I need rest from the voices. You know this my Father. Demons, go! In the name of Almighty God!"

Yusupov returned, twittery and stiff-necked, like a mad wading bird in a river.

"You drink with me, yes?" Rasputin indicated the chair opposite. "My stomach is burning. Give me sweet wine, some Madeira. That will ease me."

He struggled to his feet, feeling leaden and dizzy. He rattled his head, stretched his neck from side to side. There was a beautiful crucifix there, on the shelf: a crystal crucifix... He would have one like it for himself. His daughters could pray with him in front of it. His rough hands stroked the ebony cupboard as he would a woman's stomach. Almost rich enough to taste, this furniture.

Curtains, rugs, antique furniture, Chinese vases, ebony cupboards, tables covered with fabrics. There was a Persian carpet before a fireplace; a white bear skin hanging in front of a huge cupboard; a samovar on the table.

"You have too much vanity, Prince Yusupov," he thought aloud. "How can the Kingdom of God be within you when it is so cluttered with furniture?"

He turned away from the crucifix, to see Yusupov staring at him. The man was blanched, and trembling, pointing a stiff arm at him; and at the end of the arm, a pistol.

"Grigory Efimovich, known as Rasputin, you should look at the crucifix again and pray for your soul."

The pistol shook in his hand, reflecting gaslight from the table lamp.

Rasputin felt fear tighten in him, suck the moisture from his throat so that he could not swallow or speak. Then it was gone, replaced by a wave of warmth. He felt benign. He felt pity for the pathetic little man and sadness over what he was about to do. Was this how Christ felt at his betrayal? Rasputin would submit. This little man must fire his gun, and then we would see...

The shot sent him backwards into the polar bear skin. Its stale fur was the last thing he smelled as he fell, his face sliding downward against its bristles.

Gareth had yelled an obscenity, just before the bullet hit. Now he was stunned into silence, his inner ear straining for the hum of Rasputin's blood through veins, for the liquid thump and wash of his heart.

Silence.

Once awake in Rasputin's mind, he had felt his own self crushed. The weight and force of this man's spirit was incredible. His appetites alone blotted out most of Gareth's consciousness, so that all he had been able to do was remind himself who he was, that he was still, somehow, somewhere, aware of himself.

The bullet had done its work, silenced the massive orchestra that was Rasputin's mind. Now Gareth had to worry about freeing himself. And he felt horribly feeble, blood- and oxygen-starved. His mind, strangled to the rim of unconsciousness, now roused its abused cells, until thoughts gathered together again, like ants repairing a ruined anthill.

No pain, and really no fear yet. Not enough strength for fear to coalesce; only the sense of exhaustion striving to comfort itself.

Then the man was kicking him. Yusupov, kicking, at his guts, his head. Then on his knees beside him, grabbing Rasputin's shoulders, lifting and banging the head against the floor, crying his rage and terror through a reedy whine. Yusupov. Murderer.

Gareth suffocated again. Beneath water, pressed by a great weight.

Rasputin's eyes were stuck shut, as though he had forgotten how to use them. Then the left eye was twitching. Then the other eye twitched, and both sprang open onto Yusupov's effeminate face dribbling spittle, keening out noise.

He was Rasputin again, and he shook his finger in Yusupov's face, felt the man's lips curl behind the words.

"You BAD boy!"

Electric with anger, he leapt to his feet and lunged at the skinny fellow. His hands met cloth, squeezed on Yusupov's shoulders. Rasputin bellowed, moved his hands toward the man's throat.

Then he was staggering backward, staring down at an epaulet clutched in his hand. Yusupov had escaped, the sick little eel. He felt himself falling again, hit the floor amidst a dense blackness, out of which came words. Was it Yusupov, shouting?

"The revolver, damnit! Quick! Throw me the revolver! He is alive!"

Disbelief partnered Rasputin's fear, now that he had awakened to his death. Hollow sounds met a hollow mind, and a glittering Siberian chill washed over him. His mind exploded with a cool brilliance, and he was awake again.

He was alive and running. His feet – beneath this place where his head waved in the darkness – rattled like frozen rats tied to his ankles. He slipped, watched those rats slide sideways, pushing snow, and his hand clawed the diamond white powder.

The snow squeaked beneath him. The night sky prickled with bluewhite stars, so lonely and far. Lamplight cold on wrought iron – he recognized where his feet were carrying him. The gate. Cold, hard iron, – curlicued vanity, separating those inside from the hordes outside. He could smell their hovels, their chimneys and sweat. It clung to the city like a failed prayer.

Or was it only his mind? With the rats rattling beneath. He felt their little hearts bouncing from the ground and pounding upward. Poor, pan- icked little rats. But he was alive. They could not get him. They must not. He heard them behind, felt them gathering together by the opened door. Felt their panic too.

"Felix Yusupov!" The cry was his own. "I will tell Tsarina what you have done!"

He fell hard against the gate, felt its jarring coldness against his skin. His fingers clutched, gripped through the snow-moss on iron. He would be free tonight. He saw in his mind the warm comfort of his simple rooms – saw his daughters asleep.

Something plunged into his back. He knew its heat, and the bone splin- tering pain and the dullness around violated skin. Not a knife blade. He had felt that before, stuck deep into his gut. This was no blade. A bullet. Another bullet, sinking its teeth in near his spine. Then another hiss, as slow as a drunken fall, as if it was himself toppling forward down stairs – but coming from behind. A hiss like his fate flying, crying through the night wind. Then the explosion within his head, scarlet and purple and yellow. Electric white-blue.

Silence for two eternal seconds, and the snow falling lingeringly down- ward, an afterthought of the day's weather.

Gareth was gasping now. Inside, driving him, a thin string of utter fear where his whole mind used to be. He made what remained of himself grip tight to that string, fear petrifying into a thin branch that might just snag the shore.

How could he escape? His mind suffocated on the residue of Rasputin's death. A death so palpable that its horror beat in him now like his own heart. The heart and mind of Rasputin clawing its way back into life, leaping like a shot deer, leaping away from the black unknown, screaming away from terror toward beloved life.

Rasputin had been awake, wide awake in the freezing water. Even in the last seconds, he struggled to free himself of his bonds, thrashed his body against dumb water like a leviathan. Then he felt death approaching, coming to him across the snow that carpeted the River Neva. He saw it, once, death like a human crow, wrapped in charcoal rags, stalking woodenly his way. He caught its vermilion eye, its baleful emptiness, and thrust himself beneath again. To sink away.

Death arrived, stared down at him, its figure rippling, with the tepid morning sun behind.

'Goodbye Papa, Mama.' The thought crept through the numbness like frost, to join the snow that was death mounting in him. He managed, through an eternity, to force his arm up to his chest. He began the sign of the cross. Then his lungs filled and icy death bit into his soul.

Gareth knew what he could see. It was the Petrovsky Bridge dwindling as the sluggish river drew the body under. He could see. So he must be alive. Or did the dead see like this? Maybe a memory, replaying like a dream in the netherworld until the dead thing let go, came to terms?

Did they sit like this in purgatory? Like squatting natives sucking on a greasy cigarette, overcome with brainhum? A senseless death. A roadside daisy crushed to pulp by a timber truck.

Gareth spun ditheringly slow, a metaphysical maggot, with the dead body. A slow, aching, tango in the soul-sucking guts of the Neva, and he could not rise. Not even raise a maggot's eyebrow above the nap on Rasputin's festive blue shirt. The one he wore for special occasions.

Rasputin's hair, long tendrils reaching out to the ceiling of blued ice, snagged in silence, tearing free of the scalp. Rasputin's broken nose was crusted blood imprinted with an iron bar's chop. His eyelids turned livid and the eyes leeched their color into death's waiting atoms, bleeding to albino ivory. Rasputin's blood writes: 'There goes sainthood.'

His bobbing arm waves sadly at the Orthodox Church as the carcass tumbles slowly by. Yes. Gareth is thinking again. Think, he says. The Orthodox Church in Russia claims that a saint cannot die by drowning... Rasputin has drowned. Ergo, he cannot be a saint.

But can a drowned man become a Gareth?

Gareth's brain is blue with cold. The body is weighted down by stink. Gareth knows it is the weight of liquefying organs. But that cannot happen for some time yet. And yet, the carcass stinks. Or is it himself, his live self cocooned in the dead flesh, that stinks – his spirit's flame charring the ashes of Rasputin's life?

This cannot go on.

Can it?

Rasputin has become a barge. The sun has awoken St. Petersburg to its business, and soon the police must know, the sentries at the palace must see the blood. Soon, surely, a grappling pole will hook the Starets out of the ice?

Gareth sees a wharf. Not in his mind's eye, but real, out there. The corpse has run against an ice floe and taps against it. Tap tap. The ice responds with deep groans afar, with crunches and clicks, and the collapse of snow into frigid depths. Ripples lap along Rasputin's ear lobe, from which Gareth sees as if through a telescope.

Petrograd: Rows of tall buildings lean indifferently toward his drowned body; a tableau lit by the motionless light of a winter's morning, where the ghostly workers, the policeman, the ragged hawkers, the bell ringer, all follow their missions, as huge flakes of snow drift landward, evaporating in concert with time's markers, seconds that dissolve into gray infinity.

Gareth crawls from the ear canal to the throat, but cannot get past a scream that has plugged Rasputin's throat. He thinks himself backwards, past the dangling uvula and up the nasal cavity. He sits poised in the supine man's nostril, watching the blue ice, where the sunlight shows through frozen fans of blown snow. He watches the sun's orb flaring at them intermittently between breaks in the steep roofs as they drift silently along, now freezing to the ice floe, now nudged here, there, the iceberg banging against bridge, barge, unknowns, and the body banging dully its response, water-logged wood.

Gareth and Grigory on morning parade – would they find harbor, per-haps, at the Nevsky Prospekt? Gareth imagines somewhere warm and bus-tling, where Grigory's soul could slip into the busy day, embraced again in the warmth, noise, and flesh of his own people.

Gareth is tired of the idleness, the stilled, mindless floating.

Pan is dying and the world is stumbling into ruinous war that is the destruction of old forms of love, of courtship, of the wonderful, old-leather smell of human physicality. Gareth can hear its advance, the destroyer of the old world, a world of cavalry, horse drawn carriages, animal funk on street and farm; the world of etiquette, of eroticism under wraps, of haying with pitchforks, of walking hand in hand with the seasons. This world, entire, is uttering its death rattle through shaking sabers, tramping feet in puttees, white ribbons and soul-killing scorn, the choking throats of teenage boys in mustard-gassed trenches. The entire world has entered the pornographic realm, heralded by two festivals of carnage, and dragging itself out of that mire, finds that it has gained plastic and the atom bomb, and decimated its soul. The human soul has been blown to pieces, shredded, crippled and amputated, and still the body jumps and gyrates, dangling like a marionette pinned to the wall, praying to be fertilized again.

Gareth is absolutely sick to death of thinking. There has to be a way out, one that would not see him trapped in the battered, petrifying flesh of some waterfront worker. Or swelling inside the ego of some fat bellied, rancorous waiter in a borscht and vodka dive. He was so tired of flesh, his own and theirs. And yet he wished he could piggy-back Alexander the Great into Alexandria; could be Gandhi, or Buddha, or Fatty Arbuckle screwing a whore, or be the whore herself. Just to be in a dumb, hungry body – hungry and unaware.

He would even be Cabot. He could sit inside the pervert and drive him mad, send him off the Gardiner Expressway to become raspberry jam on the concrete.

Gareth's mind stopped dead.

The ice cracked. Seconds dissolved.

Then a rat's whiskers tickled his mind. He opened his dying eyes inside Rasputin.

One shining black eye curious, staring up a nostril. Scratching claw. A quick- pumping little heart.

Gareth stared back, peering between its yellow teeth.

Adrianna, alone – God knew where.

There was nothing else for it.

God, rat throat stank.

24

Adrianna sat on the stone and glared. The earth beneath her feet was not the earth she wanted. She knew her father was not here. The trilithons were absent. She sat near the centre of a circular ditch, which was encircled by a chalk and earth mound. She was the bull's eye on the dartboard. She looked up to the clouds, as if she would find God staring at her, or some perverse demi-god. The blazing sunlight turned her face a brilliant white-gold

"What am I doing here?" She stood and scratched her bottom where a stone chip had poked her.

"I need to find my dad, dammit!" Her cry joined the wind that meandered through long grass. She wanted something to punch and kick. She walked, to cool her anger. Her legs pulled her up the side of the mound, then turned right and marched her clockwise, around and around mindlessly.

She could not think: would not. Her mind brimmed with chattering ideas. She knew, somehow, that thought amounted to nothing here. She closed her eyes, let her mind drop out of sight, wisps of thought plummeting with it.

Her feet seemed to tread the sky, and the air exuded mist that hung above a carpet of grass that was not grass, with her feet not feet, her toes like a collection of tiny apples, shining polished in the sunlight, then washed with dewdrops, then hiding under the edge of her skirts. A bird sang, but she could not see it. And, suddenly, it was not calling sweetly but singing her anguish.

What was the use of anything? She felt a moment of madness tear through her head, and a desire to get blind drunk. She wanted to smash herself to pieces. She wanted some giant force to grab her and slam her down, so that she bounced off the chalk rocks, flailed and spun, brainless and broken, to land, shattered and dead at the bottom. But the mound was not hard enough, not high enough to annihilate her.

This was nothing but her rage turning inward, killing its host, as if killing were an answer, like one and one adding up to two. She had always been like that, she realized. Always trembling on the verge, her spirit so delicately poised at the verge of despair that it took nothing... And this was that nothing.

She sat, and the madness rent itself like a trapped mink chewing off its own tail. Why the urge to shed her own blood? A sharp knife dragged deep across her naked arm. Why the desire for such mutilation? Was she so lonely, then?

A thought came to her, spelling itself clearly across her mind.

'We each live in a time no more majestic than ourselves.'

Rigor and bone-cracking cold still blanked Gareth's thoughts, plunging frigid fingers deep. He would not have reconnected, he was sure, had the rat not breathed the stench of rot into the dead man's nostrils. Now, from inside the rodent, Gareth felt the scratch of its tiny curled claws across the eyelids; felt it balanced on its hind legs.

Gareth could hear its occasional excited whistle. A whole Rasputin to eat! The length of the Starets' carcass now showed above the freezing water, a macabre 'laying out'.

He forced his sight outward, arcing over the heavy, sad boats bellied into the ice; forced it to climb stone steps up the wharf. He had one chance – to enlarge his mind long enough to reach out and recognize the harmonies in some body that would let him safely in. There was no other way out of this spirit rigor.

He had been too close to death this time, had seen too much that one should never see. If he survived this one he would aim for home and quiet retirement. If that was possible. He had not run his course; it had run him...

He was no more that little, impetuous boy, transfixed by all creatures great and small, and besotted with the great escape. His escape was greater than he could have imagined. To the other side of the globe, dying with no dignity, suffocated by somebody else's death, and not even remembered at home.

Philomena and Clifton would be gloating soon.

25

Cabot's wrists still burned. He would kill for a scotch, here, in a world that could not spell mead consistently. They just weren't paying him enough, Buckleigh and his ghostly horde, to put up with such discomfort. Stink everywhere, and foul people with the stench of decay howling out of their mouths. And bad food: boiled meat, scraps of potato and rubbery chunks of carrot in stew, driven down the throat by gnarled hunks of wooden bread.

Here, he was an unwanted alien with odd manners to match his dress; at 'home' in Toronto, an academic non-entity. No matter where he would be, the reaction to him would always be a variation on the same theme. Adrianna's opinion of him, what Buckleigh and his colleagues thought of him, found its parallel in the bovine smugness of these hostile peasants.

Cabot pushed off from the trestle at the inn table and aimed himself toward the open door. He smirked and rebounded off bosoms, slipped on ale-slithery straw, dithered, and sloped into the night.

Silence.

What the hell had he been thinking? There was a plan.

He retched, watched his vomit fly in slow motion into the night air, orange-brown against black. He heard it pattering into the mud, smelled the acidic stink.

Moon above, a hole punched in the darkness. Same damn moon, no matter what century. And the little pork dinners grunting and huffing beneath in the mud, their backs silvering now and again in the moonlight as they scuttled. He coughed and hung, staring myopically at the fluorescent tail-end of a piglet.

All he needed was to rest, to get a good night's sleep. To energize. Then he would get something done. He wiped his moist hands against his jerkin, feeling amoebic stickiness between his fingers. He held himself still and gulped a gutful of air to countermand the throat sting that urged him to puke again.

He had to find a dark corner, pull himself under a thick hedge to wait until the Anis finally wore off. Then he would be returned to Toronto, to sleep the sleep of the pampered, maybe in Adrianna's own bed. He breathed deep, almost recalled her scent. But the feeling swam away, like a rat in a sewer, joining the slow tumble of his drunkenness.

He looked about, saw no-one and slunk into the shadow of a church doorway. He hunched up and waited. His fingers grazed against grit. His fingernail picked, picked, dirt from a joint between stones.

"Bang," he said, and belched. He pointed two fingers at a feral-looking cat as it slunk under a gate. "Bang."

By God, he would make them jump.

26

She wished now that she had never begun prying into the emanations around her. Adrianna had landed in an inhospitable portion of time and space that gripped the standing stones like a horrible changeling. A storm blew through the edge of the woods and trees threw down huge raindrops. She had torn free branches and bark and moss to form a wall against the worst of it. Then the rain hissed heavily on her and she found herself completely exhausted, with mud under broken nails and fingers torn. Starving and chilled, curled in a mess of branches and turf she had intended to form a windbreak, she was miserable, with throbbing fingers and dirt in her mouth.

She found snatches of rest, attacked continually by sudden fears – of men bursting out of the woods behind her; a shadow standing over her, as solid as a bull. She saw, or dreamed screams, groans swaying at her like fever, smelling of death. She was on her knees, her hands scrabbling through wild ground as she crawled the final few inches, stretched out for the knife in the roots and dirt – then a foot stamped down, stamped down, crushing her fingers.

She awoke to her own scream, and sweat, cold on her brow. Her back crawled. Anyone could find her, grab her. She would have been better hidden against one of the trilithons, where no one seemed to go. She did not want to be a hunting trophy for some Neanderthal or Pict. Or worse, a victim of...

Her stomach froze, crowded its chill through chest, arms, thighs. A groan pushed itself out of her, gurgling and deep at first, then keening high like the cry of a tiny animal, and she convulsed. The rain smacked toughly into her. She felt bile choking out of her gut. She tensed, as rigid as metal, tense enough to break herself to pieces. Then blackness smothered her like a huge paw, and she hung, on the verge of passing out, never falling into its mercy. She gurgled her pain through a deep current of misery. Convulsions thrust Cabot from her body and battled again and again against him forcing himself into her.

Hours, it seemed. And it might have been an entire day and night. She knelt in a bruised darkness, curled like a trilobite, her spine staring up through her damp dress. Indifferent, rain-smoked sky swept over her, over woods, over soaked stones with roots deep in the mud. Finally, she slept like the dead.

She awoke, staring at shredded leaves clutched in her hands.

Was she finally released from sickness, or would an attack come again?

If only she'd had the rage to kill Cabot when they had him tied up. She might have forgiven herself in time, and would at least know vengeance, instead of the death she now knew. How had she acquiesced to this violence? The rape, a desecration of her silent, private self – she would never return to the woman she had been.

How could it have happened? She did not invite it. Nothing in her said 'Come on, take me.' Nothing said, 'I am victim. Rape me. Tear me apart, soul from limb from spirit from childhood from happiness.'

And yet, rape had come, had punctured her quiet world, torn down its translucent walls and let in the furies – his beastly stink, his demonic noise, the blunted blade of his flesh lusting, pushing at her.

She forced herself to sit and stared into the dirt, rubbing what warmth she could into her legs. It was going to be a long wait for Gareth – any nastiness could happen. Something horrible could descend and crush her.

"That would be just about par for the course, wouldn't it?"

She said it to a pair of eyes in the bushes. A small badger, seemingly unfazed by her presence, rooting about in the wet earth. She watched badger, and heard the curtain of rain hissing away across the grass, pattering over the standing stones.

Sudden fear lurched through her stomach. What if she were stuck here now? She felt solid, and her bile had been bitterly real. She ground her teeth and her mouth formed a rictus of despair. She was caged in a dream that she was powerless to alter or release herself from. A reality in which she would grow old and die. If it wasn't real, it was as close to madness as could be, and she could not tell the difference.

What was she to do?

She pushed herself out from the darkness. Eat. Find strength and comfort in food. She began to forage, aimlessly at first, then with more concentration as her hands and nostrils found and sampled berries, leaves, pine cones. She desperately needed water. Her eyes lit up at the sight of a swarm of dock leaves, their belled stomachs holding small glitters of rain. Enough to slake her sore throat perhaps. She crawled to them and tilted dirty rain into her mouth, one after the other, every precious droplet. She sucked in and swallowed each tiny puddle, drowned ants, dirt and all. Then she sat and faced the land around her. The water cheered her, grounded her.

There was hope, then.

That was all she had. Eat, start a fire. That was a way to stay grounded, to counter the 'Stonehenge warps.' She felt better to be thinking again, planning.

Food. And now, somehow, fire.

It might be a long wait.

She dared forage further still from her little hut. But her alertness to the forest's sounds gave way again to a shapeless fear. Everywhere she faced, there was only the alien, indifferent power of nature growing. Indifferent. She was of less consequence than the badger, of a slug under a bush. There was no comfort in this primitive force. Always the horrible sense that danger moved in from behind.

Heaving breath, she crashed through brush toward the daylight and broke onto the Stonehenge plain. The sun had not come out after the rain. She looked up where anemic whiteness marked the sun's place. Other than her fear, nothing.

She walked her exhausted path up the slope toward the standing stones and swayed on the ridge, searching as far as the gloom would allow. Her eyes locked on a wraithlike motion on the moving air, far away.

Smoke! It had to be. She wiped her watery eyes clear, then stared again. And yes, there, another drifting wraith evaporating in the tree tops. She locked her eyes on the spot and walked, down the slope, then resolutely across the field, stumbling but never letting go of the spot in the trees.

Anything would be better, almost, than cold solitude.

Cabot had never had a gun before. Thanks to Buckleigh, he now held his own revolver, one he could carry with him to where law didn't exist. Better still, where he was going, they had never heard of, never even envisioned a gun.

And the police hadn't yet been invented.

He walked along the hallway leading to Adrianna's bedroom. The revolver felt like a good new truth in his hand, its firm, snub build reassuring. He held awe-inspiring power that could splinter rock, could obliterate a laugh in mid-utterance. The power of a demi-god. A cock that spit death. It felt a part of him. He felt renewed, as if a phantom limb had taken on flesh.

He laughed out loud, not caring who among the Gareth crowd might think him odd. Let them look askance, let them wonder why he was still around, the interloper. He couldn't have cared less. He had nothing to prove to them. 'To think,' he said to himself. 'Years ago, you would meet a woman, win her over, and then, unavoidably, you were taken home to meet the parents, and you always went through that wretched fear, that sense of being judged, of not quite being good enough.'

He laughed again, and banged the revolver's grip against Adrianna's door, not because he expected to find someone within, but because it felt sexy. The gun's feel, its weight alone, gave him a new boldness. He was as good as anyone now – better than most.

He pushed the door open, walked in, tapped the revolver along the surface of the dresser, then along the window sill. He surveyed the four-poster bed, the still life – fluffed pillows, side table, books on its surface forming a staircase for spiders, the remains of a blue candle, and a wind up clock ticking monotonously.

Clocks. Smug little bastards. Ticking away as if they mattered more than you. Which they did, because you were always running behind time, never getting enough done, never proving yourself, while they sang their tick tick tick into the realm of death.

Well, up theirs. That was just what he now was – a portable, compact realm of death unto himself.

"Not quite good enough, eh? Not anymore," he intoned. He grinned dryly, heard, as if from another dimension, the faint sounds of Granny

Pugh and that Uncle Huge fellow from the floor below. If they had even the slightest idea...

He just didn't give a pig's ass.

And better. They would be waiting, on and on, for their precious Gareth Pugh to come back to them, or would cling on, like Philomena and whatsisname, rabid with greed, distempered with frustration, waiting for the death certificate, for the reading of the will, each one of them smugly assured that they were better than the other because they loved more, or inherited more.

And they would get absolutely nothing.

Because he had found the will and burned it. With just a little information from Buckleigh, and a short telephone call, he had found the will. He had found a hand on the end of that will, pulling it from a wall safe and holding it up to the late afternoon light, passing it over to Cabot, who, as the 'executor's assistant,' traded it for a death certificate signed by Buckleigh. And he had stared at that effeminate, silk-cuffed hand, its manicured, bleached white fingernails, at the lawyer's balding, triangular face, and he had fired.

Two shots, and the petite lawyer was as dead as a paperweight. And Cabot had taken back the death certificate and walked out.

Easy as pie. And now he was going where they could never catch him. Just long enough for the hysteria of the manhunt to die down. Long enough to kill a few more insignificant others.

A little dance with his little pop gun, here, there and everywhere down the alleyways of time... then back here for the rest of his money, and a front row seat at the collapse of the House of Gareth. Their misery, both the Pughs' and Philomena et al. would be a pleasure to behold.

This was all getting to be too damn good. Almost better than sex.

Cabot lay prone on the mattress, inhaling Adrianna's scent from the pillow across his face. He pressed the pillow tighter, bit into the feathered guts, listened to his hissing breath in the silence. His right arm reached to his crotch. He gripped his pistol there, pointed its deadly mouth at the wall, felt the weight of its grip against his fingers and the curled palm of his hand. Almost better then sex.

Almost? Maybe better. He sighed happily. 'Baby, you're a rich man.'

27

Adrianna scanned the scrub. She could smell the smoke, saw blue-gray floating. She zig-zagged up the pine-needled slope, left, right, pointing herself toward outcrops, gatherings of rock where someone might settle or hide. Every thicket hid a hunched figure. If she was being reckless, she didn't care. Urgency elbowed aside caution. Oh God... it might be her father...

She struggled upward, desperately searching out the smoke, following like a hound.

She could see Gareth... dad, hugging her. A curl up by a fire. Words murmured into sleep... Dad completely sated of this odyssey, and a return home, just maybe... Or the strength to once again meet with that sick pervert... Finality of some desperately needed kind.

"Dad?" she called out. The word sat, dull in the unmoving air.

He would have answered. Wouldn't he? Unless he was in trouble, held prisoner.

She stopped dead. Talking with herself, yelling, getting cross; this was madness. And now the forest darkness had come. Even hope of a shadow had abandoned her. Rain. Filthy sky. Black encroaching.

A cough. She froze, listened. Somewhere, the hurried scrabbling of a squirrel...

"You know I'm here," came a voice, little above a whisper. "Just follow."

Adrianna's heart leaped. It had to be her dad. She followed the voice to a gathering of fallen trees, their huge, torn roots splayed into the air, draped with moss. She jumped expectantly around them, ready to dive into her father's arms.

But there was only a low fire smoldering, and an old woman wrapped in a cowl, sitting on a stump. She poked at the fire, encouraging a livelier flame, then smiled crookedly at Adrianna, as though smiling itself were a secret joke.

Adrianna's spine tingled to the nape of her neck. Something about this woman said 'witch.' And nothing about her said Gareth. She stared into the woman's eyes, digging after a reflection of her father.

There was a reflection – and it was Adrianna.

Deflated, she obeyed the woman's gesture and sat on the stump across from her. She stretched out her hands to the flames, unwilling to meet the crone's eyes. She could feel the old woman's steady gaze; creepy as hell. Then the scraping of iron on stone came to her and Adrianna looked up to see a pot steaming on a flat stone amid the coals. The crone offered a bowl of soup and Adrianna accepted it cautiously. Nothing smelled off, nothing sour or rotten... Its rich aroma silenced the clamor in her head. The wooden spoon went into her mouth and she almost cried from the flavorful warmth. If the witch-woman was going to kill her, she would go with a happy stomach.

Eventually feeling braver, Adrianna spoke between huge mouthfuls. "Who are you, and where am I? Yeah, Stonehenge, I know, but..." She snatched a look back over her path. Sure enough, the hulking presence of Stonehenge stood far off. Or was it a herd of cattle closer up, or woolly mammoth? She turned to the crone and her fire. "When exactly is this? I mean... Oh hell. I don't know what I mean."

"This is right now. This is yours. And everything that exists here comes into being because of you."

Adrianna left off chewing a hunk of meat that refused to surrender.

"You're kidding me! It's cold, it's empty, it's damp and miserable, and horrible. At least, until I had this soup... and... I vomited over there... I vomited an abortion!"

"Yes."

The crone offered her a face as expressionless as milk. Adrianna hated it.

"Well, who are you anyway, smirking at me ...?"

Her lips formed a shell and she exhaled, blowing her hair across her forehead.

"I'm really getting sick of this. It's been nothing but troubles and struggles since the first day. And I don't even know anymore what day it is, what month, where I am. I get hunted as a witch, raped by a pervert I want to murder, someone I should have never given the time of day. Why I didn't see him for what he was when I met him I don't..."

"So, your bad fortune not only manifests here then?"

"Oh, please. I haven't got time for that kind of lunacy."

"What kind? The truth kind?"

"Oh, call it what you like. I absolutely have no use for analysis right now. I want to know what the hell I'm doing here." She swiveled about. "This has to be a dream, an hallucination. And if that's the case..." she faced the crone squarely, tossed her words triumphantly at her. "I can bloody well undo it. I can be somewhere else."

"Try then."

The old one arranged her hands on her lap.

Adrianna stared stonily at her, shook her head and closed her eyes. She began imagining sweet things, the comfort of a hot bath, the cats stepping through the garden, a dining table laden with food, Christmas, her old boy-friend kissing her, in a time before they argued...

She opened her eyes hopefully.

The creepy woman, the dark wood, the sad fire, just as before.

'Remember Stonehenge,' her mind whispered, 'the chalk mound. Get back there, to that time, to your father before he vanished, then home.' She firmly shut her eyes. Minutes passed, sound blurred. The wind had died. No noise from across that awful fire. All Adrianna could hear was her blood hissing in her ears... Anis would help her! She must be at Stonehenge by now! She opened her eyes and felt silent tears run down to her chin. Nothing had altered.

"Not easy, is it? Not when you have not yet overcome your old self."

Old self? She felt minute underground writhings, wraiths awakening in her gut. The memory of her death-wish on the chalk mound replayed itself nakedly, showed itself for a bald, mad lie. Driving her to her end, smashed like a doll. Memories embedded deep awoke in her – trauma, fears, moments of exhilarating success that meant nothing to anyone else. Was that her old self? And could there be a new one?

"There can be," said the woman.

"Comfortable inside my mind, are you?" Adrianna snapped. But then, was her father any different...?

A. H. Richards

"You have made your time what it is, to a great extent. How can I put it? Your daily life, even in its entire span, is so very small. And your job, in this body called Adrianna, is to micromanage your existence the best way you can. Do you follow? Remember the words Adrianna, 'We each live in a time no more majestic than ourselves.'"

Adrianna nodded begrudgingly, shifting on her seat. Yes, she had heard that herself, somewhere before. She couldn't put her finger on it...

"Well then. You make mistakes, as we all do. So many ultra fine, subtle errors, in judgment, in choice, in conceptualizing. And you make some right choices, some just as subtle; some as unsubtle as a brick. Who to take as a boyfriend, girlfriend... whether to keep or push away this person who wants to be a friend... to trust or not to trust... to hit or shout, sleep and smile..."

The combination of the soup, the woman's voice, and Adrianna's fatigue made the old woman's monologue come through as pictures, a liquid, flowing movie in the night.

"Remember the saying, 'the apple never falls far from the tree?' That is heritage. As much as your own choices, it is your ancestry that makes you what you are. It is your pedigree, in the most basic sense of the term. Not simply the shape of nose, and cheek, or the size of your bum. But also the patterns of your thought, their cadence. Like the motives in a symphony. Variations on themes. Your family's themes, these, you are born with, and carry through your life. And if you are like almost everyone else, you let them shape you, without the slightest notion of it happening, let alone making the slightest attempt to learn the music, to become the artist, to create anew.

No matter, girl. There's no blame there, no harm. You are a little bit aware – and how could you not be, since you are your father's daughter..."

Adrianna bristled.

"I'm myself, not just some baggage that belongs to my father. You can't be saying that we're just property of our parents, slaves to our genetics?" She would not acquiesce to that one. "I am myself!"

The woman chuckled.

"That woke you out of your slumber, didn't it, girl? No, I don't mean that you are merely the product of gene-intersplicing. You are not simply a mix of different colored plasticine, like those dolls, those little 'eskimos' you used to make as a child."

Adrianna's mind jumped. She had forgotten all about that. She would roll out blobs of plasticine, mixing different colors into marbled, whirled pancakes. Then, she would roll one pancake into a tube, then roll around it another pancake, like layers and layers of 'eskimo fur' on a naked body. And then, when all the pancakes were on the imagined doll, she would peel them off, one by one, taking care never to tear the table-polished skin of the one beneath, never to scar it with a fingernail.

"How do you know this? I had forgotten..."

"I am your great grandmother. I am always around, near you and your father. When I am not distracted by other things, of course."

"I appear in a manner suitable, that's all. For your father, I show up as myself, because we had deep trust. For you, someone unrecognizable, so that you would not waste your time on comparisons, all the usual things we do when meeting family. I know your mind's tendencies girl – you are as much a dreamer as Gareth – and we have little time to muck about. It tires me out to do this manifesting stuff for too long."

To Adrianna, nothing seemed incredible anymore. She accepted the news as everyday truth. So she was sitting at a campfire, next to Stonehenge, in a time she could not calculate, talking with a dead great grandmother. Her father was far away. Or maybe not. Maybe just around the corner. But where were the corners? He might as well be in another cosmos. It didn't really matter, did it? Brewing the perfect cup of tea was just as important.

"So, Adrianna. Listen to me. Do not drift so much girl. I can't stay with you all day."

Just as well, thought Adrianna. Or she'd be writing a PhD. dissertation on tea brewing, or scratching her arse like an ape. This was beginning to get comical.

Great gran's voice intruded.

"Focus on this Adrianna. Think. Do you understand what I have said? Your part in the family pattern...The reiterating of the themes, the motives...?"

The old lady sat forward suddenly and spoke to her sharply.

"Do not float away. I am not your mother's womb, and this around us is not amniotic fluid."

What a strange woman, to speak so oddly. Adrianna heard herself reply, as if through a Demerol haze.

"So, are you saying that, through your ancestors, it's like you inherit psychic information, habits of thought? I mean, like whole blueprints, like jigsaw puzzles?"

"Good enough, girl. Something like that, only not so concrete, so cut and dried. I'll describe it like this. If it's a jigsaw puzzle, it is one that forms a floor pattern and, with this pieced together, even without you being aware of it, you walk that pattern that is your family history. You step out a dance that has been, in great part, stylized by your ancestors. You are invited to the dance, a pattern of movement, understanding, mystification, tendencies of thought and feeling, that they once partook of, that they helped embellish and create. Their sensibilities, and yours, become a dance that every day culminates in you. Until you die, and then your offspring carry the knowledge."

She stared plainly at Adrianna, as if willing the information to be less complex.

Adrianna floundered in the images, the internal proddings given birth by the woman's words. A weight of responsibility pressed on her confused sense of inadequacy. The image her great grandmother described... it surely meant nothing more or less than impotence... iron-clad fatalism, the only relief being a family's fashion sense.

"There's no need to be fearful. This is not a life-sentence. No absolute duties. You live as you alone wish it, only with the dance, the music of family, playing out on some substrata, as if in another room.

"It's your family psychic heritage, if you like; the psychic equivalent of what today's narrow-minded scientists would call genetic imprinting, or some such. But then, we are not ducklings, as ugly as we might feel – and we are not bound by the steps, the drumbeat, the motif. You are not bound to do, to follow, anything."

"Then why am I here? It wasn't exactly my choice." She thought back.

"My father didn't trick me into this or seduce me with promises. But, somehow, I had no choice. He asked, and the only answer I could give was yes, even though I dreaded it."

"It's not for me to tell you why. What drove you, only you can understand. And, even then, is it necessary to understand everything? I think there are more significant threads in this tapestry that you are weaving."

Tapestry, music, dance... what was it when it lay still? It was time to get back to brass tacks.

"Okay. If you can be here, and you're dead, and if this is all of my own making, then I can bring my father here, right? And then we can leave."

"It is possible. It is possible to combine two worlds, such as yours and his. After all, I was willing to come to you from my world – and, in doing so, my girl, I had to leave behind most of the trappings of my very real world, just so that I wouldn't scare the daylights out of you. So be grateful, and learn. You can combine worlds. Your father could be summoned. But here's the rub. He must want to come, as I did. Otherwise, what you would summon would be something like a fantasy, a holograph, as you might say. Something uprooted which, in the past, they called a demon, one which suffers, or causes mischief, or... "

"So teach me to summon him! What do I do? He will come. I know he will!"

Adrianna felt bright eyed again, galvanized by hope.

Old hands manipulated hers, softly undoing the little basket formed by her clasped fingers. She felt her hope sink, and her stomach with it.

"What? What's wrong...?"

"Your father doesn't want to be here just yet."

"How do you know? Why would he not...?"

"You could invite him, I suppose. See how he would respond. You never know..." She smiled her secret smile – did Adrianna see ruefulness in it? She watched the woman's stick in the dirt as she stared absently into the darkness.

"If you must, then try. At the least, you might know that I speak the truth. You would have something concrete to work from..."

Adrianna tuned her out, thought only of her father, of the pain in her heart that might signal to him. And then, there came rustling, as of something small in the undergrowth. Her badger again? She followed the crone's gaze as it linked with the source of the noise. Did she even hear a minute noise, like a click, a pop? What was it? A rush, as of blood ringing in the ears, and then that little pop, as of two things engaging.

Out of the darkness surrounding their fire, something small scurried along, hugging the border and sidling laterally, as if its behind could not detach itself from the darkness. She saw its glassy black eyes, tinged with a touch of red. If it was a rodent, it was big. It seemed to sniffle at them, alert with springing whiskers, showing a fleck of pink chin, then it was gone, sucked back into the night.

"Oh! That's horrible! Poor little thing! It looked so frightened. Why was it staggering like that, like a madness?" A rush of pity and revulsion conquered her.

"That was your father. Though you did manage to call him here, it is not what he wishes. He won't be willing to come until he has solved his problems."

Adrianna's eagerness had died out. She sat, numbed. Helplessness echoed in the darkness around her. Was she so much like him, then, in her acute loneliness? Such a pass they had brought themselves to....

For so long, solitude had been a friend, one that she could rely on. But loneliness was solitude's twin sister – starved, ravenous and empty of hope. She thought she had mastered loneliness by the time she was five, but it was staring her in the face again.

Her fingers picked twigs, let them go. Picked pine needles, dropped them.

"You came here for a reason Adrianna. It is neither meaningless nor madness. It is the family. You are our child, our pride."

Adrianna felt the sting of tears. That was all she wanted, she thought: To be loved, to have loved ones proud of her. Great gran's smooth fingers stilled hers. She touched great grandmother's knee, let her fingers rest there. She missed old gran, back there in Toronto.

"Just tell me what you think it is I must do. I suppose, then, that I can kind of decipher it all... feel it through inside me and make up my mind. If you make any sense, if it makes any sense going on..." Adrianna sighed. "I just want a cup of tea and some toast and jam. And television."

"Yes. You do have a comfortable, synthetic life, don't you, you children of the future. I almost envy you, at times."

Grandmother smiled, then sat forward.

"Your father was diverted, love, thanks to trickery by that Cabot creature, after he... Well, never mind." She stopped and cleared her mind. "Anyway, girl...

The thing is, Gareth has to travel backwards by way of the family; there is no other way. He has a purpose in mind, but thinks any and all trails will somehow get him there. That way leads only to danger, to self-annihilation. If you are not in tune with what your soul desires, what you most truly speak ... How can I put this? Well, it's a language girl, your own unique family language, more intimate than the language of species, though similar..."

She cast about, searching out the right words.

"It's something like the language of what you'd call your DNA. That is your soul's truth. The scientists can't measure it. Only you can, by using it, following through the family"

"Your father is vulnerable at this time, Adrianna. But I have faith he will come through. But you, now. We must take care of you or my time here is a waste. And I do hate to throw time away."

"Sorry. I will really try now."

And so they started. Gran massaged her scalp for minutes that felt like gloriously warm eons, and Adrianna felt herself into a unique strength, felt her spine becoming durable, yet vibrating to its very atoms.

Gran spoke finally, and her voice came like bubbling spring water. Adrianna saw sunlight and grass, felt balmy air.

"Now, you will learn to make a flower. And later, who knows..."

"Why?... Adrianna began, then fell.

She felt her fingertips submerge in cool water, felt the sun lapping its infinite tongue over her back, felt herself become both, and smelled the loam vibrant in her nostrils. She tasted sap.

28

She had made a flower, a little pathetic, timid thing, with blemishes and thorns she did not want – and the spindliest of stems – in fact, it looked like an insane daisy – but it was hers. It was her, in fact. It had risen from the earth between her cupped hands. She had taken part in a miracle, had been central to it. Adrianna cried over her little aborted flower like a mother over her newborn child.

"Okay, now. That's enough blubbering, girl." Gran's hand stroked her back. "It's easier to take in stride when you're dead, I suppose: the miraculous is much less shocking to a dead 'un, like me."

"I'd much rather be alive and sobbing my guts out, thank you."

Adrianna smiled through tear misted eyes. Her tummy had settled down now to a kind of effervescent humming that was quite tolerable – no need to be dead, at all, to enjoy this.

"What's next?"

"If you're sure you're up to it, girl..."

"I could make a cathedral!"

Gran took her hands and held them in her own, wordlessly prompting her through her flesh, her imagination. Adrianna understood. To summon such terrible potency meant a total abandonment of any fear, a complete trust in peace. One had to become that peace, and at the same time remain as brightly alert as an otter hunting in a brook. She was an unblemished child making sandcastles... the soft wind, the sunlight and crying gulls singing... She sat in the earth. Her tiniest bones snuggled down and rested. Her spine joined to the ground, then dissolved.

And as though her disappeared spine had opened a door, everything alive rushed into her with a clamoring joy. She saw animals and birds, dark forests and light, knew the smell of apples and wild blackberries and, even, spider's webs. She felt the carnival of jostling human bodies and voices, gay laughter and hoarse anger, complaint, misery; the rush of love and lust, and on and on almost until she was overcome with the dizzy weight and pulse of it all.

"I think I might be ready now," she said. "Or else I'm going to burst."

Gran's outspread hands made sweeping motions over the ground.

"It is all yours. When you have complete stillness inside of you, you will know, and you can begin..."

Adrianna sensed Gran's imprint becoming weaker. It scared her. "Gran. Don't you leave me. I'm not ready for that yet."

Gran's voice reverberated around her. She was doing a Gareth, that voice thing, disembodied but warm, nowhere and everywhere at once.

"Don't think. Just let go of yourself and play it, like an instrument. It comes into you, and flows out of you. You must be the vessel, and the mistress of the music at once. Because that will be a hunger that is true to you."

Adrianna felt a rush pass through her, like the first recognition of infatuation, the heat of sex, and then something grew beside her... a lump, stretching out along the ground, which became a ridge rising higher until it almost reached her knees. Mud fell away, and the ridge became a low wall of stones and slate slabs. Gnarled bushes grew alongside. Then there was a turnstile and on either side, a little tree, with crab apples shining dusky yellow and rouge through sun-dappled foliage.

She leapt with joy, transformed.

"I'm doing it, gran! Look!" Tears swelled in her eyes. "Gran! Oh, this is so beautiful!"

She swung about, transfixed, on the little hills furling their way beyond the stone wall, the warbling of birds coming to her on a balmy breeze, the fields, no longer cold-hardened and rain swept but plush, and bright with flowers, purple and white and marmalade gold. She turned a hundred and eighty degrees to find Stonehenge gone, and nothing but shimmering sky.

More. If this is me, then MORE! She swung slowly, her arms outstretched. She circled pivoting around her planted left foot. And she let the sublime tears flow. She made the land slope downhill to meet a grouping of cottages, their roofs thickly thatched over minute upper windows, glinting blue glass, their lower storeys patchworks of plaster and earthen brick and timber.

She brought dogs into the scene, and chickens and cats, and the badger from under the hedge, and, further off, horses cropping, their ears flicking off midges and their heavy tails swishing.

She brought smoke out of the chimneys and fire into hearths, brought the sounds of quiet business from inside houses, the scent of fruits, and horse dung and earth, and fallen pine needles. What more she could manage, she didn't know. She tried not to think, only to breathe it into existence before her soul collapsed.

Her little village. Something licked wet across her hand. A dog, chestnut brown, Labrador-type thing, with big black eyes and a wet nose that wrinkled at her fingers. She beamed and the dog's tail flailed happily.

There was something missing. The knowledge tightened her stomach. It was people. And they were what she feared the most. She could manage their sounds, their scents, a facade of the business of mankind. But to actually people this world...

She feared them, and she realized that she always had. People meant pain, meant defiling what could be so simple and good. Let them in here, and then what? Would they bring their lusts, their clumsy impulses and ignorance, their darker passions? They would, surely. They would bring violence and violation. She could not let them in.

She compromised; she created them far off. An old man, harmless and kind, sharpening a sickle at a whetstone, a jug of cider at his side, and a Border collie, asleep in the dust. Inside the cottage at his back, a cheery, rotund woman. She gave her good flour, and honey, and yeast for her bread, and the woman sang quietly as her strong arms rolled and kneaded dough.

A part of her marveled at her success. A young boy, arrived, then another, wearing rustic breeches and shirts, healthy with the dirt and resplendent sun of the lanes.

"If people must live here, they must, at least, start off with a chance at happiness," she decided. The weight of guilt would not come upon them. They would not know disillusion or shame – at least for as long as she watched them.

Were they on their own afterwards? Would their lives continue after her departure?

Then it came to her. She had been only pretending to be engaged with life since she was a tot. She'd had some bitter sorrows: Her father gone, her mother never more than an effigy of motherhood, flitting wherever she would, careless. It had crippled her. She had wept, alone, falling into sleep.

Adrianna stood rigid in the lane, clasping her arms tight to her.

In a way, she had been brave and strong. But thought became her way out, her half life. Rather than feel life with heart, and flesh, and emotion, she kept running. Her mind created a wall between herself and those who wanted to share life with her. She had done it so magnificently that she could sense no self-deception.

"You're right." Her eyes scanned the sky, the road, hoping the old woman would return. "I understand that now." She meant it. If she did not understand, then why this constriction in the throat? She had learned, and she would put what she had learned into practice. She would, truly.

Adrianna stared into air. A far off wind pushed thick clouds along; the hedgerows and grass made their particular sounds. A wisp of hair blew across her right eye and tickled her nose.

Great grandmother finally spoke.

"I think you took this chance with your father just because you subconsciously knew what it was – a chance to find a key for your life."

"A key to what?"

"A key, perhaps, to your own liberation – and not a liberation from men, as you foolish women like to think. That's not a liberation but a call to the slavery of warfare..."

"You digress." Adrianna's voice was acid. She almost felt ashamed.

"Don't play with truth, girl. You will be the loser."

"So what do you suggest I do then?" She knew she feared going any further.

"Apply the power you have found. Be creative with it."

"I thought I already had..." Adrianna shrugged at the village, the dog swishing its tail with its mouth agape, the cornflowers in the hedgerows.

"This is merely a showpiece, the product of your happy mind at the moment.

And even at that, it was withering, as your thought encroached in its perverse way. As it has always done."

"So, what must I do? Since I can't get home, I might as well make myself useful." She tried to sound witheringly facetious.

"Take action. Begin a life worth living. Find your deepest meaning."

"But..." she indicated again the village. The only real question in her mind was an enormous, stubborn 'WHAT?' She wasn't getting it.

"This creating seemed like enough meaning for you before the point that you faltered. You began to override with thinking. Once I have left you, everything will collapse into that cold misery you were in before I arrived, unless you continue to make the effort. And thinking will not do it. Thinking led you down the endless road toward your misery."

Great gran's voice came thin. She was moving off.

"Meaning and action wedded make a world that is blessed."

Adrianna did not follow. For some reason she thought of Ted Bundy, saw the spattering blood, the death hunger in him, smelled the mad arithmetic of his tortured mind, smelled it in his room.

"Now there's meaning and action wedded, if that's..." She knew Great Gran saw what she herself saw.

"It was perfection to him. That was why he was driven. He gave himself ultimate meaning."

"But that's sick. It's just sick and insane."

"I know." Her voice was as plain as milk. Adrianna's exasperation returned. Bloody riddles, she thought. Just when I was feeling happy again, she has to become Shit Disturber par Excellence. And the Shit Disturber had not stopped looking at her from her hiding place.

"What?" She yelled at the old creature.

Great gran materialized a few yards ahead of her. Adrianna immediately felt calm. 'Please stay,' said her mind.

"You must do something entirely new, Adrianna," said gran. "That is what you need to tip the scales another way."

She turned and began walking, already locked into her shawl.

"Oh come on. At least a last hint!" Adrianna stared after her back.

"Do something you have not done since you were first abused."

"First abused..."

The shock hit Adrianna in a cold, frightened place. The memory of that day surged in her, bit into her tear-filled eyes. She was a gangly twelve-year-old with an overbite. The red-haired boy with the freckles was there, the seventeen-year-old brother of someone in her school. The boy she had suddenly loved with such sharp poignancy, that morning, on the playing field. Now, the end of the day, he was there again, with his gang. He had looked so cool, to her twelve-year-old eyes, with his long red hair, his baggy pants, his supercilious air. He had winked at her. At least, she thought he had.

Then they had cornered her, laughing, pushed her back against a tree. There was a long hedgerow there, to her left, and the boys were in the way so she couldn't run through the gap. And other boys to her right. They were jumpy, laughing dry, nervous laughs and watching him. He caged her with his arms and legs, leaned down and licked her eyebrow. No kiss. A hard, wet lick. It was then that an unfocused fear opened in her. And then, he was fumbling under her skirt, pushing her to the ground, murmuring words that she could not hear, but soothing noises that told her that fear was out of place. And then, just as she waited for his kiss, their laughter erupted from behind, and his denim hips pressed into her, rubbing and burning her. Him pressing her shoulders hard into the ground, sneering down and slowly releasing a long trail of spit from his lips that slithered onto her cheek, her eye.

" Y'really thought you were all that, huh? Ya dumb, spoiled bitch. Rich bitch. Ya ho."

He was standing, swaggering like the guys in the rap videos, doing his hand signals at her as she lay, stifling her sobs, hiccupping.

"God, you so ugly, bitch. Soooooo somabitch ugly, you slag."

They were all laughing, nodding slowly as if to music on headphones. Looking sideways at the red head who gave them their cues, nodding with wooden grins and hard, hard eyes.

She remembered every word. Every nuance. And worse – every smell from his body; his ears, his spit, his raunchy sweat. She heard the jingling of his pocket chain and keys, stared at the disgusting scrap of what he called 'bling' around his neck.

Adrianna wrapped her arms around her stomach, gripped tight and stared into the old woman's back. Horror choked words.

Great gran turned.

"Do something new, that you have never done... Something you needed to do," she reminded her.

"Like what?" Adrianna coughed out desperately.

Great gran turned her back again, walked away with a nonchalant wave of her hand.

"Ohhh... forgiveness ...? Just perhaps..."

She was gone. Adrianna threw herself to the ground and sat, staring angrily, grinding her teeth. Her fists pounded dirt. Never. Never would she forgive that. Her fists pounded and dust rose. And something was happening. She stopped, listened, swiveling her eyes back and forth.

The village was leaving her, its substance dwindling as she watched. Even the cornflowers near her face appeared to wilt. In a moment they would be gone altogether.

Damn! She liked it here. It was happiness, something she could not remember knowing. She would not let it go.

She breathed in slowly, remembering the procedure her ear-candling lady had told her in Toronto... breathe in through the nose, out through the mouth, 'all the good in, all the good in ... hold it, hold it, hold it ... now ... all the bad out, all the bad out...'

She would have that world back again. And she would be happy, sensual and happy and entirely kissable. And only then would she see about forgiveness.

29

There were actually days here, just like the real thing. Days had passed into pleasant nights, and, sleeping calmly and waking every morning with a still heart, Adrianna began to have faith in her world. Nobody threatened her, or even intruded on her activities, few that there were. Her villagers went about their idyllic business – a nod of the head here, a tip of the hat there – and she passed her days blithely at first. She had herself a cottage, old-brick red, with thick thatch and timbers, and a working fireplace with a huge hearth you could sit in. She had nothing pressing to do, and no form to her days but for the pattern marked by her walking feet along lanes and hills, and by the limits of her arms' reach.

But gradually, despite herself, a disquieting darkness began to gather at the edges of her world. And then, yesterday, she had found a dead rabbit by the river, ragged and mauled, as if by wild dogs. There were no cruel animals in her world – not that she knew of – and troubling thoughts stayed with her through that day. Was it possible that unbidden evils came of their own accord? Did the bad things have an intrinsic power?

She began to falter, to lose faith that she controlled anything here. She waited in dread for the rain, as a harbinger of worse things, and wondered at herself. But the rain did not come, and she wondered if it would. Was it still up to her?

She sat on the edge of the well in the village square, sipping a cup of cold water freshly dipped from the bucket. Since day one, the weather had remained steadfastly kind, a mid-spring balm that exuded promise of a summer that never quite came. No great evil, no great good. Tepid, timid, and haunted by an unnamable fear.

It was all in her desire, Great Gran had said.

And the dead rabbit?

Adrianna drained her cup. Minutes passed. Her mind would not move beyond now – blacksmith hammering, happy yelps of children at play, a creaking cart somewhere behind her, the talk of a trio of women gathered nearby, and down the lane, the faint clang of the church bells. Just a church, with bells; no religion, no priest, the church a shelter for chickens and animals and passers by in the rain. Which had not yet come.

Days were not meant to be simply passed through like this, one day blending foggily into the next. It felt stagnant. Even this beauty felt stagnant.

She looked into the depths of the well. Somewhere, far far down, the water glittered, black and frighteningly deep. Its blackness could suck you down into madness, down there with the revolting deep-water fishes. She saw light in its blackness, once, like the flash of a fish belly turning. Why had she made it so deep? And what made it move? What lived down there? The thought clutched her insides.

She made for home. Inside, she swung the heavy stable doors to and snuggled into the fireplace, pulling her chair closer to the glowing wood. She fanned the embers and felt a primeval triumph when flames leapt up. A couple of new logs placed just right, and she sat back, willing peace of mind to settle on her. But, little by little, foreboding gathered again, whispered threateningly. There was mischief here, rottenness that demanded an autonomous life.

'There's no point to this, is there?' No point.

She shifted her feet close to the fire's edge, as if to scorch her nerves into wakefulness.

And then she had it.

"Do that something you need to do. That something you have not done since you were first abused."

She pushed back the urge to comfort, stripped her mind naked, fell into her vulnerable terror and its sharp pain. The fire was extinguished, the hearth gone within a foggy blur. Her head tilted, her eyes mere inches from the chimney flue, sight truncated, muddled in focus. A cry leapt out of her and her head twisted away, her eyes unseeing across the room. She felt ill, a bone-gnawing cold devouring her toes, her ankles, her calves, moving toward her soft thighs. So soft, so close to her centre, where blue veins made a delicate filigree under her translucent flesh.

She listened as her cry ricocheted, died away.

"Something you have not done..."

Something that curdled in her and clutched her guts venomously.

She almost choked saying it. "You must forgive."

Her eyes began to clear, as though cataracts slipped away, and with jarring suddenness the cottage returned, formed about her and centered her in itself. The smell of apples and cinnamon floated through an open window.

Forgive.

How could she forgive? At the front door she stared across the road, into the field where the apple trees had begun to blossom and the gnarled oaks wrangled with the air. She seemed to have no choice. And it made her faintly sick. Cabot was coming to her, about to appear there at the distant edge of the field. She knew he had to be here. He was coming.

Because that was where she would start.

Something she had never done...

Cabot's sexed joy had turned to boredom, then to petulance, as he reminded himself that he had, once again, to make some effort. $200,000 could buy many years of smokes, cocaine, pizza, prostitutes. But he would give all of it to be back in his apartment with just one cigarette and a six-pack and maybe a porn movie. He closed his eyes, rested the pistol on his chest, its hilt cradled in his claw, and felt himself slip groggily into dream images. An elephant striding by, and the voice of someone behind... 'The square of the hypotenuse...' Spaghetti on a plate. A man on a wharf staring into a river.

His free arm covered his eyes. A short nap, a nice, drooling nothingness, and then he would get on with it. A sweet, plush descent into the deeps. He felt infantile, as if he were five again. Five and dreaming, and in that dream, the erotic release as he pissed himself. He wouldn't care if he actually pissed himself now, as he snoozed. Nothing really mattered.

His lips turned slack, his head dropped to the side, his arm slipped to the mattress, leaving the pistol on his chest.

Three times, in his dreams, he was close to kissing her, touching her body, but things warped and she turned into something else, or geography shifted. And the third time, his fingers reached the elastic on her panties, clutched on smooth flesh, but he awoke, with an erection, to the buzz that was his full bladder.

In his dream, Adrianna had wanted him. Her desire mastered his soul, gave words to the inarticulate. His hunger made half open doors that led to secret places where ten-fingered hands could tear and probe. Doors behind which the unmet Adrianna promised flesh. Rooms into which anyone could look but only he could enter. His dream rooms, made from himself – rooms soaked in clay and flesh tones, streaked with blood sunsets like tongues thrusting into mouths, into minds...

The real sunset crept around him, an insipid imitation of his dreams, and he resigned himself to shaking the remnants of her flesh and voice out of his mind. He wouldn't go anywhere tonight. Sleep, was all.

But her whisper insisted once more, clear enough that he sat up.

"Lonesome," was all she said, but her sad, yearning emptiness tugged at him as though she had clutched his jacket, as though she needed him, pulled at him with the urgency of love. Her face eclipsed the sunset, her breathing dream-close with an intensity that made him throb again. It had to be true. Maybe this was some kind of Anis-karma at work here: She was his, simply because he wanted her. He had 'earned' her somehow. But if anything, he was bad karma personified. He smirked. What a strange netherworld this was. He wouldn't be surprised to see words become pebbles, or to feel snow boiling. So why be surprised at her change of heart? He would go willingly into her embrace.

He gathered the pistol and stuffed it into his belt. The worst that could happen was a disagreement – and he could easily overpower her. Right now, she was gagging for him: He felt the pull of her need. It was a wet dream, when the particular woman of the moment turned animal and turned her magnetic face on him, gave his lust the green light.

He tipped a pinch of Anis onto his hand and snorted it in deep. He stepped into the nowhere that separated his world from hers. A second's chill and then his feet felt warmth, and he was there. The cloying air wrapped about him, molding itself to his form. His flesh, one pore after another, acclimatized itself to the new air.

This could be his dream; it could be hers. But he saw a real Adrianna. She faced him, her cheeks, at first drawn pale, now flushing and a brightness mounting in her eyes. She crossed to him, her bare arms outstretched.

It was just like that first time, the day she had phoned him from her father's study. Her body met his, her face turned down, eyes shy of meeting his. His arms gripped tight around her. He inhaled the scent of her scalp and stared at the crooked part in her hair. They were starting over. If he had been a religious man he would have thanked God. But lust was prayer enough for him.

The birds outside her cottage had silenced, and the air held its breath – and she knew he was passing through to her. She cringed as the air in the room shifted, seemed to thicken. Then it consolidated around what she knew would be him, and she had no more chance to change her mind. She had done it, and now must play the game, even if she didn't know the rules.

Revulsion pushed against her. It disoriented her mind. Then his flesh was there.

She heard her vacant voice mouthing a welcome. It seemed to please him – she dared look in his eyes and could not tell whether it pleased or enraged her that his eyes no longer smoldered murder. They glistened, those eyes, and an insane face smiled, molded by a fantasy of love she could smell on him. Puppy dog eyes, conceit, lust, insecurity, professorial pomposity.

She would not knee him in the groin. She would not. She had promised herself. She would master herself; she would master the situation. A welcoming smile pulled across her face like a scar slowly ripped from skin.

Peace was all-important. Forgiveness. His arms crushed her. She felt his pot belly where their torsos touched. And even then, she did not visibly cringe. She was doing well. She forced herself calm as his nose snuffed against her hair like a dog's, as he flexed his muscles, pressing her to him.

Her mind slammed shut. She untangled herself from his smile and smell and reaching arms and made it as far as the hearth before he caught up with her. Before he could press in on her again, she hefted the kettle.

"Tea? Or coffee? I have managed to make stuff that tastes pretty close to them."

"Oh, whatever. Hey. Lemme help you."

Forced casual – Cabot's usual foreplay style. Adrianna strode out the door and to the pump where she began cranking expertly, shutting him out. She could feel a tincture of him within herself. It was his awkwardness. She knew it too well. It had been her own when she was a teen. The same empty, desperate mannerisms, and meaningless language. When had it first happened to him? Why? She tucked the observation away. The kettle filled, overflowed, a puddle creeping across dusty earth to her bare toes. Her arm ceased plunging.

There he was, leaning in the doorway, sparkling eyes and twitching smile. He registered her eyes on him and his body started, an anxious animal, verging on flight. His hand, his bloody, clumsy bear paw reached out for the kettle, banged against it as she pushed past.

She just couldn't help herself.

"Will you just quit it!" Her entire body flushed with sudden anger. She banged the kettle on the hob and sat, fighting her reflexes. "Don't crowd me like this."

She reached her fingers to her face, deliberately rearranging stray ringlets that clung to her forehead. Composure.

He was doing his best to saunter about. She could not anger him. Anything but that. And she must not anger herself. Self mastery was the key.

———

He had enjoyed staring at her until something in him had quailed. The thought was terrible: She could possibly want him. She might be there, always. That was an idea that always made him feel anemic and rotten inside. Torn apart by the thousand and one demands of family, of a partner, of custom and tradition and obligations and the daily grind of loving with and living with. It spilled into him like a poison, left him singled out, smothered with fear.

But by then she had reached him, and he was his old self again. His nostrils flared, sucking in the odor of her sex, feeding on the pheromonal jungle. Now this made sense. His hand brushed air within centimeters of her thigh. "Let me..." But it stubbed against the kettle, could not take it from her, and she was out of his space. This would be a pretty dance. She was obviously confused. Conflicted. Bewitched, bothered and bewildered.

He sauntered in behind her. Give her room. Give her time. Whatever evolved, he could control her. He had to. Nothing else – and certainly not love – would do. He surveyed the place, noting the woman things, the Adrianna things that betrayed her private self. Flowers and plants. Odd bits of colored stuff on one windowsill – pottery, or jewelry. There was a rustic easel angled by a back door, and on it, a half-finished painting, sky, womb, flecks of scarlet appearing here and there like driven rain. The usual girly bullshit.

Except there were no brushes, no jars of color, water, mineral spirits. And, as he turned his gaze away he could swear the images swirled, meta-morphosed... not openly but slyly... a change of shade here and there like grass under a breeze.

How had she come by this shelter, these belongings? Had she bartered, tricked the locals? How had she parlayed her way into this funny little king-dom? And – it struck him as more important – why had she come here, stayed here?

"Anything to eat? I always seem to be staaaarving." He stared at her through ravenous eyes, letting his voice descend to a low growl. She didn't pick up on the innuendo, just stared at the kettle like an old woman.

A log spat sparks at her foot. He picked a piece of gravel from the sole of his boot and tossed it at her. She looked up. He grinned.

"Coffee?" he said. And, "So, where are we? Where is this?"

"My home. I made it all myself."

She said it quietly. Probably meant it to sound humble and reverent. He heard smug. Heard her shutting him out from her secrets again.

"What d'you mean? You built it, cut the wood, fit the windows...?" Not likely. She was full of surprises... but she was no architect, no builder.

"Built it all. Here, look."

She raised her hand, palm upward and a little bud appeared, rose pink, on her milk skin. She brought it to him. He smelled it. It wasn't a rose, though it resembled one – no cloying stink.

His eyes followed her hips, fastened on her buttocks as she moved to the fireplace and poured from the kettle into a metal pot. He smelled something like coffee.

"Just made some bread," she said. "Come to the table and eat."

The table spread before him, meat, cheese, more bread, vegetables resembling asparagus, and, from a lidded clay pot, the unmistakable smell of potatoes. His nose detected something very similar to gravy. Adrianna poured two glasses of deep red wine.

This was almost as good as sex.

30

It had been two days now, and Adrianna could not rid herself of despondency. It wasn't working, this strangulated, spastic thing she was trying to do with Cabot. She didn't understand it, and it all felt wrong. The days were tipping into an absurd meaninglessness that she could neither control nor get rid of. Only two days, but they seemed like months. She was fervent and pent up. Always of two minds, she could not settle on a plan, or envision its outcome. She wondered if Cabot had begun to influence things, if his perverse spirit had begun to pollute her world and mind.

She didn't quite know why she had called Cabot to her. Forgiveness and hatred warred in her. Her manufactured sympathy rested on a seething foundation, endangered every second. Worse, most of it was his doing. How could she forgive him when her only real feeling was to despise and fear him?

Right now, he slept in the bedroom, so comfortable in his skin, cocooned against the remnants of morning chill that crept into the cottage. His snores burbled across the silent room to her seat by the fire.

He had drunk copious amounts of alcohol the night before. That should have been no surprise. She had summoned a bottle just to keep him out of her way and he staggered through Paradise, not shutting the bottle's mouth or his own for all of the two days.

She had been foolish in her naive eagerness to do the Christian thing. She despised him for his bloodshot eyes in the mornings, for his vacant gaze through the eternal hangover. She despised him for his afternoon regeneration and his growing appetite. It was then that he *would* insist, *would* be where she was, *would* let out his noises, his jokes and comments that sounded to her like the groveling of an animal. He would be wherever she was, unless he was back at the bottle, abandoning her to her gardening or another "bout of impotent intercourse," as he called her time spent with the villagers.

She peered at him from the hearth. She could kill him so easily while he snored. She crossed the room on tiptoe. She could not see his eyes, but his flaccid body showed how deeply he slept. She could kill him. In her hand, the potato peeler was a gigantic broadsword. He was sure to see it, and to hear her pounding heart, to smell her fear. But she might reach him and drive it into his throat before he had a chance.

She could.

She drew up beside the bed, and her momentary resolve abandoned her, hunted to ground by conscience. Her arm twitched, from stress, from forced restraint... She almost lost the potato peeler, but juggled it until she finally conjured it into her dress pocket. She stood over him, pressing her anger down deep into her guts.

The fireplace popped loudly, a glowing ember flying against the guard. Cabot grunted.

Reaching the plant stand at the doorway, she busied herself pruning a fern.

His croak came feebly out of the gloom. He coughed phlegmatically and tried again.

"Hey gorgeous. Tomorrow already?"

The bed's creak warned her and she was across the room before he might touch her, before she smelled his rotten breath. She would go mad; she knew it. How long could this go on? How could she expel this revulsion?

"I'm going to the river." She slung a shawl around her shoulders, snatched an apple from the table, and slipped out the door, calling back "You know where the food is, if you're hungry." Then she added, as though etiquette had a place, "You're welcome to join me later if you like."

She hoped to God it would be much later, if at all. She needed to meditate for more than a snatched minute. Halting by a lilac bush, she held a bloom to her nostrils. Its heady, heavy scent grounded her, and she set off toward the river.

Emma or Lucy would be good company. Emma, steady of gait and slow to anger, but a whirlwind if aroused. A good old friend, like Lucy, to march at her heels. She wondered if she needed a man like that, if she needed one at all. Not at her heels, but steady, kind, in rhythm with her, and protective. She wondered that she had not thought of summoning such a man. But that really meant making one, since she didn't know of any to summon. Making an old man with a dog was one thing: she had made one who remained a polite stranger to her. But to conjure up a loving partner... man or woman; much more complicated.

Better to have either cat here.

She pushed her mind back into the mists, reaching for something comfortingly idyllic in her childhood. Before the street gangs, prostitution and drug wars had taken the streets and alleys from children; before paranoia had conquered the once lovely ethnic communities, before decay had gained an immutable grip. Her Toronto was a purgatorial mire of crime, bubbling up from hellish slums. A degenerate swell of trashed houses and hard, sterile high-rise concrete.

Could she even go back to Toronto, she wondered? She couldn't remain here forever. But the city, any city of any size, how could she manage it any more? But how could she afford anything else? It was only the stinking rich who lived out in what was left of the country. And she had no car. Buses and trains as scarce on the landscape as shuttles to Mars. Everything was shut down, and promised to be for all her life. Nothing worked any more, except computers and holographs, sometimes, and teams of construction workers tearing up roads, sewers, electric lines, optic cables, still trying to get at the rot.

She was too poor to move, and too vulnerable to stay there. She just couldn't envision it.

She reached the river and sat on a root that curled to the bank and plunged into the water. Sun glittered on the water's face, and the sweet peeping of chicks came from somewhere in the reeds. She wondered if she had made the ducks. She couldn't remember any more. Her part in things was becoming foggier as the village world gained dimension.

After only two days or so of Life, she had become so integrated that she no longer stood out; she was just another villager. That was what she had wanted, she reminded herself. To not be special, to not stand out like a target. But something troubled her.

She stripped off her shoes and socks and dabbled her feet in the cold water. The sun would beat on this water through a long day, but the river would remain as cold as it was now. What troubled her? She tried to think it through, but could not start. A thin loneliness gathered in her. She found herself wishing that God lived close by – that He, She or It actually interceded. But would it intercede in this place, which probably existed in some warped backwater of the cosmos, alongside the suicides and terminally loony dead? Maybe this creation of hers was nothing but a perverse eruption of girlish vanity anyway, so who should care?

Her mind could not help but turn to Cabot, and the sense that pervaded around him. He was venomous; she knew that wasn't just her over-sensitive imagination. He wished her harm, perhaps wished everyone harm. Could she dissolve this venom by simply being extra nice to him, by flirting with him as though he mattered in her life? She had hoped to turn her own vitriol into something good, and by doing that, she had reasoned, she would manage to return him to the almost nice person he had been when she first knew him. As if the rape had been her fault.

Her hands clutched at the river bank and her fingers clawed into the earth. Her eyes fixed sightlessly on the opposite bank as she waited for her rigid body to release. Kindness, in this, was unnatural.

But if not kindness and forgiveness, then what? An eternal cycle of mutual hatred, which would surely end badly? Her heavy sigh reverberated across the water and into the trees. Nothing was simple, and nothing was fair, even in this dream world she had created for herself. She felt like the brunt of a cosmic joke. What a horrible thing it was, to try to do the 'Christian thing,' against one's own instincts!

Twigs and gravel crunched behind her and he spoke.

"Pretty nice, ain't it, this being dead business?"

She flinched as he sat down nearby, and struggled to not edge away from him. To signal dislike would only drive him all the more quickly to the alcohol, and to another nervous, broodingly dark day for her. She tried to put a bantering edge in her voice.

"We're not dead, you ass."

"I know. But feels like it, don't it? Far away from planet earth, kinda."

Why was he talking like an illiterate? Was that the 'relaxed' Cabot?

"You gonna summon your cat, or run back to Toronto and leave poor lil' Cabot here on his lonesome?"

Adrianna eyed him uneasily. Cabot pushed his face close to hers. Her skin crawled. She shut her mind down, thought of nothing but the river, the sounds and smells. She would turn up the volume on her intuition, and watch her step, and his, from now on.

Cabot's dead eyes roved over her face for a second, then seemed to dismiss her. Her ears caught his grumbled, "patronizing cow," but nothing more.

Her mind returned to the river, the sun's mild heat in the air, giving scant comfort. Then a brainwave hit her. Could it be this way because she had not thought of summer and its pervading heat? This strange life was a faulty holograph with its programming scrambled. She was the programmer.

Immediately, the notion of summer was alive in her. She felt, then heard, spring trickling, snow in thaw far away in mountains, and its fresh water filtering through earth, gathering and pushing down channels Nature had scored in the landscape. Her Nature. She felt summer burgeoning. She felt warmer, could feel the deep ache leaving her toes and calves. The water no longer held a chill. Life around her began to hum: Swarms of insects rehearsing far off downstream; then the flitting, stopping, flitting of a water boatman on an eddy near the bank. She studied its flying buttress legs, its hovercraft motion. The river's rippling tongues massaged her calves, and she laughed out loud.

Cabot looked up, half angry, half eager and his eyes latched onto her as she tiptoed into deeper water. She felt his hungry stare, and somehow, she just didn't care. She laughed and kicked a silver arced water plume from her foot.

"Come on in!" she cried. "It's summer. I've made it summer!"

He looked at her, stunned-bovine, and his stupor made her more giddy still. She suddenly felt seductive, alive and beyond his reach. Even her ungainly frog march as she struggled to stay upright against the water's weight, even that was seductive. She felt lovely again. She wanted to seduce. Her flesh, her limbs, her sexuality were no longer hurting. Everything in her rushed and gathered in a brilliant smile that seemed to have conquered her.

She flashed that smile at Cabot, and was secretly thrilled to see the change in him – a cadaver given a blood transfusion. She didn't care about his venom, or his angry sexuality; she knew she was master of the situation.

It could all turn horrid at any moment. But for now, the river curling around its banks, pushing onward unstoppably, the eager, mad drone of bees and dragonflies, the goofy ducklings charging after mother over ripples that buoyed them up like boats in a tide, everything was madly happy, urgently moving onward.

She tucked her skirt into her underwear, as she had seen the peasant girls push their skirts into belts of twine, and thrilled quickly when the water splashed and left droplets above her knees. She did not feel vulnerable, did not feel afraid of Cabot, who was now staggering a couple of yards from her, an idiotic grin twitching on his face. She was madly seductive, she knew. She had shocked him, aroused him out of his angry sulk, and she could swear she felt the grayness in him begin to fall away. They could not go back, but, just maybe, this renewal would prove to be something other than illusion, would unlock the straitjacket that was his tortured desire for her. And then, maybe, he would be released, by degrees, from the misery that he had built in his head, that had been building since the first day they met. They could both be liberated from the tainted history they shared. Couldn't they?

She pushed herself out into deeper water and dove under, springing from her toes that curled in the mud in the deep green. She surfaced yards from him as he threw himself at the river and surfaced closer to her, panting with that quivering grin on his face.

She almost pitied him. Pitied her rapist.

She curled, dived and plunged a hand deep into the river bed's loam, clutched and felt the reeds' waterlogged fingers wrap around her own. She ripped a handful of earth up into the bright air, laughed deep and flung it at Cabot. He blinked and pulled mud off his face, then bent and struggled forward, his hands scooping water at her. She danced out of his way.

She felt deliciously evil. Her forgiveness, if that was what it was, would be a seduction that would make him mad. She would make him so painfully hard that he would choke and cry out for her. It was wonderful. Her stomach told her so, plunging wickedly.

This was a new kind of tension that churned in her, something unknown. She was running, she was hunted... but it was really she who was hunting.

She hopped backwards, bouncing off one foot, then the other, enjoying the strength of her thighs and calves. All the time, she did not let her eyes stray from his body, his whitening face. The sex, the eagerness in him made her chest as tight as she knew his was. It was his sickness, his rodent-like spirit enervated by a sick desire, that sent his body flailing and raging after her. A skinny, flaccid man, no musculature, and his skin an unhealthy livor; a man who spent his life in dusty, sterile environments, his brain simmering.

She reached the opposite bank and, hanging from the turf, watched his erection as he began to wade out of the water. She watched his tight face, pinched with his peculiar, furtive desire. Always, it became anger, a kind of harried panic – her invention of summer had changed nothing for him in that way. He would always do violence to her, invited or uninvited.

She would seduce him, drag him onward, alert for that moment. Then she would stop him. Because that was what his sex would always be; violence to her. She would stop him because she was master of this world. No matter what he had learned, she was in control of this world. He was her guest. She would maintain control. And he would beg, and when she gave herself to him, this last time, he would be a slave, crushed.

She let him kiss and grope her, and she neither flinched nor shoved him away. Her teeth were chattering. Her soaked clothes clung to her. The air around her was almost as warm as Cabot's breath. But her entire body clenched through the eternal seconds of his lips, his tongue and hands pressing, exploring, dominating her.

It must not cripple her. It must not.

She withstood him nibbling her neck, felt his groin pushing against her stomach.

"Not here. Not outside."

She wanted him in private. She wanted him completely naked and as vulnerable as she would be. She would make him beg, in her own home, where everything was hers. She would make him beg before there was any kind of forgiveness.

Collapsing and slipping on the dirt, he saw her flying to the door, clinging to the door frame, her body translucent blue from her dress, with her rosy heart-shaped face sobbing out laughter, and he knew he would have her. Hysterical or not, he would have her good and proper this time. He would bang her until she couldn't breathe anymore, until she had no dignity left. He would make her cry and beg.

Her ass looked incredible. The wet dress clung like an opaque skin. He would have that off her easily enough. He threw himself after her, chuckling, hardly believing his good fortune. She was a bit crazy. If he didn't know better, if he cared, he would have been alarmed at the sound of her, at the way she moved, used her limbs. Distracted, that's what she was, with an eerie off-kilter timbre to her voice. His body prickled with anticipation as he leapt over the step.

She had slipped into the bedroom like a pale blue moth, soundless, no more laughter, and when he caught up with her, she was seated on the edge of the bed, gasping air while she fought to untangle her skirts from around her legs. His fingers gripped the top of the door frame and he leaned into the room, his groin thrust forward. He swayed and caught his breath. God! She was gorgeous! Soaking wet, black hair clinging to her flesh like trickling tar, hiccups escaping her panting bosom. Nice word, that, bosom – old fashioned and virgin-like. Virgin Adrianna, wet skin shining like marble. His hungry eyes ate her, roaming from her cleavage, her breasts pushing out of the half-unbuttoned bodice, a snatch of her nipple, to her thigh shining out from the dampness, then the folds of the dress below where the material clung to her stomach.

His eyes fed on her as she rose, came toward him, her slender fingers playing with her buttons. His eyes dared meet hers and match their dreamy gaze with his own. His arms unclamped from the doorway and made to grab her, pull her to him. He felt the kiss already, his tongue thrusting. But she slipped past him, coy. Horny little bitch. He laughed, swiveled his head to follow her legs, that gorgeous ass. 'Patient, patient, Cabot,' he corrected himself. 'Bit by bit, at first, let her do what she does, let her seduce, suck you in.' The thought of sucking turned him to melted wax. He threw himself on the bed. She was probably on the rag; had to pull the plug out and chuck it in the garbage before she took on his raging hard on. His grin almost cut his face in half. This was awesome beyond awesome! After what had happened, this was better than anything he could dream up. In the daylight, in her bed. No law, no cops, no authorities. Just him and her. Everything of hers was to be his. The tenderest parts of her, in broad daylight. Man! He ground his teeth from the sheer joy of it and, bouncing upright, yanked his waterlogged shirt out of his pants.

She jumped into the room, flapping her opened dress, and hopped onto the bed where she bounced on her knees, throwing him sideways on the mattress. He saw her fall toward the pillows and slip something under them. A condom? A sex toy. He imagined her going nuts in orgasm.

"No. Don't look!" She fell forward, her chest smothering his arm, one arm tangling around his neck, the other grappling against his reaching fore-arm. She twisted her head and kissed him, her lips misshapen, rubbery, against his unshaven face. "It's a secret, something for later." Her eyes glittered. Horny again. Probably something to shove up her snatch. Or her butt. Women liked that sort of thing. He snorted and fell on his back, pushed his body through a liberating stretch.

"Come on then, my little bitch" he growled, and his hands went to his belt buckle.

Kneeling by his leg, she pushed his hands away. Her head bowed, turned to him with those sly, coy eyes, and a demented smile twitched on her lips as her hands explored the buckle, worked it open. One hand unbuttoned him, searched out and pulled down the zipper, the other lingered on his erection. His eyes followed her every motion, reveling in her trance-like movements. She was focused only on his prick, hypnotized with it. Slow, slow movement of her body, rearranging herself, then her face moving close. Dead silence. Not a sound out of her. Her breath came warm against his shaft and he fell back, groaned, thrust his hips upward to her face.

She had stopped. She was kneeling upright, staring at his dick and waving it, laughing her deep, liquid chuckle.

He cleared his throat, wondered if spitting on the floor would turn her off. He wiped his sleeve across his lips instead. "Pants," he said, and finished unbuttoning his shirt as her hands yanked at his pant legs. He was completely naked. He wanted her luscious lips on him, wanted the heat of her throat enveloping him. Then, he would force her on her back so that her head hung off the mattress, and he would make her open up so he could force it all down her.

He had to have her naked. His hand flipped her damp skirts over her waist and thrust under the elastic in her panties. He groaned, grasping her buttock. He squeezed mightily, making her squeak with pain.

"Come on come on." Despite himself, his voice was breathy with need. "Strip. Take those off. I gotta see you naked."

She hesitated, her hands freezing at the remaining button on the bodice. She lifted her eyes to meet his. That wacko smile again. She was an absolute slut, hiding inside that dignity of hers.

He pushed himself upright, ripped the last button off and went for her breasts. But she pushed him back, steadily but gently, teasing him with her murmuring lips, her half-lidded eyes. He stared, his breathing clipped, exhaling between clenched teeth. He heard himself moan as her breasts fell free of the unhooked bra, watched his hands pull the bodice down to her waist. Removing his hands gently, she wiggled out of the dress, twisted and pulled it past her calves and, still kneeling beside him, kicked it to the floor and leaned forward.

Her heavy breasts swung against his lips as she leaned over him. His hand went to her crotch and met her underwear. He could not stand it any longer. His fingers gripped and pulled. But she remained crouched, her body taut and her knees spread wider so that her thighs stopped him pulling further. She was whispering to him, her elbows beside his ears, her breasts pressing, her lips ready to kiss, to hold him there.

He stared at her eyes.

"Jesus, my dick's gonna explode if you don't..."

"Well then?"

"What?"

"I just said what you must do." Her voice sang, slutty and coy.

He hadn't heard it. "Huh?"

"Beg me."

He snorted happily. "You slut Adrianna. Who woulda thunk it?"

"So?"

He shifted his groin, clasped his erection, ready to thrust into her. Just a few inches, that's all her ass needed to move.

"Okay. I'm beggin'."

"Doesn't sound like it." She licked his neck and he felt her saliva dribbling.

"I beg you. I beg you." Bitch. She was supposed to do the begging.

"Beg for my forgiveness. Come on."

"Forgiveness?" He didn't get it. "Forgiveness for..." Then he understood and his stomach quailed momentarily. 'Not having that,' he thought, and rubbed his prick again. Hard. Strong. No fear, not with this bitch. He was almost twice her size. Or felt like it. He grinned woodenly.

"Okay. Adrianna, I beg your forgiveness..." He was all chivalry. He was her suitor. "I beg your forgiveness for what I did."

"For raping me. For forcing yourself into me." He heard her voice scrape shut. She wasn't going to cry was she? Literally, "up her's." He'd be done with her before she had time to cry.

"Now beg me to let you into me."

That sick smile again. Toying with him. He would damn well have her. Not on her friggin' terms.

"Okay! I beg ya, alright?"

He was going to yell at her, the final scream before he wrestled her onto her back. He saw it in a flash. His bellow. Throwing her over, slamming her head into the pillows, ripping off those panties and ramming her legs back to her chest. And he would be so deep in her she gagged.

He heard a jagged scream.

This was not the way he had seen it. There was a horrible heat between his legs, and something dripping. And his scream was winding upward, snaking into the air. His mind had gone cold, shut down hard. And his wail sounded like a tiny animal, something gutted, shaking itself to pieces in fear. Then he knew it was himself, shaking, writhing on the mattress, and the keening screech was raking out of his throat.

Blood spurted over his clinging hands, far down there, between his legs. And she stood there, glowing, smiling down at him, her translucent body erect and proud. Blood trickled down her breasts, and in her hands, two things; the knife that she had whipped out from the pillow, grazing his ear, and a mess of flesh. Even under the slime of blood, he could see. It was a testicle, and a long flap of skin and vein. A chunk of his prick. The mad bitch had sliced off his balls and...

Black slammed shut around him. The screech abruptly died. Agony tore deep into him, slammed into his brain, and shut him down. His brain wrapped around her last words as he wished himself dead.

"Now, I forgive you," she said.

31

The blood from her hands joined the river, diluting like smoke. Everything was still. The birds did not sing, with the bees and dragonflies and gnats no longer there to eat. Everything was leaving, as if swallowed up in huge, soundless bites, the landscape by degrees crumbling into the void.

Adrianna ran and ran, endless running. Her heart tore at her chest. Her legs did not stop until her head swam and the urge to vomit conquered her. She found herself at the very edge of her land, staring into a fog beyond which her feet would not go. No grass underfoot in that place, maybe not even oxygen. She had willed the lovely home into place for just a few days. Its disintegration was almost complete. Soon, she would be back in the void. If she did not find somewhere to land, she might be lost forever. Caught in her misery and shame, a poltergeist in purgatory.

The land behind her crumbled away, fell into the void like molten lava. In a minute, maybe less, she would be balanced on a mere rope of turf that stretched between infinite grayness on both sides. Then she would be lost.

Where to go? And where was Cabot? She cast a furtive glance over her shoulder, expecting to hear his insane rage, the thumping of his feet. But there was not even an echo of his cry. The land swayed under her, still given form by her remaining will, but yawning towards its own annihilation.

She should have been more controlled. She could have taken the high road. She should never have summoned him. She might have forgiven and forgotten, quietly, in solitude.

No. She couldn't have. To forgive him would mean a life imprisoned, a self-loathing, life like the past, only worse. She had to try. That was all. She had to continue, to construct meaning. Surely there was, out there, a scrap of inner peace.

Her mind focused, closed around the image, and she was there once more. Stonehenge. Spring. A light breeze. She looked at her bare feet. Mud and blood mingled on them, a tarnished bronze wash.

———·———

He had hoped that the reality was virtual, that he was safe. He had wished fervently that Toronto would see him whole, unscathed. But now, a sob leapt out of his throat. He was propped in a stiff wooden chair, and blood had pooled and soaked into his jeans. He knew it must be hopeless. Then the pain caught up with him and slammed him into unconsciousness.

It might have been eternity: this might just be a new life. Someone's hand shook his shoulder, smacked him repeatedly on the cheek. Just like the movies. He was a prisoner of war, that was it, and he was being interrogated. He was whole and the distant pain was only a bullet wound. His captors would remove it. Rules of war and everything. Geneva Convention. Wake up Cabot. You're whole again; only dreaming of torture.

His opened eyes focused on the image of Buckleigh, who shoved a snifter of brandy into his stunned hand.

"Drink it." Buckleigh's voice was gruff. Cabot could hear the dismissive coldness in the two words.

"I was in bed. What am I doing in this room? I was lying in bed when I... left."

The castration rushed back to him. He collapsed in tears, his whine sounding eerily rodent-like in the bare room.

"Got you good, somebody did." Buckleigh's cheery voice compounded the absurdity that tilted Cabot's confused brain. He rocked, listening to the rodent whine as if somewhere inside it, he might find comfort. He had cried like this as a boy. And Buckleigh had no pity for him, wasted not a second of time on sympathy.

"My... dick. She cut it..." Cabot fumbled pitifully to find the zipper amid the caked blood. He stared pleadingly at Buckleigh. "Can you get a doctor?"

The irony of it seemed to amuse Buckleigh. He poked Cabot's thigh roughly.

"No problem there any more. We already looked at it. Something about this time-travel..."

Cabot squirmed at the thought of Buckleigh looking at his prick. But had he heard correctly?

"You mean, it's okay? It's not... damaged? What about the blood?" His hands hovered at his crotch.

"Not okay. Not the word I'd use anyway. But as I've said, this virtual traveling does strange things. Seems it's cauterized your pecker, my friend. What's left of it."

"What's left?" Cabot felt like dying again.

"That's what I said." Buckleigh took the snifter from him, refilled it. "Yer John Thomas is pretty well finished, me lad, out of commission, certainly, as far as sex goes. You might be able to piss out of it, I don't know. But, look on the bright side; you're not going to bleed to death. And you've still got one of yer ballocks."

Renewed rage galvanized Cabot. He forced himself upright and swayed unsteadily in blood-stiffened pants. "Gimme a gun, a knife or something. I'm going back. That bitch has to be..."

"You want revenge. Of course you do." Buckleigh's voice was conciliatory, belying a face clouded with contempt. He opened the door on his burly orderlies. Cabot then saw what Buckleigh's girth had been covering; Gareth lay on the cot, as comatose as the day he and Adrianna had first studied him. Cabot looked from Gareth's body to Buckleigh, to his two attendants.

"Sorry, Cabbie, old chum." Buckleigh beamed.

The attendants tore at Cabot's clothes, thrusting hands into his pockets and pants.

"You really have cocked this all up, from beginning to end. I can't for the life of me think why I was deluded enough to give you this opportunity in the first place. Complete cock up. Days and days gone and you've achieved nothing but getting your own prick sculpted."

The attendants snorted. Cabot submitted as they turned him over and pinned him down, his throat pressed into the chair back.

"Got it." They jammed him in a seated position. He didn't resist. The last of his energy was spent. Buckleigh slipped the Anis in his jacket pocket. Maybe it was over, Cabot thought hazily. Maybe that was the way he should play it. He slumped lower in the chair, allowed his head to droop and his burning eyes to close. Blessed sleep. It would be so good.

"Okay. You're in charge," he muttered. "And I still got some money coming to me. Coupla hundred thousand, right?"

And Adrianna would have to come back some time. She couldn't stay out there indefinitely. And when she did, he would be mended. And armed. He promised himself.

Buckleigh barked a dry laugh of disgust.

"You'll be lucky to get gas money home kid! Two-hundred effing thousand! Don't make me laugh."

Cabot stared, dumbfounded, the blood hissing in his head. His upper lip twitched. All that work, and no payment, the reward he had anticipated so often?

"You didn't finish the effing job, you... you stupid turd!" Buckleigh's reddening face strained out of his tight collar. "Now I have to go finish it! You eff up and I have to get trained and do the job myself. You have no effing idea how much credibility you cost me! Now I have to salvage it. For all I know, it could kill me!"

Buckleigh's fat hand flashed out, gripped Cabot's hair and yanked viciously at it, then slammed him back in the chair. He stormed out of the room.

"Keep him right here!" he snapped at the orderlies. "I've got plans for his pathetic ass!"

32

Her guilt plagued her until she vomited. She threw herself into a run, pushing her chest against the still air, around the stones in the opposite way she had gone before, in futile hope that she could undo the past few days. She ran until her eyes blurred and the blackness framing her sight closed down the light, and she finally collapsed.

When her mind spoke, reminding her that she lived, her gut heaved and she retched up something almost alive. A multihued, plastic thing, tarry black with slashes of blood-red over bruised and sickly flesh.

She knew it for what it was: the aborted coagulation of her guilt and horror. It was Cabot, and psychotic rage, and torn flesh. It was the hank of his penis she had let drop from her slimed hand.

It was the pain of having no-one to turn to.

Did the stones know, she wondered? Did they forgive? She was aware of them standing around her. Behemoths, formidable progenitors of time itself, or guardians of that something – more horrible and more beautiful than she could comprehend – which conceived the universe, the womb, the sex of man and woman.

She was sitting on the earth. And the earth was a womb. It had accepted her sickness, and she supposed that was enough of a cure. Bitter medicine, but one of her own making. The best antidote to poison was the poison itself.

She tasted bile.

"I'll just rest here for a while," she said aloud for the benefit of the stones. "Then, I must drag dad home. Enough is enough."

The wind huffed. The stones made no response. They had no stake in anything she did.

"How the hell do I find him then?" she barked at the nearest trilithon. "You tell me, standing there so bloody smug."

She stared skyward, her cheeks and eyes prickled by the spitting rain, and spun slowly with her mouth open. The sky was a smoky gray spiral that went on forever, tunneling upwards through sad gloom.

The drizzle clung to her hair. The cold wet was keeping her half awake. She remembered her father: carrying her on his shoulders in the Fall, when she would stretch tiny fingers around big fat apples and fight them loose from the tree. Her dad lifting her high enough to knock horse chestnuts off with a stick. He had taught her how to play his childhood game of 'conkers,' tapping a hole through the rich glow of the chestnut's skin and threading a shoelace through. It always pained her to see the chestnut's wounded flesh at the end of the game, but she was vehemently proud of her aim, satisfied when her conker smashed his 'prize chestnut.' They were all his prize chestnuts; he always said that. It made her even more earnest, and she would jump on the spot, her gangly legs flying this way and that. And he would always laugh delightedly, that warm, burbling laugh of his.

She always remembered him best that way, towering above her, a blur of a man, turned to shadow with the sun somewhere behind him. As if he was made by the sun, born from it and set down there on the earth in front of her to remind her how proud, how majestically happy a human should be.

And where was he now, this naïve, old youngster? She knew, suddenly, that he would return! If not now, then soon. The stones had surrounded his image, cupped it in their field of power and presented it to her. A holograph, that was all, but her father, healthy and happy, striding out of the gray toward her.

She laughed, exultant, and spread her arms, then began spinning in the same direction she had walked, that seeming age before. Lightness swarmed her head, reaching from the roots of her hair to an empty space between her shoulder blades. Something transcendent and meaningful was always signaled to her like this, a familiar dizziness that seemed to set her beside herself, silently observing. Familiar because she had known it before now, before Stonehenge or her dad's insane errand. It used to happen in her violin recitals, when she practiced, and when she danced. An airy disconnection from the earth, as if some cosmic umbilicus was feeding her the milk of beautiful lunacy.

She stopped.

He had said it was the key, Stonehenge. This stone hieroglyph spinning its solitary mile through space. Wherever he was, he would read it, and come.

———•———

A long, featureless time had passed, and Gareth had gathered his wits. He recalled staring at shadows near a camp fire, and then the winter aching cold where Rasputin signaled disinterested heaven. It was as if St. Petersburg had its own hungers. Perhaps a time, a space, became attached to its rats, its trees, its people and buildings, in just the same way that humans attached themselves to their lives, by sentiment, and need, and desire. And fear of what was beyond.

His own fear had coalesced into a barrier.

Summoned by his own daughter, invited to join her, he had become liquid from fear. He was afraid. What if he made another mistake? Because he could not see the mistakes for what they were. Could not find his way in the darkness. Did not know anymore.

What did he know? He knew that he had touched a piece of rag in his pocket and had flown into Rasputin's life like a windblown crow. They had to be connected; and he smelled filthy Cabot, maybe Buckleigh, behind that.

And he, Gareth Pugh, was no better; hiding from his own failure when to remain hiding meant obliteration. An obliteration that this rat would ultimately feel, when, some time, it could no longer scuttle through these black sewers.

Then suddenly he knew that there was nothing to fear. He remembered his garden back in Toronto, the dawn, the start of all this. He had seen death, distant and sweet, then; something secretly cherished. It was a promise, his particular death. He knew he could face that, and its sweet time was not now.

His trembling spirit shut its inner eye for a moment's blankness. It found the key. He floated and became the spirit of floating, a particle, a wave. His internal eye saw Tintern Abbey, its obdurate remains, with sunlight glistening in its pitted face like molten gold.

Gareth entered laughing, wafer thin, a letter stuffed through a letterbox. A peal of minute bells and a glimmering light following him became the voice of a nearby brook. A door in the air slipped closed against its frame like a slab of ice caressing its brother, then became a mischievous puff of wind that sent Adrianna's hairs prickling along her bare arms.

"You won't believe what has happened since we parted."

She pushed him to arms length and they kneeled, staring through tears.

She swayed onto one elbow and breathed into tall grass that flowed away from the stones. It seemed to go on and on, bending at the horizon's curve.

The two of them together made a larger, peaceful world.

"You look older," she said at last.

"I am," he said. "And you would be too." And he began describing his encounter with Rasputin, and finally withdrew the scrap of Rasputin's coat and tossed it over his shoulder. "All done," he said. "All used up now. Someone got their money's worth."

"Cabot?"

"Yes. Him and Buckleigh, I'm guessing."

Adrianna looked at him maternally. She finally felt unwaveringly bonded with him. He was a vessel of strange perfumes, an alchemy of oddness that had somehow evolved to the very verge of deep artistry, to the verge of a brilliant language that she realized she so needed; that even the world, perhaps, would embrace.

She told him of her meeting with his grandmother and how she was taught to manifest living things. She described her village, the robins, cardinals, thatched houses, kindly farmers and sun-drenched sheepdogs. Gareth sat, his huge blue eyes registering everything she said with childlike acceptance. He simply accepted it, as if she had just given him a plate of baked beans. Then, dark memories of Cabot threatened to rebel against her resolve to silence and her mind stopped, locking Cabot out. She could talk or think no more.

As if on cue, their eyes wandered in the same direction, to the edge of the stone circle, and there she was, sitting silent, her fingers stroking a growth of sedge. Gareth lowered himself beside her and squeezed her arm reassuringly while Adrianna stood, her heart still pounding from their reunion, smiling uncertainly. She was the first to speak.

"Great gran?"

"I'm awake love. Hello Gareth." Her head turned upward. "You barely made it that time, my boy."

She motioned them to sit, then heaved a sigh. She wasted no time.

"You'd do a lot better, Gareth, if you'd stop climbing into strange dying people. Stick close to home, to your own family. They can protect you – they belong where they are, and are gifted like you."

Her hand stroked Adrianna's then, and gave it a squeeze. They might have been on a beach in Wales, eating ice cream and riding the donkeys.

"You've had your share of trouble too, Adrianna. Far too much. I hope this final trip can help heal you."

She and her father spoke in chorus.

"Final trip?"

"You must finish this, of course," began Great Gran.

Adrianna could not help herself.

"Finish what? Everything's been askew since day one. There's nothing to finish." How could you finish a mess but by quitting?

"Is there anything to finish, dad?" He would have the final say. She was committed to that.

Gareth patted his grandmother's hand, then pulled Adrianna gently to him. She lay out, resting her head in his lap and stared up to the sun with her eyes closed. Pink eyelids. Faraway sounds she didn't need to give name to. Golden heat comforting her bones. Her mind swayed gently, as if on water. Her dad and Great Gran had fallen silent. Everything was just the sun and their breathing. Blissful rest.

Her father's voice rumbled around her.

"Can't we stay like this forever, gran?"

Adrianna grinned. It did her good to hear her father become the child. Her heart softened even more. Bliss or no bliss, she would go with him if he asked.

"I wish we could, my love. But, you know, even death is work, some-times." She chuckled, then rearranged her bottom on the grass. "So what is it to be, my loves? Finish, have done with it properly and for good? Or go home, mend and try to forget you tried at all?"

"You put it that way, there's not much choice, is there?" Adrianna laughed.

"I'm going. There was never any doubt there," said her father. "But I'll go alone this time. Let Ade go home to recuperate. It's not fair to her, any more of this."

"No way!" Adrianna was adamant. "You go, I go too." She looked at gran. "Where are we going, anyway?"

Gareth pulled a shred of grass and chewed on its tip. "Next stop, God, I suppose." He remained as glib as always. "But Ade, I really think you should stay home. It's safer."

"I'm not so sure," said gran. "The state, mind and body, that Cabot's in, she will be anything but safe."

"Survived did he? The shrunken bastard." Her father growled. "I thought I'd tied him so tight he'd…"

"It's worse than you think dad. He and I met again, and…"

Her father's face was stone as he stared at her, searching into her eyes. There was a rage in him she did not want to see.

"I…" The horror of it was still with her. She bowed her head. "I took care of him myself."

Gran took her grandson's hand and shook it. "Bring her with you, love. Home is not safe. And if that doctor catches up with you, at least you will be together. Alone, you are each much more vulnerable."

She smiled through bright sunlight to Adrianna.

"OK." Adrianna got to her feet. "Let's go." She brushed grass from her bum.

"Right then." Gran squeezed Gareth's leg. "Off we go then."

Gareth nodded silently. Then, "You have a plan, don't you? Traveling through the relatives perhaps…?"

Gran nodded, pulled Adrianna to her other side and wrapped her arms around their shoulders.

"Some of your relatives died in nasty ways. Your distant relation, Geraint Morgan, now, perished in the charge of the Light Brigade, so don't do him. Then there was his nephew, Dafydd."

"Dafydd Morgan? A really bad poet, keeps peacocks and llamas?" said Gareth.

"Read about him have you? Daft as a brush, is our Dafydd, but quite spiritual, in his own mad way. Not much blood connection there, a cousin of a cousin's brother or something. And it's the blood connection that matters, you'll see. But there are distant cousins used to visit with him on his estate. Your thrice-removed cousins Wyn and Arwen. Perfect match for you two, really. Get inside them, one each, curl up like little bedbugs, and you should be safe. They're not your style perhaps – rather timid – but lukewarm will do you good right now. They have good hearts.

Wyn, especially, is a religious man, and the estate is a spiritual place, despite the canticles and magic and Mr. Mathley... Now, you stay away from him, mind."

"Mathley? You mean Alun Mathley, The Last Angel, as he calls himself?"

Adrianna looked at her father with a "how come you know so much?" scowl.

"Yes, love. That's why Wyn and Arwen are a safe bet. Cautious, and gifted enough to not be taken in by the glamour. They quite naturally abhor it."

"Ok. Enough dithering." Gareth breathed deep. "Time for a visit to Wyn and Arwen."

"Nose to the grindstone, then." Adrianna swallowed a breath.

Out of a singular blot of pewter cloud, a corpulent mass of blue-gray flailed, yelling in forty different directions at once, then finally righted itself at low altitude and glanced off a medium-sized trilithon. Bouncing and scrambling a few yards, the mass finally managed to stand upright, puffing and glaring blind.

"Damn! What effing century am I in now?" Buckleigh snapped. Fat fingers impatiently brushed bracken from his front, then untangled briars from his disheveled hair. At the outset a focused, confident man accustomed to success, Buckleigh was now two hundred and seventy-two pounds of squat, filthy, crimson irritability contemplating failure. His whirlwind visits to over nine centuries had been a decided displeasure.

He was a Buckleigh, nevertheless, cheered by possession of a gun, and a clamoring desire to use it.

33

"God has walked on these hills. It was His feet, see that flattened the points of them."

Wyn smiled down, pleased as Punch at little Hermione's laughter. She tugged his hand, pulled him along after the others.

"Did he make it all rainy and cold too, silly?"

"Of course. Even God has to pee from time to time," said his sister Arwen.

"But when he farts, it's warm," said Hermione.

Wyn's feet would go no further. He stared at Arwen, stunned at the language. Arwen shrugged. "Not my child."

"Come on!" Hermione danced impatiently, a whirl of burgundy coat and cream colored blouse that flashed in the grayness like the sole remaining scrap of daylight in this sad afternoon.

Such an innocent little imp. But what a mouth! Farts, indeed! Wyn's boots thumped down the footpath after his sister and the girl, and his hand finally closed on Hermione's free one.

Arwen watched Dafydd's motley group, not too far ahead. This weekend there was that Mathley, who fancied himself a warlock, and that tall, scraggly-looking painter and Blavatsky's acolyte, Auguste or something: All a touch on the insane side. "Perhaps we would be better off in the gang," suggested Arwen and pulled Hermione with her. Their ectomorphic selves would benefit from the body heat and shelter. Whatsername, that other Blavatsky sycophant...Cecilia, that was it... her ocean-liner girth would block the wind. It was an acceptable trade; Cecilia's shelter from the storm in return for pretending awe over her lamentably daft pronouncements on the cosmos.

Hermione thrust her filthy little spaniel into Arwen's arms.

"Keep Angus warm. Poor little thing, he's shivering, look!"

The spaniel squirmed, as always, and whined. Angus indeed. They should have named him Angst. And the little charmer was wet through, coated in dirt from the pathways. Arwen winced as a gritty, cold paw poked through her buttoned blouse, thrusting against her stomach. Stupid animal. Arwen rearranged the beast until it finally shut up and rested its chin on her arm.

At least its belly was warm.

She hated Sundays in Wales.

Come to think of it, she hated Sundays almost anywhere. London was just as grim. But Paris was lovely, even on the most somber days of autumn.

"There will be good brandy back at the Morgan home," suggested Wyn, as if reading her mind.

Brandy on the one hand, and puffed up, bullet-headed Mathley on the other; Hermione on one hand, and huge Cecilia, all purple and deep blue, like an insidious illness waiting to germinate; and those horrible plays and ceremonies they all kept inventing... but, on the other hand, Huxley and a few odd fellows who could always be relied on to voice a compelling thought.

"Yes, there's always good brandy," said Arwen

Adrianna snoozed, lulled to sleep by Wyn's amiable drone, pulled along into stuporous dreams. Wyn was warm. It was nice. She found some warm rest and made like a bedbug in Wyn's brain.

At Davydd's rambling palace, Alun Mathley was meeting mildly soused resistance to his urgings for a black mass that evening, something he called "The Rites of Eleusis."

"Alun's not a bad sort," Auguste was saying. "If you like your friends notorious and pretentious. But a mass? I don't know, old man. I mean, the sacrificial maiden would be fun, what? But all that demonic mumbo jumbo..."

"The Rites of the Useless, you mean? Or is that, The Rights of the Useless?"

Auguste barked happily, nodded at the joke. He was, once again, pressing his hip against Wyn's as he slurred into his ear. And that damn waxed mustache prickling him again. It made Wyn uncomfortable, smiling through the morass of drunken amiability that always sloped into parties at about this time of the evening. Now, to expect him to tolerate this pervasive, ambiguous sexuality, that was too much. He left Auguste peering over a potted rhododendron at Cecilia's gigantic behind enveloping a Chippendale chair. She was ready and eager for the Mass– and stared droolingly at a corpulent Mathley as he fussed and fidgeted at his box of tricks. He had erected a portable podium of some kind, ignoring equally the jibes of the non-Spiritualist onlookers and the painfully tactful hints from Dafydd that the time and place were not right.

A few besotted guests who had succumbed to curiosity hung about near the heavy embroideries and drapes, tilted against little boy statuettes who flaunted their cheeks and periwinkle pudenda. Wyn escaped as far as the doorway that led to the billiard room, where the fug of cigar smoke repelled him.

Hermione's voice came from behind a tapestry. She slid out from behind it, with Arwen in tow.

"You must stay Wyn, or we will die of boredom." She reached, on tiptoe, and whispered in his ear.

"Father and mother actually take all this seriously, Wyn. That horrible man..." Her head indicated Mathley. "He was at our home two nights ago, for dinner. And they all went off, mother and father and him, to their secret room, dressed up ridiculously in robes and gold snake headbands and such... I think they've gone mad. And mother, why, she's even more anemic than ever lately..."

Wyn knew her mother's look. That delicate face, with its huge, beautiful, green eyes that seemed to smoke in a head two sizes too big for her fragile frame; her head nodding as she playfully rolled her eyes, nodding like an overweighted flower on a stalk. Nancy Maitland was like a wraith expecting to die, a target for demons, walking amid the smoke that plumed from the permanent cigarette that accompanied her in its long, slender holder.

Nancy leaned against the cherub with the winkle scrotum and watched Mathley and the gathering audience airily, her hand absently stroking the crack of the cherub's alabaster bottom.

Hermione navigated them into a hole between an archway and an aspidistra, and picked at Wyn's leg urgently. He looked down, and, seeing her cross-legged, imploring him in that silent, hungry child's way, felt his resolve disintegrate. He fell into a heap next to her.

"There we are," she said. "I have to hide. But I have to watch. I can't help it Wyn. You see, mother's taking part in the Mass, and daddy."

Hermione finished, ever so maturely, "To tell you the truth, I'm thoroughly ashamed of both of them. But I'm morbidly interested. Aren't you?"

Wyn groaned. "No, just moribund, hopefully." He waited to die. His backside prickled, falling into bloodless sleep. That was a start.

Mathley, The Last Angel, looked like The First Ponce. It was unbelievable that he would wear that triangular head-dress in public. And then, a long dressing gown affair, with lumps of fur showing through – apparently a decaying leopard skin to complement the moth-eaten curtain look. He was taking himself quite seriously, muttering some incantation with his fists clenched, turned upwards to the sculpted ceiling.

The candelabra threw down mercifully poor illumination. But Mathley's sinister voice could not so easily be dulled.

"... Thee, therefore, whom we adore, we also invoke. By the power of the raised lance!" Mathley bellowed. "I am the flame that burns in every heart of man, and in the core of every star. I am Life, and the giver of Life, yet therefore there is in me the knowledge of death."

Wyn's hairs stood on end. He privately feared that the hocus-pocus and demons were real. But the worst was the perverse desperation at the core of the words. It was the filth that flowed beneath. It was the dirty, masturbatory childishness of power lust. His lip curled in disgust.

"I am above you and part of you. Your ecstasy is mine. It is my joy, to be your joy..." said Mathley.

Hermione's head lifted sharply. She watched the trio with sudden intensity. Wyn touched her shoulder and met her blank stare with a quizzical look. She turned back to the invocation, waving her hand at him impatiently.

He waited. The tone of the ceremony lightened, Mathley's voice rising a few intervals into a calming lilt.

"They didn't do it," said Hermione.

"What?"

She rested her chin on her knees and spoke confidentially to both of them, tugging them close.

"They did it at my house, but they did it differently. I watched them, in secret. They thought I was asleep in my bedroom, but I wasn't. I sneaked all the way down to the cellar and spied on them through the keyhole. It was... I don't know... it felt all creepy, all sort of slimy."

She looked up, studied the trio for a few seconds.

"It's not at all the same now. At home, the fat man was moaning, and he had his robes open, and his thing out, poking out like a banana or something, under his fat stomach. He kept stroking it and rubbing it and singing like that, and then mother and father kneeled..."

Arwen hissed at her. "That's it! I've had enough. And so have you. Come on!"

She stood and pulled her out of the room.

Adrianna felt relief as they walked into the silence of the library where a fire crackled in the midst of a huge, ornately carved fireplace.

She felt Wyn's sadness, knew the tearing poignancy the man felt. The sharp sadness of wanting to be father to a little girl, to love beyond anything else, to keep her from harm, to give your all.

"Let's forget about that fat man, shall we, and your mother and father with him, just for tonight? Let's play a game or something," said Arwen.

Wyn felt a compulsion to kill her parents. He was a stupid man, sometimes. But there was still time for him to become a father, to have his own family.

"Let's go eat some cakes, shall we?" said Arwen. She fluffed Hermione's hair and the three of them raced, and she smiled at the bright chuckle that followed behind, and the dainty clack of Hermione's dress shoes on the polished floor.

They stared at fruit flans, custards and cream, and chilled chocolate surfaces that perspired in the warm air. Wyn let Hermione win the largest piece of chocolate cake and slather it in whipped cream. He bit decorously into his custard-fruit tart.

"You must eat like a lady, Hermione."

"You mean like you?"

Always right, always bright, she was, thought Wyn. If only age, bringing wisdom, did not trade for it your youthful courage, your naive power of spirit. It really was quite demoralizing, exhausting, if you thought about it.

"It is always refreshing to apprehend their happiness, isn't it?"

The voice sounded quietly across the floor.

Wyn and Arwen turned simultaneously to face... someone who wasn't there. Who was that? The hallway was empty, the entire household seduced into the ballroom. Hermione posed, on the verge of giggling, next to a leather wingback chair. She was pointing to the top of a barely visible head.

Arwen strode over to them. "Found her. She's not a ghost."

Wyn stood in front of her and struggled to put a name to the face. Beautiful woman, face like a heart, with Slavic cheekbones.

"Don't tell me. I'll get it." Wyn's hand slapped his forehead. "Mary. No, more exotic, begins with an M, has a Y in it."

"Well done." The face lit up with a softy blessing smile. "I'm Myfanwy. Myfanwy Aberconway. I'm distantly related to you both. If you remember."

"And you've been sitting here quietly all along? I'm sorry, we didn't mean to disturb your peace," said Arwen. She loved silence herself.

"There are far more disturbing things around and about us. No need to apologize. I was just cleaning my mind in here. I need to be alone quite regularly, otherwise my mind becomes oppressively cluttered. People, their thinking, desires, all the mess of the human world."

Wyn understood. It was exhausting, being acutely aware of the oddest dynamics in human life. He and Arwen had never known what to do with that part of their minds.

Inside Wyn, Adrianna was all ears. She didn't know quite why, but Myfanwy's presence indicated something portentous. And that name. If Adrianna's mind had been a stomach, it would have plummeted. 'Aberconway. Holy crap Gareth... Aberconway.' He would have heard, for sure, camped out inside Arwen.

"I have something to tell you that you need to know," Myfanwy said. "My mother is the sister of Blodwen Aberconwy, who is the first born of Daniel and Bronwen Aberconwy, who you might have heard of, or read of in the various family bibles of relatives. I think your father has one, in which there is quite an extensive family tree. The family's ancestors go back as far as the birth of writing, it seems: though you will see the name spelled different ways – Anglicized Aberconway, Welsh Aberconwy – and even linked to Conwy Castle and such."

"Yes, you're right, Father has a huge family bible in his study," Arwen concurred.

Myfanwy's eyes held Arwen's and Wyn's. "Your minds are like ours, our family's." She continued. "You are somewhat psychic, both of you. And, perhaps luckily for you, since you don't seem to want it much, your portion of it is slight and manageable."

Wyn couldn't tell whether he was happy at the thought, or put off. Slightly psychic. It sounded a bit soppy to him. Like being slightly strong.

"But I have a feeling this is not the point of what you want to say to us." He studied Myfanwy's beauty luxuriously.

"You are right. And forgive me if what I say is difficult to swallow."

Hermione slid off her chair and advanced on the cakes.

"You two, Wyn and Arwen, have a gift for translating all this ethereal noise I speak of ..."

"Ethereal noise?" Wyn said.

"Yes, put simply, our cosmos is full to the brim with it, always vibrant. It almost translates itself, so to speak, into human form, or animal form when it manifests in our dimension, and then we do the rest, fashioning, tailoring, according to our inspiration and need.

"I say this now as encouragement, but also as a warning. Any contact with the occult is not for either of you. It is a danger to you."

"But I don't play around with occult things. I despise it, I..." Wyn was shamefaced.

"But you are intrigued, fascinated, and, in moments of anger, tempted into living out the illusion that there is some part you can play in uncovering its untruths, its perversions."

"Well, I suppose... You may be right. But it's only a whim, after all. Nothing that is a danger to me. And Arwen couldn't care less..."

"Now," Myfanwy leaned into them and spoke almost under her breath.

"My friends Gareth and Adrianna are different."

Who? Wyn had been enjoying her focus on himself. He wasn't interested in talking about this Gareth.

Arwen, though, was suddenly alert. "Ahaah!" she cried, then fell back in her chair, waving a hand. "'Scuse me, please go on."

"I felt that you knew something," smiled Myfanwy, and rearranged herself more comfortably.

"He has powerful psychic gifts, Gareth Pugh does, and they have almost destroyed him on occasion. Its shape has remained ambiguous, but its force has been both ravenous and protective."

Wyn zipped through his mental file of relatives and friends; he really didn't know this Pugh.

"Gareth's power, and as she is learning, his daughter Adrianna's, are huge with potential. So huge, that life for each of them has been a continual process of getting lost, orienteering in darkness a land that they cannot chart, so to speak.

"Because of this, we need to help them to get back to the deepest centre and find out what this driving strength is, to find out how to apply it to Life."

Wyn cut in.

"Okay. I can't disagree with you because I know nothing about this kind of thing. I haven't even read much Freud. But, who are Gareth and Adrianna? Why are they so significant? And to me and Arwen, specifically?"

"They are family. Part of the family's destiny. If we don't help them, we have failed as much as they have."

"So what is this destiny?" Arwen muttered from a lowered chin. She was thinking deeply, thought Wyn. She always slumped like that when she was thinking.

"And what can we do about it?" said Wyn. "We're not priests, or Alun Mathleys ... I mean, do you want us to meet them? You want us to visit them?"

"That would be difficult. He isn't born until 1950, and she..."

Wyn started. "Okay. Now I'm completely lost. This conversation has just leapt off the deep end, and I'm in my knickers without a water ring."

"That's not important. What is urgent is getting Gareth and Adrianna on their way."

Arwen remained silently brooding. Wyn spoke. "First of all, we have no idea what that means. Second, this could just be more spiritualist bunk, so, with all due respect, why should we care? And three, I badly need to urinate."

"Ignore your bladder for now. Adrianna has met you, Wyn, although you probably haven't had the faintest hint, and Gareth has met you, Arwen."

"Look, I really do need to pee."

"I'll be blunt then. Gareth Pugh is inside Arwen right now, and Adrianna inside you. You are their mode of transport."

Adrianna felt Wyn's body chill, goose bumps prickling along his arms. She suddenly felt the same panic. Wyn wasn't a car. He was human. She couldn't control him. And yet they had been asked to put their complete trust in these two. What if they crashed, went insane? She could only freeze her mind and sit, acutely aware of the fear, of cold perspiration.

"Inside me?" Wyn squeaked.

Myfanwy rushed through all that she knew, of Gareth's and Adrianna's recent journeys, their near failures. Wyn forgot he even had a bladder. His mind had lurched over sideways. It would be good to be home with his violin. Or maybe not. He would have a disembodied woman for close company.

After his mind had reeled its yawning orbit, after he had watched it fly away to pinprick size, then boomerang back to him, Wyn surfaced on a gap in Myfanwy's narrative, found that his bladder had revived with a vengeance, and stumbled to the nearest bathroom, where he voided in ecstasy. Then he perched on the counter, his tired mind striving to keep him from complete denial.

He couldn't feel Adrianna inside. But he had felt some unique sensations, of late; inexplicably hilarious moments, stifling laughter over notions, words in conversations, somebody's appearance or manner. And, just as inappropriately, sudden urges to fly, to jump off heights; or the need to curl up in warming sleep and listen. Listen to what? He thought he knew now. His subconscious must have discovered Adrianna's presence. He wondered if they could converse

"Go home," Myfanwy had told them. "Cleanse yourselves ... church, or meditation, a hot bath and prayer, or a long swim... whatever suits you best."

And then, with fresh minds, they were to pore over the family 'bibles,' their generations of ancient photographs. "Making avenues for Adrianna and Gareth," was the way she put it.

There were healthy ways for their visitors to go, apparently, and others that would sap them and eventually cause them to disintegrate. In such a dangerous cosmic world, the most natural path was innate: It was the family. And it was their job to study the family so that Adrianna and Gareth could see, and seeing, no longer be diverted by bad options.

Wyn and Arwen were to help get them to the next gate of their destiny.

"We must help, or we all fail," Myfanwy had said before departing the room.

"We are our brother's keeper."

And she had kissed each of them on the cheek.

34

The family bible had been cajoled from an aunt. They had to make a significant find, tempting enough to move the two ghosts along.

"We had better hop to it," sang Arwen, who was obviously enjoying herself. "I hope my Gareth is paying attention. Gareth-Tape-Worm, sit up and pay attention now," she sang gleefully.

Wyn slid the tablecloth aside and laid out the bible. Outside, in the back garden, starlings whistled and pecked, and a tough looking robin yanked professionally at a desperate worm. The sun was bright. He wished he were out there with his shovel and hoe, instead of in here digging up dust and old bones.

Adrianna knew they had no time for digressions. Myfanwy was absolutely right. They had been barking up the wrong trees. It was along the family line that their path ran.

Before Adrianna's eyes paraded pages of sepia and tea-colored prints. Most were frightening. Stone-eyed crones in tight black bodices, thousand-buttoned, ogling from under laced cowls out of dim rooms crowded with doilies and bric-a-brac and stuffed couches and chairs looking like dormant buffalo. All the rooms the same, and all the men and women similarly wooden, caught in states of indignant alarm or grim piety. Each couple whaleboned and waistcoated so tight, and with lips so tightly pursed, that not a drop of love could be lost by any of them. Adrianna felt her gut sinking. She couldn't survive inside one of them. And there was no time to fiddle here.

She sensed the power snaking through the family, looking out through the eyes of particular women. Here was where the strength lay. It didn't travel through the entire family, but through the maternal side, one matriarch linked to the previous. It shunned the males, avoided the entire paternal ancestry. Her mind ran ahead of the pictures and script – as Wyn furiously flipped pages to keep up – slipping into the head of a white-fleeced toddler, or in the ample bosom of a new bride. The line traced the gifted matriarchs, to whom she was somehow connected. A line of hidden royalty, it seemed to her, disguised as governesses, house maids, self-effacing wives.

For hundreds of years, they had managed to protect, if not quite to nurture, this secret that was born in them, as it had been in her. Generation following generation of peculiar women, some whose glittering eyes showed how they loved their gift, women well-kept; others who had succumbed to a strange, faceless fear, and stared into the lens out of strange torpors, out of lives of waiflike terror or consuming distraction.

There was something in her father, she knew, that echoed the demeanor of their men. Stern defensive lines of quiet, stubborn husbands, brothers and fathers forming protectively around the women, appearing as if they were summoned spirits, gathering in silence while the magician with the photographic box and the flash powder set up his trick show. Smiths, miners, farmers, the odd shop-keeper and bank official, and even a composer, all of them faced the camera with frank, large-jawed strength of purpose, as though posing for a picture were a sacred duty among many others. And God help you if you dared insult the daughter, the mother or wife with a lewd look, a cocksure remark, a wink. Every one of them, even the skinny composer, looked as though they could box your ears and knock you down without drawing a heavy breath.

Inside Arwen, Gareth knew he was with the family now, and trust calmed him. The secret matriarchs and their devoted guards connected him to the first root of things. At least, as close to that root as they and he could ever be.

Wyn got up, rubbed the blood back into his numb rear end, and took the kettle from the hob. Adrianna shut herself up while Wyn made tea.

The book lay open at a page of photographs recent enough to have escaped decay; her parents, naturally, were not among them. They were not yet born; mere germs in the cosmos. She scrutinized the photographs – blowing on the tea, sip, savor, then stare again – through Wyn's absent gaze.

There was a fine picture of a rugged ancestor, in the nineteen-twenties or so judging by the hump-backed motor car in the blurred background. A slim man, but tough as old boots, wearing his worn-out Sunday best, a jacket and waistcoat, a scarf wrapped around his neck and smoothed down his chest, a decorous tongue of silken wool, and, crowning his gray-mustached face, a tweedy cap with a little front brim. The man's mouth turned up at one corner, as if he were suppressing a good, throaty laugh, and his eyes showed kindly through a weather beaten, grimed face. A miner, out to the park of a Sunday afternoon, with chapel over and done and a few hours of liberty before Sunday dinner and night. Adrianna turned her mind to other pictures. The darkness, the seemingly eternal toil and weight of their lives pressed on her.

Then, finally, Gareth let out the psychic equivalent of a yell.

Arwen's teacup hit the wallpaper and shattered, painting an ochre stain down faded ferns. Wyn's spastic arm returned to his heaving chest. Adrianna rocked with the pounding of Wyn's heart.

"Bloody 'ell, 'Wen!" Wyn picked up the broken crockery, threw it in the rubbish can in the pantry, then returned to the dining room with a new cup and saucer. "Can't you be a little more controlled than that? We've not got many cups." His hands still trembled with aftershock as he poured a second cup of tea.

"Sorry. It's the first time for me too. I think Gareth over-compensated."

"For what? Your thick head?"

"Play nicely, now," purred Arwen.

Wyn sipped his tea, breathed heavily, counting his heartbeat down to a normal pace.

"Can you hear me now?" Gareth's words barely rose from his mind into the vocal range.

"Hmmmmm? That you?" said Arwen.

A little louder then.

"Arwen is a simpleton."

"I heard that."

"Just testing." Gareth studied the page.

Adrianna's mind joined him, and they stared into one photograph intensely, heedless of the domestic noises around them. The picture showed a sturdy, buxom woman in her late middle age, standing behind a kitchen chair. Though her wide skirt fit the part of governess – a simple, heavy cloth that was as starched as it was colorless – the jacket she wore looked fit for the Queen; full-length sleeves that rippled like water, and a bodice with buttons like cherries.

The inscription under the picture was in a graceful, controlled hand that spoke of a painstaking and happy mind. It had to be her own hand, reading simply, 'Bronwen Aberconwy, Bristol.' Aberconway: Not a monastery but a woman. The thrill of certainty flushed through them both.

Then they felt the tug, and knew they were on their way, and, almost before they could prepare themselves, they were hovering over a railway platform. The sign said Bristol, and the air whispered 1873, and there was Bronwen, deferential, as suited her position, bobbing her goodbyes to the Master and Wife, and allowing the two little girls to cling to the free hand not holding her purse tight to her bosom. No embroidered jacket this time but a rough coat that might have been sewn from a canvas sail, a heavy, durable piece of armor well suited to the rigors of a Victorian train journey.

The children kissed her goodbye and she almost let a tear fall. She loved her employers as much as her own family and felt her heartstrings tugging, even though her absence would be short. Almost too short, indeed; a rushing, racketing charge to Clevedon on this new railway, completing a journey that might have previously taken a day in what now seemed mere minutes – and then the comfort of home for one day, one night, and another morning before clambering aboard once more and hurtling back to Bristol. If it were not for the good comfort she found on either end, she was sure her heart would have quailed and died from the noise and urgency, the very speed of time.

Bronwen cooed her final farewells and clambered to a seat, where she sat staring primly ahead for a second, for the entertainment of the girls, ignoring their calls, then lost her composure and broke into a tearful smile and waved sadly.

She disliked the train, as she did all machines; malevolent creatures that could not be trusted. And yet, this being her second trip on a locomotive, she left Bristol with the confidence of a seasoned traveler.

They were in the open country before she had finished counting through her sons and daughters, imagining who would meet her at the station in their Christmas best.

With so much thinking and emoting going on, Gareth's own mind lurched with surprise when her interior voice first spoke.

"Going to introduce yourself then? All the polite visitors do, you know."

Them. She was talking to them. She was aware of them, and they had tried not to make a sound. Gareth stammered introductions, and his mind closed on the details of their life. How would she comprehend the 21st century, or mind-traveling, or that they were the latest in the line, from Blodwen and Iris Morgan, through Mildred Morgan and Cecil Pugh...?

"I have been expecting you." Her voice calmed and teased them at the same time. "While I'm not capable of seeing as far forward as your time, I pay regular visits to my grand daughter Myfanwy, who, praise be, has not yet married and so retains her sense and faculties and has time to concentrate both."

Here was a woman, and a blood relative, whose fingers could trace their very roots, could follow the secret undulations of their like minds.

"And why shouldn't it happen?" she said, as if to dispel any vestiges of insecurity that lay rooted in them. "All the doctors in the world, and Mr. Pasteur himself, would not be so bold as to claim knowledge of everything under the sun and moon. And we Celts know a thing or two yet that they can't pin into a specimen box. And neither fearing of it, nor scoffing at it, makes it any less true."

'Well said,' Adrianna thought. Although, to state anything of the kind in her day would brand her a cornflake, or a charlatan.

"Ah, well, 'tis no different now, rest assured Miss ..." Her thought hung, waiting for the surname.

Adrianna gave her the family name, Bronwen mused on it, then stored it in a recess of her humming mind. She looked out over the passing fields, the ploughed ground they charged past, free of Bristol's sad tenements crowding the outskirts of the city. Her mind eagerly envisioned her eldest son, Dai, his rough lips pecking her cheek and brawny farm-laborer's arm reaching for her luggage.

"But there's no time for digression," she told them both. "You need a guiding hand. Rather, a guiding spirit. And your instincts were right. No-one better suited, and closer at hand, than Bronwen Aberconwy."

Bronwen coughed. "There's really no time to be shilly-shallying about now. I understand through Myfanwy that some kind of nastiness is in pursuit? Malevolent minds distilled into one evil creature."

She rearranged her ample rump on the hard seat, then happily arranged her arms on her lap like someone about to take tea.

"Now. I can send you back a little way, or a long way, as you deem best. A little would be to my own mother, Elen, but that would only be thirty years or so, and then she would have to send you to the next stepping stone, which would be my grandmother Myfanwy, then Olwen, I suppose, although she is a bit on the flighty side, born just a bit more tup than the rest of us and prone to getting herself tucked away in a sanitarium for weeks on end... so maybe little steps is not the way to go... so many eccentricities and bits of history to wade through..."

'And the Big Step?' said Gareth's mind.

"Well, that depends on how strong you feel you are. Only you can know that. It takes a combination of strength of mind and courage bordering on the foolhardy... but yes, I could send you, post haste as it were, back to, say 1670 or so. Sian would take care of you there. I could send you no further, I'm afraid. The deeper past is just a fog that I have not dared encroach upon."

"I would be very grateful if you would send us as far as you can, as safely as you can. We've had more than a few mishaps on the way to you. Can't afford another," said Gareth.

"Then it is fortuitous that you had the good sense to choose me. Anyone deeper in time than us is just words on a page; none of these things they called photo graphs. Without the image of a specific relative to anchor you, well, that would mean a lot of wasted time. My goodness, I still recall my first tries at going back there. A young woman, I was, blessed with some schooling beyond sewing and churning butter. I used to sit there, on the window bench, daydreaming over my books, and then, one day, off I went like a bee, in a positive fox trot down the ages – so speeedily, I do swear it, that this train crawls by comparison..."

217

"But the task at hand," urged Gareth.

"Ah, yes. Forgive me. Well now. You just sit tight and let me concentrate. Sian, Sian."

Bronwen let her eyelids grow heavy and flutter shut. "Won't be long now."

35

They plunged, along with their stomachs, and hoped for the best. Abruptly shocked by the sight of her fingertips in the dead fluorescence of moonlight, Adrianna stared into their whorled prints. They reminded her that she was someone, a thing more significant, surely, than a clothes pin or an apple; significant enough that she wouldn't be abandoned to an empty death, cast off like flotsam on the quantum surf, swirled down the cosmic u-bend.

Gareth spoke to her gently, reminding her of the crucial thing at these times: Common-sense turned to fear, which became an impenetrable lead door. Forget sense, common and uncommon. Forget the habit of time. A ghost, not recognizing walls, walked through them with ease. Certain that time did not exist, they could simply walk through what was not there, and be anywhere.

So it was goodbye to the moonlight, goodbye fingertips. She was weightless density, gliding like an iceberg with the real gravity of herself somewhere down there in the deep black. Was it cosmos or water? Were the ripples moving in a fluid substance, the glittering white-gold fragments simply the waves reflecting sun? Or were they stars, moving away from her down their own tunnels of space, flaring into non-existence like fireflies? She did not know who she was, or what, or where.

Bronwen's inner melody thinned, then trailed away.

Adrianna's eyes searched into liquid blackness, but found no purchase. There was no up or down, no here or there. And the rushing wind that was not wind sounded like blood and a heart pumping in her ears. And she had no ears. No heart. No blood. She was a holographic crow banking in a motionless sky. She was crowblack, and then the blackness itself. And still she was moving, as if onward, though backward, if Bronwen was true to her word.

She heard her words again. "You must lose your body. Forget any desire to manifest, because when you desire, then you are there, and I will not have the power to reach back to you to pull you out. I can only launch you, and carry you like dust on a sun mote. Any manifesting beyond the density of dust, and your motion will end. God alone knows where."

Adrianna knew she must float at the border of the universe of mind, beyond the very reaches of logic. They would land, Bronwen said, inside Sian's mind, and, from her, push deeper back to a mind that sat at the very edge of consciousness. They would know when they had landed. And then they must be silent, for eons if necessary, until that little mind awoke to them.

And so they went on, passing not through real worlds but, sight focused inward, through lands of imagination. Through arctic regions where time hung suspended in regal icebergs; through the soft lands, the Amazon where the steam of fertility stung, through the heart of a many-petalled flower, ochre and rose, that breathed open in rhythm and slept in rhythm. Adrianna saw an ocean's fingers stroking at Land's End, felt its rime washing her mind. A distant ringing of bells in a captured sky, with angels singing from a golden nowhere. She saw herself afloat on the wind, then she was falling and saw up close a checkered tablecloth, a laden fruit bowl spilling grapes at dusk.

They spiraled through memories, through dramas they could not own or recognize, drifted alongside banks of histories that stretched higher than Niagara, then overturned like huge boats turning belly up. Then their minds stopped. And a woman called Sian knew they were there, making an imprint less than her own baby's sleeping breath.

They had done it. They floated in Sian's consciousness, an idea in embryo. And she, with maternal intuition, knew a spark of something alien in her, something new, akin to the nudge of conception.

"It's only us," they thought to her, following Bronwen's instructions. "Bronwen told you we were coming." The words did not seem to get through; Adrianna could feel her searching within herself, a slowly swirling hand reaching for silt, fishing blindly in a rock pool. Words would not do. God alone knew what language they spoke now.

And when was now? She fought the urge to open her eyes to the world outside, locked everything in herself in stasis. It was good that she was not fighting alone, that Gareth's will also countermanded her impulse to awake here, to alight here.

Adrianna heard his mind as if it were another hemisphere of her own. And he spoke to Sian with images, imagined them harmless; better yet, naked and luminous, like angels. He imaged them as benevolent creatures, the kindest of chimera, incapable of penetration. As comprehension dawned in Sian, he repeated images of Bronwen to her and her mind settled into relief.

There was something indescribably beautiful about Sian that tempted him to open his eyes and mind to her time. His mind saw hair silken and long, the color of sun-bleached wheat, and pale skin where light freckles surrounded glass-blue eyes. Perhaps just a little peek, just to see if he was right? He would only allow sight, no hearing, no sense of touch. Only for a second. He opened his eyes within her and looked out of hers.

He saw nothing. Only the pale vermilion of closed eyelids, crossed erratically by floating phantoms, blackish blue. The retinal universe, a tideless ocean of amoeba and light.

Sian's mind stirred. "NO!" it said, and closed itself.

He felt Adrianna's metaphorical smack. "I resisted. How dare you!"

"Thee must be away. There is no time," came Sian's voice again. "The Brute One would have you dead. He comes, and his servants. I see them, like locusts fanning out, spying the circles on the water. And you are the pebble at its centre. They will find you eventually. Now GO! Do not venture further than this world however; God is the next and only door you can arrive at."

Her mind closed down, and they were jettisoned into the blankness. A still lake that held terror in its infinite depth – this was alien country. They felt its tide sucking them on like corpuscles in a bloodstream, dragged toward the heart. The filigree of memory began to break. Adrianna's fear turned her sight backward, created fingers to clutch at something. But her fingers gripped air as memory veins snapped one by one until there was nothing. And they were in it.

Momentum drank them in. It was as if Sian's mind pulsed through and past them like a river, ocean bound. It aimed into a beyond to which no mind could give shape, where the island called self became an absurdity. Merciless, implacable blackness, surrounded them, forever endless, no matter their speed or direction. Memories of bodies had turned to smoke long before; now even a fragment of thought suicided. Until the mind was a pinprick, then less.

Fatigue alone spoke, like rot inexorably creeping into wood, its fingers dragging them to final rest, to nullity. It ate into their spirits, and even though they were metaphysical, they felt the sudden alarm surge like an electric poison. Soul fatigue, like metal fatigue, dry rot.

Would Sian kill them? Had she already? Had she lost them eons back?

They felt a scream, a razor blade slicing an eyeball, and knew it was themselves. It was their limit and their terror.

There came one nudge. A pulse. Sian.

She said "Leap." And they knew instantly what was demanded of them.

Here, there was nothing left but invention. Where the germ sprouted from nihilism. First alpha... then ... beta... then...

God! It was endless!

Adrianna was a fish gulping its last ever bubble of oxygen. After this, something worse than death.

Make something. Anything. She felt her mind join with her father's and become pregnant with hope, with hunger. She looked outward, invented with him a fantastically blue sky, supported by one fledgling cloud, and they leapt for that cloud. It was their portal, their dream door. And then they were aloft, insisting on a blue sky and a cloud that held up the world.

Just one step through the portal. Simple, said their mind. Make it simple.

They burst into light-speed, flashed out in all directions into a hanging stillness that sounded like one continuous, unwavering note. A soft note, almost like a trumpet; almost like water running, like the vocabulary of all the winds gathered into one voice. And yet, silence, suspended.

Everything said one thing. Wait.

Twinned, they hung like an atom perceiving the orbit within itself.

36

Adda performed his shaggy limp through green jungle. Straight out of his cave on a jaunt, with lianas still dripping scarlet and blue amoebae. Powder-blue birds shot like missiles through the air. Heavy-winged creatures dropped about his walk, bellies sagging with meat, looking, to the newcomers, like the aborted clay models of a child. Adda had barely registered them. His mind reacted to the sliver of pain within him that was their arrival, like a hand obliterating a biting gnat, then dismissed the stab as hunger.

Somehow, either within this Adda creature's mind, or outside, everything seemed to be happening at once. Adrianna saw, in Adda's mind's eye, mastodons making churches out of themselves in secluded glaciers, bending under the crippling weight of horns. Through a gap in the leaf canopy, she saw pterodactyls rowing by on huge leathery wings. She saw apes and deer, and a huge aurochs cropping grass in a clearing. And amid this primeval world there was Adda, humanoid and ecstatic, an anachronism.

They had waited, as instructed, and then the world had exploded. Into laughter. Just one long laugh caught up in the flood of the universe, this Adda.

Short and stocky, all grin and gawp, Adda swayed through the forest dark, reveling in the feel of damp earth on his leathery feet, wet leaves and grit on his naked claves, nettle sting flaring on biceps. Coming upon the raucous battling of a stream with its village of rocks, Adda leapt the ribbon of silver without the slightest hesitancy, and when his body missed its mark, plunging a leg into deep water, he gurgled happily and dragged himself onto the bank. No fear of drowning; so he either had never experienced it before, or he just didn't care. Gareth was betting on the latter.

Adda clambered and hopped and wriggled on through the bush, and his nostrils flared and stopped, flared and stopped, as inquisitive with myriad odors as were his darting eyes over the birds that flew between trees and bush, ferned floor and foliage canopy, mere brushstrokes of scarlet, yellow, and green.

Adrianna lay, gobsmacked by the profusion and heft of Adda's sensory information, her mind curled in self-defense against its continual barrage. She watched with Adda's glittering eyes, smelled with those huge nostrils, and her head echoed with more sound than she could decipher. The land pulsed without let, and Adrianna tossed about like abandoned luggage in the belly of a ship. Her head would have ached, her ribs have bloomed with bruises had she been flesh and blood. Adda's world pressed on her more viscerally than anything she had known in her travels. Adda's mind and senses reveled, drank greedily, as though he had just been born, whole and innocent, with a huge, hungry mind. Which he was.

Adrianna wished for pain killers.

The world rampaged on.

No one had invented the word hirsute yet, but they would have to. Adda's furriness was shocking, just a few steps short of gorilla. Thick legs, snug even to the ankles in dark hair, where there showed a couple of inches of flesh down to the toes which, once again sprouted patches of equally dark fur. As he made his aimless way through the forest, Adda's fingers continually scratched into his fur, answering a nip here, an itch there. And the visitors trundled along, wondering just how they were to galvanize some attention in this distracted animal.

It was not simply the thrill of the moment which attracted his attention, or the barking of the apes that plunged alongside or rolled crazily into the brush, or the reedy melody of flittering birds, the saw-cawing of demented toucan-like creatures sitting halfway up trees that peeled bark. It was other things, strange things that no-one should be able to see.

Adda saw things that made him stop dead. A bloodbath sky, the coming of gods, human commerce and architecture, the ripping apart of flesh and silence. Then he was an inconspicuous hermit, brain as sharp as a carrot, sitting in classic Greece. Painted statues with rings around the eyes watching fig trees fruit.

And then, Adda pulled up short, a tang clinging faintly to his nostrils. He jammed his fingers into his nose, then breathed deep. Who was that animal in the dark who had smelled so sweetrank, but also like him?

Finally! Adda sat and rested his back against a tree trunk. No longer the rhythm and noise of the sinews and limbs. Just quiet, a few insects buzzing around his body, a tree here and there shedding bits of twig, an unwanted leaf.

"Hello," Gareth tried. Adda dreamed brainlessly, occasionally lifting his fingers to his nose. A sense of smell so acute that Gareth could catch it too. He knew the scent, knew it well. But he would not enlighten Adda. He would have to open that Pandora's Box himself.

"Hello," again.

But it was not Gareth, or Adrianna. As addled as her mind was, Adrianna knew she had not spoken.

The voice insisted.

"Earth to Gareth. Earth to Adrianna. Helloooo."

"Adda? You speak?"

"Not Adda. Though I look like him, temporarily. Think again."

Suddenly, Adrianna and Gareth were outside, ejected unceremoniously. There was Adda and there was the forest. And Gareth looked down at his translucent feet and saw the faint denseness of twigs through them.

"Bloody 'ell," said Adrianna dumbly.

"That comes later. Right now things are nice." The voice spoke with a tinge of threat.

"Who are you?"

Adda blinked at them, smiled, then stood and offered a hand to shake. Stunned, Gareth gripped the leathered paw, and stood motionless, mesmerized by the creature's eyes: For a second violet, they shifted hue to hazel, lavender, electric blue, even amber, then back to a forget-me-not blue.

"I've been called by many names: Nobodaddy, God Biology, Demiurge, Allah, "I am that I am", Yaweh." What-was-Adda pressed His hands on their shoulders, urging them to sit.

"I don't get sensitive about names. No living creature can get my name right, except by being absolutely silent; then I say my human name, my elephant name, my meadowlark name, and the creature who hears it is momentarily blessed. Then, of course, life returns to normal, blahblahblah, racketracketracket."

"You talk a lot for a God." Adrianna's head spun.

"THE God, thank you." The words hit out bitterly.

"Never mind... If you don't know – doing what I like is one of the nice things about being here. I could talk for hours non stop and there wouldn't be a thing you could do to halt it. You couldn't even stop listening. That's the power I have. You respond when I have stopped, because my silence compels you to speak. Even though my silence means the whole universe is listening. You're compelled to. I'm the Magnet: you're the iron filing. That's how the conversation goes; magnet attracts or repels, iron filing obeys, magnet, iron filing, magnet, iron filing. That's how it goes here, anyway. Precisely here, I mean, as opposed to a multitude of other heres.

"It wasn't exactly my design. Not down to the nth degree, anyway. You set the laws in motion, you envision their potential, and once the Word is out of your mouth, there's a new Law having its own way with the universe."

God clamped his lips together and stared stonily. Everything about Him said 'speak.' Gareth's mind was off camping somewhere, chasing apes through rampant ferns.

"Sounds like a funny setup," he said.

"No more funny than the way I've allowed you humans to govern yourselves. Free will has freed a pestilence of ills."

"For which we blame you." Gareth grunted tacit concurrence with what he imagined was God's distemper. While he thought, his right foot worried stones out of the undergrowth and tapped them about. Their damp, tumbling sound, and the forest's massive silence was unnerving.

"Oh," said Adrianna, suddenly. "Where are we? I suppose you're here, there, and everywhere, but us..."

Something snuffled nearby in the undergrowth, a something with, by the volume of it, a nose the size of an anteater. Further off, a bird, or something, cried out experimentally into the quiet.

Sensing their discomfort, God tilted his head, twitching Adda's ears like those of an intent cat.

"Not getting the results you wanted, Gareth? A little too nonsensical for you, am I? Looking for something more Scriptural? A nice philosophical-question-and-answer hour? Or blacker still, a burgeoning storm over forty fathoms, water and sky like lead? I can oblige."

Gareth, tempted by a facetious, "Surprise me," bit his lip.

"I can hear every word, articulated or not," said God. "Come, follow me. I'll change for you and we'll walk."

God slipped out of Adda. They both looked down on Adda's limp form, crumpled at the foot of the tree.

"Will he wake up? Is he ok?" asked Adrianna guiltily.

"Certainly. You're thinking I shouldn't have used him that way. Well, truth be told, there's nothing there to be used. Empty as a broken egg."

"Huh?" said Gareth, intelligently.

"He is Me, you see. I gave him a name. Adda the acorn, he is. But he doesn't exist in the way you understand. Not yet. I wear him when I come down here to play. Need to get physical once in a while, feel the thrill of muscles and limbs and such. Sometimes I'm a man, like Adda, and others. Sometimes I'm one of scores of women; all in My head, all Me. All part of the experiment; trying to decide between the apes I've grown to love and perhaps a new species I've been toying with. Adda, among a few others, is something halfway between." God looked Gareth and Adrianna up and down. "I toyed with the idea of your type, your evolution. And I suppose you're proof of the choice I finally made... I suppose I alter him somewhere down the line. I can't remember now. The excitement of meeting you two, I suppose. Not thinking straight today."

God's tone spoke volumes. Apparently, a gaily-colored cockroach might have pleased Him as much. So, was the human race the product of God's Bad-Hair Day?

"You remember the future?" Adrianna's brain was stymied.

"Off and on. Lately I've been choosing not to though. I think it's just the thrill of pretending time exists. Being in the 'present' becomes more poignant then. Though I am the All in All, He Who Cannot be Named. I warn you: don't think I am just playing for your sakes. I could be playing for mine also. Abraham will learn this, but he'll get it all wrong. He's pretty dense. Or will be."

"So you know all this? The future, the past, petty cruelty? "

"Of course. I am a jealous god and I move in mysterious ways."

'As you are now,' thought Adrianna

"We must walk then, and have our talk," said God, who was now some flying insect. Buzzing happily, the insect roused himself, then flashed and became anthropomorphic once more. He poked Adrianna where her ribs should be, and she felt the fingertip like a pole jabbed into flesh. He stepped with resolute calm, fluid limbed, and with very biblical sandals on His feet, now sporting a toga and a veritable sail of a gray-white beard.

"Is this better? More what you would have me be?" he asked Gareth sarcastically.

"I wouldn't have you be anything but what you are, and I don't think you're some Walt Disney grandfather."

"Point taken. Just playing Devil's advocate..." God ruminated, a very Walt Disney finger crooked over old man lips in a cartoon face. "Nevertheless, Gareth Pugh, Adrianna, I will not show you all of Me. You could never apprehend the "I AM." "

Gareth thought, 'Try me,' and recalled the painful yearning that he had known since infancy, since he could form words and pictures. If not desire for God, then what had it been?

"I came a long way, through more than twenty years of struggle, to do just that," he tried, though he felt much less than up to the task. "So tell me, please… is this your natural form, for example. Is this all of you? It seems absurd…"

"Not all of me. No. Not much of me, in fact."

"Well why do you appear in such absurd manifestations?"

God coughed. "Because you have a sense of humor. In fact, you, both of you, and your humor, are making me this."

"So you're telling me that you are merely a projection of our inner mind. Of man's mind…?"

"No."

They waited. Nothing more was forthcoming.

"Well," Gareth insisted. "What are you?"

God sighed. "Every living creature already knows."

That didn't help.

Gareth pulled up, the foggy angst of his years coalescing: years that were nothing more than the razor's-edge balancing act of the suicide, years sucked dry of any joy or desire for joy. Everything done wrong; desiring the wrong things, expecting that he would somehow thrive on innocence and art, and knowing instead a drawn out shame compounded with rage, filtered down, through the years, into a bitter resignation.

"Suffer the little children to come unto me," said God, as though that melted Gareth's boyish angst.

Adrianna balked. "The little children get crushed, and worse," she said… "And anyway, you never said that; Christ did."

"Oh, that idiot!" said God.

"Why idiot?" Adrianna rankled, but restrained her disgusted anger.

"He was my son, and he preached the wrong things. The metaphysics of that separated us. Remember "Adonai. Adonai"….Well by then…actually, a decent time before that, I had washed my hands of him. I AM THE ALL IN ALL and he can never reach me, for you or himself. He was of me, but he became stupidly egoistic, bedazzled by himself."

"I don't think he ever was yours, because…"

"Why, little girl?"

"What were you in the Old Testament? A jealous God, one who killed, who had people sacrifice one another, attack one another… ambiguous to the point of deceit…"

"I, ambiguous?"

"All that nonsense, I am that I am. When it is us who are that we are. We are part of the universe, as much as you are. You know, knew this, but demanded unthinking devotion to yourself, with all our heart and body and soul. You demanded suicidal abnegation…"

"So what? I'm worth it, in your vernacular." God tore a shank of bark from an impossibly white birch tree and flapped it menacingly at her. "You, too, must bow before me; that I swear. But go ahead, have your little speech. Then you will see the real me."

Adrianna sat calmly and crossed her legs, wordlessly challenging this wrathful God. Her outer demeanor belied her inner turmoil. She just couldn't begin, couldn't find the words. There was something about casting out devils...

"I will tell you the words." The honeyed voice of what might have been a woman, might have been all the trees and ferns and moss and rocks around her, spoke inside her, bringing a calmness that melted all anxiety and turmoil.

Adrianna recited the New Testament words as if by rote. "And all the people were amazed, and said, Is this not the Son of David? But when the Pharisees heard it they said, this fellow does not cast out devils, but by Beelzebub, the prince of the devils.

And Jesus knew their thoughts and said to them, Every Kingdom divided against itself is brought to desolation; and every city or house divided against itself shall not stand..."

"And maybe they were right," God retorted. "Christ was always an upstart. "The Kingdom of Heaven" and all that. Who was he to promise that? The Kingdom is mine and mine alone. He could not speak for me, or for all those who yearn for me now. I, alone, decide. I Am the Power without which, nothing... I AM..."

"Can I finish now?"

"Blather on, young girl. It means nothing."

Gareth sat under a tree, watching beatifically, as if transported, a personified smile.

Adrianna continued nervously, as if blathering were necessary to get everything out before she lost it.

"Well... You are a Jealous God. A warlike giant of the universe who protected the Jewish tribes who lived on the periphery of the rest of civilized society..."

"I'm glad you imply that they were civilized also. Had you not, my wrath..."

"And that's just the point. You are a jealous, warlike God, possessive and demanding constant attention. While you were being that, Jesus followed with a narrative of love."

She pushed her simple logic further toward its end.

"Christ said that a house cannot be divided by itself. And yet, while he performed miracles of love, you used miracles as conjuring tricks, to bamboozle, to cow people into obeying what you needed. That was certainly not the human love that your supposed son personified. He was the opposite of you. He divided the house, if there ever was one. By his acts, he renunciated the Old Testament and its volatile, violent God. YOU."

"This Christ person didn't speak your language. He wouldn't have it, even though the Jews wanted him as a vengeful King. He would not be you. He never was of your house!"

"Stupid girl! He was no longer of my house because I washed my hands of him," God repeated menacingly, and moved with sudden violence toward her.

Gareth lifted himself up and smiled.

"Shall we walk a little?" he said gently.

"Yes, walk a little." The voice sounded like honey, a lullaby voice that filled the trees, the brambles, the very air itself.

"Oh God! That bitch!" moaned God with exasperation. "Worse than Eve! Stubborn whore insists that she governs all, even gave birth to the cosmos itself. Doesn't know her place, that slut!"

"But I do," returned the honeyed voice. "You alone are God-Biology, nothing more. The director of merely a part of what comes from me, Sophia...even without my desire. I am love. I am forever..."

"You are the Whore of Babylon!" bellowed God.

No reply. No sound. Just the milk and honey of a perfumed forest.

"Stupid, uppity whore. Yes, let's walk. AWAY."

Gareth moved slowly, clutching a tight back. He surveyed the branches above.

"Lord God," he said, "Can you help me break off that branch? See? It's bulbous on one end, perfect as a handle. I need a cane."

He gripped the handle and it slipped loose from the tree with the resistance of a baby's arm. Gareth tested it, walking a few steps on the uneven ground. The walking stick was thick, the handle fitting into his curled hand like an apple. Gareth checked the tip for wear. Would it dig? he considered, thinking of Elspeth.

The honeyed voice sang once more. "Dig for her..." Somehow, her voice directed him. "I will make her appear for you."

"You just CANNOT do that!" shouted God. "This is mine, all of it. It's my rules!!"

Silence, yet something like a wind song, washed away God's ire.

Gareth rammed the stick's point into the earth. Loamy, heavy to shift with the stick, it was softer than he expected. He stabbed and stabbed again, dotting a web of deep holes. He fell to his knees and scrabbled furiously, dragging up handfuls of earth, piling them again and again. Pouring sweat stung his eyes. Then the earth began to show the ivory white of her face. He gasped and stopped dead. His insides prickled as he stared at the apparition before him.

Elspeth lay in the dark earth like a child bedded down, her eyes shut, her body curled as if within the peace of a sleeping newborn. An untrammeled spirit; a mind unmarked by thought. Gareth kneeled by her body and, as gently as he could bear, enfolded her in his arms. His spirit screamed, a rage of loss. And love. And then quiet.

He let his head touch hers and rest. He imagined breathing, and he was breathing, exhaling trembling breaths that passed over her cheek like kisses. Behind him, the wood was silent, time stopped. He curled closer to her, buried his face deeply beside her breast and rested his head on her arm. It was warm, as though she breathed and would wake to find him there.

Time passed, and she did not open her eyes, nor flutter an eyelid or nerve.

Time passed and he lay curled into her, breathing more softly each second, until he had breathed himself down, almost to where she was. Almost death.

Eons later he returned to himself and the forest. Shock, forever loss, flared inside him. He would have to return to earth, where the wall could never again be penetrated. Except like this, to the dead, immobile, sleeping thing. Elspeth was gone to him, and even in his own death... it would make him sleep deep, like her, and he might never ever see her again. Never. Dead was dead, and was horrible. The most heinous injustice to man's existence.

"Sophia?" he wept. "Is this how it must be? Did you do this?"

"I cannot," came the honeyed voice, as of sun flickering through foliage.

"It is not in me. I am nothing but growth…" She would have said more, but that Gareth, with grimly tightened teeth, swung his stick. Its clubbed end smashed into God's skull. It dug deep and Adrianna heard bone crunch and collapse inward.

"That's for Elspeth's death!" he screamed.

"I love you" said God, metamorphosing into Adda. "Despite Elspeth, I love you."

"Stolen words," said Gareth. "Why is Elspeth trapped here, in the mud? Is this her world now?"

"She remains there because she must."

"Why?"

"That is the Law."

"Who made that law?"

"I did."

Gareth clubbed Adda into flesh, blood, sinew and bone. Around it, he scored a line with his stick, then stamped and stamped Adda's remains into earth.

Nothing. No leaves stirred. The wind choked into its throat. The sweet voice did not breathe.

Then they saw it and teared up.

It was a gazelle. Beautiful with its full eyes, its twitching ears and pointed step.

Gareth hesitated. Adrianna gripped his arm. "Perhaps there are awful consequences from this…. It could be Her."

"It is not." That lambent voice filled them.

"I love you," said the gazelle. "Don't heed the whore."

"Dad!" cried Adrianna. "Stop this. We have to get home. You have met this God thing, and Elspeth. You're done here."

"This is the first step." Gareth's chest heaved. "Otherwise he would block us. He still has the strength, I can feel it."

He aimed through tearing eyes, aimed at the gazelle and swung. "This is not real," he encouraged himself.

The gazelle collapsed onto its broken front legs, and mercifully expired quickly.

Adrianna cried. Gareth knelt beside her and held her hand.

"Is it over?" she whispered.

Then their ears began to fill, like water with the scent of honey, ferns and patchouli that captured the air.

Gareth whispered. "I think this is God, at his most fundamental, he is Kronos, eating his own young. He is the God that we have created, along with Satan. We created them out of terrified, wounded minds; half born and driven by utter violence."

Perhaps, Adrianna thought, suffering was sewn into the very heart of existence, was the off-beat to the heart's on-beat.

"If so," said Gareth, hearing her mind, "then life is perverse, and God is its demiurge."

37

"I am Sophia, creator of the planets, the cosmos, the earth, woman and man in their essence, which humans have separated from that essential called love, into a place seen as Eden, where trickery, violence and self-loathing began to be born... Sadly, though I created God as your keeper, he became merely a demiurge with a huge ego, as you have seen, now and through the ages. Then, in this process, you became him and he became you, until you both created hell, and began building it, first in your minds, and now, in the flesh of the world."

Gareth fell to his knees, aghast. His hands clawed at the air, as though rending something would let some answer in; something he could understand, could hold to himself as a manageable truth.

"But I can never have that back. That thing I believed made the world when I was a child. That miraculous thing I had as a child. I'm so far gone, so disconnected. I've made it all too damn complex. And where did it come from, this perversity, always adding two and two and coming up with three-hundred?"

"From your killing hunger," said Adrianna, with a happy fortitude. Certainty was with her, guided her mind and words.

"Huusshh, Gareth." Sophia's voice infiltrated his pores, cleansed his worries, which blew away like layers of dead skin. Gareth's gut righted itself, lay calm. For a moment, he was home, on a deck chair in the sun-dappled garden under his tree, and close by, Adrianna and the cats moved, and all was right with the world. It was something he could not trust. Destruction would come – as it had with his grandmother, with Elspeth, with the absolute death of love, the dearth of love he had known with Philomena.

"It's all here," said Adrianna. Her arm indicated the forest, demanding nothing, not even his consciousness of it. "Sophia fits. We fit."

Gareth leaned against a tree root as thick as his leg and stared into the glittering air. "But we can't STAY here. We must return to that hell." His mind whirred in the stopped air, an uninspired gyroscope.

Sophia's voice resonated calm.

"There is one more choice you must make. One more death. I am sorry."

Two creatures hovered before his face, more minute than they had ever seemed on earth. There was a bee on the left and a bluebottle fly on the right, unmoving, their wings a blur.

"You see these final apparitions. And Gareth, you must make a choice."

Gareth's stomach plummeted; his bowels tightened.

"Now consider. I will put it simply, because the hardest part will be your choice to kill.'

Gareth and Adrianna felt the forest sigh, the air an inbreath of deep sorrow. Adrianna looked at Gareth, who hung his head.

"Now. The fly immunizes us against all matter of sickness and virus. Its life is among the offal, the dead, the filth, and then in your sugar bowl, crossing your eyelids at night, landing on your lips by day. Though it is annoying, sickening to some, it is performing its job to perfection. This is its job, to immunize humans by degrees, generation after generation.

Then, the bee makes honey. We eat the honey and momentarily feel joy. But the bee is like a bullet in flight, untouchable – its sting burns and can live within your skin – some, it can kill."

"I know. I know the choice. One of them is an old god." Gareth's voice was barely audible.

"An old god?"

"Ancient. Answering nothing but the primeval in us." He watched them hover. Immobile, as if hanging from invisible cord, their wings hummed near to absolute silence. But Gareth heard them as a clatter of mechanics.

"You must choose and kill I am afraid. You must choose between your instinctual horror of decay – because it helps us live; is the off-beat to the heart's on-beat – and the existential decay, the possible uselessness of the honeyed sweet of the bee, who brings only momentary joy."

Gareth wavered.

"Your choice, to kill which apparition, will answer all."

236

Adrianna's jaws ached from gritted teeth. The air was pure pain, jammed with impotent love for her father.

"Please choose…"

The sweet voice tore at him. Her insistence felt like poison. Perhaps God had been right. Perhaps she was the Whore of Babylon… of everything. The poison in him hated her. Her challenge was not his to answer. It was impossible.

She wasn't listening – or could not hear his thoughts.

Perhaps she was not evil but liberation. Perhaps she was nothing like liberation, and like nothing he had ever known. A black hole of deceit…

Suddenly he felt free and swung. The fly, hard as a pebble, flipped backwards, jetted through the air and smashed into a tree. Gareth stared into the guts on his club.

He turned weakly, all but choking into weeping. "Is He gone? Where has He gone?" It was wrong, terribly wrong. All around him and in him became a vacuum. The dead did not hurt. It was the living who suffered a living death. Terror gripped him. Panic gathered inside him, a spinning ball of stone. He could not move. He was lost.

Adrianna's breath caught in her throat. Had Sophia hidden her vengeful self? Had the end of them both come now?

Everything had emptied. The forest, the air, the scents of everything. Life spoke the word bereft, and Adrianna and Gareth sank to the earth.

Gareth dropped the club, stared, neck bent, at the place where he should have seen his legs. He saw haze. His ears rang with the secret pump of blood.

"I've killed him then…" He was more evil than Judas, than Satan. He had been horribly wrong. Suddenly, Sophia was frigid – the honey gone.

Then she came back, sweet.

"You only seem to have. He will be back. He always comes back."

Adrianna gulped, shocked with an unformed idea. Then it came.

"So others have come? Others have come and killed Him before?"

"Only in their dreams. In their astral fictions. Only you have come as yourselves, to the real place."

"But God… the bitterness, the hatred?"

"That was both of you combined. He was you."

The air breathed again.

"Gareth, you killed the rage in yourself. Adrianna, the bitter, deep anger of solitude's fear. Don't worry, since it seems to matter to you. He will come back. Billions recreate him, instantly. He comes back."

"The bee is my symbol. It is the land of milk and honey and far beyond. It is the truest love. It is your truest cosmic liberty, which you earn by living. By knowing. By joy. Remember me when you meet it on earth."

Her voice was honey again. But an arctic chill pulsed behind, pushed against the warmth.

"You need some visions, for a reward. Because you have chosen. And you have chosen right."

Gareth and Adrianna sobbed simultaneously, one tight sob, and fell to kneeling, emptied.

Deepest cold plunged through them in a bitter flash.

They stood on a high hill at night. A camel's hump, at the foot of which flowed the dark tan, moon-glowing fields of grain. Or were they people? They heard a sound of rushing, as of a million tongues, or of wind through grain. There was no time to distinguish if one, or both, existed below; for above them, out of a black that glittered like jet, there came masses of flying stars, surf-waves of stars of different colors advancing silently and at light speed, like fireworks exploding, spitting fiery trails. They kept on, rising out of infinite distance. Something profound, something eternally desirable dwelled in the stars. No. Not in the stars themselves, but in the meaning of their display. Not in the dancers, but the dance; making all bliss. Gareth, then Adrianna, fell to their knees, bones and sinews become water as the display continued to and through them. The stars, and the space around and between them, were sacred. They knelt in silent awe, inarticulate, mere dots on infinite white, but fearless.

On earth, Adrianna saw, she was a continual self-made tale, the little self that told itself to everyone. Now she was the absence of word, of name. She was naked, and invulnerable. Death, even, would not change that.

Untroubled, roused from an empty sleep, her unknown mind, that huge percentage of gray matter unused, had come awake, had suddenly become aware of itself, and reveled in the cosmos. She was little Adrianna, standing next to little Gareth, who she saw had a spray of stars imprinted on his forehead. He turned his face and looked at her in silence. 'So do you' said his insides.

They joined hands like sky-divers, twirling gently. Their bodies traced an arcing orbit in the black cosmos. At first outlined and filled with bright color, they became light itself. They were pulsing light-forms in natural embrace, kaleidoscopic jellyfish, opaque with a light that seemed to have no source, even in themselves.

But they were wrong; they knew that they had not seen properly. They had thought they were forms joining, but saw that they were two parts of something splitting, a bifurcating amoeba. They felt the searing pain, slow and attenuated, of their farewell. His mind filled with their foresight that brought their future loneliness alive and touched each of them, terrorized them so that they gasped and almost surrendered. But implacably, calmly, they continued separating, a necessity that neither would challenge pushing them on.

It was death, and a part of Gareth cringed and shrank to a dry husk, desiring nothing but to be overlooked, spared its gloomy eye. And yet it was far beyond him to tear his own away, and he devoured every motion, every flash of color and light, and even the lingering pain, as though the air itself demanded it. Pain was of no more account than the bursting of a distant star.

There was a light figure, immense beyond comprehension, pure potency. Dynamic, fluid, it encompassed everything in sight, every particle of the cosmos, and every photon of thought that flickered where their bodies might have been. And it continued to grow and to separate, a cry of agony and a cry of glory all at once, not a thing that felt either, but the agony and glory itself. Not two things in love, or of love, but love itself, infinite and eternally potent. What they saw, what their cells inhaled and embraced, was the verb, not the noun. It was infinite potency, sublime and meaningless, purest virtue and perversity, distilled to their essence. The sun, and prayer, and love; bestial murder, betrayal, a child's guts spilling in mud. It all pumped blood, swirled and lived.

Exhausted, Gareth screamed out for rest, and when it came like a blessing, he fell into its embrace. But they still had not banished the ugliness.

Horrific faces, spiders under a microscope lens, deep sea fish with bulbous, sightless eyes glowing opaque, loomed over images of pure bliss. Brilliant water slaked the thirst of every cell, every emotion, while reptilian thoughts and black emotions seethed through veins like hot mucus. They were bursting, cracking apart like leather eggs, blanched in a fierce sun, and together they were the genesis of a minuscule blue flower, the very thought of the flower itself, born under still, protecting water.

Sophia's voice came to them mercifully.

"It's not easy, is it?" she said. "And this is all a human can bear. I and my sisters bear this a millionfold, manifestations beyond count and naming."

Suddenly, unaccountably, they felt infinite density. They felt hunger like that of a black hole. But they knew no fear. There was a black hole devouring everything as if it were fuel. Everything. And the fuel's conduit was Stonehenge.

"Black holes consume your dreams." Sophia's voice rang in concentric waves.

They absorbed the process in wonder. They saw countless dreams floating through the ring of Stonehenge, spiraling upward; and the black hole sucked them in. They saw inside the hole, where the dreams separated of their own accord, like oil and water obeying natural law. Like images finding their kin, the dream colors twisted to form dream strands, which formed ethereal floating spirals. Still more tones and colors joined the blackness and intermingled.

They knew the physics of it, the positive and negative polarization of dream thoughts and urges, lusts and visions in their most elemental form. They understood how colors could shriek, or reverberate like cellos, how sound transformed into love or hate, into profoundly muscular forces that rocketed on like hunger itself, to bullet over the black hole's threshold into a new, black vacuity.

They saw dream strands by the millions, like DNA spirals, exiting the black hole, spiraling into vacuity like viruses. They saw spraying whiteness, an absence of color in their world, now the amalgamation of all color in another, spraying semen-like into a febrile blackness that hummed and clutched. They saw the black vacuity become hunger itself, saw it buck and cling and cry like a woman in orgasm and in birthing, and they knew, their minds vacant with awe, that they witnessed the birth of a new world, somewhere.

There were, beyond the black hole, infinite configurations of new worlds being born. And when she and Gareth were turned to face the blue and lonely and familiar earth, Adrianna cried. Around the earth, in a dimension no telescope could ever hope to see, black holes twisted dream threads, and the earth pulled them down, an umbilicus of visions, of absolute, ravenous truth for which the earth hungered.

Gareth, then Adrianna, fell to their knees, bones and sinews become water as the display continued to and through them. The stars, and the space around and between them, were sacred. They knelt in silent awe, inarticulate.

"Are you lonely still?" asked Sophia.

38

Adrianna was still crying when she opened her eyes in the grass under Stonehenge. It felt beautiful. She saw her father's tear-stained face next to hers. He stared into the sky, a sublime smile balanced on his face like a butterfly alighting. It flickered, then left, and his face turned to hers.

"Hello, love," he said, and his human smile returned, twinned with twinkling eyes.

Their two faces turned upward again. Two sets of eyes followed an armada of clouds tacking across an oceanic sky.

A hoarse yell, rising in volume and pitch, followed by a jellyfish thud, butted them out of their reveries. Unwilling to move, they looked between their feet and there, framed between Gareth's size tens and Adrianna's eights, a bulbous entity rolled, righted itself, then puffed and cursed itself upright. Their shock subsiding, Gareth and Adrianna grinned, almost pleased to see him: it seemed that nothing was impossible lately. Then his baleful eye caught them as the gray cloud he had dragged behind him mingled with the air, pulling it a shade darker.

"What you two smirking at?"

Buckleigh's wrinkled suit waddled closer. He loosened a shoe, shook out a stone, replaced the shoe and tugged something from his jacket pocket. A pistol, shaped like the body of a stealth fighter. Buckleigh jabbed it at them like a two-edged, beautiful sword.

Adrianna's head turned from the gun to her father's face, his warped eyebrows screwed into a stunned perplexity so comical that she had to laugh. Her gaze returned to Buckleigh just in time to receive the stinging fullness of his backhand.

"No effing giggling from you, my girl!"

He turned menacingly on Gareth, and pushed the pistol to his forehead, forestalling his attempt to rise.

"Not an inch!" he cried, and spluttered into a whooping cough. Gareth and Adrianna remained frozen.

"Surprised to see me?" Buckleigh spat into a handkerchief, screwed it up and wiped his perspiring face.

"You must have thought you were way ahead of us all the time, hey Pugh? Thought our grasp of things, our methods, were all too crude to amount to a pile of crap, hey? Well, surprise surprise. We've passed muster in this one. You should have signed on with us when we offered."

He paraded before them waving his gun.

"Had no idea, did you, that we could tap into your brain, anyone's brain, and simply via electronics and holographic principles, begin drawing images of thought? Crude, they were, but they were the foundation of everything that followed. And now…"

"Now," said Gareth blankly, expecting nothing good.

"What? No curiosity? No eagerness to see where you and your kind have taken us? Well, I'll tell you. We've become astronomers of the interior. Brain telescopes, we call them; not simply tracking and detecting brain activity any more, but constructing living maps of the human interior cosmos. You knew it was there, though you saw it outside yourself at first. We followed you on that, until you had your breakdown, that week you found that it was all inside you. Remember? You couldn't see any difference between the cosmos out there, and the huge, insane space inside your mind. And then you went a bit mad and started writing about it, and started that stupid school of yours, feeding everybody Anis to get them off. Thought you'd actually sent them off into the cosmos, didn't you; thought you all were on your way to breaking the barriers between dimensions, crossing that singularity and swooshing off into past time?

"Well, we knew what you never stopped to verify." Buckleigh wondered for a second if Pugh's psychic faculties could detect a lie this big. No matter. It had to be said.

"It's all an illusion – whether you see it as an interior cosmos or a real one, out there. We've done the math, Pugh, and again and again it tells us that the whole thing is the product of a deluded mind. A triggered mind, that's all.

"Remember that headgear you developed? Nothing more than a crude rip-off of Dr. Persinger's God Helmet. He knew the facts of his invention, and abandoned it. Persinger knew, it's all in your head, all a product of electrical triggers. All a matter of mapping the brain and zapping it in the appropriate places. The good old bicameral mind hearing itself masturbating; that's all there is to it."

"Sure of that, are you?" said Gareth glibly. "You've thrown millions into simply bolstering your own ignorance. I'll tell you that much."

Buckleigh turned on him.

"You poor, pitiful old coot. I'd feel sorry for you if you weren't such a damn nuisance. You have no idea how we tracked you, how we began our work, do you? Gawd, you were in such a mystified funk, those days, you didn't even know we'd knocked you out for two days. Well, next time you scratch that freakishly large head of yours, stop somewhere around your temporal lobe. You'll find a nice little metal implant, about the size of an apple seed, which we donated to the cause. Allowed us, eventually, to target you."

Gareth ran fingers along his head, then grinned a brave face up at Buckleigh.

"One more piece of metal here or there, no bother to me at all," he said gamely.

Buckleigh raised his pistol.

"I have a feeling this pop-gun could install a piece of metal that would bother you immensely. Both of you. Now, I want you to do something for me. I want you to undress."

Adrianna started, then stared, disbelieving, into the grass.

Buckleigh shoved her roughly with his foot. "Now!" he barked. "Not tomorrow! I didn't want to damn well come here, y'know, and the effort has not improved my outlook one bit!"

It didn't really matter, she thought. Anis would die out and its absence spirit her away. Wouldn't it? Just this time? It wasn't far now. She would return to her bedroom, and that would be that. Bedroom and visions enough to transform every day into something better than mundane.

"This really isn't necessary, you know," Gareth began, drawing Buckleigh's eyes from Adrianna's undressing. "We could quite easily come to an arrangement. I don't know what you plan to do to us, but I'm sure it would make things more complicated than they need to be. We can just go back to Toronto and…"

"As if we'd trust you back home! And don't stop undressing, either of you, unless you want to die right here." Buckleigh was enjoying himself. "No deals. We can't trust you to keep your mouth shut or your pen still. And, smothered or not, delusions like yours have a way of gaining currency and momentum with the unwashed masses.

"But I don't need to tell you that," Buckleigh huffed. "You saw on what side your bread was buttered years ago, didn't you? What a great way to make a killing, and a following, come to that. Always did have a bit of a messiah complex, didn't you?

"Well, sadly for you both, delusional or not, we can't risk your nonsense getting out to the world at large. You survived once. Remember that dumb kid who overdosed? Ha ha, I see you do. Well, he was our doing. Our plant. He reported everything you did direct to us. Problem was, he began believing your crap, began trusting that damn Anis of yours and talking you up as some kind of pioneer, a hero. So he overdosed. We made sure of that, and paid his parents a hefty sum to sue you.

"You were lucky then, got off light, and that was thanks to us. We were merciful, after we'd put the wind up you. But we won't be this time. Too much on the line. And I'm the one who has been entrusted with the final solution."

"I've got news for you." Adrianna sat upright, her stiff body a challenge. "He was right. We both crossed that barrier. And even a retarded hen like you should be able to do the same."

Buckleigh puzzled for a moment; where had he heard that phrase before?

"Just another kind of mental trickery; self-delusion writ large, that's what this is," said Buckleigh. "You've both imagined this scene, and I've tapped into the mental image, that's all. But, since you believe so much, then there's one option to save you from dying right here. You both find yourselves a nice century to go "live" in, and never, ever set foot in the 21st century again.

If you return to Toronto in the flesh, or anywhere in the decades to come, we will locate you and kill you. As it stands now, the story is that you both went comatose, Anis overdose again. When your family gives up on you they will be gone. There will be no inheritance, no tidbits for any of them. A counterfeit will, giving all your crap to the University of Toronto, and the bottom-feeders will abandon the hunt. And you, to silence. Not murdered, not even dead – just forgotten, shipped out of a hospital one day like used linen. Your histories finished, as if they never happened."

Buckleigh sat cross-legged, held his left index finger to his nose and blew snot into the grass. "Effing bloody volcanoes. You know, I must have gone back to pre-history before I made it here." His sleeve wiped the residue from his upper lip. "Quite the bloody goose-chase."

With sudden violence, the air behind him cracked, and Cabot leaned over Buckleigh. Hard metal made a sickening noise against Buckleigh's skull and Cabot stood wide-legged over the man's collapsed form, holding his bloodied revolver.

"You can't kill 'em, Bucky old man." Cabot grabbed Buckleigh's gun and tucked it into the back of his pants. "I won't have it, you pompous effing fool."

Gareth's heart leapt. He looked at Cabot hopefully. Maybe he wasn't so useless after all.

"Just sit there on your fat ass, Bucky." Cabot pushed his face against Buckleigh's bleeding ear as the man began to come around. "You'll do no killing today. If this is a friggin' day at all."

He stood, stretched, and stared about him. "Can't tell when or where we are any more. Still... not to worry."

He produced a small sack from his pocket, and from it pulled three lengths of cord, then squatted next to Buckleigh and tied his wrists behind him. He dropped Buckleigh's gun in the sack.

"No gunny, no funny, eh Bucky?"

Cabot waggled his revolver beside the man's ear. He grinned at Gareth and Adrianna.

"Okay. End of the line, just like the movies. Bucky Boy made his first, big, big mistake when he backed out of the deal. Then, cocky bastard that he is, he neglected to search me fully. Thought I had Anis in just my pocket. Bloody eejit!"

"Cabot...?" Adrianna dared a smile.

"Hello?" His voice was taut with spite. "You there now, are you? All of a friggin' sudden? Interested, concerned, ready to talk, hanging off my every word? I bet you are. I bet you're listening pretty seriously, aren't you?"

He pressed a finger to his lip.

"What do I do? Shall I patronize him? Should I speak at all? What do I do to stop him from being:

a) violent

b) sexual

c) vengeful

d) insane, or

e) all of the above? Am I right?"

Cabot whinnied with pleasure. "Well, Pugh One and Pugh Two... What next?"

"I just..." Adrianna began.

"Did you? Just. Well, let me tell you. Let me enlighten you. You just didn't. You just won't. You're dead. That's what, just."

"But why? Cabot, be reasonable..." Gareth protested.

"WHY?" Cabot's voice sprang eerily upward. He turned, sour mouthed, to Gareth. "Because she, just, cut half my friggin' dick off!" He hissed the last words, then stood rigid, his revolver aimed at Adrianna.

Gareth wiped the shower of spittle from his face and locked his eyes on Cabot's. The man was mad, and only one thing mattered, stopping him from hurting Adrianna.

Gareth spoke, squirming forward.

"Please, Cabot. Tie me up. Leave me here to die with Buckleigh – shoot me. But don't hurt my girl. Please don't blame her. Whatever happened, ultimately it wasn't her fault. I dragged her into this. I dragged you both into this. Take your revenge on me, not her."

"Hold STILL! And shut your FACE! Listen, Mr. Privilege, to me, Mr. Nonentity Academic. And you keep your ass still too!" He rounded on Buckleigh, then Adrianna. "No moving until I say. You are allowed to breathe, and that's all!

"Now, do you know the slightest thing about me, Pugh One? You dragged me into this, did you? Well, I'll let you know, you didn't. Your

247

bitch daughter got yours truly involved. Your bitch daughter played it coy, slut that she is, for months. And it was your bitch daughter who called me for help. Me. Mr. Effing Nobody."

He spun to Buckleigh. "Right, Mr. Effing Buck-Shot? Or did you set us up? Did you pay her to invite me into this game, just like the offer you made me? Which one of you used me the most, Bucky, Pugh-One or Pugh-Two?

"Well, I'll let you know, in these last few seconds. The answer is, none of the above. I knew what was going on. Me, dumb working-class Cabot Greenway. Born in Scarborough, land of infinite strip plazas, land of eternal, meaningless gang warfare, land of synthetic hills stinking of landfill. I grew up in a place where you got beaten senseless in shopping malls or gutted in an alley; not educated, not enlightened. A place to overdose, to prick your last collapsing vein in the room next to where your darling mother shags strangers for the rent.

"I got into this, and I got here, just like I got anywhere else before you idiots fell into my life. Raised myself by myself. Got where I am in life no thanks to anyone else. Genetics? Don't make me laugh. Daddy was an alcoholic, mummy dearest a whore. Public school was a laboratory crawling with rats. When they got electrified enough, beaten enough, starved enough, they ate each other. No food, for thought, or anything else. It was a JOKE, a NIGHTMARE! And not a single thought wasted on the likes of me.

"But where am I now? Tenured prof., Bucky's Jag, right Buck? Holographer, money for the deluxe Virtual Bitch, no end of toys; and more. Respect from all and sundry, and a nice advance from Bucky for a job soon to be well done. Didn't expect that, eh Bucko? Funny how simple a locked desk can be, with a decent crowbar. You think you, any of you, used little me?"

Cabot spat at Adrianna and languidly waved the gun.

"Now, what to do, and in what order? I might be tempted to blow you away first, Pugh-Two. But you know what? I won't. Come to think of it, I might not shoot you at all. Because I know just how to make you suffer the most. I can make you suffer even more than I have. With what Buckleigh has paid me, well, let's just say that I've got nothing to worry about. I've done with suffering. But not you, Pugh-Two. You're just starting."

He swung about, aimed at the head, and squeezed the trigger once, twice, three times. His laughter broke dryly through Adrianna's strangled cry as she threw herself over her father.

"Look, he even bleeds. I wondered if he would. Not quite human in this place, you see; I figured that out a while ago."

Adrianna froze around her father's body, her throat gurgling misery. "You should have shot me!" she cried. "Not him! Not my dad!" Her eyes stared unseeing toward Cabot. "Why couldn't it be me? Whyyyyy!"

Cabot sneered, mimicking her voice, then calmly turned to Buckleigh and shot him once.

"One bullet's all you're worth."

He sat, his gun in his lap, and began breathing, and exhaling hard, forcing the Anis out of his body. A few minutes passed, Cabot performing his exhaling technique. Emptied of Anis, he moved away, a figure shrinking away from a mirror, then vanished.

Buckleigh lay, eyes open and motionless, blood gathering on his waistcoat. Adrianna, smeared with her father's blood, sobbed, and wrapped her fingers around his head.

39

The room where the cot lay was dark, the body untouched. Buckleigh's two bruisers appeared to have packed up for the night, or they had run off to escape Buckleigh's wrath at their failure to hold Cabot. The thought added to Cabot's pleasure. Finally, everything was going right.

Life was full of irony. Everything going right, just when you had half your dick torn off. The only witness, a woman who would suffer forever and dare not say a word. Who the hell would believe her?

He turned on the lamp and stared at Pugh's sleeping body. He could do it. He could pump a cylinder of bullets into this second body of Gareth Pugh. Cabot saw the blood spatter the walls. Saw himself wiping its fine spray from his face. He saw Pugh's blood gather, form a thick pool and drip slowly, in heavy gobbets, to the dusty floor where a shriveled spider corpse lay on its back. But maybe he didn't need to kill at all, although it would be a fine conquest. Maybe the body, like the spiders, would just dry up and blow away.

He would have some scotch and consider what to do.

"This was where you came in," said Cabot to himself. "Musta been your destiny, your calling, Cabbie old chum. The slut called you to resolve things; to help. And you will. All resolved."

He stared at Gareth's corpse. "I'll be happy to help you shuck off this mortal coil, what's left of you," he grimaced.

Cabot surveyed the room. The heavies would have to clean up the mess. They would have to cover up the murder too. They had no choice, something he would make very clear to them. He had hidden the remainder of Pugh's Anis in his car, along with Gareth's writings, photographs and nanocds. And more besides. The Foundation would pay well for that.

First, though, a good drink, or five. He would raid Pugh's study. He reached the hallway and stared about, mindless for a moment. The air was

kronos duet

almost empty – no noises from other floors, the faint thrum of city traffic as familiar as the sound of a fridge in his kitchen. He could go home soon.

Outside the windows, big, ugly looking moths were batting their wings against a light that shone down onto the asphalt below. A shiver slithered across his shoulders. He hated the outside at night. He hated the denuded, lunar places, where people got beaten up under fluorescent street lamps, got their bloodied faces ground into stones and broken bottles. Wilson's Candy Factory was just the place for a gang war. With Gareth and all the others gone, it would rot and the only humans for whom it would mean anything would be the street kids who murdered and fornicated in its many shadowed places.

Cabot turned to face Gareth's study door. He'd smash open the booze cupboard with his gun.

Brainlessly drunk, gun in pocket and half-empty Glenlivet bottle swinging, Cabot pushed Pugh's door open with his foot and stepped into the room. The claw around his throat was not in the plan. Neither was being carried across the room and crammed into the armchair. Cabot, choking scotch, squeaked alarmed protest. Old Spice stench came from the square bastard who pinned him, black forearm hair bristling against Cabot's chin. A hard smack set his head ringing and he tasted blood coagulating somewhere in his nose. He gasped tight breaths that leaked bloody mucus into his throat. He had pissed himself.

The other guy stared down at him, then stepped aside to reveal Buckleigh nursing a bloody side, and Adrianna, still naked, drawn and sickly, her eyes raw red from crying. Her wrists were bound, the cord fastened to Buckleigh's belt. Cabot's brief pleasure at her naked body left him as a fist rammed into his solar plexus.

Cabot wheezed, felt a residue of urine, or blood, leak into his pants.

"Not dead yet, me," smirked Buckleigh. "Ribs hurt like effin' hell, but the bullet passed clean through." He held up the blunted bullet between thumb and forefinger, then tossed it into a corner with a grimace. He tugged brusquely against his cord as Adrianna slumped to the floor. "Bloody women. No sense at all."

251

He dropped the cord and advanced on Cabot, his pistol menacing. Cabot's groin dripped. Two pairs of hands pressed him in place.

"Looks like Pugh won't be coming home," said Buckleigh. "We left him melting into the grass." Buckleigh's bloodshot eyes stared into Cabot's. "And since you did so well, I've got a little surprise for you." He pressed the sweaty stock of Cabot's weapon into Cabot's right hand, then manipulated Cabot's index finger around the trigger. His eyes indicated Adrianna, where the gun barrel now pointed.

"Don't squeeze yet, don't do anything rash, or we will, all three of us, batter the remnants of your pitiful spirit right out of you. Along with guts and cartilage and such."

He sidled to a position behind Cabot, his sausage fingers massaging pain out of Cabot's stiff arm. Cabot stared ahead at the exhausted creature in the corner. Now that his chance had come, he was not sure he could shoot her.

Buckleigh's hands massaged flexibility back into Cabot's arm, bent and straightened it, turned it inward, then straight once more, all the while cooing reassuring noises into his ear.

"Relax, that's it," he murmured. "It's almost all over now, almost done, and you'll get your reward, I promise. Just relax the arm, get the finger right. I'll tell you when."

"Now!" He twisted the arm brutally. The shot crashed bluntly against eardrums, cordite stench floated in the air, and Cabot's carcass curled spastically on the floor, a flower of blood blooming from his fragmented skull.

Buckleigh waited, watching Adrianna as the noise of the gunshot subsided and became the sound of Adrianna retching. He plunged a thick finger into his right ear and manipulated it furiously, battering a sudden itch.

"Here's the story," said Buckleigh at last. He recounted the steps as if solving a Clue game.

"All of this because of a woman." His eyes bored into Adrianna's still figure. "She finds Cabot up here, seduces him, beds him, then Gareth Pugh wakes up, walks in and, lunatic that he is, tries to castrate our poor Casanova."

Buckleigh smirked at his two thugs as they listened, calculating the situation thickly. "Cabot murders Pugh." Buckleigh waved Cabot's snub-nose at them. "Nasty gun, see? Then, in a fit of cowardice, he takes his own life…"

Better get some of the idiot's blood on this woman's bed sheets. And a trail of it down the hallway. Tear that groin area open again too. Oh, and don't forget to tie Pugh's hands. Cabot forced him into this room, made him lay out on the cot... And change into your medical drag. Gotta go through the motions, if only for the visitors. I'll telephone the police chief and we'll get the ball rolling."

Buckleigh crouched beside Adrianna, wrapped his huge hand around the back of her head, and rocked it from side to side.

"Wakey wakey Princess. You've got some police to talk to. So we will have to synchronize stories. That is, unless you have a better explanation for this."

40

From her corner of the warehouse, the windows framed a segment of the city at dusk. Signal lights on the unused railroad track came feebly alive with the reflection of car headlights, then died out. A concrete bridge spanned the entire length of the window; beyond it, a squat factory, continually alight. On either side, streetlights stretched their attenuated necks into the sky. The Canadian flag fronting a gas station sagged like an old sock one moment, flapped free and cracked in the wind, only to sag again. It was that kind of evening.

Mottled clouds stretched across the sky, while from the far north winter's sting moved in. October soon, and her father truly gone this time. She could not undo it. The awful gap his death made in her life could never be filled. The undeniable fact stared her down every minute – he would never again enter this room. A few months gone, and she still did not dare recall his voice. The void still clung to her.

Silent tears traced her face, dripped from her opened mouth as she sobbed. She grit her teeth, tried to shut her mind against the pain. The doctors knew, and even she agreed, that if she didn't take great care, she would fall into depression's abyss, and perhaps not return. She owed it to what remained of her family to stay alive, to surface from this spirit suffocation. And she knew she had to take her leave of this place, no matter how it would tear at her heartstrings. And she cried soundless tears.

She sat immobile, planted in the centre of her pain, and let the tears slip down her cheeks, refill, slip, each one a repeat of agony and, just maybe, a minute particle of release from it. She knew she would have to cry for months, perhaps years. And she could not even pretend to see an end to it somewhere in the future. But it was her pain alone, and she would find some way to accommodate it, to accept it into the rest of her life. She had to wake up some time. She had her father's work to do.

She rose from the desk and walked to the ruined latticework of the cupboard bar. She picked at the pieces of wood. It was a jigsaw all right, and some of it had turned to mere splinters, some blown away. No-one had disturbed the room since the police inspection. There might be enough left to fix it. She owed that to her father's memory. It had been one of his favorite antiques.

She wouldn't ship it to England though, even if she could convince Buckleigh to release it as part of her 'inheritance.' He was king here now, until his organization completed the purchase and renovations of the building. Then, with the Pugh Museum of Mentalism complete, (a cheap nasty title, completely trivial – no doubt their intention), some agent would be designated curator, a tacky gift shop opened, and all of Gareth's history, his work, buried under a slag heap of kitsch and commerce. Even her upcoming book on his life would no doubt be heavily butchered and censored by their choice editor. Price, twenty dollars – a paperback printed by some completely unknown and forgettable publisher, relegated to the discontinued bin of sad, failing bookstores no-one ever went to.

The Foundation had sewn everything up. Highly efficient, she had to give them that. Nothing could leak out.

Not even the money in Gareth's will was to be found, or the crappiest knick-knack in this sugar-dusted candy store. The will had conveniently disappeared, so whatever cash resided in his bank account returned to the government in one way or another. Short of the things she could secrete in her luggage, or ship surreptitiously to England, nothing of this would be hers, or the other Pughs. The only positive thing; Philomena and the German relatives got nothing either.

And the man who met God and Sophia, She behind the demiurge – the man who had discovered that the mind could fly beyond the speed of light and survive, who had taken her through time and back again? Spied on, plotted against, ambushed, desiccated, gone. He was sprinkled ash down there, under the tree by the pond. Fertilizer, a nourishing feast for worm mandibles.

There was no indignity in that. He had joined the sun.

Her hands dropped the shards of wood that she had been toying with blindly. Outside was lilac twilight. The sun had fallen for the night, cued the long darkness she hated so much. She had to choose, for countless tomorrows, what pieces of the merciless outside world she would face. Her life was the mere commerce of bones and flesh with silence. One day, she might return and truly engage with life. She didn't know.

'Go back to the cupboard.'

The voice was the slightest of whispers, but her heart leapt and battered adrenalin through her body. She recognized it. She stood as still and silent as she could manage. Her breath stuttered in and out. Her ears rang.

'To the cupboard, Adrianna.'

It was Great Gran.

A whine escaped her throat and tears welled, then trickled.

'Go on sweetheart.' Gran's voice coddled her like an infant. 'Go on love.'

Her nose was running and she couldn't locate the Kleenex box.

'See what your father left you, love. Inside the cupboard.'

Her hand passed the splinters. Behind, a small bundle rattled woodenly. She pulled the package into the light and unwrapped it. Two spoons. One was carved from one solid piece of wood; two segments, joined by wooden chain links. Without a single cut to indicate that they might have been joined, the pieces formed a spoon end, and a medieval looking flat handle, hieroglyphed with Celtic geometry.

'That is now yours. It was mine, and my mother's before me. I gave it to your daddy when he was a little 'un. He says you are to have it and to protect it for all your life. And if you have children... then, it is your choice who you hand it down to. You will know.'

'Dad, is he with you? Does that happen? I mean, I don't believe in heaven, but...' Adrianna's tears burned again. 'I'm more than willing to believe. If I could say hello. Can he... can he speak to me ... or ...?' Her mind could not think, but would not rest.

'He cannot speak right now. His spirit is still shocked, a bit feeble, love. But don't you worry. He only needs to wait and all earth's residue will melt away.'

'All? You mean, he'll forget me?'

'No love. He will only forget what he chooses to. The rest he will treasure, like all of us.'

Adrianna fingered the second spoon, her eyes sightless as she thought herself beside her father. Perhaps just a piece of her spirit could reach, could nudge him again, let him know she was thinking of him.

'He's perfectly okay, love. You see, he knew the end was coming some time before it arrived. Had a vision, you see, and was quite reconciled to it, quite at peace. Only the brutal nature of it, you know... things like that hurt even the spirit that has passed over. For a bit. But Elspeth is with him often, and he is jolly enough.'

Adrianna sighed, breathed in, sighed again, letting the tension out of her body, releasing its grip on her heart.

'Thank you, gran. And please thank dad. I love him so.'

'He knows, my duck.'

A soft silence floated between them. Adrianna could almost hear breathing. She saw Gran's crooked smile, her baby soft cheeks. Dad's mum was the same. Funny how your skin and lines on your face mirrored your spirit, your kindness or bitterness.

'What about this other spoon?'

It was simpler than her own; a stocky little thing carved all of one piece of speckled wood, rubbed smooth by hands that must have traced its delicately crenellated edges, passed over the simple criss-cross pattern surrounding the half moons cut out of its handle. She could almost feel the eyes caressing it, could almost feel the secret pride in their hearts.

'That is for your gran, my love – Gareth's mum. So you see, you do have a good reason to go to Wales. Get away from here for a bit love. Let the bosom of the family give you comfort. You will come alive again, there. And you know they won't push you, not gran or Uncle Huw. Go there love, and give his mum her little bit of her son.'

Adrianna held the spoons against her breast and gazed into air. The room was so silent, and not a creak from anywhere outside the door, no hum from downstairs.

"Thank you," she whispered. "If you're still there."

'I am,' came Gran's voice in her head. 'And there's one more thing for you. For your journey now, and more journeys to come.'

'What's that?' Adrianna's heart sang. She needed nothing else.

257

'You may think so, but your dad is pragmatic, more than you knew. Now, go to the cats' room, and under their cat litter box…'

'Yuck! That stinking sand pit?'

'Indeed. Put your spoons in your room, then get a nice little shovel, and off you go. Your father says it's in the dead centre, and to never mind the stench. That's its disguise.'

The sand box reeked acridly of cat piss, and Lucy had just deposited and partially buried a huge, warm turd. She banged joyfully against Adrianna's shins, escaped the room and raced up and down the hallway, skidding on the carpet.

"Stinky cat. No wonder you have a pug nose. Whew!" Adrianna rolled Kleenex into two tubes, jammed one up each nostril, then advanced on the poo-pit with her garden shovel.

"Not exactly a day at the beach." The shovel pushed through four-inch deep damp litter, freeing a puddle of fresh urine. She turned a shovel full of litter over it, then scraped the mess aside. More or less at the centre, fossilized turds broke under her shovel. A few more energetic thrusts and she could see the floorboard beneath. She dug, coughing litter spores and gagging. Then the shovel blade met an iron loop. She yanked on the handle. Crumbled litter rolled aside, and the skin of ordure cracked like pie crust.

There, under the trap door, a metal box, somewhat the worse for cat pee leakage. She pressed the button on its face and was surprised that the well-oiled lid popped open.

Adrianna sat in the litter and stared into the strongbox. It was filled to the rim with neatly packaged bank notes, fifties and hundreds. A note, scrawled in Gareth's hand, read, "Happy re-birth day, love. Spend it wisely or unwisely. And have faith. Then I will be happy." Signed by dad, with a bad ink drawing of herself under crossed kisses.

"Well," breathed Adrianna. "The Foundation will never get a whiff of this."

Wilson's Candy Factory was alive with hammering and drywall dust, its foundations hopping to the thunder of front-end loaders and pneumatic drills. For all the technological advances of this lubricated hothouse they called the world, the wreckers and builders still cherished their connection to prehistoric brutality. The air was hammers and sweat and colorful cursing against everything dear; gridiron concrete and metal, poking bones, and tramping boots.

It was all alive, and all dead. Carpets ripped up, salvaged when someone remembered to, or tossed into battered skips; rough plank floors thick with dust and boot prints. Old doors unhinged, handles salvaged by prowling antique dealers, debris thrown from windows to explode on asphalt below.

The museum rooms had been emptied, their treasures carted to storage, their walls gutted, smashed back to bare brick. And over it all, the silt of hundreds of years of candy manufacture leaked from ceilings above, through floorboards to workers below. And the mice above and rats below hid from the cacophony and carnage, and waited.

Gareth's tree, planted in the back surrounded by a mosaic of colored stones, would not survive the winter, its largest limb ripped aside by a reversing truck, and its roots, poking up through the wrecked earth, glowing an eerie yam-potato color in the failing light.

Buckleigh struggled along floorboards dangerous with loose nails and abandoned hand tools. Groaning through the pain of his bullet wound, he hugged an entire suit of armor tied with twine.

He deserved his prize, and everything else he had secreted in the building. He had served Pugh, that effing idiot, for many years, keeping him healthy, lengthening his sorry life. So that was that.

And the government? To hell with them. What they didn't know wouldn't hurt him.

Buckleigh picked up speed – he was about to drop the damn stuff – as he passed the cool shadow that was Gareth. He felt the temperature change and stopped, awkwardly teetering, looking for an open window. He couldn't unlatch one, but if it was open and handy, why the hell not? He could toss the whole shebang out to the parking lot three floors below.

But no dice. Cold draft leaked from somewhere, but not a window. Buckleigh committed himself to a moderately loud 'Bugger!" as he reached the freight elevator.

He grimaced and blinked stinging sweat from his eyes. Didn't bloody help. He cursed again, staggered closer and let out a fart. Damn cats! The black-and-white one was performing a dainty figure-of-eight synchronized with Buckleigh's legs. Emma, the marmalade-colored female sat out of range, her eyes locked seriously on him.

"Piss off, pussies!"

Buckleigh kicked out at Lucy's behind and found nothing but air. The damn bitch had slipped round to his planted left foot and circled it insolently. And now the marmalade bitch had stepped between him and the freight elevator.

"Bugger off!" he blared. He shook his head violently, showering sweat on them.

Then the cool breeze thickened, aimed and ran.

Gareth peered into the open shaft. There, deep in the factory basement, sprawled Buckleigh's impossibly twisted body. Thin light showed up the crimson blood as it flowed and intermingled with the polished armor. Buckleigh's broken body looked like an illuminated capital in an ancient bible.

"Well kitties." Gareth's voice purred over their backs. "You hide out up here for a few days. Food in the storage room. Adrianna will come back for you, and then you're off to Wales."

He surveyed the abandoned silence of the sad hallway, the tremor of streetlight reverberating, a kind of death.

"I'll be back tomorrow morning. I much prefer the sunlight."

And the cats' eyes drank in his going.

Ω   END   Ω

ABOUT THE AUTHOR

Having traveled Europe and the U.S., fallen in love with (and in) Paris and lived in Japan, I now make my home in Ontario, Canada.

I love cats as pets, and all animals as sentient creatures. I think this is why, when asked at around age nine the name of my greatest hero, I answered "St. Francis of Assisi." Tarzan came a close second: I kid you not. (I also harbor a crush on a hybrid historical/fantasy Joan of Arc, but did not know that at age nine: It has never done me any good.)

I believe resolutely in the sanctity of fundamental human rights, kindness, and Nature in all its life forms. My great grandmother was Native American. That, and my Welsh birth and ancestry, I consider blessings.

While writing Kronos Duet I was saved from penury by a generous writing grant from the Arts Council of Ontario (bless all who work for her!). I now work as a full-time author and free-lance editor. I have published fiction, essays, short stories, and literary criticism.

My two Masters degrees: in English Language and Literature, and in Library Science, attest, if nothing else, to my self-discipline – and perhaps to a masochistic streak.

73508395R00148

Made in the USA
Columbia, SC
12 July 2017